"Wow! *Heading Home* is that rare n[...]
and keeps you flipping pages to the very end—the stunning, ca[...]
end. Forget everything you think you know about apocalyptic thrillers. This one will enthrall you and force you to rethink what it means to be brave, to believe. In *Heading Home,* John Robinson's bold storytelling, limitless imagination, and formidable skills as a wordsmith come together to both entertain and enlighten. A fabulous read!"

—ROBERT LIPARULO, AUTHOR OF THE DREAMHOUSE KINGS SERIES

"John Robinson delivers a novel that strikes the heart with what true faith is all about. A taste of the past, a mission for the present, and a glimpse of the future will keep the reader in suspense and anticipation."

—DIANN MILLS, AUTHOR OF SWORN TO PROTECT

"No one knows the day or hour of Christ's return. But what if we knew the week? When Christians all over the world hear the words *this week* whispered to them by God—all at the same moment—mass evangelism breaks out all over the globe. Longtime friends and retired Army buddies, Nick Castle and C. T. Barnes, feel led to contact the men in their old unit—to warn them of what's coming. As miracles and conversions increase, the devil grows angrier, determined to wreak as much havoc as possible before the church of Jesus Christ is raptured. Nick and CT are targeted for death along with their families and friends. They race against time and the evil devices of the enemy before the last trumpet blows. This taut thriller will keep readers on the edge of their seats as author John Robinson delivers one of the best 'end of days' novels ever written."

—NANCY MEHL, AWARD WINNING AUTHOR
OF THE IVY TOWERS MYSTERY SERIES

"*Heading Home* is the flip side of *Left Behind*—on steroids."

—ERIC WIGGIN, AUTHOR OF BLOOD MOON RISING

"*Heading Home* is a tightly woven story with many happy endings. That's my kind of book."

—HANNAH ALEXANDER, AUTHOR OF THE HIDEAWAY SERIES

John Robinson
Heading Home

Charlotte, Tennessee 37036 USA

Library of Congress Control Number: 2010928330

ISBN: 978-0-9797485-8-5 (softcover)

Cover and interior design by Marisa Jackson.

10 11 12 13 14 15 16 17 18 19 — 10 9 8 7 6 5 4 3 2 1
MANUFACTURED IN THE UNITED STATES OF AMERICA

DEDICATION

For Barb

All my love,

All my life.

Part One :
Vietnam 1972

CHAPTER 1

THE SAVAGE THUNDER crashed like cannon fire, rattling the metal Quonset hut. Nick Castle shook his head to clear it and looked back at the large man seated before him.

"Say again, sir?"

Colonel Rugg's sigh was deep and heartfelt. "Corporal Castle, I'm growing mighty tired of repeating myself. You've been in-country for almost a year, as near as makes never-mind, and you're telling me you're still having a problem ignoring our little summer storms?"

Little summer storms? Nick bit back a caustic reply. Cincinnati had little summer storms. This rotten monsoon had been raging unchecked for nearly five weeks, and he'd never been so wet in his life.

The moisture seemed to have a mind of its own as it seeped its way into nearly everything; even the boxes of cereal in the company mess tent were soggy. To make it worse, Nick's olive-drab socks and underwear had gone black and slick with mildew, and the oil-soaked sweat covering his face and body made him feel gummy night and day.

Reining in his thoughts, he returned to the matter at hand. "Sorry, sir. I'll do better. You were saying?"

"I was saying, corporal, that I just now got off the phone with General Mannon. Things may be on the mend here. Finally. Turns out he's cooked up a scheme that just might help us with our funding problems."

"That sounds good."

Rugg's grin was devilish. "It seems he's been in contact with the editor of some newspaper in London. The general persuaded them to send a reporter over here to write a story about our unit. A real human interest piece. When it's finished they plan to syndicate the thing back to the States. Maybe it'll stir up a little homefront passion for our poor cause."

Nick's ears perked up. *A reporter? Yeah, that might work. A news story might be just the ticket.*

"How can I help?"

Rugg smiled, cat and canary. "You and I are the only mother's sons around here with any brains, corporal. So I'm making you our goodwill ambassador."

"I don't understand."

"When this reporter—Ames, I think his name is—arrives, I want you to nursemaid him. Personally. You're to hold nothing back. But at the same time I need for you to do your best to present all of us here at Quon Tre in as good a light as possible. Can you handle that for me?"

Nick kept his trap shut. Those seemed to be two mutually exclusive things, but he simply nodded at Rugg to continue.

"Anyway, that's what I called you in here for," the colonel said. "We're running out of options, and for the first time in a year I'm seeing some light. Not to put too much on your shoulders, Nick, but between you and me this is about the last chance the 7th of the 115th has to get funding. If this story doesn't fly, then pretty soon neither will we. Got it?"

Wisely Nick didn't say what was really on his mind—that Rugg could be a stone rat when he wanted to be. The colonel never called him by his first name unless he was up to something, and the pressure he was exerting simply wasn't right.

In spite of that he found himself saying, "Got it, sir. So when does this guy arrive?"

"Two weeks from today, the twenty-fifth. By that time the rains should have stopped completely. I'm sure he'll be wanting to talk to our pilots and ground crews, and gaze in wonder at our slicks as they take off and land in highly dramatic and blood-stirring ways—" here the colonel's ice-blue eyes twinkled shamelessly "—so the general made arrangements for him to be here then." Rugg pointed at the younger man. "But until then keep this to yourself, corporal. I don't want you blabbing this to Dooley or Barnes or anyone. Not yet. You leave that to me. I'll tell the whole unit myself when it's time."

"Yes sir. Anything else?"

"That's it. Dismissed."

.. .. ..

SHUTTING THE DOOR OF THE OFFICE BEHIND HIM, Nick glanced at the young man leaning against the hut, his ear pressed against the hut's frame. The torrential rain thundered down on the metal awning they stood under like a thousand insane kettle drummers.

"Yo, Dooley, you catch all that?"

"I sure did." Corporal Dooley's eyebrows rose as he straightened. "A limey reporter. To check out this little old flea-bit outfit. Guess old Mad Jack Rugg still has some pull, huh?"

Nick's shrug was noncommittal. "I'm not sure how much good it'll do, but at this stage anything is worth a shot."

"You got that right. Speakin' of which, did you hear about poor old number five, and Cap'n Albertson?"

In the 7th of the 115th Air Cavalry, each helicopter had been given a number rather than a name; the glory days of the old Army Air Corps were gone for good. Number five, a one-man Bell scout ship and a creaking relic from clear back in the Korean conflict, was the oldest of their fleet, and Albertson its pilot.

"No, what?"

Dooley shook his head sadly. "Finally bit the dust, man. I heard Chief Makris give it last rites hisself. And Albertson was short, only had ten days left on his ticket, so the colonel done cut his orders this mornin' and sent him on back to battalion for reassignment."

"No wonder Mad Jack is grabbing at this news article thing. If we're running out of slicks and pilots, we're running out of time."

"I heard that," Dooley nodded.

"Could be he's right in thinking General Mannon might be looking out for us rather than himself for once."

"Mannon?" Dooley shook his head again. "He hates Mad Jack, and you know it. If that skinflint's doin' us a favor, I'd like to check out what cards he's holdin' in his other hand."

Nick was about to reply when the rain suddenly slacked off, the way it does in monsoon country. It was as if the water pressure in the sky had abruptly dropped fifty percent.

He and Dooley looked at each other. The rain hadn't changed its volume or intensity in the last five weeks. Now this. Maybe it was an omen.

"Huh." Dooley stuck his hand out from under the awning and then stepped out into the downpour. The boy stood ankle deep in the mud, staring up at the brightening sky. Looking over at his friend, his rainsoaked grin was huge.

"Hey, man. Change is comin'."

CHAPTER 2

THE SMELL. DEFINITELY THE SMELL. That was the first thing that struck Trevor Ames on exiting the Huey helicopter at Quon Tre airbase. Previous journalists had remarked on Vietnam's peculiar odor, but those reports hadn't done it justice.

The air around him was heavy, fetid and oppressive, like none other the Brit had experienced in covering hotspots around the globe for the past fourteen years. Not even the hint of a breeze stirred the clammy air as hot sweat instantly glued his clothing to his body like plastic wrap. This was no climate for a pudgy man like him.

And where the devil was his escort? He'd been told back in Saigon, before he'd boarded the noisy beast he'd come in on, that someone from the American forces was going to be here to give him an official welcome.

Ames was craning his neck around to see if one of the soldiers huddled under a nearby open-sided tent was to be his guide when he felt a light tap on his right shoulder. He turned abruptly.

Before him stood a freckle-faced, tow-headed boy in faded jungle fatigues. He didn't appear to be more than fifteen years old, but the reporter knew that couldn't be right.

"Mr. Ames?" the young man shouted over the diminishing roar of the chopper's blades. Ames nodded his assent.

"I'm Dooley, sir," the boy hollered. "Colonel Rugg sends his compliments. He also said to get you over to HQ and he'd be finished there as soon's he could. He said he woulda met you here hisself, but he had to rip up some silly idiot back at battalion, and it just couldn't be he'ped."

Ames suppressed a chuckle. *Huck Finn lives.* This boy—Dooley, was it?— seemed entirely too laid-back to be a combat soldier. He would never have done in the RAF, Ames's old outfit, or even in the army of America's halcyon days. No wonder the Yanks were losing this war.

"Lead on, young Dooley." The reporter's tone was expansive as he mopped his face for what seemed like the thousandth time since he had landed in

Vietnam. "You wouldn't happen to know where a man might catch a drop or two while we're waiting, would you?"

"Well, there's nothin' around here—officially, that is—that I can tell you about." Dooley grabbed Ames's bags and began striding off toward a far Quonset hut, talking as he went. "What with Mr. Charles bein' so active these days, we're supposed to remain in a state of 'situational readiness,' as the colonel puts it. So Slopehead Annie's bar's been closed for goin' on a week now."

"Mr. Charles?" Ames stumbled over the tough grass and stones of the camp, and he found himself having to struggle to keep up with the young soldier.

"Yeah, that's what we're callin' the Cong these days. Early on in the war he was the Cong or just the VC." The boy hawked up something and spit it to the side as they walked. "Soon's he started waxin' our tails on a reg'lar basis we started callin' him Charlie. Now that this deal's about done, he's been gettin' bolder. These days we call him Mr. Charles because he is about two-thirds bad."

Ames looked sideways at his companion. "What do you call the other third?"

Dooley kept gazing forward as they walked. "Worse."

After what seemed to the reporter to be a mile's walk, they reached the door of the metal building. Painted in bright red above the door were the words *7th of the 115th Air Cavalry. Death Delivered Daily.*

Inside Ames could hear someone yelling, pausing, then yelling louder again. He nodded toward the sound. "Colonel Rugg, I presume?"

Grinning, Dooley bobbed his head. "Yessir. Told you he was tearin' somebody at battalion a new one. Poor feller. I hope the colonel at least left him one good leg." The smirk widened. "That man's a holy terror, I kid you not—and today's one of his good days."

Ames had the feeling the boy was having him on a bit, but he didn't mind. It was always the same; no matter what the branch of service, your CO was always the worst.

Chuckling insolently, Dooley knocked twice. The volume of swearing inside suddenly increased, quickly followed by the sound of a phone slamming down.

"*Come!*" The voice that barked the command sounded like it had been baptized in Drano.

Dooley swung the door open, half-bowing, flinging his arm in an "after-you-Alphonse" sweep. "Mr. Ames, I give you our leader, Colonel John Taylor 'Mad Jack' Rugg, movie-star handsome, scourge of southeast Asia, and a man among men. May God have mercy on your soul." With that he jammed his hands in his pockets and sauntered off, whistling tunelessly.

Ames blinked. No doubt about it, this outfit was *loose.*

The man behind the desk stood up. And up. He was massive, standing at least six-five, redheaded and crewcut and wide as a semi. The newsman noted that the officer possessed the type of body that at first glance appeared to be fat but was in reality smooth, hard muscle. Ames had the feeling that it was a mistake not a few men had made, to their regret.

"Mr. Ames? Colonel Rugg." The man shoved a huge paw in Ames's direction. "Don't let Dooley fool you. The kid's a wisenheimer, but get him behind a minigun and he's burnt sin."

Shutting the door, Ames took two steps forward and gripped Rugg's hand in a quick shake. "I admit I was wondering about him. About you, too . . . and your outfit. My editor seems to think there's a story here for the *Observer.* I doubt it, but you're welcome to try to convince me."

Rugg motioned to a chair in front of his desk. "Good. We'll talk. Sit, sit, please." Reaching into his desk drawer, he withdrew a longnecked bottle containing a clear liquid. He held it out.

"Vodka? Sorry it's not chilled, but it *is* the real deal. A Marine we pulled out of a firefight a few weeks ago stole it off a dead North Vietnamese officer. Where he got, it I haven't a clue. Maybe from one of his Russian handlers." He peered at the label. "Unpronounceable name, but smooth as a baby's butt."

Ames nodded. "I believe I will, thanks." While the colonel procured a couple of glasses and began to pour, the reporter continued taking in his surroundings. "Rather spartan, I should think. Your corporal Dooley said there was no liquor to be found on the base."

Rugg winked as he handed Ames a tumbler filled nearly to the brim. "There isn't. You're imagining this." Holding out his glass, he smiled. "To home."

Ames touched his glass to Rugg's. "Home." Taking a delicate sip, he winced. The stuff stung like a nettle but seemed to burn some of the gumminess out of his throat.

With a sigh, he settled back in his chair. "So tell me, colonel, is there a story here?"

Setting his glass down, Rugg took his time as he stretched back, lacing his fingers behind his head. "That depends, Mr. Ames. What are your bona fides?"

Ames met his gaze without flinching. "I'm an old RAF man, although I never saw combat. After I'd mustered out I went to J-school, courtesy of the service. After graduation I got a job as a stringer with the *London Observer*. When a full-time slot opened up, I grabbed it. Because of my time in the service, my editors felt I might do well covering an IRA uprising in Belfast." He took another sip of his drink, which went down easier than the first. "I impressed them with it and got other assignments as time went along. Since then I've covered stories in Angola, Pakistan, Libya, and the Sudan." He pulled at his already-open collar. "All less humid than this."

Rugg seemed to be taking Ames's measure. "But never Vietnam?"

"No, first time here." Ames drained his glass.

The colonel looked away and out the window, pausing for a moment. When he spoke again, his voice took on a metallic tone.

"We call this place The Land of the Bad Things. When it's not hot and dry, like now, it's hot and rainy. The enemy's called this lousy dump home for thousands of years, and he knows every blade of grass, every tree, every cholera-infested ditch. He's dug hundreds of tunnels for his troops. Some of them are so large they even contain hospitals and theaters. He's also cunningly constructed booby traps. After watching one man get blown up in front of you, you dash off the trail toward safety, only to die in another one."

Rugg still gazed outside. "Children will come up to you wanting gum or a chocolate bar. As you smilingly fish one out of your ditty bag, those same laughing children will drop a homemade hand grenade down your shirt." Ames winced as Rugg went on, "You literally cannot tell friend from foe, and to top things off, we've been given explicit orders not to win this conflict."

He turned back with a scowl. "Mr. Ames, I've proudly served in the United States Army for the past twenty years, man and boy, and I've seen service all over the globe. This is, hands down and by far, the most Godforsaken place I've ever been. I have no doubt you're a fine journalist, a sterling fellow, and a credit to England. But believe me, *nothing* has prepared you for Vietnam."

"Is this where I'm supposed to swoon, colonel?"

Rugg's stare continued for another second. And then without warning he threw his head back in a raucous laugh that shook his entire frame. This went on for quite a while. Ames watched silently as the man gasped and convulsed.

After several moments the show slowed and finally ceased, and Rugg wiped his tearing eyes with a yellow-stained handkerchief. "Oh dear, oh dear. I almost did myself an injury, as you English chappies put it." He wadded the rag. "Mr. Ames, you're all right. I think we're going to get along famously."

"I trust we are, colonel, else my editor is likely to be miffed."

"Miffed." Rugg cocked his head to one side, grinning strangely, his eyes dancing in mischief. To Ames he suddenly looked very dangerous indeed. "Well, we wouldn't want that, heaven knows. No. We would not." He leaned forward and said in a harsh whisper, "Would you like to know why they call me Mad Jack?"

Ames nodded, mesmerized by the change. Rugg's unblinking gaze was unnerving.

"I'm on my third tour here. When they first assigned me to Vietnam, I was woefully unprepared. All spit and polish, no nonsense—by the book, if you're familiar with the type. About six weeks in, I knew I'd been had. It seemed Washington had decided in its infinite wisdom that we were to fight our battles here with one hand tied behind us, and the ways I'd been taught of waging war were now unacceptable. I had to make a choice. Right there and right then I knew the only way I was going to finish my time here with all my neurons still firing in sequence was to junk the Army way and do it my way."

"And did you?"

"I did. And it worked so well I knew I'd found my place in this world. When my tour was up I signed up for another one. Then another. More still if they'll let me. But always, ever and anon, on *my* terms."

Relaxing a bit, he steepled his fingers. "This unit has won more citations than any other in the history of air cavalry simply because I run it the way I think it should be run. But we've paid a price for that."

"A price?"

Rugg jerked his head toward the bustling outside. "I suppose you've noticed that we're not at full strength here. This is by design. Not mine, I assure you. Higher ups."

"Like who?"

Rugg scowled again. "Never mind. Thing is, body counts notwithstanding, my unorthodox methods seem to have mightily riled someone in the upper echelons, and we're starting to feel it. With implacable determination we're slowly being phased out. Helicopters, pilots, ammo, parts; you name it, we're short of it. In popular parlance, we're a maverick backwater unit in the closing days of a war most people would just as soon put behind us. And the problem with that, Mr. Ames, is I'm not so sure that whatever story you end up writing is going to help us much. I think the days of *Why We Fight* went out with Frank Capra. Okay. Fine. I'll accept that too."

Abruptly Rugg stood. "But it doesn't matter. The 7th of the 115th continues to get the job done, and done well, because as far as Mr. Charles is concerned, we are simply death incarnate." The soldier's spread fingers contracted into fists. "The brass tolerates us, Washington despises us, and the enemy fears us. I wouldn't have it any other way. My boys are the best. So am I."

Grabbing his glass, Rugg took a deep draught of his vodka, then wiped his mouth with the back of his hand. "There's your story, Mr. Ames. Write it."

CHAPTER 3

TREVOR AMES TOOK A SLOW LOOK around the shack that Dooley had led him into. The place seemed to be built of nothing more than flattened fuel cans and mosquito netting.

"You actually live in this—this hovel?" Ames was appalled. "What happened to your tent?"

"We don't call 'em hovels, Mr. Ames," Dooley replied. "We call 'em hootches, and yeah, this is where I live—well, me and three other guys, that is. Our tents got liberated by somebody a while back, and they ain't sent us any more." He shrugged. "We dunno who did it. But if Colonel Rugg finds out who the thief was, he will, and I quote, 'take that poor, silly miscreant and send him out into the bush, naked, with pictures of John Wayne taped over his nether regions, and encourage Mr. Charles to do with him whatever seems right and prudent.' " The boy's grin was humorless. "And I wouldn't put it past him, Mr. Ames. I surely wouldn't."

The reporter wrinkled his nose at the funk that permeated the squalor. Old food, mildew, stale body odor—the place was disgusting. "So who are your roomies, Dooley? Ernest T. Bass and his kin?"

The young man slapped his knee in raucous laughter. "Good one, Mr. Ames! Naw, it's just me, Frankie Malone, Nick Castle, and Mr. C. T. Barnes. Nick was the one that was s'posed ta be guidin' you around, but you gettin' here a day early kinda got that screwed up. He'll be here directly, though."

"Did I hear you call this Barnes fellow Mister? Isn't he a soldier too?"

"Yeah, sure he's a soldier. It's just that that's what he likes to be called, by his full name, Mr. C. T. Barnes." Dooley lowered his voice. "Mr. C. T. Barnes is a nigra, doncha know, real big fella, kinda quiet and awful nice, until you get him riled up. Then you better run for cover. That's for true, you bet."

"And all four of you are doorgunners?"

"Yessir. See, the 7th of the 115th ain't a real big outfit to start with. And what with the war comin' to an end they got us down to four slicks mission ready and two that ain't that we just use for parts. So the way things shake out is you got us gunners in one hootch, the pilots in another, Chief Makris and his mechanics in a coupla others and maybe forty or so other support people."

"What's this minigun the colonel mentioned? Something new?"

"Yeah," Dooley allowed, growing excited. "Pretty new. New for us, anyhow. They're what replaced the M-60 machine guns we was usin'. The minigun is really a Gatlin' gun, see. Six rotatin' barrels and she spits out almost six thousand rounds a minute. Screams like the end of the world and looks it too, just a long, red stream hittin' the ground and a sound like banshees dyin'. Whatever it touches, it dissolves, purt' near."

Ames cocked his head. "You sound like a man in love."

Before the boy could reply, a figure burst through the door of the hootch. The intruder was a tall young man, dark-haired and well muscled, holding something high in his left hand.

"A chicken!" He laughed. "Can you believe it, Dooley? A real, ring-necked banty rooster. I found him down by the stream, strolling along like he didn't have a care in the world. Well, he does now. Who are you?" This directed at the reporter.

"Nick, meet Mr. Ames, the newspaperman from London. He's gonna make us famous!"

The young man strode forward, thrusting out his right hand while keeping a firm grip on the rooster's neck with the other. "Nick Castle, Mr. Ames. A pleasure. Sorry I'm late. I hope Dooley here has been keeping you entertained."

"You're not late. I'm early," Ames answered cordially as they shook hands. "And Corporal Dooley here has been a veritable fount of information."

"A fount. Well, he is that." Nick cocked a thumb at the smaller man. "Dooley has the gift of gab. If we could ever get him to shut his pie-hole long enough, he'd make a swell doorgunner."

"Yeah, that's right," the Southerner retorted. "And if Nick would ever let us forget he's a rich boy blueblood, he'd make a swell human bein'."

Though the words were harsh, Ames had a notion they masked a genuine affection between the men. He'd run across it before; it sometimes happens between two completely opposite types in wartime. The reporter's feelings were confirmed as each soldier grinned wickedly at the other.

"So, chicken-boy," Dooley mocked, "what do you propose to do with that fine, gorgeous animal?"

"Well, you being from good rebel stock, I figured you'd either date it or cook it."

"Me?" The other man faked shock. "My granny could cook a chicken that'd make you weep. I just eat 'em, that's all."

"Okay, you sold me." Nick shoved the rooster at him. "Since you're still the newbie here, you take this to Cookie and tell him to do us proud."

"Newbie? I only been here two days less than you." Muttering, Dooley grabbed the rooster and headed toward the door. "Okay, okay, I'm goin', but only because I want to, not because you're tellin' me to." Still protesting, he trudged off.

Nick turned back to the reporter. "What newspaper do you work for, Mr. Ames?"

"The *London Observer*, corporal."

"Call me Nick. As you can probably tell, we aren't real big on the social graces around here."

"All right. My first name is Trevor. And what do I call young Dooley?"

"Just call him Dooley. I'm sure he has a first name, but none of us know what it is. He guards that secret like the phone number to Ann-Margret's beach house. And don't expect him to call you Trevor. Dooley's from the South and won't call you by anything other than your last name. At least for a while."

"Yes, I rather figured his geography when I heard him describing this Barnes fellow."

"Don't let him fool you. Dooley's no more racist than I am. It's just the way he was brought up." The other man's eyebrows rose in humor. "Besides, nobody's been able to figure out Mr. C. T. Barnes since he got religion."

Ames frowned. "Since he what?"

"Got religion. You'll see it for yourself when you meet him. He's down at the motorpool right now, helping the guys try to get one of our two Jeeps running. The man looks ferocious, and still is when he's in combat, but up until six months ago Mr. C. T. Barnes was the meanest mother ever to wear olive drab. He'd fight you for no particular reason, especially if he was stoned on reefer. He hated everybody. Himself most of all, I guess."

"So what happened? Or should I wait for him to tell it?"

"Oh, he'll tell it all right, if you give him half the chance. Sometimes even if you don't. All I know is, a few months back something happened."

Ames was intrigued. "What?"

"You tell me. The hate was gone, he said, and the pain. Don't get me wrong, the guy is still an excellent soldier, but when the mission's done, he shuts it off." Nick's smile now was puzzled. "You're a newspaperman, Trevor, a chronicler of all things curious. What could cause a change like that in a human heart?"

CHAPTER 4

AMES VAINLY TRIED to come up with a reply but never got the chance. At that moment another figure, even smaller than Dooley, sauntered in. But where the youngster's face had seemed fresh and open, this man's looked hard and pinched.

The new arrival ambled over, his suspicious gaze never leaving the reporter's face. "What we got here? A do-gooder from the Red Cross?"

"Down, boy," Nick directed. "This is Trevor Ames, a reporter from London. Mad Jack brought him here to do a story on the unit. Trevor, Frankie Malone."

"A pleasure, Frankie," Ames said, offering his hand.

The other man's face darkened in a scowl. "It's Corporal Malone ta you, newspaperman, till I say otherwise. You're probably a commie, like all the rest a' the Brits."

Ames was struck dumb at the slur against his homeland. The look froze on his face, while his right hand remained angled out like a department-store mannequin.

When he lowered it, Nick scowled. "Frankie, you're an idiot. Did you check the ammo crates that came in like I told you?"

"Not yet."

"I'd suggest you do it."

Malone stood rooted to the floor.

"*Now*, man."

Scowling, Malone stomped back out through the door of the hootch and into the compound, muttering curses all the way.

Ames watched him stalk off, then turned to Nick with a wry smile. "He seems pleasant enough."

"Don't let him get to you. Frankie's like that with everybody. Before he was assigned to us, he was a tunnel rat."

"Tunnel rat?"

"They do the job no sane man would, going in and flushing Mister Charles out of his holes. But I heard his last time in, things went bad. Now he's finishing out his hitch with us. Frankie's all right, but he does take some getting used to."

"No doubt. Perhaps there's a way I can get some good quotes out of him nonetheless."

"If you can do that, you're the greatest reporter since Walter Cronkite. No, make that Walter Winchell."

"Winchell? I'm surprised you've heard of him." Ames curled a finger on his chin. "You'll forgive me for being blunt, my boy, but you seem—I don't know—beyond this place somehow."

"You mean because I'm educated?"

"Perhaps. I did notice the other two men both obeyed you. That's odd, seeing as how all three of you hold the same rank."

"It has to do with seniority, at least here it does. I suppose it's that way because we're such a small unit. The seniority order goes Mr. C. T. Barnes, me, Dooley, then Frankie."

"I really should begin making some notes, or my editor will have my skin." Ames pulled a pen and small notepad from his shirt pocket. "I'll start with this. Are you planning on making a career of the service after you're back stateside?"

"Over here we call it being rotated back to the World, and no, I'm not. Dooley's crack about my being a rich-boy blueblood was true enough."

While Ames wrote, Nick took a seat on the edge of his bunk. "It's no secret I disappointed my dad by not letting him help me avoid service over here, but not so much that he wrote me out of the family business. When I get back, my position with our firm in Cincinnati will be waiting."

Ames arched his eyebrows. "Firm?"

"Manufacturing firm, actually. All kinds of things. You know those little plastic doo-dads on the ends of shoelaces?"

Ames nodded.

"Eyeglass screws? Battery-powered Christmas candles? Cat litter scoops and stereo knobs?"

The reporter nodded again.

"Castle Industries products all. Those and at least a hundred others I could name. All that's waiting for me when I get back to the World. Not as exciting as getting to shoot holes in nasty little men dressed in black pajamas, but still . . . "

Nick's voice trailed off as a sudden heavy tread stomped into the hootch. Ames stopped writing and looked up. As he did so his jaw dropped. Before him stood the biggest, blackest man he'd ever clapped eyes on. This behemoth was so huge he made Colonel Rugg appear frail by comparison.

The giant stepped up to them. "Hey, Nicky. Hello, sir. My name's Mr. C. T. Barnes." He stuck out a hand that looked to be as big as a Smithfield ham.

Ames took it gingerly. "Hello. Trevor Ames."

He hoped his shock didn't show. He also hoped his hand wouldn't be pulped into batter. Surprisingly, Barnes shook it quite gently, twice, before releasing it.

"Trevor is here to do a story on the unit," Nick explained.

Barnes nodded, and then cranked his turret-like head toward the other man. "Make sure you spell my name right." Lowering his voice to just above a rumble, he gritted, "It's Barnes, Mister C period, T period, B-A-R-N-E-S. Got it?"

Before Ames could answer, Barnes stretched his hand past Ames's head to the bookshelf behind him and plucked off a Bible. Tucking it under his arm, he left the hootch, humming something familiar. After a moment, it came to Ames: "Jesus Loves Me."

"Whew!" He gave a nervous laugh and ran his hands through his thinning sandy hair.

Nick returned a slight smile. "A force of nature is our Mr. C. T. Barnes. If he made your bowels loose now, you should have seen him before."

"Before he got religion, you mean."

"Yeah, that." Nick stood. "Well, c'mon Trevor, old bean, and let me introduce you to the other inmates around here. It'll probably be the last chance you get to talk to them before we go up tomorrow."

They left the hootch together and made their way over to Chief Makris in the maintenance hut.

CHAPTER 5

AFTER CHOW THAT NIGHT, Ames decided to take a walk over to the colonel's quarters. Something undefined churned in his mind. He thought Rugg might be able to help him sort it out.

"No problem, but make sure you stay within the compound, and within the lights," Nick warned. "For obvious reasons."

Ames agreed, and after a leisurely five-minute stroll found himself before the HQ hut. He noticed a lone light burning. After a moment's hesitation, he knocked lightly.

"*Come,*" Rugg's voice boomed.

Ames entered to find the colonel slouched at his desk, papers strewn in front of him. The man appeared oblivious of his visitor as he continued to write.

Ames softly cleared his throat. "Mind if I sit, colonel?"

"Sweet Mary," Rugg muttered distractedly, " requisition forms from here to breakfast . . . " He looked up. "Hmm? Oh yeah, sure, sure, sit, Mr. Ames. Don't mind me. I'm just quietly going insane. Ever hear the phrase 'an army moves on its stomach'?" He snorted. "That may be true as far as it goes, but the pavement it rides on is made of paper."

"Problems?"

"No more than usual. Trying to make fifty cents do a dollar job." The colonel slid the papers to the side, shaking his head. "We're down to four slicks in this unit that are airworthy. The other two have been stripped of so much that in a few months all that'll be left of them will be their metal frames. They'll make some Vietnamese kid a dandy set of monkeybars after we *dee-dee* outta here."

Ames's ears perked up. "Any idea as to when that might be?"

Rugg leaned back in his chair, eyeing the reporter lazily. "Off the record?"

"If you insist."

Looking up at the hut's metal ceiling, Rugg sighed. "Well, this is just between us girls, you understand, but I don't give us another eighteen months." He swung his gaze back down. "It's 1972, for pity's sake. We've had troops in country in one form or another since 1957. Over fifty-eight thousand casualties and very little winning of the hearts and minds that I can see." He shook his head again, his tone disgusted. "No, I think it's time we put this one in the loss column, trundle our weary behinds out onto the team bus, and head on down the road."

There was a lull, then the reporter said tentatively, "That's the reason I felt I needed to stop by and speak with you, sir."

Rugg spread his hands. "Say on, Mr. Ames. The night wanes."

"Colonel, I wish to ask you a favor. I know there's a mission laid on for tomorrow." Ames took a deep breath before plunging in. "With your permission, I'd like to go up."

This time the silence stretched even longer. Then Rugg cocked his head.

"Up? You mean as go up in the air, flying around in a helicopter with my boys? That up?"

Ames swallowed hard. "That's precisely what I mean. If you are right, this may be the last chance anyone from the media might have of seeing how you fellows really do in action."

Rugg shook his head. "No chance in this world, Mr. Ames." He waved his hand toward the back wall. "Remember all these citations? We don't need to prove anything to anyone."

"Yes, but—"

Scowling, the colonel leaned forward. "Your position, as I see it, is mainly that of a PR flak. No offense, but what you're supposed to do is write us up in a good light so you can sell more newspapers and maybe we, indirectly, might get some badly needed funding. Win-win for both sides." Rugg frowned again. "That plan does not include combat joy rides for civilians. No sir. Discussion closed."

Ames's thoughts raced. The desire to go up with these men into harm's way had suddenly, and seemingly of its own volition, gone from idle speculation to serious intent; just like that, it had burst over him like a wave. Journalistic objectivity be hanged, he wanted to go UP. *Sell it, man.*

"Colonel Rugg, you are absolutely correct. I know that nothing I could write would add to the glory your unit possesses. I also know the only reason I'm here at all is as a favor to your CO, General Mannon."

"You know that, do you?"

"Yes. I'm aware he happens to be good friends with my editor. They served together in Korea, and my being here is simply an effort on the general's part to try to help your unit get the funding it needs through a puff piece." Ames's smile was a slash. "I may be a broken-down drunk, colonel, but I'm not stupid." He licked his lips. They felt as dry as cactus. "May I tell you something? Man to man, something you may appreciate?"

Rugg nodded, intrigued.

"The moment I set foot here it was almost as if a light had clicked on inside me, some long-dormant spark. Earlier today I told you I was in the RAF, serving as a weapons officer, if you can believe it. I suppose it was in my blood."

"Soldiering will do that."

"My dad fought in the Battle of Britain, flying Hurricanes. After the war he would entrance us children for hours with tales of battling the Luftwaffe. But I was never given the chance to use the skills I'd been taught. And I wanted that chance."

Realizing he'd been rushing his words, Ames stopped for a breath, meeting the colonel's icy blue eyes. "My father got his opportunity. I never got mine."

Rugg remained mute, and Ames finished up in a headlong rush. "I'm not asking to *fly* the bloody helicopter, colonel, or even to man a gun. All I want is the chance to *see* combat, to smell it, to hear a shot fired in anger. You, if anyone, should understand what I mean." Laying both his hands on the scarred oak command desk, he held Rugg's gaze. "That's all, sir. I won't ask again."

The silence seemed to Ames to last a fortnight.

"By-y-y God," Rugg drawled at last. "Quite a speech, sir. Yes, quite a speech. But you've missed the big picture. Should you die a flaming death, your problems would be over. Mine would have hardly begun."

"What do you mean?"

"I mean a formal inquiry would be convened. The subject of that inquiry would be why a decorated AirCav colonel would allow a civilian, a foreign civilian at that, to talk him into going on a combat mission. And that would just be the beginning of the festivities."

"But—"

"That'd be followed by a foregone court-martial of yours truly, with its attendant loss of rank, pay, and benefits, at last finishing up with my disgrace and public censure. Not the way I'd like my career to go out. You see what I'm saying here?" Rugg drummed his fingers on his desk, staring intently at the reporter.

Ames held his peace, feeling the tension tightening.

Suddenly the colonel relaxed. "Ah, screw it!" He slammed both hands down sharply on the desk. "You're right, Mr. Ames, I know *exactly* what you're saying. Truth be told, combat can be a lot of fun. And what's life for if you can't have any fun? Besides, always trying to be Mannon's good boy is giving me cramps."

He poured a cup of coffee from a battered pot on his desk. "Yeah, I haven't royally ticked the good general off in a long while, and Lord knows the poor fella needs it. Keeps his bowels open. This little stunt you're proposing may put blood in parts of his brain that's never been there before. Mr. Ames, you just hit the lottery. You'll go up with us tomorrow, yes you will, and I trust you'll see some heat."

For once Ames was speechless.

Rugg leaned forward, eyes dancing, his face twisted with that same crazy grin Ames had seen earlier. He flung his arms to either side.

"Mad dogs and Englishmen!" Throwing back his head, he laughed and laughed.

CHAPTER 6

AMES HARDLY NOTICED the walk back to the gunners' hootch. Part of him was elated; another equally wondered what sort of fool begged for the chance to see combat.

Entering the dwelling, he found Nick asleep on his bunk, Dooley and Frankie playing cards, and Barnes sprawled across a tiny folding chair, reading his Bible.

"This world is just too small for me," the giant said with a sad shake of his head.

"Hey fellows, how goes it?" Ames's voice was a bit too bright, a bit too loud.

Dooley glanced up from his game. "Mr. Ames, you got the look of a man that's heard his mother-in-law just went over a cliff in his brand-new Caddy. Kinda sick-like, but happy. Right?"

"You're not far wrong." Ames cleared his throat. "It, uh, well . . . it appears that I'm to fly with you men tomorrow."

Dooley laid his cards down, bugging his eyes as he gave a low whistle. "Lord-a-mercy. You didn't. You *volunteered?*" He shook his head. "My, oh my."

"Yeah, well, you ain't ridin' in my slick, chump," Frankie sneered from his side of the table. "You're a piece a' bad luck just waitin' ta fall."

"Malone, did your mother have any children that lived?" This from Nick, who evidently wasn't asleep after all.

Frankie threw his cards to the floor. "Screw alla ya! Doncha get it? I'm *short!* Forty-one days and a wake-up and I'm gone! And I *don't* like the idea a' this Brit commie bringin' in bad karma!"

"Karma," Nick snorted. "That's plain stupid. Frankie, I'm shorter than you, and you don't hear me carping."

"And I'm shorter than both'a ya," Barnes rumbled. "Nineteen days. 'Sall right by me, though. I think Mister Ames should do what he want. He's a grown man."

"Ahhhh, the hell with this." Frankie shot to his feet, knocking over his chair. "I'm goin' over to the motor pool. Get a sandwich and some decent conversation. You guys are crazy." Crashing the door open, he was gone.

There was a moment of embarrassed silence before Dooley spoke up. "I'd like to apologize for Frankie, Mr. Ames. He don't mean nothin' by it. He just gets like this the nights before we go up."

"I don't doubt it," Ames said. He cocked his head. "How about you, Dooley? Are you ever scared?"

"Only all the blessed time," the boy said. "It's never really gone. Just some of us handle it differ'nt. Me, every time we go up I shake like a dog tryin' to pass a peach pit for about five minutes, then I'm fine."

Ames turned his head. "Nick, you?"

Nick propped himself up on one elbow. "Well, yeah, fear's always a part of us. It depends on how you use it. You can either let it keep you frosty or paralyze you. I go with the former."

Ames looked over at the giant. "How about you, Mr. C. T. Barnes, ever any fear?"

Barnes slowly closed his Bible, marking his place with a massive thumb as he regarded Ames with a flat gaze. "Nope. Got God with me." With that he began to read once again.

"Whoa." Dooley grinned, impressed. " 'Nuff said, huh?"

.. .. ..

AN HOUR LATER and twenty dollars poorer, Ames couldn't spot exactly how Dooley had cheated at cards, but was nonetheless convinced the young soldier had. Ames made his way over to the VIP tent. Apparently it was the only one the thieves had missed.

Stretching out on his old wood and canvas cot, he tried to relax. It didn't seem to be working. After an hour he got up and took a pill, seeking to calm his increasingly quivering stomach. He hoped he was ready for this.

When at last he dropped off to a fitful sleep, he dreamed. He dreamed of flames, of fear, of Hurricanes.

CHAPTER 7

DAWN CAME WITH A GENTLE SHAKING. Ames opened one bleary eye. It was Nick, poking him on the shoulder.

"Trevor? Time to get vertical, my man. Chow's hot, and then we have a briefing with Mad Jack at 0800. C'mon, let's go."

Ames slowly climbed off the cot, stiff and red-eyed. His neck cracked as he turned his head from side to side. Not a good night, not at all. He hoped it wasn't a sign.

After an unremarkable breakfast, he made his way to a small hut, made even smaller by the full complement of helicopter aircrews and Colonel Rugg.

The colonel nodded at him, noting his haggard face. Rugg's smile never reached his eyes.

"Mr. Ames. I trust you slept well. Allow me to introduce our pilots. They got back from a briefing at battalion just last night. Warrant Officers Milburn, Torelli, Bates, and Gaddick."

All four men muttered their acknowledgment, but disapproval seemed to radiate from them in waves.

"You'll be going up in number one, with Corporal Castle, Warrant Officer Gaddick, and me." Rugg grinned savagely. "A question, sir?"

"Well." Ames nervously cleared his throat. "Yes. What, uh, do we have laid on for today?"

"First thing we're going to do is ferry some medical supplies to a MASH unit about forty klicks northeast of here. After that we fly our usual patrol, see what's what. It's rather like fishing. We may either tie into a lunker or just drown worms. You fish much, Mr. Ames?" Rugg took a long, slurping sip of his coffee, his eyes never leaving those of his guest.

"No, I don't," Ames allowed. "Not since I was a boy."

"Too bad. Fishing around these parts is pretty good, providing some passing enemy patrol doesn't make you the catch of the day." Rugg set his cup down. "Well, that's what we've got 'laid on,' as you put it. How does that suit you?"

Ames was about to reply when Bates spoke, his eyes narrowed. "Colonel, before we go any further, I would just like to be on record as saying I'm opposed to taking a civilian up with us."

There were mutters and nods of assent from the other pilots. Ames gulped down his bile. Suddenly he wished he were someplace else. Anyplace else.

"I appreciate that, Warrant Officer Bates, I surely do, and your comments are duly noted. But Mr. Ames has his own reasons for flying with us, some of which actually have to do with the writing of his story. Anything else?" Rugg looked around. "No? Fine, let's get it done."

.. .. ..

AMES, HIS EMOTIONS STILL IN A WHIRL, slowly walked around the helicopter with Nick and Gaddick while they completed their preflight checklist. They watched a ground crewman loading ammunition into the minigun's magazine. The man made a final check before cycling the action and safing the weapon.

"Eighteen thousand rounds of Uncle Sam's finest, Trevor," Nick said. "Enough for three minutes of fire."

"Three minutes?" Ames looked appalled. "Good heavens. That doesn't seem like very much. Does it?"

"Three minutes is a lifetime in combat," Nick replied. "Besides, we always bring some back. I've never fired it all yet."

.. .. ..

TWENTY MINUTES LATER the four helicopters were airborne, on their way to the MASH. Ames had said little so far, as he watched, entranced, the endless green jungle canopy flashing below. If one discounted their purpose in flying over it, the view could almost be considered breathtaking.

His stomach problems had finally eased, and the beating of the rotors overhead was pleasantly monotonous. *Perhaps this would be—*

A light tap on his shoulder jerked him out of his reverie.

"Kinda pretty, huh?" Nick motioned toward the jungle below. "Like it?"

"Very much. Quite a countryside." Ames gestured above his head. "Not as noisy as I had feared. These helmets we're wearing are marvels."

"I know. The commlinks inside each one let us talk with each other as well as with the other crews. It helps pass the time, and the chatter doesn't bother the colonel." Nick bent forward. "I think he kind of likes it."

"Yeah, well, I don't." This from Frankie, from his doorgunner position in slick number three. "That fruity Brit makes me nervous. Why don't you ladies just shut up and neck?"

"Anybody for throwing Frankie through the hatch?" Rugg said to no one in particular.

.. .. ..

AN UNEVENTFUL HOUR LATER the supplies had been off-loaded at the MASH, and they were once again airborne. Overhead the colbalt sky stretched out cloudless, and at three hundred feet altitude the wind rushing by the slick's open door made the heat seem almost tolerable.

It was now mid-afternoon. Ames wondered if they had dodged the bullet, as the Yanks put it. He was relieved. Perhaps just being in the vicinity of combat had been enough to slake his morbid curiosity.

They passed over a muddy brown river, flowing south.

"Lot of silt," he remarked.

"Runoff from the mountains," Nick replied. "Monsoon season is only two weeks past. It'll stay like that for another—"

"Quiet!" Rugg barked. "Listen to this." He made a minute adjustment on the radio.

"—day! Mayday! CQ! CQ!" The voice coming over the commlink sounded tinny and faint. "Please, anybody there? Over!"

"This is AirCav flight Baker-Alpha-Tango one-seven, Colonel John Rugg. State your name, position, and status. Over."

"Thank God!" The relief in the soldier's voice was audible, and the confused noise Ames was hearing in the background suddenly resolved itself into the rattle of small-arms fire, explosions, and screams. "This is Gunnery Sergeant Yancey Wheeler, USMC, Firebase Alice! We're under attack! Taking heavy casualties and requesting evac now!"

Oh no. Ames's bowels cramped. Cold sweat popped out on his forehead, and his mouth went dry. Was he ready for this? He knew what he'd said, but—

"Roger that," Rugg confirmed. "Wait one, over."

"Man!" Frankie groused. "Now we gotta rescue some ground-pounders? That's just great!"

"Shut up, Malone." Pulling a case out from under his seat, Rugg opened it, extracting a plastic foldout map. Quickly he located the firebase. "Got you, gunny. We're ten klicks south of your position, ETA three minutes. Have you called for an airstrike from the *Kitty Hawk,* over?"

The sergeant hollered back over the din, "They jumped us too quick. Sappers, a slew of 'em. Ran a truck, crashed through the gate. Our main comm systems were shot to pieces before we knew what hit us. I'm on an old field telephone now."

They heard an explosion over their headsets.

"For God's sake, colonel, hurry! They're tearin' us apart! I've got nine of my people left, three of 'em wounded! There's forty-seven dead, including our CO!"

"You got it, son. Out." Rugg turned to Gaddick. "Put the spurs to her, son, or I know some jarheads that are gonna be flat outta luck." The pilot goosed the throttle and the slick lunged ahead. Rugg spoke again, louder. "Two, three, and four, you heard it. You all know the drill. Follow us in, staggered attack formation. Mr. Ames, keep your head down and your mouth shut."

That wouldn't be a problem. The reporter was nearly popeyed with fear. This was really happening! Why hadn't he refused this whole bloody assignment from the start? His throat felt like it was packed with cotton batting, and cold rivulets of sweat meandered down his chest, his face, and the backs of his knees.

"What happens now?" he croaked. Nothing good—of that he was certain.

"Go easy, man," Nick soothed. "You're going to give yourself a thrombo. Breathe deep now, okay?"

Ames, nearing panic, could only nod wordlessly.

"I've done this before," Nick went on, "and believe me, a hot evac is no fun. You need to keep your head on straight. SOP is to send two slicks down to pick up the men while the other two orbit the LZ and lay down suppressing fire. Then we grab the guys and *dee-dee.* Piece of cake." He smiled encouragement. "So, like Mad Jack said, sit tight. This shouldn't take too long."

"One and three will evac!" yelled Rugg. "Two and four will cover! Clear?"

There were assents from all the pilots. Through his headset Ames could hear Frankie muttering dark oaths, psyching himself up. Barnes was praying softly, seemingly at total peace. Nick was quiet. And Dooley . . . Dooley was singing, "Gimme Shelter."

For the next minute Sergeant Wheeler gave the colonel a nervous running report while the slicks swept low along the muddy river, pounding for all they were worth, their landing skids only feet above the surface. Wheeler and his troops were sheltered behind sandbag revetments at the rear of the compound, their last line of defense. They were down to their final few rounds of ammo, out of grenades, and it looked to Wheeler as if Mr. Charles was preparing a final rush. Rugg assured the sergeant that relief was now only seconds away. The man gulped his thanks, sounding on the ragged edge of endurance.

Ames's stomach lurched in terror as the slicks banked hard left into the next bend of the river. Throttles wide open, they burst like thunder out over the treetops.

Below them lay a scrambled nightmare. A furiously burning truck, obviously the one that had blasted through the gate, crouched in the center of the compound, flanked by the charred corpses of the driver and his comrade. Where the grill had been was a blackened hole. One of the Marines must have taken it out with a rocket-propelled grenade.

Various still-smoking craters littered the ground, some containing remnants of men. Agonizingly, an NVA pulled himself by his elbows away from one of the craters, his legs gone at the hips, his intestines dragging behind like dirty pink and green streamers.

Ames shuddered back his nausea, horrified at the full extent of the Marines' situation. The firebase perimeter had been completely broached by what appeared to be nearly three hundred Vietcong and NVA.

The enemy seemed on the verge of capturing the area, but the price exacted by the defenders was sickeningly high. Nearly two hundred attackers stretched out either dead or dying, intermingled with the bodies of almost fifty Marines. Russian AK-47 rounds continued to zero in on the hapless surviving grunts, ripping large chunks out of their sandbag wall. Any second now—

Deliverance.

Spotting the helicopters swooping in, the Marines broke out in ragged cheers. In response, the enemy weapons swiveled around, opening up in the slicks' direction.

Four miniguns from above answered in kind, laying down a seamless curtain of fire. All around erupted curses, shouts, and screams, both from the ground and the air. The noise was horrendous.

Like the end of the world.

In slick number one, Ames covered his head with his arms, drawing up his feet. *Madness!* Baring his teeth, he panted sharp, shallow breaths, groaned in dismay at the sound of enemy bullets smacking against the slick's skin like metallic hail. His bladder let go, but he no longer cared, too frightened for shame. This was it. He was going to die.

Over his headset erupted sounds of pure pandemonium. Rugg bellowed commands at his pilots, while Frankie, hanging on to his blazing ripsaw mini-gun, screamed obscenities. Barnes calmly spoke what sounded like a psalms as he decimated enemy targets. Inexplicably, Dooley yelled out the names of state capitals while hurling devastation through the enemy ranks.

Nick was the only one silent. Ames stared at the young man as again and again he grimly depressed the minigun's trigger, seeking one target after another. The gun's six barrels spun in a roaring, blinding blur, sending a red tongue of fire lancing out and down, cutting enemy troops in half before they ran three steps. The carnage and cacaphony seemed endless.

Ames gulped in relief. The landing zone was clear. For the moment.

"One and three, cease fire and go get 'em!" Rugg yelled.

Using a deft touch, the pilots of the two slicks hovered their craft a moment longer, the long landing skids scraping the tough sawgrass, carving narrow furrows. Then they were down.

A huge cloud of dust, grass, and debris spun skyward from the blades' furious windmilling as the doorgunners frantically motioned to the Marines. That was all the encouragement they needed. Falling back as they fired, drag-ging their wounded, the grunts clambered aboard the slicks while Nick and Barnes lay down a blistering covering fire.

Sergeant Wheeler, blackened and bleeding, lunged forward, grabbing Rugg by the shoulder. "What about my dead?" he ground out, his voice hoarse and raw.

"We leave 'em."

"Colonel, that isn't acceptable! A Marine does not leave behind his dead!" Wheeler's outrage was clear even above the hammering of the guns.

Rugg swiveled in his seat. "Look around, gunny! We're full up! We either leave 'em or join 'em. Your choice!"

The two soldiers locked eyes, Rugg's expression belying his harsh tone. With a sob and a curse the sergeant tore himself away.

Gasping and coughing, the Marines stared at Ames with haunted expres-sions. The smells of sweat, fear, blood, and cordite rolled off their bodies in waves, the stench assaulting the reporter's sinus cavities, making him gag.

This is what you wanted, don't forget, he reminded himself, again and again. *Everything you wanted.*

Looking over their shoulders, the pilots made a frantic check of their passengers while all four doorgunners kept up their pounding fire into the rushing enemy, exploding them into red mist and body parts, exacting sweet revenge.

"Go!" bellowed Ames at last, nearly wild with fear. "What are you waiting for? Everybody's in! There's no more time! For God's sake *go, go, go!*"

As if obeying his command, slicks one and three lifted, beginning their dust-off, the insane screaming of their rotors spooling up.

And then only twelve feet off the ground, slick three heaved and rocked as the murderous rounds probed upward to riddle the Plexiglass canopy, smashing through and jerking Warrant Officer Torelli's body around like a drunken marionette. Brutal fire raked the fuselage from nose to tail, severing fuel lines and control cables, seeking the kill.

The doomed slick seemed to hang suspended for a moment. Then it heeled over and plunged sideways into the ground. Instantly it exploded, thowing flames and jagged steel forty feet outward, a rolling orange and black ball of burning aircraft fuel marking its grave.

Horrified, the other aircrews and their Marine evacuees watched a writhing figure rolling helplessly in the flames before flopping free of the crushed wreckage. As he staggered to his feet, Nick saw that his body was completely sheathed in blazing hellfire.

Dooley.

"No!" In one motion Nick threw off his helmet, unsnapped his safety harness, grabbed a medical blanket, and leaped through the open doorway. Dropping the five feet to the ground, he rolled once, then sprang back to his feet to make a dead run toward his friend.

Shrieking, Dooley thrashed in unbelievable contortions on the ground as he desperately tried to put out the fire that was consuming him. His unearthly screams filled the air, so loud that blood poured from his throat.

Falling to his knees, Nick threw the blanket on top of the writhing man, using his hands to smother the stubborn flames, oblivious to both the pain from his hands and the AK-47 rounds thudding into the ground all around them until he had Dooley safely wrapped in the blanket and in his arms. Vainly Nick tried to shut out the image of how horribly burned his friend was. All that counted now was getting to safety.

"Cover us!" he screamed, clambering to his feet.

He stumbled back to the waiting slick, protecting Dooley's body with his own while enemy bullets missed him by scant inches. Frankie and Barnes fired furiously over Nick's head into the enemy troops beyond, who dropped behind their dead, keeping up a slashing rain of return fire at the remaining slicks.

Just as Nick reached number one, a wet, slapping sound filled the air and, hard on its heels, a shriek. Frankie fell back away from his gun mount, flesh and entrails hanging from his midsection in tatters. Screaming in agony, he began mindlessly clawing at himself.

Glancing back, Nick caught a glimpse of the soldier who'd shot Frankie turning to run. He didn't get far. The Marine crouching next to the little gunner opened up on the fleeing enemy with a burst from his M16. Two of the bullets tore off the NVA's jaw. The third blew out his heart.

Nick hurled Dooley through the slick's open hatch, felt hands jerk him roughly up. Halfway inside, his vision exploded as a bullet grazed his skull, carving a deep channel through hair and scalp. The air expelled from his lungs in a gasp, and he collapsed across Dooley's convulsing form, face to face, as the smaller man's scorched eyes rolled back in their sockets.

From a distance, through a red haze of pain, Nick heard Rugg screaming, "They're in, Gaddick! Move! Move!"

Then conciousness faded as below them the earth tilted and swung and fell away. They were above the guns, above the death, lifting higher.

Heading home.

PART TWO :
CINCINNATI, PRESENT DAY

CHAPTER 8

NICK CASTLE GAZED across the mahogany conference table, directly into the calm brown eyes of a killer. Honshi Yamato didn't look the part, but then corporate raiders seldom did. Appearances aside, men like Yamato were as fatal to companies as a poison, and Nick warily regarded the proposal lying on the table in front of him with all the caution a man would give a pit viper.

He took a deep, cleansing breath before he spoke. "Mr. Yamato." He tried his best to keep his voice calm. "As I told you earlier, I'm simply going to need more time to—"

"My time is finished," Yamato interrupted, sitting up a bit straighter in the black leather visitor's chair, his expression stern. "Mr. Castle, the hour grows late. I wish to finalize this matter before tomorrow. Many matters at home require my attention."

He placed both hands flat on the table. The edge of it barely came to his sternum. Like most Japanese, Yamato was slightly built. He was also snowy-haired and stooped, showing every one of his eighty-plus years. In fact, he looked like everybody's idea of a kindly grandfather.

But the eyes, Nick thought, *the eyes ruin it all.*

They were the eyes of a much younger man, a man who'd grown up on the merciless docks of Tokyo. Sixty years ago, Honshi Yamato had acquired a small marine salvage business and then through extortion, arson, and occasionally murder had parlayed that business into one of the world's largest financial concerns. His flagship company, the Yamato Group, was always hungry for more. In years past it had sunk its claws into a dozen Western businesses, slaking its thirst on their life's blood.

Now the beast cast a ravenous eye toward Castle Industries.

Yamato breathed deeply and evenly, slowly tapping his pen on the table's surface. It took a moment for Nick to realize the psychological trick; the old man was using his pen as a metronome, tapping it in time to the ticking of the Howard Miller grandfather clock standing against the far wall, establishing dominance.

Two can play at this. Nick never broke the stare with Yamato, but with a mocking smile on his lips began tapping his own pen in counterpoint with the old man's.

Yamato didn't catch on for a few seconds. When he did, he stopped his tapping with a scowl.

"Mr. Castle. As I was saying, the hour—"

"Grows late," Nick finished. "I agree. We're both growing tired. If I may make a suggestion, let's meet back here tomorrow morning at around ten. I'll have brunch catered, and maybe we can get this issue behind us at last." He indicated the phone by his hand. "May I call a cab for you, sir? Perhaps you'd like some help outside?"

Take that, you fossilized crook.

Standing, Yamato narrowed his eyes. "I have my own driver. Also I am not as frail as you would doubtless hope. Come!"

His two aides had jumped up at his command, and now all three strode toward the door. Reaching it, Yamato touched the handle and turned.

"I wish there to be no misunderstanding," he said, his voice cold. "I know you plan to spend the night trying to come up with a way to stop me. Be assured, you will fail. I *will* put Castle Industries under my group. Your attempts to delay the inevitable are both pathetic and pointless. The facts are simple."

Yamato's demeanor was chilling as he began to tick off the points on his skinny fingers. "One: Your board of directors has voted to make Castle Industries a publicly traded corporation, beginning tomorrow. Two: The initial public offering of common stock is to be five hundred thousand shares. Three: Those shares are to be available tomorrow morning at the opening bell of the New York Stock Exchange. Four: The selling price floor is to be twelve dollars per share. These are facts."

The old man folded his hands placidly across his abdomen. "What I have done is simply to finesse the system, putting into motion certain forces that will assure that by the close of trading tomorrow I will have aquired fifty-one percent of all Castle stock. In sum, your company shall be mine."

"To strip out, break up, and sell," Nick said tightly.

"Perhaps." The Asian man's nonchalance was maddening. "As majority stockholder, I will do with it as I please. My final offer—" he pointed to the bound document on the table "—removes you as CEO of this firm and places you under my authority as plant manager."

Plant manager. Nick silently ground his teeth.

"Sign it, and you are assured of employment for the forseeable future," the old man said. "Do not sign, and you are out completely, as of tomorrow. With my global contacts, it will be child's play to see that no one hires you for any position, up to and including men's-room attendant. Think on that, sir, during your night season."

He again turned to go. One of Yamato's aides was pulling the door open when Nick called out, "Hey."

The old man stopped and pivoted with a sigh, all pretense of civility gone. "What is it now?"

Nick narrowed his eyes. "You may be a ring-tailed wonder as a business-man, Yamato, but you seem to have forgotten a key rule of the game: Never underestimate the competetion. Worse than that, this time your reach has exceeded your grasp. Something tells me this has gone beyond a simple act of business piracy and into the realm of another thing altogether. A showdown, if you will. Your god against mine." Nick's smile slowly grew into a grin. "Care to lay any bets, old man? I'll give you Vegas odds."

Yamato stood silently quivering, his eyes daggers.

"I thought not. Get out. And don't let the door smack you in the butt."

The other man plastered on a death's head grimce. "Mr. Castle. You cannot imagine the pleasure I have at the thought of you either writhing under my thumb or selling carnations in winter on Fountain Square. It mat-ters little to me which. Until tomorrow." He bowed slightly, his aides aping him, and then all three were gone.

As soon as the door clicked shut, Nick slowly leaned forward, at last drop-ping his forehead on the table with a groan. "Lord help me." He stayed like that for quite a while.

Ten minutes later that prayer was answered in an unlikely way as the door swung open once more.

"Yo, Nicky." CT Barnes quickly looked around the room. "They gone?"

Concern filled his face. Except for his graying hair CT looked remarkably the same as he had nearly forty years ago, bigger, if anything.

"You all right? You look lousy."

"Thanks. Yeah, they're gone. Until tomorrow morning." Bone tired, Nick sat up straight and sighed. "Man, what a fight. I wish I'd thought to put this on pay-per-view. We'd have made a fortune. Maybe even enough to buy out Yamato, get him to go bother somebody else."

He gestured to one of the chairs encircling the huge table. "Oh, well, pull up a rock. Always room for my favorite security chief. The night's still young. Who knows, maybe we can put our heads together, figure a way out of this unholy mess."

"Who says the night's young? Don't look now, but my watch says 11:30." Shaking his head, CT sat down next to his friend. "You've been in this room over six hours with Yamato and his trained chimps. All that time, and still nothin'?"

"Nope, nada. This one's going down to the wire." Nick rubbed his face, then slowly rotated his head in a circle, listening as his neck vertabrae crackled with tension. "This is insane. When the board voted to go with an IPO on the stock, the main reason was to help build a better retirement for our employees, give 'em a shot at owning some of what they work so hard for. I had no idea it would draw a shark like Yamato, none at all."

He blew out a breath. "Stupid, huh? Guess I'm slipping. I dunno . . . maybe it's time to hang it up, let Yamato have the thing, go fishing in Cozumel. Too many battles for too many years."

CT grinned. "Tired of corporate combat, huh? Wish you were still flyin' slicks out of Quon Tre?"

"Uh, no. Business warfare may be rough, but it rarely draws blood."

"I know a Japanese industrialist I wouldn't mind seein' bleed a little bit." Reaching over, CT grabbed Nick by the shoulder, giving him a gentle shake. "C'mon, bro, snap out of it. There's gotta be a way to beat this greedy little despot."

"Greedy little despot. I swear, CT, you amaze me. You come back from Nam, snag your GED, go to college on the GI bill, get your BA in electronics, and then you go on to achieve your master's in business security. All that education, and what do you use it for? Just to insult people more fluently." Nick shrugged. "That said, you're right. Yamato *is* a greedy little despot."

CT rested his massive forearms on his thighs. "There's a way, Nick. Gotta be. I've spent the last fifteen years here as your righteous right hand, the best time of my life. I'm not finishin' out my career pourin' tea for some twit. That simply is not gonna happen."

Both men fell silent for a bit, gazing out at the city below through immense plate glass windows. The executive offices of Castle Industries took up the entire thirtieth floor of the prestigious Whittaker Building in downtown Cincinnati, and tonight's view this clear September evening was never prettier.

"Take a good look." Nick sighed again. "Barring a miracle, tomorrow Yamato owns this, and I'm out of a job."

"We, Kimo Sabe." The big man jumped to his feet. "No way I'm workin' for that yardape, no way. Write it down."

Nick dug the heels of his hands into his eyes. "Why don't you head on home, check on Sarah and the kids. Give 'em a kiss for me. They've probably forgotten what you look like."

"Nicky, Nicky. C'mon baby, toughen up. I got the feelin' the Lord's got things under control. Gonna be all right." The giant stood up to stretch, his fingers almost brushing the ceiling tiles above. "I'm leavin'. You too. Go on home, see Maryann. After that you oughta mellow out, read a book, stack some Zs, somethin'."

"Yeah." Nick stood as well. "I suppose you're right."

As they left the conference room, Nick paused to take in a final look at the well-decorated area before flipping off the light. All the years he'd spent building the business up . . .

There had to be an answer to this. There *had* to be.

CHAPTER 9

THE TOP WAS DOWN on Nick's Lexus as he sped along I-74 toward his home on the west side of the city. In spite of his trials, his spirits were already better. He'd weathered storms like this before. Well, maybe not exactly like this, but still pretty rough.

Shaking his head, he smiled. It was a good thing the Lord had never promised a life of ease for His kids, but only the promise that they'd never have to go through it alone. Nick was living proof of that.

And then, as he drove, almost of their own volition his thoughts drifted back to those first hard, gray hours at the field hospital he'd been taken to. At the pain he'd endured, the revelations he'd been told, and the hope he'd been given.

.. .. ..

HE GROANED, putting a hand to his head. Bandages? Sharp pain flashed, and he opened his eyes wide. What?

"Easy, man," a voice above him muttered. "Go easy."

Nick could barely make out a massive figure hovering over him. He blinked. Blurry.

Using the backs of his hands, he rubbed crusted matter from his eyes and blinked again. The figure materialized into that of Mr. C. T. Barnes.

"Hey . . . " Nick's tongue felt thick and rubbery, his brain shot through with spiderwebs. He shook his head to clear it. *Augghh. Mistake.* " . . . where am I?"

"MASH 812th." Barnes rumbled a low laugh. "Guess you usin' some of those supplies we brought over, bro."

Nick made a floppy motion with his hand. "Water. Dry. Gimme a drink of water."

"Sorry, man, but the nurse says only ice chips for now." Barnes brought some over in a clear plastic cup, gently placing a few between Nick's lips.

He pulled them into his mouth, then settled his head back on the pillow. "Better. Thanks." He cleared his throat. "How long have I been here?"

"Three days." Barnes hooked a stool with his foot, slid it over and sat down. "You feel up to talkin'?"

"I think so." Nick swallowed again, trying to focus on his friend. "Mr. C. T.—"

"Hold it." Barnes held up a meaty paw. "Stop right there, Nicky. The Lord done been dealin' with me about that. I ain't gonna go by that no more."

Nick had no idea what his friend was talking about, but nodded anyway. "Okay. So what do your initials stand for, then?"

Barnes looked sheepish, a first for him. "Don't laugh, awright? It's Crispus Thaddeus."

A pause. Nick wasn't sure he'd heard him correctly. "You're kidding."

"Nope. Truth."

"I think I'll just call you CT."

Barnes grinned, his wide mouth an expanse of yellow teeth. "So does my momma." The giant's grin faded as his tone grew somber. "Like I said Nicky, we gotta talk."

That sounded grim. "I have the feeling I'm not going to like this."

"I have the feelin' you gonna hate it."

Nick gulped. "Dooley?"

"Alive. Frankie too."

Frankie?

"Yeah. Dude got nailed 'bout the same time you did." Barnes sighed, a huge sound. "Guess I'd better say it all. Sure you up for this?"

"Say it!" Nick barked, more sharply than he'd meant, and the pain made him wince. "Sorry man. Just . . . just say it, okay?"

Barnes laid a beefy hand on his friend's shoulder, nearly covering it. "Okay. Well, the ride back to base was mighty hairy. Number one an' number two took bad ground fire, an' number two was shootin' black smoke like crazy. We didn't think it would even make it back but it did, all three did. The colonel'd already called for medevac slicks to be waitin' for us at Quon Tre, an' two was. Soon as we landed, they loaded the three wounded Marines an' you an' Dooley an' Frankie an' Mister Ames on 'em an' they dusted off back to here."

Nick tried to sit up straight. Again the pain jabbed him. "Him too?"

"Hey, man, lay back an' lemme tell it, huh?"

"Okay." Nick lowered himself back down with a hiss between clenched teeth. "Trevor was hit? How bad?"

"Naw, man, nothin' like that. He wadn't hit." Barnes lowered his voice, looking from side to side, before muttering the next. "See, the thing is . . . he gone nuts."

"What!"

"Shhhh. Yeah, Mister Ames, he snapped. He was here for a hour gettin' checked out, then they evacked him to the *Kitty Hawk,* let them Navy shrinks take a whack at him."

Nick slowly shook his head. "Unreal . . . He went nuts? I don't get it. He seemed like a pretty together dude. I just can't feature it."

"Feature it, bro. You know the drill, some guys cain't handle the music. We both seen it happen. Too bad, too. I kinda liked Mister Ames."

"Yeah, so did I." Nick paused. "So what about Dooley and Frankie?"

Barnes looked at the floor a moment before speaking. When he did, his voice was soft.

"Bad, man. Real bad. Both of 'em on the *Kitty Hawk* too. Heard they got Dooley in a burn unit. Heard they was flyin' him right on over to the States, to Walter Reed. Orderly here tol' me they got specialists there, s'posed to be the best in the world. As for Frankie . . . "

He seemed to struggle for the words. "Lot more simple. That AK did a number on him, man. Liked to have blowed his insides out. They saved him, but the docs are sayin' Frankie's never gonna walk again."

"Oh, man—"

"That ain't all. Here's the real kick in the slats. Our unit's bein' decommissioned."

"Say *what?*"

"Yep. If I'm lyin', I'm dyin'. Got this from Greer, you know, the company clerk. Dude got this straight from the top, General Mannon hisself. Seems Mister Ames goin' nuts is some kinda major PR foul-up. Mannon's tellin' anybody that'll listen that Rugg had no written authority to send Ames up with us."

"So what?"

"So the 7th and the 115th is bein' erased, and Colonel Rugg's bein' courtmartialed. And Rugg's a good man, too good for this." Barnes blinked. "Always good to me, any rate."

Nick couldn't believe his ears. This was getting worse by the second.

The giant went on, "The colonel's already over at battalion to stand trial, but it'll go quick, open and shut. Word is they got him in their sights, and ol' Mad Jack's a goner. Inside a week he'll be in civvies again. Or in Leavenworth."

"Man, don't say that! I know for a fact he was set up in this deal by Mannon and his editor pal. Trevor said so. And we all know Mannon's had it in for Mad Jack because he wouldn't toe the company line. Mannon was just waiting until the colonel did something he couldn't abide. I guess he saw this as his chance to get rid of him for good."

"Don't mean a thing, man. The brass wants Rugg's guts for garters, an' they gonna get 'em. And you're right, this is just an excuse to do what they been wantin' to do for a long while."

Nick pondered for a moment before saying, "So what about us? What happens to us?"

"Who knows?" Barnes shrugged. "I only got two weeks left. They'll fix me up with some kinda grunt work, I guess. Stackin' ammo crates, workin' in the laundry, somethin'."

"What about me? Heard anything on that?"

"Yeah, heard the nurses talkin' about you. They said you have a concussion and are s'posed to be in here for at least another coupla days. Make sure your brains don't fall out, I guess. Then after that, I dunno. You only got, what, about another three weeks left yourself, right?"

"Yeah, about."

"Egghead like you, Nicky, I wouldn't sweat it. They'll be findin' a good use for ya, bro." Barnes brightened. "Hey, maybe they'll send you out to count mines!"

Nick started to laugh, and then grabbed his head with a groan. "Oh man. I can't do too much of that. Jeez, Louise, this has turned into a real mess, hasn't it?"

"You said it. Bad end to a good unit."

He was about to reply when Warrant Officer Gaddick stuck his dark, curly head in the tent flap and beat him to it. "Hey, Castle, how's it going, kid? The head and hands, better?"

"Yeah, they are. Thanks."

"Super, super." Gaddick turned to the giant. "You about done here, corporal? We need to shove off." From outside came the muffled sound of a woman's laugh. Gaddick half-turned in mock annoyance. "Stop it, Maxine."

"Yes sir, comin'," Barnes said.

The laughing continued, and Gaddick's head disappeared.

Barnes smirked. "Phil Gaddick, ladies' man. That's half the reason the dude flew me over here every day, to flirt with the nurses."

Nick felt a sudden lump in his throat. "You've been coming to see me every day?"

"Sure, bro," Barnes grinned. "Even conked out you was better comp'ny than Gaddick."

"Listen, you'd better catch your ride while you can. Unless you want to bunk the night in here with me."

Barnes gave a mock shudder. "No way, baby, not me. Not hardly. I'm gone."

The big man was turning to leave when Nick called out, "CT? I just want to say . . . Well, thanks. For everything."

"You got it. You rest now. I'll be back tomorrow, same time. We'll talk about your visitor."

Nick frowned. "My what?"

"Tomorrow." With that, Barnes flipped back the tent flap and was gone.

Chapter 10

NICK FOUND HIMSELF at a four-way stop in one of the better parts of town he usually drove through to get to his own neighborhood. Not for the first time he looked to his left and regarded the huge brick church hulking there on the corner. The light on the sign at its front was out, and he couldn't seem to recall right then what it was. Some off-the-wall denomination, he was pretty sure of that: Unitarian, Universalist, Eckankar—something like that. Some feel-good-do-your-best-and-it'll-all-work-out pile of uselessness whose main draw was sending people to hell in plush cushioned chairs.

It was exactly the kind of place Lieutenant Minch would have felt right at home in. Nick smirked as again his mind went back to that Vietnam field hospital. Good old Minch. Whatever happened to that yahoo, anyway?

.. .. ..

AN HOUR OR SO after CT had departed, Nick was floating in a painkiller-induced half-slumber when he heard a cheery voice. Someone was standing next to his bed.

"Knocky, knocky! Corporal Castle, are you awake?"

"Wha? Whoozis?" Nick propped himself up one elbow, the pain in his head somewhat abated. He gazed at his visitor blearily. "Who're you?"

"Hello, corporal!" The man gave a toothy grin. "My name is Minch. Lieutenant Alan Minch. I'm the hospital chaplain."

All Nick's internal radar instantly switched to full red alert.

"How are we doing this afternoon?" the man continued.

The ever-dreaded editorial 'we,' Nick thought.

"And are we enjoying our stay at Ptomaine Central?" The chaplain laughed at his own joke, such as it was.

Nick stifled a groan. This plump, birdlike guy with the long nose already bore all the earmarks of being a major pain.

Nick discarded several replies that would have landed him in the stockade, instead saying neutrally, "Sir, I'm doing well."

The man was staring at Nick's head bandages.

"Real good," Nick said.

The staring continued.

"Fine as frog's hair."

This guy was staring ropes.

"Sir, was there something you wanted?"

Minch jumped, and then tittered.

Oh boy, Nick moaned inwardly. *I'm really, truly not up for this.*

"Sorry, corporal." Minch pursed his lips. "It's just that, did you know they've shaved half your head? It looks so . . . odd. I'll bet when your hair starts to grow back it's going to itch like the very dickens."

Who let this idiot in here? "Sir, if you could—"

"My job is to guide the patients here," the chaplain broke in. "To give spiritual insights. Succor, if you please."

A sucker? What?

"Yes, I just wanted to stop by and introduce myself, and to let you that know I'm here if you have questions."

"Questions, sir? Regarding what?"

"Well, about God, of course." Minch fluttered his hands. "What else?" Then he tittered. Again. "God just happens to be my specialty."

"Is that a fact?" *I'm going to have some fun with this. Besides, I'm bored.* "Well, sir, maybe you *can* help me out here."

"Of course," Minch smiled, plopping himself down on the same stool Barnes had used.

"I have a friend, another gunner as a matter of fact, who got religion a few months ago—"

"Got religion?" Minch broke in again. "Is that what you said?"

Bingo. "Yes, sir. Maybe you can give me your slant on that." *This ought to be interesting.*

Minch rolled his eyes in a smirk, and then leaned in closer, laying one sweaty hand on Nick's knee. He tried not to pull away. The lieutenant's breath smelled like a gruesome blend of garlic and Juicy Fruit.

"He's a fundie, then?" the man smirked.

"A what?"

"Fundie. Fundamentalist." Minch lowered his voice. "A Bible thumper." This last was said in the same inflection as *baby killer.*

"Well, sir, I don't know—"

"Of course, you don't. The silly fools will be the ruination of us all." Minch plonked himself on the head with a forefinger. "The mind, corporal. That's the ticket. Unenlightened thinking has doomed your friend, I fear."

Says you, Nick thought.

The chaplain went on, "A wise man once said it: You are what you think. Mind and spirit, ruling together. Mind is spirit, and so is God. You've heard it said that God is spirit, true? So it follows that God is all and all is God." Minch beamed pontifically, his homily complete.

"You don't say." Nick leaned back.

"Yes, corporal, I do say."

"Rocks and fish, kitty cats and cactus, roses and rats, you and me . . . everything, all is God."

"Yes, that's right."

"Everywhere, transcending time and space."

"Young man, you're a quick study." The chaplain leaned closer, smiling. Sweat beaded his upper lip, nose now inches from Nick's face. "Perhaps when you're discharged we can talk about this more . . . privately." He gave Nick's leg a squeeze.

"So all is God, lieutenant," Nick looked him right in the eye, "including those Vietcong we chopped into dog food?"

Narrowing his eyes, Minch leaned back, sliding his hands from Nick's body.

"You disappoint me, corporal. But that's all right. Words no longer shock me. I've heard them all. They even mocked our Lord." He shook his head. "You seem to have a good mind, boy. Don't waste it pursuing myths."

Nick closed his eyes. "Maybe you'd better leave, sir. I'm getting pretty tired." He grew quiet, waiting, and then heard Minch clear his throat.

"Of course. You've been through a lot. We'll speak again." There was the rustle of tent flaps as the chaplain left.

"Not if I can help it," Nick muttered.

He heard a laugh and opened his eyes. The sound had come from a young orderly making beds; Nick hadn't even known he was there.

"Good one, mac!" the private chuckled. "What a moron. Never heard a real person use the word *fundie* before." He expertly folded the sheet corner flat. "That bird's only been here a week, and already it seems like a year. Replaced our other chaplain, a good man. Lot of us here think this new guy is a little—" The private rocked his hand from side to side. "You know? Dude gives me the willies."

"Me too. And I just met him."

"Yeah, if you're gonna have religion," the soldier continued, finishing the bed, "make it one with some fire in it, like we have back home. That'll do a man some good, 'stead of that fool's balloon juice." He stood and dusted his hands, looking around. "I'm done here. You need anything before I take off, corp?"

"Nothing. Thanks." The orderly left.

Nick now had a pretty good idea of what Barnes wanted to talk about tomorrow. The question was, how had he known the strange chaplain would be paying a visit?

.. .. ..

BEHIND HIM A HORN HONKED, jerking Nick out of his reverie. With an apologetic wave to the other driver, he pressed down on the accelerator and smoothly pulled away.

CHAPTER 11

HE WAS ONLY SIX BLOCKS from home when the attack hit. Like a concrete block dropped from a great height, hot fear, sudden and urgent, seemed to smash into his conciousness. Dark and demanding, for just a moment it commanded his attention, filling him utterly.

Years of experience told him what to do. Without taking his eyes from the road, Nick whispered a quick prayer, full of strength and faith. For a moment longer the fear tried to hold, its centipede legs gripping tighter, and then suddenly it was gone, blown away like a leaf in a cyclone.

With a laugh of relief, Nick accelerated once more, his gray hair flying every which way in the wind. This was nuts. Living the lifestyle of faith, to many, was insanity incarnate because to the natural eye nothing had changed. Tomorrow morning was going to come as scheduled, and Nick still had no earthly idea what to do about Yamato. But God did, and that was enough.

How did people who didn't know the Lord even make it these days? He didn't know. And he also knew that, absent a friend like CT Barnes, it could have very well been him who'd made a partnership with hopelessness.

.. .. ..

THE NEXT DAY following Minch's visit passed uneventfully. Nick rested, ate, and did a bit of nurse flirting himself, trying to keep from glancing at his watch every three minutes. If Gaddick was true to form, he should be landing by 1500 hours, bringing Barnes with him. Nick wasn't even aware that he was dozing once again until he sensed rather than heard the big man enter the tent.

"Yo, Nick."

He jerked fully awake with a start. "CT! Dude, I was having a fabulous dream. That cute little Portuguese nurse and I were—"

"Save it," Barnes said with a smile. "I can't listen to such things no more."

"Okay, but that nurse sure is something. Connie, I think her name is. Whoo-wee. Yowza."

"I bet she is, Nicky." Barnes deftly changed the subject. "So whadja think a' Minch?"

Nick scowled. "Minch. Even his name sounds like somebody who squeaks when he walks. Where'd they dig that guy up?" Cautiously he sat up straighter. "And who told you about him seeing me, anyway?"

Barnes rumbled a laugh. "Ain't he a caution? Ol' Minchie was in here the first day when I stopped by, and you was still asleep. I come in here and there he was, mumblin' and leanin' over you like freakin' Dracula or somethin'. I tell ya, bro, my guts twisted like a worm on a hook. Dude may be a lotta things, but a preacher of God he ain't."

"Tell me about it." Nick shook his head. "Listen, I don't know what this thing you're into is all about, all this Jesus stuff. All I know is you're sure different than when we first met. And if what you have is one end of the spectrum, then Minch is way over on the other side."

"Well, I dunno about no spectrums," Barnes shrugged. "All I know is what Jesus done for me. Took out the hate, man, and the drugs and the pain of losin' ma daddy—all gone, like they never was."

"Yeah? Gone where?"

"Dunno." The big doorgunner rubbed his nose. "Sea a' forgetfulness, I s'pose."

"The what?" Nick tried not to laugh; he didn't want to offend this man who was giving so much of himself to him. But, come on. The sea of forgetfulness? It sounded like something out of Dr. Suess or a kid's game.

"Yeah. The Bible talk about it. Says God takes all your sin, all your bad stuff, and casts it into some kinda sea or somethin', where even God hisself cain't remember it no more."

Barnes leaned forward on his chair. "I ain't real clear on it, Nicky. Sometimes that book works out ta be a pure-D puzzlement to me, but my momma wrote me and said if I keep at it, it'll keep makin' more and more sense, and maybe I might end up talkin' better too." He nodded decisively. "Gonna make somethin' a' my life, man. I'm gonna get me a education when I get back to the World, get me my GED, maybe even more. But I got to read the Bible every day, Nicky. You should too."

"Yeah, well . . ." Nick was suddenly uncomfortable with where this conversation was going. "Maybe I will someday."

"One a' the reasons I stopped by," Barnes said, almost shyly. "Here. Wanted you to have this." He shoved something wrapped in newspaper and string into Nick's hands.

"What is it? This isn't my birthday."

"Call it early Christmas."

Nick shook his head as he began tearing off the old newspaper. Trying to understand how Barnes had changed so completely from the way he'd been could end up being a lifetime pursuit.

He pulled the gift free. "Aw, a Bible. Cool, thanks." Then he stopped, peering at the condition of the book. He opened it up to the presentation page. "Hey, wait a minute CT, this is yours. It's got your mother's inscription in it."

He tried handing it over, but Barnes took a step back. "Keep it. I'll be gettin' another when I get back to the World. 'Sides, you'll be needin' it to look at after we talk."

Nick laid the Bible down alongside his leg. "Okay, you've finally got my curiosity up. Let's hear it."

Barnes's face grew stern. "Don't want no curiosity, fool! I'm wantin' your *attention.*"

Nick gulped. "You've got it."

The big man began pacing back and forth at the end of the bed. Suddenly he stopped, fixing Nick in a stare.

"You ever think about dyin', man, how it might be? Checkin' out, and wonderin', hey, is that it? A long sleep? Or maybe not even that. Maybe just a blank, nuthin' at all, just winkin' out?"

Nick swallowed before answering. "Sure I do. We all do. You know that."

"Not me," Barnes said firmly. "Not no more."

"What do you mean?"

"I mean I found out this life here, this right now?" Barnes smacked his forearm several times, loudly. "This ain't nuthin' but the pregame, man. Real life don't even start till you're dead and gone."

"Huh?"

"That's right. It says so, right in that book, more than once, too. See, everbody gonna live forever someplace, slick, heaven or hell. Thang is, you get to choose where. God give everbody that choice. Heaven or hell, acey-deucy, and God done give you the winnin' hand."

Nick's head was spinning, and it wasn't because of the painkillers. "Hold the phone here. I went to church as a kid, and I never heard any of this stuff you're going on about."

"Nicky, they's churches, and then they's churches, dig? Church ain't nothin' but a buildin', man. *We're* the church. People that loves the Lord. That's all. Goin' in a church don't make you a Christian anymore'n goin' in a garage makes you a Buick."

Nick grinned at Barnes's words. This stuff was real to him, all right. "Okay. Let's say you're right. So how do you do it?"

The giant grinned, showing that same huge mouthful of yellow teeth. "Now we're gettin' to it. The story don't change, only the people. Story is the same ol' same ol'. You just say you're sorry for your sins, ask Jesus to come into your heart, let him do the changin' on the inside, dig it, and he will. He always does it right, too, dude, first time outta the box." He shrugged. "And that's it."

Nick stared. "What do you mean, that's it? That's all? Just ask Jesus to come in, and he does it, wham, just like that? Instantly?" He shook his head. "I don't know, man. It seems too easy."

Barnes's look now was almost fierce. "Easy it ain't. What you got to do is soak it up and be willin' to live for him. He'll work out all the rest. It's like when I handed you my Bible. I coulda stood there all freakin' day with it in my hand, but you had to reach out and take it from me, dig? That's the onliest part you got, is takin' that free gift he's offerin'." Barnes paused, breathing like he'd run the hundred in six seconds flat, his eyes seeming to bore holes. "So whaddya say? You want in or what?"

Nick squirmed. He hadn't remembered this hospital bed as being so uncomfortable the night before. "Well, what you say makes a lot of sense."

"Makes the onliest sense," Barnes broke in.

"I dunno . . . I'm going to have to think on this some. Give me some time, okay?"

"Time." Barnes lowered his eyebrows, his voice now seeming to come from somewhere under the tent floorboards. "Time's the one thang we ain't got, slick. Blood clot break free in your skull and wham!"

Nick flinched.

"Be all over, baby. Leastways on this earth. But your troubles'll just be startin', man, and they'll never end." Barnes paused again, and then asked softly, "You remember how it was with Dooley? How it was that day he got caught on fire, how he was jerkin' and screamin' and cryin'?"

Nick turned his face away and didn't answer.

"Sure you do," Barnes said. "I'll never forget how quick you leaped outta that slick to get to him. Bravest thing I ever saw. Only took a few seconds, but to poor ol' Dooley rollin' around on the ground, it musta seemed like years."

Nick remembered, all right. Trying not to was the hard part.

"Now imagine hell and havin' Dooley's pain all the time. It never stops, never gets better. It just . . . never . . . stops. And Torelli—how much time do you think he had to get right with Jesus before Mister Charles blew him clean outta his socks? Don't play around with this Nicky. God's got a great life planned out for you, man, for me too. It's time we start livin' it."

There was a long pause, and then Nick drew a shuddering breath and turned back to his friend. It was if something hard and dirty deep inside was breaking loose and washing away. The big man's words had detonated like a bomb in the center of Nick's heart. All doubts and arguments were gone in the light of this gentle giant's simple faith.

Barnes was right. It was time, and past time. "What do I need to do?"

The giant smiled. "Here's how momma said to do it. Just talk to Jesus like he's a real person 'cause he is, Nicky, the realest person you'll ever meet, and ask him to come into your heart. Tell him you're givin' your life to him to make of it what he will and to please take away your sins. It's easy as pie."

"Okay." Nick closed his eyes for a few seconds, and then he opened them with a grin. "I did it just now as you were saying it."

"Yow, baby! Welcome to the fam'ly!" Barnes slapped a huge hand on Nick's shoulder, and as he did so Nick's eyes nearly popped with the impact. The giant grinned sheepishly. "Sorry, man, I got carried away. You're my first convert!"

Nick rubbed his throbbing shoulder. "Yeah, well, don't kill me my first five seconds of being a Christian. I have no idea what my dad is going to make of this."

"Your dad! What about Minch?"

The two men stared at each other, and then both burst out laughing so hard a nurse came in to see what was the matter.

.. .. ..

WHAT A DAY THAT HAD BEEN. And things had only gotten more interesting.

As Nick drove on, his thoughts shifted forward a few years, harking back to the day he'd assumed control of Castle Industries in 1985. When he'd returned from the war in 1972, he'd been more than a little concerned about what his father would make of his newfound faith. His fears had proved groundless.

Henry Castle did at first wonder whether Nick's change was to be believed. Maybe it was just a phase. He'd gone through them before. But after many days of closely watching his son, Henry was finally convinced that, whatever had happened, Nick's experience had matured him like nothing anyone could have imagined.

As an added bonus, Nick's prowess with business was everything the elder Castle had hoped for. His energy was unflagging, his curiosity and love of learning boundless, his integrity and ethics beyond question. When at last Henry began asking him questions about what his war experience, Nick was only too happy to explain, but slowly, taking into consideration the man's stoic ways.

And it worked. Henry Castle was the first to put his trust in the Lord. Nick's mother, Eileen, followed six weeks later.

Unfortunately, both of Nick's parents were killed in an automobile accident just days after his mother had come to the faith. At the time Nick was vice president of Castle Industries, and because the firm was still family owned, the mantle of leadership naturally fell to him.

One of the first things Nick did was to hire his old friend CT Barnes as head of security. CT's fame as a level-headed troubleshooter was already well known, and he'd jumped at the chance. The two ex-soldiers were still as different as hot dogs and steak, but their friendship only grew stronger through the years. So did Castle Industries' profits.

And they'll continue to do so, Nick thought grimly as he wheeled into his driveway, *Yamato and his crap notwithstanding.*

CHAPTER 12

HONSHI YAMATO DECADENTLY SMOKED a final cigarette as he relaxed in the bedroom of the Omni Hilton's presidential suite. To him, most Western things were dung, but over the years he'd managed to acquire a neverending need for American cigarettes. Marlboros.

Minutes earlier the old man had commanded his two aides to stand guard in the hallway outside his door. Yamato's orders were, as always, quite specific: No one was to approach closer than fifteen feet to his person without one of the aides turning them right back around again, preferably without force. Also no one, under any circumstances, was permitted to be in the room with the master until he'd given them permission to do so. This was his private time, the time he cherished above all else.

The time before a kill.

Stealing a last glance at the sleeping city through the huge window, the old man slowly drew the curtains closed, mashing out his cigarette in a crystal ashtray. Then he undressed and padded over to his closet where he drew out a single item of clothing. It was a black silk robe, his most treasured one. What set it apart from the others was the adorning crest of his family's longtime guardian, a filagree of a highly ornate crimson and gold dragon slithering down the back and encircling both sleeves.

Reverently Yamato drew the robe on over his emaciated body, tying it shut with a rich golden sash. Then striding over to the Chippendale desk, he sat down. On it lay his laptop, already powered up and plugged into the room's com port. Fine sweat beading his lip, Yamato ran his hands over the keys, thin fingers dancing. In moments he was on his company's Web page.

Everything was in readiness.

Various shell corporations he controlled had all been given orders to begin purchasing differing amounts of Castle stock at tomorrow's opening bell, but only upon his sole authorization. A code the old man had devised many years earlier allowed him the ability to consolidate all buy orders into one, that order to be executed by him at his command. So it stood: two hundred fifty-five thousand shares of Castle Industries stock, more than enough to secure controlling interest, were a push of the Enter key away. Yamato held his finger an inch over that key.

And stopped.

I am samurai. Samurai. A samurai can hold his sword out from his body all night long without tiring, and what is this beneath my hands but a sword? A sword to execute my judgment and my will.

It always pleased the old man to rape Western companies, doubly so when they were owned by Christians. *Christians.* The word almost made him ill. Any country that would use nuclear weapons on his revered homeland, and then have the temerity, the *gall*, to send missionaries to tread that same sacred soil after the war was over, smiling, forever smiling, telling the poor moneyless dock rat that he was wrong, wrong. No. Yamato would not have their smiles. *This* was his destiny.

The tingling he received from the proximity of his computer felt almost sexual. And why not? Sex was power, after all. A different sort, yes, but still power.

And as in sex, Yamato was the taker. The spoiler of all not his. His foolish aides would never understand, could never understand. That was why they always had to leave him at these times. Only another warrior could truly realize the depths of his desire.

And of his hate.

Yamato would let that hate build to a crescendo, all through the night. Because at its end the hate was more than his life.

It was his song.

And the song sang deep. Deep and strong, deeper than longing itself, the hate sang inside Yamato's marrow and in his joints. It empowered him, lifted him, gave him strength and purpose when most men his age still dreamed of the girls they'd had in their youth.

But not for Yamato. Never for Yamato. He was samurai.

And he would hold this position until morning.

CHAPTER 13

PULLING HIS CAR INTO THE GARAGE, Nick got out and locked it, then went on through the inside door into his house. It wasn't large as some people might think fit a company president, and it was a little worn. That wasn't surprising. He and Maryann had bought it nearly twenty years ago. They'd loved it, though, as well as their nephew Blake and niece Tracy, who'd come to their family as children when their parents, Maryann's sister and her husband, had died in a plane crash. They'd grown up there, and both kids were away at college now, Tracy a senior and Blake a freshman.

Nick walked the few feet across the inside doorway on plush cream carpeting. Maryann was still up, reading. Hearing him enter, she jumped up out of her chair and ran over to take him by the hand. She gave him a quick kiss, and then leaned back, examining him critically.

"It's about time! Are you all right? How did the meeting go?"

He gave her a longer kiss in return, breaking it with a grin. "Chatterbox. The answers to your questions are, in sequence, yes and not well. Say, do we have anything to eat? My stomach thinks my throat's been cut."

"Eat? Aren't you going to tell me what happened tonight? Did everything get settled between you and Yamato?" Her blue eyes almost sparkled with questions.

"Settled? Well, yeah, after a fashion." Nick moved from the family room into the kitchen, Maryann following, doing her best to hold her tongue.

Opening the refrigerator, he pulled out a jug of milk and poured a big drink. Then clutching his glass in one hand, he stuck his head back in and rooted around.

"I thought you said we had some leftovers or something, hon. At this stage I'd even eat CT's cooking." His voice brightened. "Hey, how about some country ham? Do we have any of that left? I could use a sandwich."

"Nicholas James Castle!"

Wups. *That* voice.

Maryann's tone held an unbreachable command. "Stop what you're doing, right this second, buster! Put that milk away before I empty it down your pants, and tell me what's going on!"

Nick, knowing he was outgunned, carefully set his glass on the counter. "Well, it turns out Yamato's playing a little different game than we thought. He really does hate Americans, Christians most of all. The old croc as much as told me he plans to destroy the company, but I really felt something break through tonight. I can't say how, Maryann, but I know God's going to do it. It's just a matter of staying out of his way." Now Nick grinned. "This is going to be good. Bank on it."

She took his hand. People had always remarked on what an attractive couple they made, Nick tall and dark, Maryann smaller and more delightfully rounded. Even though they'd been married nearly three decades, their love for each other seemed to grow steadily stronger every year.

Maryann's gaze was so guileless and pure and filled with trust it made Nick's mouth go dry. "Okay, I'm standing with you. I agree that Castle Industries is safe, in Jesus' name."

"Yep." Nick cleared his throat and grabbed his milk, flinging the refrigerator door open once again. "Now as I was saying. About that country ham . . . "

CHAPTER 14

YAMATO GLANCED AT THE CLOCK on the laptop's screen: 8:59 a.m. He couldn't have been prouder of himself. He'd sat motionless in this same position, his finger poised above the Enter key, for over nine hours. He nodded once, gravely; he was samurai indeed. Only a few more seconds now, and another Christian company would be his.

And then he would kill it.

The electricity tickling his loins felt quite pleasurable. *Power. Pure power.* Nothing else, no aphrodisiac ever concocted could cause his aged body to react in such a way. It was only a force of his will that was keeping the trembling from showing on the outside, through his finger, for the next few seconds. Just a few moments more, and he would engage that key and destroy Nick Castle's life.

His breath coming stronger now, he began panting like a wolf. Nine o'clock. *Do it.*

Yamato commanded his finger to move . . . and nothing happened.

What? The old man tried again, but it was like it was set in stone. *What is this?* Sweat popped on his brow as he made the effort to move his finger just a bit, just a centimeter. Nothing.

And now here was something truly horrifying. It felt as if a huge hand, steel-like, had grabbed his wrist, encircling it, bearing down.

Sudden hot pain flashed like fire, like burning acid, coring Yamato's left arm. The pain spread up through his shoulder, up and up and up, and then down through his fingertips. The old man's anticipatory victory pant had become a labored and erratic gasping.

A scorching, crushing blow struck Yamato's chest then, agony unlike any he'd ever known, a pain that smashed the universe aside and made his eyes bulge and his sanity flee. Through it Yamato tried to make his body move, away, *away.*

And then all at once and with great force his body did move, and he found himself on the floor. But not just him. Somehow he'd grabbed his laptop on the way down. He wasn't sure how, he wasn't sure of anything now, but there it lay before him, broken into pieces.

Yamato opened his mouth wide for a scream—for his aides, for help, for release, for his torment to cease. But only a wheeze emerged.

The pain doubled. Then doubled again. And then doubled again. He felt like a man being crushed beneath blue-hot rollers. This was insane! If he could only get a breath, just a small one, just one. Make this elephant get off his chest, crawl away.

To his shame Yamato realized he'd voided his bowels. He was now rolling and gasping in his own filth. Unbelievably, the pain grew yet more terrible . . . and then his vision began to darken.

I'm dying. The thought broke over his consciousness in wonder. *It ends here. No!* he fought back. *Not yet, not yet. . .*

Yamato vainly struggled on. Even in his final moments he would not allow himself the indignity of calling upon that Christian God whom he'd hated, would not avail himself of that disgusting thing those cursed missionaries had called grace. No. His pride would see him through this. It always had. His pride . . . his . . .

Finally the old man's gyrations slowed, ceased. His breathing stopped. His eyes became fixed upon . . . something . . .

And it was only then, as he felt the first hot, rushing licks of incredible, mind-scorching fire blasting every atom of his body that Yamato realized the full scope of the truth.

And of his error. To his unutterable horror he realized he'd been wrong.

He'd been wrong, he'd always been wrong, and now forevermore would be wrong, just like those cursed missionaries had said would happen.

And this pain he was enduring had only begun.

CHAPTER 15

AT THE SAME TIME Yamato was breathing his last, the entire executive staff of Castle Industries found themselves crammed into Nick's office, listening to David Plumb, Nick's stockbroker, on the speakerphone as he watched the NYSE reports coming over his system.

Everyone leaned forward in their chairs, full attention on the device, all of them unconsciously doing their best impersonations of the RCA Victor dog. Nick shook his head at the sight. On the other end of the line Plumb had remained silent.

"So far, so good," they then heard him say. "It's 9:02 and nothing's moving on the big board yet about Castle . . . wups, hold on a sec . . . okay, I'm seeing the first shares are gone, a hundred of them . . . another five seventy-five . . . there go a hundred and ten . . . no big buys yet, these all seem to be smaller investors, mom and pop type . . . okay, another two-fifty . . . another three seventy-five . . . Yamato hasn't made his move yet, why, I don't know."

As Plumb's nasal monotone droned on, the office staff began to fidget and glance at one another. Was Yamato playing some kind of sick game with them?

CT mopped his brow, jiggling his knees up and down, sweating BBs. Combat was easier on the nerves than this. Then with a snort he shook his head. No. No, it wasn't.

The minutes crawled by while Plumb dispassionately recited the stock figures like a prizefight announcer on Prozac. "Okay, it's 9:50. Nearly twenty-three percent of the stock issues gone. Yamato must still be at breakfast."

No, thought Nick in sudden clarity. Whatever was holding up the old pirate from making his move was definitely something he hadn't banked on.

Secretaries moved in and out of the office now like wraiths, barely breathing. The atmosphere inside grew as thick as pancake batter. When one of the junior account execs discreetly coughed, it sounded like muffled artillery fire.

So the morning passed, the hours going away, the mid-September sun slowly making moving rectangles of light along the floor as Plumb droned on.

Nick stretched, his eye catching that of CT. Both men shook their heads. This seemed to be taking forever.

The speakerphone suddenly crackled again with Plumb's voice. "Okay . . . okay . . . the pace is picking up now . . . issues are going in smaller lots, but at a faster tempo, twenty shares here, forty-five . . . forty-five . . . there goes another twenty-five . . . Wait a minute . . . now wait a *minute*, here . . . holy Moses, we're coming up on . . . forty-eight percent gone, and still no move from Yamato!"

The broker was finally beginning to show some animation. Nick had begun piping Plumb's running commentary over the PA system an hour earlier, and by now everyone in the entire company had stopped work.

"Forty-nine percent!"

" 'Potter won't close us up today, George!' " somebody joked, incorrectly recalling the famous line from *It's a Wonderful Life*.

Everyone in the room cracked up. It was incredible. They were witnessing a miracle.

A secretary silently slipped into the room, making her way to Nick's desk, where she handed him a folded piece of paper. He took it from her without seeing it.

Plumb was fairly screaming by now. "Forty-nine point three percent gone . . . fifty point eight . . . Oh, my God, *fifty-one percent!*"

The room exploded into cheers. Castle Industries was saved. All over the company, papers were thrown in the air as coworkers hugged and kissed and slammed each other's backs beet red. Tears coursed down almost every face in the office.

Nick threw his head back, shooting both arms straight in the air with a holler. "Thank you, Lord!!" The noise in the room doubled.

After a few more moments he opened his streaming eyes and realized he was still holding the folded piece of paper. He opened it.

Mr. Castle, it read. *I was personal secretary to Honshi Yamato.*

Was?

Please excuse this note, but I understand you are not taking any calls this morning; I probably know the reason for that. At any rate, it is my duty to inform you that Mr. Yamato's other aide and I found our employer on the floor of his hotel room at 9:55 this morning. He was quite dead. The hotel physician has listed the cause of death as a massive myocardial infarction. I believe this is also known as a heart attack.

I do not know what pull you have in the spirit realm, but I thought you should know the final look on Mr. Yamato's face was one of abject terror. I bow to your god. Congratulations.

Hideki Suto.

Nick blinked and stood, holding up his hands for silence. "Folks! Folks, please . . . thanks."

The people in the room quieted down, faces still shining. Most of them would be hoarse by tomorrow.

"Well, what can I say? This victory we've seen today wasn't due to any of our puny efforts. I know that. And I also know that not all of you are Christians, but for those who are, thank you for your prayers." Nick felt his throat closing with emotion. "This paper," he loudly went on, holding it high, "was brought over just moments ago by one of Yamato's aides." He paused. "The old man's dead."

A moment of shocked silence filled the air, followed by collective gasps and murmurs.

"Yeah." Nick shook his head. "Weird. I figured God was going to give us a win in this, but I didn't know he'd do it by Yamato dying." He paused again. "I really don't know quite how I feel about this."

"I do," CT broke in. "Yamato was an evil, twisted dude, just like Haman in the book of Esther. God ended up takin' ol' Haman out, and he's done the same with Yamato. The fact that both of 'em are barkin' in hell right now should make me sad, but I gotta say, it doesn't." The big man grinned from ear to ear. "The Jews celebrated when Haman bit the dust. I'd say it's only right our lovin' boss does the same for us by givin' the whole company the day off tomorrow, with pay. Whattya say, Mr. Castle?"

Nick held his hands out in mock surrender. "You've got me over a barrel, Mr. Barnes. I can't very well go against biblical tradition. Okay, you've got it. I'll call Maryann. You tell the troops."

With a pump of his fist and a "Yes!" CT shot from the office, faster than a man of his size had any right to move.

CHAPTER 16

AT HOME THAT NIGHT Nick and Maryann, along with the Barneses, were still giddy from the day's euphoria.

"I just can't believe it—the guy dropping dead in his hotel room like that." Sarah looked over at Maryann. "Kinda like what God did with King Herod, huh?"

"A lot of people think God doesn't do those sorts of things anymore," Maryann replied. "I guess we're finding out differently."

"Especially in this time we're living in. Some people call these the last days." Nick shrugged and took a pull on his cream soda. "Could be. All I know is we're seeing what bibical scholars have been predicting for centuries. We're smack up against eternity. Every promise God made in his word is being fulfilled in this last little sliver of time we're in."

"Yeah," CT broke in excitedly. "We're seein' it. The glory's bein' poured out like never before. It's decision time. So I guess that would have to include more of the devil's junk, too."

"Well sure," Sarah said. "Just look at what we're seeing here locally in our own church. Salvations by the truckload—and at the same time more filth in the world than anyone has ever seen. Something's gotta give, and soon."

"Yep." Nick stood. "And speaking of church, we'd better move if we're going to make it to tonight's service on time."

CT checked his watch. "Man. Near on to 6:30. We've been yammerin' like politicians for goin' on an hour now."

Maryann went to get their coats from the hall closet while Sarah called the babysitter to check on their kids.

CT looked out the window and gave a mock shiver. "Looks mighty cold out there tonight. Guess I'll have to break down and go ahead and wear my new mink coat. Good thing I just happen to have it with me."

Nick rolled his eyes. "Mink. A grown man—man being the operative word—wearing a mink coat. To church yet. Have you no shame?"

CT's grin grew even more huge. "None at all, my brotha, 'specially when it comes to wearin' fine threads."

Nick shook his head in mock exasperation. "You only talk that way when you wear furry animal skins."

"You'd best be nice to me," the big man shot back, "or I'll be the first security chief you ever saw sportin' a 'fro and platform shoes."

"Oh, boys," Maryann called out from the foyer. "Can we continue this in the car? Nick, let's take the Caddy tonight. Sarah, you and CT can ride with us if you'd like."

CT's mink fell nearly to his ankles. He smiled. Let Nicky flap his jaws. He knew he looked *fine*.

Still going for mock-tough, he turned to his friend. "Who she callin' boy, white-bread?"

"Just get in the car," Nick sighed as they walked out onto the front porch. Locking the house behind them, they started down the steps. "And mind you don't shut the door on your lovely coat when you get in. That would break my heart."

CT gathered up the garment before climbing into the back seat with Sarah. "White people." He carefully shut the door. "What was God thinkin'?"

CHAPTER 17

BY THE TIME THEY REACHED THE CHURCH the lot was almost full, so Nick had to park clear at the back end of the parking lot addition. God's Community Church had been deeply into a mighty move of power the past few months, and its growth had exploded. In just the nine years since Dr. Frank Wasson had taken over as senior pastor the church had gone from a membership of twelve hundred to over four thousand and was now adding as many as two hundred new members a month.

In this they weren't alone. Reports had been coming in worldwide for the past year from churches of all denominations; any group of believers willing to preach an uncompromised gospel was in a period of incredible growth, that growth consisting mainly of the previously unreached. As Sarah had put it, there were salvations by the truckload. Conversely, many churches prattling on about a social gospel and the joys of pop psychology and situational ethics stood vacant or close to it.

It was becoming obvious that people were hungry for something real and lasting. And places like God's Community were ready to feed them a gospel feast. Unfortunately, New Age cults and their ilk had also targeted these same hungry people, with some success.

To add to this, perversion was running rampant, with the media and Hollywood having sunk to new depths of strangeness and depravity. Politicians flaunted their immorality, daring the public to do anything about it. The specter of greed stalked the planet, while diseases thought long extinct had once again exploded on the scene, now even more virulent than before. Clearly a final battle was shaping up. Something had to give.

On a night like this, in the middle of both jubilation and heartbreak, the GCC, as members called their church, was a good place to be. Tonight was the first installment of Fresh Fire, a yearly weeklong series of meetings hosting various guests and musicians. The main thrust of this year's conference was on personal evangelism and a deeper call to a tight walk with God.

Even from out in the parking lot, still fairly far from the church building itself, both couples could hear the swelling of music and the tumult of praise. The air of expectancy was tangible as they found themselves almost double-timing it to the doors. With the way God had been moving lately, this year's Fresh Fire had all the indications of being a barnburner.

The four friends entered the foyer and walked straight into a solid wall of sound. The service had been going on for only a few minutes, but already the orchestra and three-hundred-voice choir were blasting praises skyward. Nick looked through the door glass to find the auditorium packed with nearly five thousand men, women, and children, all lost in joyful and noisy worship.

He scowled. "I knew we should have left earlier. We'll be lucky to find seats together."

"Hey, man, it was you that told me luck just stood for Living Under Christ's Kindness. And look, bro, the Lord's been good to us tonight." CT pointed. "Over there, four seats together, right in the back row."

"Honey, grab those seats," Nick told Maryann. "I'll be right back. I've got to go see a man about a horse."

"Me too," CT said. "I have the feelin' this one's gonna go long tonight, and you know how the pastor hates for people to disturb worship by gettin' up in the middle of service to go."

The two men were walking down toward the men's room when Sarah called out, "Yo, CT, you sweet thang! I thought only women went to do that together!" She and Maryann dissolved into howls of laughter.

CT and Nick pretended they hadn't heard.

.. .. ..

THEY WERE ON THEIR WAY back to the sanctuary when Nick stopped and began chuckling.

"Must be pumpin' nitrous oxide through the vents," CT muttered as he gave his friend a puzzled look. "Wanna tell me what you're ha-ha-in' about, man?"

"That!" Nick cocked his right thumb back over his shoulder toward the bathroom door. "Yamato said a bunch of stuff to me last night, most of it not worth hearing. But one of the last things he said before he left was that when he got through with me, I wouldn't be able to get work even as a men's room attendant." He grinned. "Too bad for him. Guess my job at the company is still secure."

"Yeah, ol' Yamato is the one that's through now. Over and done with."

Nick's smile slowly began to fade. "I really shouldn't be laughing, I guess. Unless Yamato got right with God before he died, he's in hell right now, burning alive. He's been there for nearly eight hours. To him it must seem like eighty thousand years." He paused, remembering.

CT's reply was soft. "Kinda like Dooley, huh? What he went through."

"Yeah." Nick blinked. "And just think, after eighty thousand years really have gone by, Yamato'll still be on fire and screaming . . . " His words trailed off again.

CT put a kind hand on his friend's shoulder. "You all right? This thing with Yamato is really gnawin' at ya, isn't it?"

"What?" Nick shook himself out of his reverie. "Sorry. Not Yamato. Well, not just Yamato, but people like him. People bound for hell, unless somebody gets to them with the gospel first." He looked up, a strange look on his face. "I've got something I want to run by you, an idea I just got as we were standing here. Let's talk about it after the service tonight." He started walking back toward the sanctuary.

In two steps, CT was matching Nick's stride. "What about?"

Nick glanced sideways at his friend. "I think I'm going to do you like you did to me back at that MASH in The Land of the Bad Things. I'm gonna make you wait until later."

"Oh man, now ya got my curiosity up."

Nick stopped and his face right up in the bigger man's. "Don't want no 'curioisity,' fool!" he barked. "I'm wantin' your *attention!*"

The look on CT's face was priceless.

Nick slipped back into his normal voice and posture. "Are you going to keep standing there or what? Let's go on in."

A step behind Nick as they found their way to their wives, CT shook his head. For the CEO of a major manufacturing firm, sometimes Nicky could be a real trip.

CHAPTER 18

NICK COULDN'T SPEAK FOR THE OTHERS, but he couldn't remember when he'd enjoyed a service more. Two hours in, and not a soul had left. They were having too good a time.

It was weird, he thought. Back before he'd become a Christian, it was inconceivable to him that somebody could actually like going to church. But as CT had pointed out back in Nam, there are churches, and then there are churches. The music tonight had been first-rate, as was the guest singer. Pastor Wasson had preached like a house afire, and now they were praising once again.

Nick was in the process of singing along with a famous old chorus, the one about Jesus never letting go of his own. When it happened.

On Tuesday night, the twenty-fourth of September, at exactly 9:15 p.m., the rules forever changed.

He felt two words go off deep inside, but quietly, almost like a soft hand grenade.

This week.

What? He shook his head. *Where'd* that *come from?*

The chorus was repeating—albeit a bit disjointedly—when Nick again heard the voice. Louder this time. More insistent.

This. Week.

He stole a glance at Maryann. She wasn't singing anymore, which was more than a bit odd for her. His wife had her head cocked to one side, as if listening. Nick noticed that the singing was now growing really ragged, both from the choir and the people. What was happening?

CT shot an elbow into Nick's ribs about that time, none too gently either.

"Yow!" Nick winced. "What?"

"You hear that?" the big man whispered. "Two words just now? Or am I goin' nuts?" A look of wonder filled his eyes.

"I heard it, yeah," Nick answered slowly. He motioned with his chin. "Take a look. We're not the only ones."

A general muttering was beginning to rumble through the congregation by now. It wasn't an upset sound, but more a puzzled one. The music finally petered out completely and stopped.

The muttering grew louder.

Pastor Wasson stepped behind the podium. He had his mouth open for several seconds before he seemed to find any words.

"Um. Hello?" he finally managed. "Please, folks, could I have your attention here?"

He got it. Every eye in the place locked onto him, and the pastor smiled, unsure.

"Uh . . . you know, I've been preaching for over forty years, and I'll have to say, I've never experienced anything quite like this." He cleared his throat. "Could I ask everyone to do something for me? Could all of you who just heard a word from the Lord, please hold up your hand?" Wasson held up his right hand, eyebrows raised, a look of expectation on his face.

Nick and Maryann looked around. They'd put their hands in the air; so had Sarah and CT. Then all the hair on the back of Nick's neck stood up as he realized nearly every hand in the building was slowly being raised.

A collective gasp ran though the crowd as they all noticed the same thing.

Wasson put his hand down and gripped the podium. "Okay. Anybody not get anything? Be honest, now."

A few hands tentatively went up, no more than a hundred.

"Okay," the pastor said again. "Now here's the big question. Anybody want to tell us what it was exactly that they heard?"

There was further murmuring mixed with some nervous laughter as it became evident no one wanted to speak out. Then slowly Sister Eula Todd, nearly ninety-five years of age and easily one of the oldest persons in the church, shakily stood to her feet.

"I'll say it, pastor," she said softly, and with a quiver in her voice that was not entirely due to age. Not this time. "It was just two words, right in here." She tapped her heart. "This week." And she nodded once, sealing it.

Nick was finding it hard to breathe. His knees felt like water. Gripping Maryann's hand, he glanced nervously at her. His wife looked as if she was about to pass out.

A buzzing started in the congregation as everyone began speaking at once. It went on like that a few seconds before Wasson held up his hands for quiet. "All right, listen up," he said, his tone deadly serious. "I don't know about you, but I'm gonna seek God's face about this, right here and now. I'm not getting up until I get some answers. Anybody who needs to leave, now's the time to do it."

Are you kidding, pastor?

Nick was right. Not a single person left. Most were already getting on their knees, some in the aisles, some turning their pews into altars.

Nick, Maryann, and Sarah all knelt in front of their pew, burying their faces in their hands. There was no way CT could kneel down next to them, and now he couldn't even make it into the aisle, so he merely folded his huge hands under his chin, still standing, and closed his eyes.

For the next few moments, quiet reigned. No one prayed aloud, no one moved. All that could be heard was the soft, sibilant breathing of nearly five thousand people seeking answers.

Then . . .

Pastor Wasson shot to his feet, his eyes fairly popping. "I know what it means," he croaked. "I know what it means!"

He gazed upward, hot tears flowing down his face. "Oh, my sweet Jesus, it's really gonna happen!" He stared out at his flock. "Don't you get it, people? Don't you *understand*? It's happening this week! He's coming back for us *this week*! This week . . . *my God, this week we're going home!*"

Both of the pastor's arms flew straight up over his head, as if he'd just witnessed the biggest touchdown of his life. In a way, he had.

"Home!"

The word detonated like a nuke.

For the next five minutes the place went absolutely berserk. The reality of the pastor's words had rocked the congregation to its very core. At last Wasson held up his hands for quiet. He sounded as hoarse as the rest.

"All right. All right now, listen up. Before this place went ballistic—"

Here the noise threatened to start again. He held his hand up.

"As I was saying, before we all started yelling our lungs out, I noticed that a hundred people, near as I could tell, had said they hadn't heard the Lord reveal anything to them. Now, here's what I believe the reason is for that. I think it's safe to say only Christians heard this word tonight."

Nick realized he was nodding in agreement.

"And not just here, either," the pastor said. "I believe it was heard all over the world. I'm gonna have to study on this some, for sure. Every one of us needs to seek God's will about this. But that still leaves us with those hundred folks I just mentioned."

He leaned over the podium. "So listen up, and listen good. Some of you out there have never made Jesus Christ Lord of your life. Others may be professing Christians, but your walk sure doesn't show it. Okay, I am gonna say this just once, and I am not gonna beg. This evening, time has flat run out. God's made his intentions as clear as a nail in the well water. There's no more time for debate, for arguing, for procrastination. All that's done. Over. Jesus could return seven days from now or in the next three seconds.

"So here it is. Anybody, and I mean anybody, not 100 percent sure of their walk with Jesus, come down front *now,* right here, and let's get it settled tonight, forever." Wasson pointed at them, his finger looking as big as a ball bat. "Come on, do it now!"

They did. In less than fifteen seconds the entire front of the huge sanctuary was jammed wall-to-wall with a hundred or more seekers while the rest of the church cheered them on. Nick and CT and their wives, everyone, all screamed themselves ragged with high praises to God.

Because here it was.

All of them knew, against everything common sense was trying to tell them, that their pastor had called it dead on target. God had revealed something tremendous to his people, something incredible and without precedent. Judging from the experience of everyone in this congregation, undoubtedly Christians everywhere, all their brothers and sisters worldwide, in the very same spark of an instant had been given the same marvelous gift, an insight no one would have thought possible.

The heat in the church had grown stifling. As if on cue men began opening the emergency exit doors and throwing wide every window.

The pastor grabbed the mike again, grinning hugely. "Folks! Folks, while the altar counselors lead these people down front to the Lord, I want you to hear something. Listen! Hear it? It's coming from outside!"

"I don't—" CT began, then he said, "Wait a minute. I do now!" He grinned at the others. "Guys! Do ya hear that?"

Out in the street, through the open doors, they could hear the blaring of horns from passing cars and the voices of passersby calling out praise to God.

Pastor Wasson laughed, "Well, listen to that! Let's join them!"

They did. And how. Nick wasn't sure but that he heard the angels joining in.

But the overriding thought he couldn't shake, even while glorifying the Lord with every atom of his body, was *why?* What could God's purpose be in revealing such an amazing thing?

And the reply he heard was a whisper so soft, so deep, he nearly missed it. *For Dooley. For them all.*

CHAPTER 19

THEY RODE BACK to Nick and Maryann's house in a haze. It was a miracle they didn't wreck a dozen times over. They finally pulled in the drive, and Nick shut the car off, his hand shaking. They sat there for a few moments, still a little punchy, before he looked back over the seat.

"You guys want to come in? Talk about what we're supposed to do next?"

"Oh, yeah." CT nodded. "I would say that's somethin' we oughtta do. Most definitely."

After they all were inside, seated in the den, Nick drew a deep breath and said, "I guess there's no need to rehash what we were given tonight. We pretty much heard it all. But I do feel we need to discuss what's next, what we—"

"There's one thing we need to talk about, right now," Sarah broke in. "And I think it's pretty serious."

CT looked over at her. "What's that, babe?"

She leaned forward in her chair, clasping her hands tightly out in front of her. "Y'all don't get mad at me, now, but . . . how do we know that what we got tonight was really from God? I mean at the end of the service, after we'd finished praying, Pastor Wasson told us all to go on home and seek the Lord's face about this some more, and that we should meet back at the church tomorrow night. Assuming there is a tomorrow night. So the question, I guess, is, how do we know we didn't get, like, hypnotized or something?" She shook her head. "What bothers me the most is that what we heard goes against the Bible."

"What do you mean by that?" Maryann asked.

Nick and CT leaned forward, both listening intently. This was something that hadn't occurred to either of them. Sarah was a sharp gal.

She pulled her little New Testament out of her purse. "Let me find it here. I'm not so good at finding scriptures just when I want them . . . Here it is. Listen. This is Matthew 25, verse 36: 'But of that day and hour knoweth no man, no, not the angels of heaven, but my Father only.' " She looked up. "See what I mean?"

Maryann frowned. "She's got a point. Maybe what we experienced tonight was really nothing more than an attack from the devil. It's strange to think so, but it could be."

All four fell silent, wondering if maybe they'd been duped after all.

Then Nick snapped his fingers loudly, sitting up straight in his chair and smiling. "Wait a minute. I think I know the answer. Sarah, read that first part again."

"Okay. 'But of that day and hour knoweth no man—' "

"Stop." He looked at the others. "Don't you get it? No man knows the day or the hour of when Jesus is coming for us. The day or the hour. It didn't say we wouldn't know the week."

A slow grin split CT's features. "Son of a—that's right, Nicky! Oh man." He wiggled in his chair like a kid. "Oh man!"

Maryann looked at her husband, cocking her eyebrow. "Okay, hotshot, you've answered that. Now answer this. Any ideas as to what we're supposed to do now? Other than kicking our witness into overdrive, that is?"

Nick nodded. "Yeah. That is, I think so. It has to do with reaching the lost, obviously. I think we all got that." He stopped, searching for the right words, and then said, "Hon, I bet we all could use some coffee. I know I could. Would you bring us some?"

"I'll help you," Sarah said. They headed for the kitchen.

CT waited until they'd left before speaking. "Does any of this have to do with Dooley? Right before service, you said you had an idea, and you said we'd talk about it later." He grimaced. "Well, I got the feelin' we're all out of laters."

"That's a fact," Nick agreed. "Yeah, earlier tonight I was going to say we ought to try to find out where he is, see how he's doing, maybe pray for him. But now I know that was just the start. I think we're supposed to find all of them and make sure they're ready to go."

"All of who?"

"All our bros," he answered quietly. "All our bros from the 7th of the 115th. Dooley, Frankie, Mad Jack . . . and Trevor Ames."

"Mister Ames?" CT frowned. "He wasn't one of us."

"I know. But going into that hot evac must count for something. Besides, I think we're supposed to find him too."

CT shook his head. "Ain't gonna be easy. That trail is over forty years old. He's probably long since gone back to England, and God knows where the others are."

"You said it. God does know, and I believe he's going to help us find them."

"Okay, point taken. But we got a bigger problem than that."

"Say it."

"Time, man. We only have seven days, tops, to find 'em all."

"Well, old buddy," Nick leaned back, lacing his fingers behind his head, "let's take some inventory. You've earned a master's degree in business security, which I know for a fact includes courses in finding missing people. You've had fifteen-plus years of real-world experience. You've got the tools; you've got the talent. Use 'em, already. That's what I'm paying you the big bucks for."

The giant's face darkened in a scowl.

Nick put both hands in front of him, palms out. "Joke! That was supposed to be funny."

"Yeah, well, it ain't. I'm good, but I don't know if I'm that good."

"Consider it a challenge then." Nick leaned forward in the chair, earnest now. "I didn't say it would be easy. But we have to try." Suddenly he felt a hot stinging in his eyes. "We have to know, man. We have to know this time that our bros are going to make it all the way home."

CHAPTER 20

THE BIG MAN WAS ON THE VERGE of replying when they heard a crash. Glancing in alarm at each other, both men shot out of their chairs and ran to the kitchen. There they found Sarah slumped at the kitchen table, weeping, her face buried in her hands. On the opposite wall a large coffee splatter ran down in rivulets. Lying on the floor below that stain lay the smashed remains of a mug.

Maryann stood behind Sarah, her hands on the other woman's shoulders. As the men skidded to a halt, she turned to stare at them. Tears ran down her face as well. All the while Sarah continued to sob quietly in her chair.

The men stood goggle-eyed, Nick especially aghast. "What the—?" He would have rather taken a beating than see any woman cry, Maryann most of all.

CT knelt beside Sarah's chair, softly touching her arm. "Hey, babe, what's the matter? Hey, now . . . "

Nick started toward his wife. "Honey, what—"

"Oh, it's all right for *you!*" The vehemence in Maryann's tone made Nick take a step back. She glared down at CT, pain filling her voice. "And as for you, how could you! Good heavens, you and Sarah still have little kids at home!"

Nick was totally out of his depth by now. He held up placating hands, mind racing to assess what in the Sam Scratch had set these women off.

Sarah angrily shrugged CT's arm away. He looked up at Nick as if to say, What? *What?*

Nick shook his head a millimeter. *Better defuse this, and fast.*

"Uh, Maryann," he began again. "Maybe—"

She cut him off. "You don't have idea one what has us so upset, do you?" Again she looked down at CT, her eyes flashing. "How about you, rock'n'roll, any clues?"

"Uh . . . " CT quickly duck-walked backward. He wanted to get clear of the kill zone of whatever bomb these ladies were about to drop. He was no fool. He didn't stand up again until he was next to Nick.

"Okay, boys, since you're both too dense, I'll tell you. Sarah and I—"

She stopped as Sarah finally lifted her head, her face wet and eyes red and puffy. Moisture glistened on her upper lip. CT thought it prudent not to mention that just then.

"Sarah and I heard all about your plans from in here—your plans to find your old army buddies," Maryann started again, more softly. "Oh, Nicky, I know the hell you both went through that last time. What happened to those poor boys, the nightmares you had for years. I think the idea of finding them is terrific. We both do."

She patted Sarah's shoulder. Sarah nodded and wiped her face with her napkin.

"But don't you see?" Maryann looked pleadingly at the men. "This week something beautiful will take place. Something . . . Tell them, Sarah. I can't."

The other woman straightened in her chair. "What she's saying, guys, is we wanted to experience this together, as families. Don't you get it? CT, the kids and I don't want you and Nick to be God knows where, away from home, when . . . " Gasping, she leaned forward, breaking into tears once again. Maryann jammed her fist against her mouth.

"Aw, honey." Nick stepped forward and took her in his arms. At first she stiffened, then with a sob relented, burying her face in his chest.

"Shhh. It's all right. Look at me, now." He lifted her chin with his finger, smiling into her eyes. "I do understand, Maryann, but that won't happen."

"What?" She sniffed. "How do you know that?"

Nick released her and sat down at the table. CT lowered himself into the next chair and Maryann took the fourth, completing the circle.

She took a breath, looking at her husband. "Okay. Again. How do you know that?"

"I don't," he said. "That is, I'm not completely sure of it. But I do know the Bible says that God'll give us the desires of our hearts—his desires becoming ours, I mean." Nick took her hand. "And this is important to all of us. Souls are in the balance here. But I really believe God's got it planned out so CT and I can complete this mission and still be back home in plenty of time so we can all leave together."

"Mission." Sarah narrowed her eyes at him. "Why are you calling it that?"

"Because that's what it is," CT interjected. "It's the last mission for Nicky and me. The most important one."

He gazed at his friend. "You're right, man. Those guys are our bros, Mister Ames included. I'm in. All the way. Let's go bring 'em home."

CHAPTER 21

THE NEXT MORNING found the two men in Nick's office. Except for the low mutter of CNN on the television, quiet ruled. The place was nearly deserted; Nick had forgotten he'd given the whole bunch of them the day off with pay. He and CT had come in to go over strategy.

"Okay, I think we're straight on this," he said. "You're sure that buddy of yours at Social Security will come through for us?"

"Yeah, I don't think we need to sweat that one. Old fraternity bros, dig it? He owes me big for bein' his sponsor all those years ago; guess now's the time to collect. If any of those guys are drawin' SSI or vet benefits, we'll know where the checks are goin'."

"Okay, and I'm going to check with the VA." Nick frowned. "Speaking of which, do you remember that Portuguese nurse, Connie something, back at the MASH 812ᵗʰ?"

"Yep." CT grinned at the memory. "Remember you had a thing for her, too. You and half the doctors there."

Nick shook his head. "Old news. Anyway, we need to locate her. I think she said she was being transferred to a VA hospital back home not too long after I was to be discharged."

"Lotta Connies, man. How do you figure to find her? And besides, what for?"

"Simple. She was there when we all came in on those medevac slicks. Maybe she'll remember us, or maybe she would've known a corpsman on the *Kitty Hawk*—anything to start the thread. I sure hope your info comes through first, though." Nick sighed at the thought of the enormous task that lay before them. "Like you said, lots of nurses named Connie. Consider this just a backup plan."

CT was about to reply when something coming over the television got their attention. Nick grabbed the remote and turned up the sound.

" . . . reports coming in worldwide, so yes, I would say, Ron, that this is definitely not just an American story." The reporter standing in front of the

White House pulled her coat closer around her. "And there's still no word from the administration regarding official response to any of this. It appears they're willing to let it play itself out a bit more before issuing any statement."

The gray-haired news anchor pressed his earpiece in tighter with his finger. "One last question, Diane. Much has been made recently of the so-called religious conversion the president is said to have experienced several weeks ago. Any comments from him regarding his personal view of this?"

She smiled. "No, I think after the pasting the civil liberties groups gave him over that rumor, he's taking a rather low profile."

The camera cut back to the anchor. "Thanks, Diane. To recap for those of you just joining us, there is apparently an ongoing worldwide uproar among evangelical Christians. Late last night they received a message from God. Supposedly." The anchor didn't bother to hide his smirk. "To expand on this rather shocking pronouncement, we now go to our New York studios and our correspondent Barry Kane. Barry?"

The scene switched.

Kane, fortyish and nattily dressed, could have been the news anchor's clone. He was relaxing in the farthest of three swivel chairs arranged in a loose circle before a plain blue background. Seated in the other chairs were, respectively, a bearded, rotund, Left Bank artiste type and a smiling grandmotherly woman.

"Thanks, Ron," Kane said. "On my left are two of the world's foremost authorities on what we've been hearing. The first is Dr. Alan Minch, former dean of students at the Yale Divinity School and presently pastor of the prestigious Union Free Church in Manhattan."

Nick and CT both stared at each other, eyes bulging. *"MINCH?"* they said together.

"Now I've seen it all," the big man snarled.

Minch nodded and smiled at the camera, but one could detect just the tiniest bit of boredom in his eyes.

Kane went on, "To his left is Ruth Ella Pierce, head of the International Society of Gaia. Ms. Pierce—"

"Please!" the woman interjected, eyes twinkling as she showcased an absolutely perfect set of teeth. "Call me Ruthie! Everyone does!" She wriggled her fanny in her chair, as if she were completely tickled to be there and couldn't wait to tell what she knew.

"All right . . . Ruthie," Kane smiled in return. "We'll do that. Ruthie is considered an expert on the occult and New Age ideas. She received her training at the Edgar Cayce Institute for Advanced Psychic Research in Virginia Beach and is presently on staff at the Gnostic Peace Center near Taos, New Mexico." Kane turned. "Dr. Minch, we'll start with you. Any credence to what we've been hearing?"

Minch crossed his legs and leaned back, looking down his aquiline nose and giving his best William F. Buckley impersonation. His smile registered about forty-three degrees Fahrenheit.

"Mr. Kane, the ravings these evangelicals have been spouting for the past half-century have been embarrassing in the extreme for us mainstream Christians. Their failings are as painful as they are well-documented." He spread his hands. "Let's enumerate them. These people are homophobic, xenophobic, intolerant, grasping, rude, crude, hypocritical—all these things and more. Even more galling is their insistance that Jesus Christ is the only way to heaven. That idea is preposterous and offensive, not only to Christians like myself, but also to my brethren of all faiths."

Minch pointed a forefinger heavenward. "As Jesus so aptly put it, 'in my Father's house are many mansions,' not just one, as they would have us believe."

Lacing his fingers across his ample midsection, he seemed every inch the tolerant cleric. "So to answer your question, Mr. Kane: Did I recieve any 'divine message' last night about being whisked away sometime this week to a place that has yet to be proven even exists?" He shook his head. "I most assuredly did not. And not to put too fine a point on it, I would wager no sane person did."

He paused, and then lowered his voice. "I will tell you this, however. I wish there really would be a cleansing of these rabble-rousers from the face of the earth. Religion might then accomplish something truly grand."

"Thank you, doctor," Kane said. "Ruthie, any comments?"

"Yes, Barry," she giggled. "A lot! Stop me if I start to ramble!" The old woman then calmed down a bit. "Seriously, what I've been hearing makes me both joyous and sad."

The reporter raised his eyebrows. "How so?"

"Well . . . " Ruthie pursed her small lips. "I'm saddened, as any caring person would have to be, that in this day of enlightenment and love any group of people would feel constrained to make themselves feel superior to others regarding some supposed sins they had committed."

She clucked her tongue in disapproval. "Yes, I know the term is archaic and fraught with doom, and one would think that in the dawn of this new age it would have long since been discarded. Unfortunately that word and its proponents have wreaked and continue to wreak havoc among all peoples of faith and goodwill. As Dr. Minch put it, would that those haters were gone."

She began wriggling even more rapidly. It was plain that she was trying to give the appearance of being girlish, with the unfortunate result of making her look like an older lady who needed to go right now.

"That's why I'm sad," she stated. "And here's why I'm glad!"

Kane leaned back a bit as though he thought this woman was on the verge of either telling something wonderful or exploding, and he wasn't sure which.

"As both priestess and prophetess of Gaia," Ruthie said, "I am privy to certain vibrations, vibrations which, if interpreted correctly, can give wisdom. And here is wisdom: Yes, these poor, misguided souls will indeed be taken away from Gaia's presence this week, but not for their pleasure and certainly not to some mythical 'heaven.' " The woman's smile grew radiant. "No, Mr. Kane, Gaia is removing them to their complete and final destruction so that the new— the *real*—Messiah can come to us at last!"

She fluttered her eyelids and bowed her head. After a few seconds more it was apparent that was it for Ruthie. Minch stared at his shoes, his hand over his mouth. He was going for studious but obviously was trying to stifle his laughter.

"Well." Kane sat up straighter in his chair. "Thank you. And thank you, Dr. Minch." He faced the camera. "Barry Kane, reporting live from New York. We now return to Atlanta."

Picking up the remote, Nick snapped off the TV. "Well, I'll be dipped. I guess now we know how our disappearances are going to be explained."

The big man laughed as he shook his head in disbelief. "Whatta load a' monkey puke. And Minch! Talk about a blast from the past!" He laughed again, harder. "What can I say? Some necks were made for stranglin'. Guy like him, all he needs is a sign hangin' under his chin sayin' I'm Better than You. Hit Me."

"Yeah, and what about Ruthie? She wasn't as sweet as she'd like everybody to believe. Butter wouldn't melt in her mouth as she brought down the knife to cut out your heart. The thing to remember is who our battle is really with. Not those poor dopes, that's for sure."

"Yeah, that's true. Speakin' of which, you know, maybe it wouldn't be a bad idea to call Pastor Wasson, tell him what we're gettin' ready to do. Have him agree in prayer with us before we start. Cut off problems before we got problems, dig?"

"I knew there was a good reason I hired you besides your startling good looks," Nick said.

"And my mind, Nicky." CT leaned back in his chair, examining his fingernails. "Don't forget my mind. Just like a tripwire."

CHAPTER 22

WHILE CT HEADED ON BACK to his own office to try sweet-talking his old frat buddy, Nick began working the phones, trying to get a lead on Connie Whoever. His first call was to the Pentagon and the Bureau of Army Personnel.

The phone rang once before being picked up. "Personnel, Mrs. White."

Good, a civilian. Nick felt hopeful. He'd heard a while ago that the Army had begun farming out some of its more mundane projects to civilians. To no one's great surprise, he'd also heard that they'd been having pretty good success with it. At any rate, he thought he'd get farther with a nice lady than he would with some grizzled old sergeant.

"Hello, Mrs. White. My name is Nicholas Castle, and—"

"Excuse me." The line went dead. Nick waited. After a few moments the woman came back on. "Yes, and you are . . . ?"

"Nicholas Castle, and—"

"Does this pertain to Army business, Mr. Kestrel?"

"Castle. Nicholas Castle." He drew a breath. *Steady now.* "Yes, Mrs. White, it does, after a fashion—"

"After a fashion? What is that supposed to mean? Are you being smart with me, mister?"

Nick tightened his voice. "Of course not, ma'am. It's just that I—"

The woman sniffed. "You are aware, of course, are you not, Mr. Kissel, that this line is only for official Army business, and—"

Enough. "Hold it." Nick's voice grew CEO hard. "I want your supervisor, and I mean right this microsecond, sister."

So much for civilian efficiency. Again the line went dead. A few moments later a different voice, this time a man's, answered. "Personnel, Sergeant Alverez."

"Sergeant." Nick rubbed his neck. It felt as if a croquet ball was buried in there. "My name is Nick Castle. I'm wondering if you can help me."

"I'll give it a shot, Mr. Castle. What's it about?"

"Just this. In early 1972 I was assigned to the 7th of the 115th AirCav, Vietnam, and was wounded late that year. While I was recuperating in the MASH 812th I met a nurse named Connie something. I'm trying to get a line on her. That's it. Your Mrs. White wouldn't let me get that out."

Alverez chuckled. "Mrs. White. Yeah, don't I know it. She's pretty good at records. I just need to remember to keep her off the phones. Her people skills aren't the greatest." Then he said, "Wait a minute. The 7th of the 115th . . . not Jack Rugg's old outfit?"

Nick sat up straighter in his chair. "That's the one! Did you know Mad Jack?"

The sergeant gave a short laugh, an oddly sad sound. "Yeah, I knew him. Still do." Another pause. "He's my brother-in-law."

"*What?*" It was hard to picture Mad Jack Rugg as being anybody's brother-in-law.

Suddenly Nick had a thought that brought him up short. This was just like God. He and CT had been prepared to slog through who knew how many hours to find Connie Whatzit, and then, whammo, here he was talking to Mad Jack Rugg's brother-in-law. Amazing.

"Here's the deal," Nick said. "On that last mission several of us were wounded, and an English newspaperman named Ames lost his mind. I guess really I don't need to find Connie, but I do need to find those men, Mad Jack included."

A note of caution crept into the sergeant's voice. "Mind telling me why, Mr. Castle? There's a reason I'm asking."

Nick stopped for a second. How much should he say? And the answer came simply.

Just say it all.

"Sergeant, did you watch the news this morning?"

"Yeah, I did. Why?"

"Did you see the story on the—" Nick licked his lips and started again. "The message that came from God last night?"

"Yeah." Even more caution. "Why do you ask?"

"I was one of those who heard that." There was silence on the other end, and Nick rushed on, "So since I think this thing is really going to happen, I want to contact my bros and make sure they're ready."

There was another long pause, and then he heard the sergeant clearing his throat. "My foster parents used to talk about that when I was a kid. Maybe I need to give 'em a call today . . . " His voice got louder. "Sorry, sir, just woolgathering. Listen, Mr. Castle, I need to tell you something about Jack, why I'm cautious about letting people meet with him."

"All right."

"That last mission you guys went on, where this Ames guy broke down. You heard how Jack's CO left him twisting in the wind?"

"Yeah, I did. I heard he was facing court-martial."

"Faced it and lost, Mr. Castle." Nick could hear anger in the man's voice as if it had happened yesterday. "Jack's worst fears came true. His rank, his pay, his benefits, even his Army career—all gone in one afternoon."

The sergeant stopped, as if considering his next words. Then he said, "Mr. Ames wasn't the only one who lost his mind. Jack did, too. Mad Jack Rugg is now just that. Mad."

Nick slid back in his chair with a groan. "Oh man. Oh, that's awful."

"Tell me about it. Jack came home, but he never left the war, if you know what I'm saying."

"I know exactly what you mean. So where is he now? Can you tell me that?"

Alverez grew evasive. "Well, I don't know . . . I don't know if he'd even want to see you. His wife, my sister Patrice? She takes care of him, and it gets bad sometimes. Jack acts it all out again. The mission. He starts screaming about someone named Dooley. And Frankie." The sergeant paused. "And you, Mr. Castle. I guess you would be the Nick he keeps screaming about. Then he slumps over and cries like a baby. It about kills Patrice each time he goes off. So as far as seeing him—"

"Sergeant Alverez." Nick's voice was soft. "I know you don't know me from Adam. But I'm asking you to trust me, and believe me. Jesus Christ is coming back this week. You're free to believe that or not."

"Well, I don't. Sorry."

"Whatever. I have a leading that I'm supposed to see Mad Jack and Dooley and Frankie Malone and Trevor Ames and tell them God can save them and heal their pain. I'm going to do that very thing, sergeant. With or without your help and blessing. Either way, do it I will."

Alverez blew out some air. "You sound like a man on a mission, Mr. Castle."

"Call me Nick. And you bet I am." There was a long wait, during which he prayed silently in desperate hope.

Finally Alverez spoke up. "Okay. I don't know why I'm saying this, but okay. And by the way, call me Manny."

Nick grinned in relief. The croquet ball between his shoulder blades began to shrink. "Okay, Manny. Thanks. What I need from you is Mad Jack's address and phone, plus the addresses and phone numbers of the others. And I need them like yesterday."

"Jack's and Patrice's I have right here in the computer. The others were who?"

"Trevor Ames, though that one may be tough. Trevor was British, and he worked for the—oh, what was it?—*London Observer*. I would guess they're based in London, but I don't know that for sure. He never said where he lived when he wasn't on assignment, never really talked that much about himself, period. Typical reporter, I guess. Next would be Frankie Malone. Maybe Frank or Franklin; it could even be Francis. I think he was from New York; he sure had the accent. And Dooley—uh-oh." Nick stopped.

"What about him?"

"That's just it. I don't know his first name. He never told us what it was. It should be listed in our unit's records, though."

"Well, now, there might be a problem with that," Alverez said. "When Jack lost his job the 7th of the 115th was decommissioned, and the unit's records went into the inactive files."

"So access those, then."

"No can do. Because of budget restraints they were never put on microfiche or disk. And the building they were stored in burned down two years ago. There's nothing left of your old outfit but what you guys who were in it still have in your heads."

That was bad. "What about hospital files from the MASH?"

"Depends. If your guys were admitted, then yeah. How bad were their injuries?"

Nick winced, remembering. "Awful. Dooley was burned, and Frankie was shot up."

"Probably did a triage and evacked them straight to a carrier. Which one was close?"

"The *Kitty Hawk*."

"There you have it," the sergeant said with finality. "The doctors at the MASH probably took one look at them, got them stabilized, and then flew them right on over to the ship. In all likelihood they didn't even record their dogtag numbers."

How many more roadblocks could there be? "Okay, we'll have to ask Mad Jack about it and hope he's lucid when we do."

"Yeah, well that's another problem," Alverez said. "Jack doesn't talk anymore. He hasn't for the past year or so. Just screams your names and cries. It's about to kill Patrice. She's not had an easy life by any means. We were separated as kids when our parents died. I was placed with a naturalized family, while Patrice lived in filth in Juarez. Marrying Jack was the only good thing that ever happened to her, and now this. It's about to kill her, I'm telling you."

Nick blew out an exasperated breath. "Yeah, you said. Well, do what you can, Manny. Call me back ASAP with whatever you come up with. Here's the number." He gave it to him.

"Okay, got it. I'll get back to you as soon as I find out anything. You going to be there? This may take several hours."

"Yeah, I'll be here. And Manny?"

"Yeah?"

"Talk to your folks about this tonight. There's still plenty of room left on this evac, but not a whole lot of time."

CHAPTER 23

NICK LOOKED AT HIS WATCH. Again. Nearly 11 a.m. Manny had sure called it right. Over two hours, and still nothing. CT had finished up with his friend quite a while back. Getting Social Security records, other than your own, was just a wee bit illegal, and CT's friend said he would do what he could. But it would still take some time.

To pass the time, Nick was finishing the draft of a memo to all the company employees. For those who weren't Christians, and so would miss the rapture, existence here on earth would go on for seven years more. And for at least the first little bit of that time life would be fairly normal. So he was, of all things, making sure those folks would get paid next week. After that they were on their own. Plus he couldn't be certain that there would even be a Castle Industries a week from now. Who knew?

His vice president of operations, Gary Kilgallen, was a Christian, so he'd be gone. As would the three assistant vice presidents. And the treasurer. And the chief legal counsel. Come to think of it, there weren't any officers of the company except for the comptroller who weren't Christians. So what should he do? Put an ad in the trade journals?

WANTED: PERSON TO TAKE OVER DUTIES AS CEO OF MAN-UFACTURING FIRM. POSTION TO LAST SEVEN YEARS OR LESS, FULL STAFFING AUTHORITY GIVEN. PAGANISM A PLUS.

He shook his head.

"What?" CT asked. He sat in one of the chairs facing Nick's desk, doing his own paperwork.

"This," Nick said, throwing his pen down on top of the memo. "Is this insane or what? I keep having to tell myself that it's real, that we aren't just going down to the Smokies and will be back next week." He gave a dry chuckle. "In less than a hundred and fifty-six hours we're going to be in heaven. Can you believe it? This is really, really hard to get my head around."

"Tell me about it. You know Billy Montgomery, that kid I hired as my assistant last year?"

Nick did, of course.

"He really took off fast. I'm proud of him. With just a little more trainin', I think Billy could run security as well as I can. Well, he ain't gonna get it. The job's his in less than seven days, ready or not." CT scratched at his chin. "Thing is, I've witnessed to that boy till I'm hoarse. No dice. The kid's good, but cocky. Says he's an agnostic." He started back on his paperwork. "In less than a week he's gonna find out if he's a good one."

Nick was about to reply when the phone rang. He snatched it up before the first ring was done. "Hello, Manny."

Alverez laughed. "How did you know it was me? Couldn't it have been a business call?"

Nick leaned back in his chair. "I'm not taking any today. My staff has the day off." He winked at CT. "So, anything?" He switched the speaker on so they both could hear.

"Okay, first things first. I talked to Patrice about you wanting to meet with Jack. It took some convincing—she watches him like a mother hen. But finally she said okay. I'll give her a call and set it up."

"All right!" CT said.

"Hey, who's that with you?" Suspicion again.

"One of the good guys," Nick answered. "Say hello to CT Barnes, another old doorgunner. He was with us that day."

"Pleased to meet you, Mr. Barnes. Okay, let's see, next, next . . . Okay, Franklin Edgar Malone. Present address 249 Boyle Street, Newark, New Jersey. No phone."

"Does your information show how he's doing?" Nick asked.

"No, just the address and the fact he's drawing both SSI and vet disability. That's how I found him."

"Huh. Jersey." CT grunted. "Well, I thought he sounded like he was from New York. Close, though, right across the river."

"Have you ever been to Newark, Mr. Barnes?" Alverez asked.

"No, just knifed a guy from there once, that's all. It was back in my rowdy days."

There was a pause. "Uhh . . . okay. Next. Trevor Ames. Now this one took a bit of doing. I called the *London Observer*. Over there it's already afternoon and on the phone the place sounded like it was coming down in pieces. Anyway, I finally got some kid to tell me that last night's, well, message, was big news, and he said he'd try to help me if he could. I had him access their system, and it turns out that Ames does still live right outside of London."

"Is he working for them now?" Nick asked.

"No. According to what they have, the Navy flew Ames to Bethesda Hospital in Maryland the day after he'd been brought aboard the *Kitty Hawk*. Bethesda had him for a week until his paper paid to fly him home. He was then released from his contract with them under their medical retirement clause. He draws a small pension, and that's about it."

"Address and phone?"

"12 Harrowgate Lane, South Essex, London. No phone."

CT shook his head in disgust. "No phone. Two for two. Looks like Nicky and me are gonna rack up a whole bunch of frequent flyer miles we're never gonna get to use."

"And right here's where I ran out of luck," the sergeant said. "I accessed both SSI and the VA, and I found seventeen Dooleys, all in the right age group. Eight served in Vietnam, the rest in other places. Of the seventeen, none of the guys had been burned. Gunshots, landmines, punji sticks, you name it. No burns, though, and none of them had ever set foot on the *Kitty Hawk*."

"So where does that leave us?"

"You tell me," Alverez snorted. "Even Walter Reed has no records of him. I have one trick left, but again, this'll take some time. How old do you figure Dooley was when you knew him?"

The two men looked at each other, shrugging.

"I don't know," Nick answered. "It was hard to tell with him. He looked like a kid, just a farm kid. I know he was from the south. I don't know—what do you think, CT, maybe seventeen, eighteen?"

"I turned twenty when I was there, Nick."

"Yeah, and I turned twenty the day I left the MASH. The staff made me a little cake to take with me. And I know Dooley was younger than us, so I would say—yeah, maybe eighteen."

"All right, then," Alverez said briskly. "Here's what I plan to do. I'm going to access the records of all Army inductees with the last name of Dooley and having birthdates ranging from 1 January 1955 to 31 December 1956. I'll then narrow the search to those from the southern states who were sent to Vietnam." The sergeant paused. "You know this is going to take a while, gents."

"Maybe I'm a bit slow, Manny," CT said, "but that gets us Dooley when he went in. It doesn't tell us where he went when he got out."

"That's because you don't understand the southern mind, Mr. Barnes. You're from where?"

"Gary, Indiana. So?"

"So," Alverez replied, "you were born in Gary, Indiana but you're living in Cincinnati. These southern boys, as a rule, tend to go back home when they leave Uncle Sam's employment. So figure if, say, Muskrat, Arkansas, sent Dooley to Vietnam and he ended up in your unit, he probably returned to Muskrat, or close to it, when he left."

"Sounds like a generalization to me," CT growled.

"Mr. Barnes," Alvarez shot back with some heat, "I'm doing what I can."

"And we appreciate it," Nick jumped in. He glanced at CT, shaking his head. "We really do."

"Okay." The sergeant sounded somewhat mollified. "I'll be in touch."

They hung up, and Nick looked over at his friend. "Almost blew the deal, there. We really don't need to be antagonizing this guy. He's just trying to help."

CT sighed. "Yeah. Sorry. I guess I'm gettin' antsy. I need to get out of here for a while, catch some rays."

"Do that. Go up on the roof. I'll stay here and wait for Manny's call."

CT sighed again, briskly scratching his head. "Naw, man, I'll wait, too. Don't mind me, I was just poppin' off." Then he scowled. "It's just that I'm not lookin' forward to flyin' clear over to England and back, I'll tell ya that for free."

"Want to stay here in Cincy? Go over your paperwork? Check timesheets?" Nick grinned. "Watch cartoons? Braid your leg hairs? Strangle Minch? Tell you what, you stay here, and I'll bring you back a nice present."

CT faked a punch at Nick's head. "Jerk. No, I'm in it till we win it. 'Whither thou goest, I will go,' and all that."

"Why, CT Barnes!" Nick fluttered his eyes. "Sarah was right. You *are* a sweet thang!"

This time he barely slipped the punch.

CHAPTER 24

THE REST OF THE DAY HAD DRAGGED, and now it was late afternoon. With Manny rooting through reams of Army records for Dooley, the two friends were trying to figure out who to see first: Mad Jack Rugg, Frankie Malone, or Trevor Ames.

CT had a world atlas open on the desk. "I dunno. Here's what I'm thinkin'. Manny told us Mad Jack and Patrice live just outside of St. Louis, Frankie's in Newark, and Mister Ames is in London. I say let's get the longest leg done first, seein' Mister Ames. Then Frankie, then Mad Jack. Dooley, I guess, we save for last."

Nick leaned back, rubbing his eyes. "You're not going to believe this, but we just wasted an hour we really can't afford. I think that what we should have done is prayed about it first and asked God where he wanted us to start. If he's given us the green light to do this, he really should be consulted."

"You're right." CT blew out his cheeks. "Man, I feel like a bonehead."

"Me too. Just chalk it up to youthful enthusiasm. Well, we know what to do."

Both men went quiet, Nick with his eyes shut, CT staring at the floor.

Then the bigger man looked up. "I think I know."

Nick opened his eyes. "Me too. We almost had it right: Ames first, then Mad Jack, then Frankie, and finishing up with Dooley."

"I got the same thing. Guess that would be confirmation. We'll do it that way. And speakin' of Dooley, I sure hope this Manny guy comes through—huh." CT paused, stroking his chin. "I just had an odd thought."

"What?"

"Have you noticed we only seem to have a leadin' about those guys we mentioned? You and I both know the unit had a lot more men than that. I wonder why God hasn't told us to find Gaddick and Greer and Cookie and all the rest."

"Good question. And I don't know the full answer. Maybe he's having other people contact them, while we're to stick with the guys we knew best."

"Yeah, maybe. Could be."

"The first thing we need to do is to call Betty Zane," Nick said. Betty was the company travel agent. "I'll tell her to book us two tickets to London in the morning. She also needs to get us a car while we're there."

"Better tell her to get us a big one. That flight's gonna be crammed enough. Which reminds me. You gonna be a cheapie or book us first class?"

"We might as well go whole hog. It's for sure we can't take it with us."

CT nodded. "Good deal."

"Let me call Betty first, then I need to reach Maryann." Holding the phone to his ear, he said, "How about you guys eating with us before church? We can ride over together afterward if you want."

"Thanks anyway, but I'm gonna head on home. Sarah wants to take the kids with us tonight, so I think we'll grab a bite to eat at a restaurant first. Ever since we adopted them from Honduras, we've been educating them in the finer points of American cuisine. We're up to Chinese food now. Little buggers love those noodles."

"Not a problem. Speaking of kids, we called our nephew and niece last night."

"Whoa. Kinda late, wasn't it?"

"Are you kidding? Remember back when you were in college, how little sleep you got? No, they were up, all right, and cranked up tighter'n Dick's hatband. We tried both dorms, and neither was there, so Maryann phoned Tracy on her cell phone. Sure enough, there they were at Pizza Pete's, along with about a hundred other students, having calzones. After we told them about you and me going to find our bros, they said to go with their blessings and that they were leaving this morning to drive back up here."

"Good kids, Nick. Ours too." CT stood. "Well, I'm gone. We'll see you guys tonight. Where you gonna be sittin'?"

"Anywhere but under the balcony overhang. That low ceiling always makes me feel like I'm in a submarine." Nick started to dial. "Figure the center section, maybe in the middle. We're going to try to be there early. I have a feeling the place will be packed to the rafters."

"Save us a couple seats if you can. I think we'll hit the Lotus Garden for supper, and I know the service there can be iffy. Good pad thai, though."

"We'll do our best. See you tonight."

CHAPTER 25

CT STRETCHED OUT WITH A SIGH, his legs fully extended. They still didn't reach the bulkhead in front of him. The jet flew high over the Atlantic, its powerful engines just a whisper. The soft leather seat he reclined in caressed his rear end lovingly like a catcher's mitt, making him nod blissfully. No doubt about it, first class was the only way to fly. He nudged his friend.

"What?" Nick put down his Bible.

"This." CT waved his hand around. "I thought we were gonna be stuck on some ratty, overcrowded domestic flight. But British Airways!" He closed his eyes, utterly content. "We're walkin' in tall cotton now, son."

"If the comptroller knew how much this was costing, she'd have kittens."

"Well, no worries, mate, as that Aussie vendor used to say back in Saigon. You could always write it off on the taxes." He barked a laugh, opening his eyes. "Not that we have to pay 'em! Yee-haa!"

Nick chuckled. "Yeah. And if the IRS doesn't like it, they can always come on up to the throne room so we can discuss their concerns in person."

Both men grinned.

"Home, we're goin' home!" CT sang—croaked—joyfully. "Home this week, baby!"

One of the flight attendants strolled up. "May I get you gentlemen anything?" The flat A's of her Cockney accent could be clearly heard above the airplane chatter.

"Thanks, but nothing for me," Nick said. "CT?"

"That meal was mighty tasty, miss." CT arched his eyebrows in hope. "You wouldn't happen to have another steak or two back in the galley, would ya?"

The young woman smiled. "Yes sir, I believe we just might have a few left. Would you like me to get you some more?"

"Yes, please." She left, and CT grinned enormously. "You know, Nick, a man could get used to this."

.. .. ..

FIVE HOURS LATER their flight touched down at London's Heathrow airport. Nick had been there as a boy, but didn't remember it being so crowded.

As their plane rolled toward the jetway, CT looked out the window and gave a low whistle. "Take a gander at that." He pointed. "What's that all about?"

Nick peered past him with a frown. The tarmac was crawling with what appeared to be armored personnel carriers at various locations, along with British troops in full battle gear shuffling next to them.

The two glanced at each other. "What the—?" Nick muttered. He touched their flight attendant lightly on the arm as she passed. "Excuse me, miss, but do you know what's going on?"

"Yes, sir, I do." Her tone was somber. "It's coming over the radio now. Those soldiers have just now arrived, and more are due shortly. I think their being here has something to do with that . . . message . . . people have been talking about."

Again both men looked at each other. "What do you mean?" Nick asked.

"I'm really not supposed to say. Are you gentlemen going to be in London for a while?"

"Maybe a day, maybe longer. What is it you're not supposed to say? I think we have a right to know."

Crouching down next to him, the woman quickly glanced to either side. "I heard there have been threats from various groups to do the airport harm," she whispered. "Satanists mostly, the pilots are saying. There are a sizable number of them here in England. We're the ancestral home of Aleister Crowley, you know."

CT frowned. "Who?"

"Crowley was one of the granddaddies of modern satanism," Nick explained. "Dude thought he was the Beast of Revelation."

"Huh. So what does that have to do with the message?"

"I'm sure I don't know, sir. My niece is married to a closet satanist, and I can tell you they're odd ducks. It doesn't take much to set them off."

"Who are they looking to harm?" asked Nick.

"Anyone they can, I suppose. Traveling Christians would be my guess. This excuse is as good as any." She pursed her lips. "Every one of them is quite mad. Hence all the troops." She stood. "You gentlemen watch yourselves now."

Nick smiled. "Thank you very much. We appreciate the warning."

As she turned to go, CT spoke up. "I'm curious, ma'am. What did you think of the message?"

"I'm ready," she beamed. "I have been since I was twelve. How about you gentlemen?"

CT's grin, in return, while not as radiant, was nonetheless a pretty yellow. "Us too!"

As the attendant began proceeding toward the rear of the plane, checking her passengers, the big man frowned. "Weird they have troops protectin' the place instead of cops."

"Remember where you are," Nick returned. "Until pretty recently, English cops didn't carry weapons. I heard that's not true anymore, though." He shrugged. "Maybe somebody felt soldiers would do a more thorough job of guarding the area than the police."

"Yeah, maybe." CT frowned again at the soldiers nervously milling around outside. "But those kids sure look young to me, trainin' or no. Hope they know which end of the tube the round comes out of."

"So do I." A bell dinged softly, letting them know the taxi was now complete and the passengers could gather their bags and leave the plane. Nick glanced again out the window. "Let's pray we can find Trevor fast and get back home. England doesn't look overly friendly to me."

CHAPTER 26

THE TWO MANAGED TO CLEAR CUSTOMS in a surprisingly short time. Nick wondered if it had to do with the threats; maybe the airport was processing their travelers quickly to get them away from danger. At any rate, thirty minutes after they'd landed, he and CT were tooling down the M1, one of England's major highways, toward London and South Essex.

The big man smiled as he sniffed the car's rich leather interior. "A Bentley! Man, Nicky, I gotta say, when you set out to spend money you put Sarah to shame."

Nick regarded his friend. "What else was I going to squeeze your carcass into—an MG?"

"A Rolls Royce Silver Shadow would have been all right, I guess."

"I guess it would have!" Nick snorted. "I told you this trip would make the comptroller have kittens, but I didn't want her to go into cardiac arrest."

"Just messin' with ya." CT perused the map, shaking his head. "Hard to believe I used to be able to read a jungle topo map, but I can't tell how to get to South Essex from this thing."

"Well, figure it out quick. I'm having a hard enough time trying to remember which side of the road is ours."

"You're doin' fine," CT replied, and then belched. "That was good steak, but now I'm hungry again. If you run over any little English fish and chips guys, be sure to let me know."

.. .. ..

WITHIN AN HOUR they were hopelessly lost.

"This is fun," CT said dryly. "I think that's the third time I've seen that same cow. You sure Mr. Ames is from England?"

"Yeah, smart guy, England." Nick cut him a sideways glance. "I should have brought Maryann. There's a lady who knows how to read a map." He peered out the windshield. "You can be replaced, you know."

"Doin' my best, man. Want me to drive?"

"No way. I've seen you drive at home. Why do you think Maryann and I always ask if you guys would like to ride with us to church?"

"I guess the truth finally comes out—hey, wait a minute. You did say South Essex?"

"Yeah, why?"

"I think that's the sign back there."

Nick slowed the car, moving into the emergency lane. "Are you sure? How could we have missed it three times?"

"Dunno man. You're the drivin' ace. I'm just the navigator."

After executing a sharp three-point turn, they found themselves headed the other way.

"Go slow," CT said, watching. "We're—wait, there it is." The sign ahead read South Essex, 2 km. "Okay, we've got it now. Two klicks to South Essex. The map shows Harrowgate Lane is before we get to the town, off to the right."

A few minutes later the road forked. They both saw the sign at the same time, but CT felt compelled to point. "Harrowgate Lane, this is it. What's the number again?"

"Twelve."

Slowly they drove a hundred yards or so, watching, then they saw it. The house—cottage—was tiny and rundown. Gray now, it was impossible to tell what color it had originally been.

Pulling their car into a grass-rutted drive, Nick shut the ignition off. They strained their ears to listen. They could hear the ticking of the car's engine as it cooled, but nothing else. The neighborhood was deathly quiet.

"Guess let's go knock." Nick said.

Getting out of the car, they gazed around. There were plenty of houses, but that was all. No children, no lawnmowers, no dogs. Nothing but an overcast sky and a feeling of gloom and loss.

"Man." CT pulled his suit coat closer around him, even though the temperature was in the low sixties. "Where's Stephen King when you need him?"

"Pretty strange, all right. Come on, let's get it done."

They walked across the small overgrown yard and up two creaking steps onto the porch.

"Mind your step." CT gingerly moved around a rotted floorboard. "Mister Ames's house doesn't look all that safe."

Realizing there was no doorbell, Nick rapped soundly on the frame. They waited. No answer. He knocked again. Nothing.

The two men looked at each other, both thinking the same thing: long way to fly to find an empty house and a deserted neighborhood. Nick was just starting to knock once more when suddenly the door was violently jerked open.

"*What?*"

Both men stepped back involuntarily. The slight figure standing before them was as caved-in as the house. The man's white hair was matted down, and the odor rolling from his body was newsworthy.

"What do you want? Can't you leave me alone?"

Nick leaned forward. "Trevor? Trevor Ames?"

The man said nothing as he regarded Nick with quivering lips and rheumy eyes. Suddenly those eyes opened wide, and fear shadowed his face like an eclipse. He moved to slam the door.

"No sir, *not* part of the plan! You're dead!"

CT reached out, stopping the door with a palm. The old man staggered back into the house, nearly falling, catching himself at the last instant. Nick and CT followed him in.

The inside of the house was like the man himself, collapsed and foul smelling. Every shade was drawn, allowing only speckles of gray light to filter in through the tears. The furniture was stained and torn, the carpet filthy.

Moaning, the old man fell into a decrepit Queen Ann chair and put his hands over his face. "Go. Away."

Nick knelt beside him. "Mr. Ames . . . Trevor. It's me, Nick Castle. Remember?"

The old man shook his head, hands still covering his mouth, his voice high and muffled. "Not part of the plan!"

"What plan, sir?" CT asked softly.

Ames jerked his hands away from his face, eyes wild. "The plan! The *plan!*" His voice dropped to a mumble, and he took on a lost and haunted look. Then he grinned. "Colonel Rugg called it right, by Godfrey, yes he did. He said all we needed was a plan. A man with a plan with a goose! Loosey-goosey! Loosey-goosey!"

Suddenly he began to shriek, "*I didn't want my eyes on a plate! No plans, you get plates!* Pip pip, old sock, no harm, no foul. I'm trying to be clear . . . " Bending over, he began to sob.

CT looked at Nick, heartsick. "Good Lord. He's gone. Maybe we'd better—"

Nick tightened his jaw. "No. We can't leave him like this."

CT started to reply when they both heard the sound of another car coming down the lane. The big man parted the thin curtains and lifted the shade.

"Huh." He turned to Nick, who remained kneeling before Ames. "Cops."

"Cops?" Nick stood, still holding the weeping man's hand. "Are they turning in here?"

"Yep. Wonder if Mr. Ames has been causin' problems."

Nick let go of Ames's hand and walked over to the peeling door, opened it, and waited while a large car with the words *South Essex Constable* on its side pulled into the worn drive and came to a stop. Its two occupants emerged, one a beefy, florid-faced man, his partner smaller and younger but with the same coloration.

They regarded Nick with wary eyes as they made their way up onto the porch. "With the asylum, are you?" the older man asked. "May we come in?"

"Please," Nick said, stepping aside. "But no, we're not from any asylum. We're friends of Mr. Ames. My name's Nick Castle, and that gentleman there is Mr. C. T. Barnes."

The bigger man and CT sized each other up like alley cats.

"Americans, eh?" The younger man removed his hat and smiled. "My name is Alastair Woodhaven. The big chap eyeing your friend with bad intent is my brother Neville. We're both constables with the village."

CT scowled. "I figured that, Woody, from the car and uniforms." Scornfully he glanced at Neville. "Would you mind tellin' your brother to look someplace else? People givin' me the hairy eyeball make me nervous. You can't tell what I might do."

The older man pulled his head back a tiny bit, his smile frosty. "Don't muck with us, boyo. We're in the process of serving final papers on your friend, which he ignores at his peril. Maybe you'd like a tour of our jail, eh? An attitude adjustment of sorts. Do you both wonders. Are you game?"

"Hold it, hold it," Nick said. "Let's start over, shall we?"

"Let's do that very thing," Neville replied sharply. "All right, gentlemen, your passports, please."

Sighing, the two men dug in their suitcoat breast pockets and handed the documents over.

"Let's see now . . . Nicholas James Castle, Cincinnati, Ohio. Also we have one Crispus Thaddeus Barnes . . . " Neville looked at CT. "Crispus Thaddeus? Could this be your real, Christian name, Mr. Barnes?"

Nick saw his friend's fists beginning to ball up and his eyebrows lowering. Lightly jabbing him, he CT gave a small shake of his head.

"Also from Cincinnati," the older policeman went on. "So why are you here in lovely South Essex, bothering our poor Trevor Ames?"

He continued flipping the passports lazily, and Nick motioned to them. "May we have those back?"

"All in good time, chum. That depends on the answers I get."

The younger man spoke up. "Neville, perhaps—"

"Quiet, Ally," Neville barked, not taking his eyes off the two. "Well? I am waiting, gentlemen."

"All right," Nick sighed again. "Here's the condensed version. Mr. Barnes and I served in Vietnam together. While we were over there, we met Mr. Ames, who was covering a story for his newspaper. We came here to visit him. The end."

"The end." Neville rubbed his chin thoughtfully. "I wonder. Did you know he was mad, then, before you made the long trip over?"

"We knew," CT rumbled.

"And so you spent quite a lot of money and came halfway around the world to spend the day with a lunatic." Neville's smile held no humor. "Wouldn't you call that a bit odd, sir?"

"Constable, I really don't understand why what we're doing here is any of your business." Nick's normally banked temper was finally beginning to flare. He'd had about a gutful of these two already.

"I'll tell you," the older man snapped right back. "One word. Terrorism. Did you happen to notice that our airport was overrun with troops? Did you figure it out?"

"I understand there've been threats," Nick said. "From cultists."

"The very word! And now you see our dilemma. My brother and I have been given orders down at the station house to be on the lookout for suspicious persons. Our village may be small, but it's ours." Neville's tone turned menacing. "And we intend to keep it."

Placing his hands behind his back, he began to do that heel-to-toe rock policemen all around the world seemed to do unconsciously. "And so, while on routine patrol, what do we see on this godforsaken lane but a shiny new Bentley? In front of a madman's house, I might add. And driving that Bentley we notice two men we've never before encountered. Do you see where I'm going with this?"

"Yeah, we see," CT answered coldly.

"So perhaps you'd like to . . . amend your story, eh?" Again Neville's smile was cold. "Expand it for us, if you would be so kind."

The two Americans glanced at each other, wondering how much to say, wondering if the "asylum" that Trevor was bound for had a cell for three. They both prayed silently and quickly for wisdom. And as before, the answer again came quickly. *Just say it all.*

"All right," Nick said, "here's the long and short of it. You've heard of the message from heaven, I suppose?"

Neville quit rocking. Both policemen shot looks at each other.

"Yes, Mr. Castle," the older man said slowly. "I daresay we have. The point being, sir?"

"The point being that Mr. Barnes and I are Christians, and we came here to make sure our friend was ready to go."

There was a long pause, and then Alastair blew out a quick breath and a laugh. "Well, praise the Lord! I heard that message too!"

Neville glared at his brother. "You may have, Ally, but I did not. You've been pushing your idiot religion on me for years, and I've had enough." He pursed his lips in disapproval. "This is simply some sort of mass psychosis."

"It's not—" the younger man began.

"Yes, I know, it's not a religion but a relationship," his brother finished for him. "I've been hearing that for years as well. It's still utter nonsense." Neville narrowed his eyes at the Americans. "Perhaps in the light of all that's taking place, it would be best if I took you both down to the station house for questioning. How would that be, eh?"

"Oh, get off it!" Alastair growled, his patience gone. "If you take them down, then take me down as well! Don't you see, you fool, we're out of time?" He drew a breath before going on more calmly, "Now, I'm going to talk with these gentlemen. You are free to stay and listen or go sit in the patrol car. Choose."

They waited, and then with a sneer Neville threw the passports on the floor. Turning abruptly, he stomped outside and down the steps. A moment later Nick and CT heard the patrol car door slam. They were amazed at how easily the younger man had handled his brother.

Alastair looked down briefly, shaking his head. "Idiot," he muttered, then he looked up at them with a smile. "Now, let's really start over." He held out his hand. "Alastair Woodhaven."

They all shook hands, the atmosphere lighter by degrees.

"Man," CT said. "Your brother is one major pain in the neck."

"Oh, I don't know," Alastair replied. "Most people have a much lower opinion of him."

All three laughed, and he went on with a rueful smile, "I love my brother, gentlemen, I surely do, and I've witnessed Christ to him for many years, ever since we were boys together, playing in these very woods. One of Father's good friends was a missionary to Africa. He'd told us of God's love when we were small. I accepted it, but for some reason, Neville rebelled. And as I said, we're out of time."

"I know it's rough," Nick said. "CT and I'll keep you both lifted in prayer."

"Thanks. I'm believing Neville will come to his senses before it's too late. I'd hate to see him accept Jesus after we're gone." Pain filled the young constable's eyes. "I don't think my brother would make a very good tribulation saint."

The big man nodded. "Most of us wouldn't. Now about Mr. Ames . . . "

They all turned to look at Trevor, who was rocking silently on his haunches in the corner of the room.

"You said something about taking him to an asylum?" Nick asked.

"Yes, today, as a matter of fact," Alastair replied. "You've noticed this neighborhood, have you, how quiet and deserted it is?"

"We sure did," CT said. "It was almost like the rapture has already happened."

Alastair's countenance grew dark. "Not so joyous as that, I fear. This entire three-block area was condemned six months ago. They're putting a bypass around the village. Everyone was given a tidy sum of money for their places, Mr. Ames included." He gave the old man a pitying look. "He's been our resident eccentric for many years. We English do treasure our eccentrics. He has a sister, you know. Honoria Peet."

"A sister?" Nick asked.

"Yes. She's a widow and lives in town, right above the apothecary shop. Honoria has been keeping her brother's money in trust. She's willing to take him in, but he's refused to leave." Alastair shook his head sadly. "Today was his last day. The county magistrate had papers drawn up to have Mr. Ames committed if he again refused his sister's offer. Neville and I were to meet with the asylum officials here and take him with us."

CT's eyes grew wide. "Man, talk about God's timin'. No wonder he had us see Mr. Ames first. Tomorrow he would've been gone."

The young patrolman studied them, an unsure smile on his face. "It seems I'm missing something. How does the fact that you're both here change Mr. Ames's situation?"

"That's simple," Nick answered. "How familiar are you with scripture?"

"Not so much as I would like," Alastair allowed. "Why?"

"I'll tell him," CT broke in. "See, Ally, right before we came over here our church was in the middle of a revival. Matter of fact, Nicky and I and our wives were in the service there Tuesday night when we got the word about the rapture happenin' in the next seven days. One of the things Pastor Wasson brought out that night was what Psalm 105, verse 37 says."

"You've got me hooked, Mr. Barnes. What does it say?"

"I've got it memorized. 'He brought them forth also with silver and gold: and there was not one feeble person among their tribes.' See, a lot of biblical scholars think the exodus is a type of the rapture and that God is gonna follow the same pattern."

Nick continued, "If that's true, then the glory we've been seeing poured out this last year, worldwide, is the culmination of history. A lot of us think that before the rapture hits, every one of God's people is going home healed. So our reason for being here is simple. We want to make sure Trevor is both in his right mind and right with God before Jesus comes."

"Mister Ames isn't the only one," CT added. "Nick and I are seein' three other men in our old unit to make sure of that too."

Alastair whistled. "You have a job ahead of you, gentlemen, and little time to do it. Is there anything I can do to help?"

"Yeah." Nick's voice was tight. "Make sure Neville stays outside while we pray. If keeping unbelief out while prayer was going on inside was good enough for Jesus, it's good enough for us."

"Don't bother about him." Alastair waved a hand in dimissal. "Neville's spoken his piece. Now he'll stay out there and sulk until I come fetch him." A hopeful look came into his eyes. "I wonder . . . would it be all right if I stayed and watched while you and Mr. Barnes prayed?"

"All right?" CT laughed. "Don't look now, but you're joinin' us!"

Alastair nodded, his smile tentative. "Very well. Count me in. I'll follow your lead."

They gathered around the old man. Nick and CT's fervent supplication sounded strange to Alastair's ears, and his heart pumped at a furious rate. He was sure he'd never participated in anything quite like this. Then it was done, and he found himself saying amen with the others.

Hardly daring to breathe, they all looked at Ames. For an endless moment, nothing happened.

Suddenly the old man drew a shuddering breath. He shook his head once, twice. Alastair found his breath jamming up in his throat. Ames slowly rose from his haunches, Nick following him up.

"Corporal . . . Castle . . . ?" Ames' voice was papery, unsure.

"That's right." Nick placed his hands on the old man's shoulders. "It's me, Trevor."

Ames gazed at the other two men. "And Mr. C. T. Barnes? You're here as well? I'm sorry. I don't know the other . . . " He shook his head. "Corporal Castle, is it really you? Where in the world am I?" Gingerly he put his hands on his head. "My mind . . . It appears to be clearing . . . "

That did it. All three men began whooping and hollering and slapping each other's backs, as Ames watched them blankly. Alastair yelled as enthusiasticly as the others, joining in a decidedly unreserved show of joy.

When they finished, Nick was out of breath. "Trevor, you're home. In England."

"Home?" Ames gazed at his hands and clothes. "What's happened to me? I . . . How did I get to be so old?"

"It's a long story," CT replied. "But you've been here for a while, Mr, Ames. The war's been over for years."

"Trevor. Look at me, now." Nick leveled his gaze. "I'm going to say something hard. It'll be the hardest thing you've ever heard. Okay?"

The old man gulped, nodding.

"You've been insane for nearly forty years."

Ames stared, incredulous. Forty years. For a moment it looked as if he would collapse. But the moment passed, and he said, "I can—I *must*—believe that, corporal. I have no choice." He licked his lips. "It happened when we flew that last mission, didn't it?"

"Yeah," Nick said softly. "Do you remember any of it?"

"I remember . . . I was horrified. The noise . . . and the smells . . . I was wondering how my dad could have ever lived through such a thing. And I remember poor young Dooley. How brave you were. The screams, I remember . . . "

So did Nick.

"And gunfire. Then you got shot." Ames looked up, haunted. "And that's all. That's all! A . . . fog . . . seemed to settle on me. It was endless. Time ceased to have meaning. Just a . . . drifting. And then . . . then I saw a hand in the fog, reaching out to me. It had a hole, nearly the size of an almond, right here in the wrist. And I knew that I *must* grasp that hand, or I was well and truly lost, forever. I reached out for it, and I grasped it . . . And when I opened my eyes, I saw I was gripping *your* hand, Corporal Castle."

The old man blinked, unsure. "That's odd, isn't it? I awakened . . . here." He gazed around, his eyes wide. "What's happened to my house?"

"Constable Woodhaven will explain it all to you," Nick told him. "But here's some good news. He's taking you to your sister, Honoria."

"Honoria." Ames seemed to choke on her name. Then "Oh God! My house . . . my *life!* It's all gone!" He began to weep.

"Trevor!" Nick's tone was sharp. "Look at me! Here's the most important part of all, and you need to listen up."

Ames wiped his nose on his sleeve, drawing in a ragged breath. After a few more seconds, he nodded.

"As a reporter, you'll appreciate this. The biggest news story this world will ever see is going to happen in less than a hundred and twenty-five hours. And you'll be here to witness it."

Ames blinked, digesting the words. Then he nodded again.

"Last Tuesday night God let all the Christians in the world know that Jesus is coming sometime this week, to take us home."

"Home? Do you mean . . . heaven?"

"Yep. And after we're gone, a man called the Antichrist is going to rise up and enslave the planet for seven years. At the end of that time, Jesus will return to depose him and to cleanse this world. And Trevor, for anyone who comes to God during those seven years, life won't be worth living."

"Won't be worth a bucket a' warm spit, Mr. Ames," CT broke in. "Be hunted down like a dog and probably die for your faith."

"But there's a way to avoid the hell that's coming here," Nick said, "and that's to accept Jesus Christ into your heart right now and leave with us when he comes. Jesus is the one who delivered you from your prison of insanity, Trevor. Will you trust him now with this?"

"What you are telling me is familiar, corporal," the old man said, his voice small. "Or should I say, Mr. Castle . . . that is, Nick . . . " He took a breath and went on, "I covered a story on the born-again experience many years ago. I'll confess I judged it harshly. My life before I went to Vietnam was less than sterling. Less than . . . exemplary. Drinking, you know." He looked up, eyes glistening. "Do I have time?"

"Yep," CT said passionately. "All ya gotta do is ask."

There was a pause, and then, "And so I shall." With a final wipe of his nose, he said, "Let's proceed."

.. .. ..

AFTER LEADING TREVOR AMES IN THE PRAYER, all four men were overwhelmed. In the midst of the filth and squalor, God had come through again, just as he promised.

"I haven't cried this much since I was a boy," Alastair said, laughing through his tears.

"Nor have I, constable," replied Ames. "Nor have I. Ah well . . . "

The old man looked around at his house, as if seeing it for the first time, and not liking what he saw. Shaking his head, he sighed, lost in memories.

Then he dusted his hands on his thighs. "Young man, I suppose I'll need to take you up on your offer and accept a ride into the village. My time of living in this place apparently is through." He gave them a tentative smile. "You know, of course, this is all going to require a good deal of explaining to Honoria."

The other three laughed. Closer than brothers now, they all walked outside. Nick and CT saw that the patrol car had theirs blocked in and realized that the Englishmen would need to leave first. There were more grins and handshakes and slaps on the back as they saw the men off.

Neville appeared awestruck as his brother and Ames climbed into his car. The older man's mouth hung open, and he regarded them with bulging eyes.

"Hey, Ally, see what Neville has to make of Mr. Ames!" CT called out as the vehicle pulled away. "And make sure he shuts his mouth before he swallows a bug!"

The car's noise faded in the distance, and then it was gone. Silence once again ruled the day. Nick led the way back inside.

Taking one last look around the crumbling old cottage, CT said, "Kinda like an old cocoon after the butterfly has flown, ain't it?"

"Buddy, you're a poet." Nick knelt to pick up their passports, then rose and headed to the door. "All right, time to roll. One down. Three to go."

CHAPTER 27

BY THE TIME THE TWO MEN ARRIVED back at Heathrow airport, it was nearly 9 p.m. Seeing that they had some time before their flight left, they decided to stop at an authentic English pub for a dinner of shepherd's pie and sausages, which both completely enjoyed.

That meal was now only a fond memory. The airport crowd was horrendous, just astoundingly bad. It seemed as if half of England was trying to board planes, while the other half was disembarking. And above it all loomed the menacing presence of armed troops, watching everyone with baleful and suspicious eyes.

"What time's our flight leave?" CT yelled above the din.

"Nine-fifty. Gate 26," Nick answered. "We'd better hoof it; international flights can be tricky with their boarding procedures." He looked around for an airport map, then gawped in despair when he saw how far away their gate was. "Man, this is worse than O'Hare. We should have brought running shoes."

CT's reply was flat. "Uh-uh, Nicky, not me. Troops this nervous see a very large, extremely handsome black man hotfootin' it through the airport?" He gave a slow shake of his massive head. "No way, baby. I wanna get translated, not resurrected."

"We don't seem to have a choice. Come on."

As they began double-timing it to their gate, CT looked over at him. "Do you feel that?"

"Yeah," Nick nodded. "Something's up at home. I've been feeling weird ever since we left that pub. We need to call our wives." He increased his pace. "I wish I'd thought to bring my cell phone. I left the fool thing back in my office."

"Mine's on the fritz. Sarah was supposed to take it in while we were gone to have the guy see what's the matter." Then he smiled, "Be cool, bro. We can grab a pay phone after we get checked in at the gate."

By slapping shoe leather, the two men made it to Gate 26 with five minutes to spare. Nick was winded, while his friend wasn't even panting.

"How do you do it?" Nick bent over, gasping out the words. "You're the same age as me, and I know you don't work out any more than I do."

"Superior gene pool, bro. While your forefathers were tendin' shop, mine were bein' chased by lions. Tends to make ya speedy."

Nick straightened, trying to find a departure screen. His mouth nearly fell open when he finally saw one. "Aw, no!" He pointed at it with an accusatory finger. "Man, I do not believe this." Their flight showed as cancelled.

CT's shoulders dropped. "How can they cancel us? Why?"

"I don't know. Listen, I know it's a pain, but go get in line at the ticket counter and find out what's going on. See if they can get us on another flight out. Tell 'em we'll take anything. I'm going to call home, see what's up there."

"Okay. Make sure Sarah and the kids are all right, huh?"

In a few minutes Nick returned, a scowl on his face.

"Well?" CT asked.

"Nothing. Couldn't get a phone." Nick plopped down onto a hard plastic chair. "There are six phones right around the corner. The only problem is three are broken and there's a line a mile long for the others." He rotated his head, trying to get the knots out of his shoulders. "What did the ticket agent have to say?"

"Good news and bad. The reason our flight got cancelled was a bomb threat. They got dogs in there now goin' over it, but no way are we flyin' out on it anytime soon. I did manage to get our tickets switched to another carrier." CT looked disgusted. "Unfortunately for us, not a good one; some no-name banana-republic thing. The ticket agent says it's a trashed old 767, so I hope you're prayed up. To top it all off, they got us three rows apart, right in the middle. Gonna be jammed, man. And it leaves in less than twenty minutes."

"What gate?"

CT pointed back over Nick's shoulder. "Gate 1. Clear back that way. But the thing is, we gotta board now."

Nick groaned again as CT pulled him to his feet with a bark. "C'mon on, soldier, off your butt and on your feet! Move it! Move it! Move it!"

They both began running back down the concourse.

"Hup! Hup!" CT yelled, arms swinging.

"You . . . remind me . . . of . . . Sergeant Krantz . . . " Nick huffed, "my . . . DI . . . at Fort . . . Sill. . . . I . . . didn't like . . . him either."

The big man wasn't even sweating. "Want me to count cadence? Always helped me."

Nick gasped again. "Shut . . . up."

CHAPTER 28

SHUDDERING, Maryann put down the kitchen phone with shaky hands. It was nearly four in the afternoon, and they'd just gotten the sixth disturbing phone call since lunch.

"Sarah, are the kids occupied?"

Her friend peered around the corner into the den. Toby and Tina, the Barnes's six-year-old adopted twins, sat quietly watching cartoons. She looked back at the other woman. "Yeah, hon. Was that another one?"

Maryann hugged herself, even though the house was warm. "Yes. Another breather. This time he chuckled right before I hung up. This has simply got to stop. I wish the guys were back home."

"Want to pray again?"

"Yes—no—I don't know!" Maryann covered her eyes with her hand. "Maybe we should phone the church, get some prayer on this. Anything!"

"I'll do it," Sarah said, taking the phone and dialing it. She waited. She knew the church had call waiting so she just let it keep on doing its thing.

Finally someone picked up. It was Zoe Gennaro, the church secretary, and she sounded hoarse. "God bless you, God's Community Church."

"Zoe? This is Sarah Barnes. Girl, are you all right?"

"Oh, Sarah!" Zoe sounded relieved to hear a friendly voice. "What a day. I've been taking calls since breakfast."

Sarah motioned for Maryann to pick up on the extension in the master bedroom. While she was on her way, she asked the young woman again, "Are you all right, sister?"

Zoe began to cry. "No. Oh Sarah, it's awful. It seems everyone that's called in has needed prayer for one thing or another. Sickness, accidents, one crisis after another. The oppression is really bad. But that's not all." Sarah heard Zoe blowing her nose, then the girl whispered, "Pastor Wasson and the others have been getting death threats!"

"What?" On the other extension, Maryann gasped.

"Who from, baby?" Sarah asked. "Did they say?"

"Yes. He said his name is Sangre de Diablo. I don't know if that's his real name, but he says he's a satanist and his name means the devil's blood. He's called three times already today."

"Have you phoned the police?" Sarah asked. "Do they know about this guy?"

"Yes, I've called." Zoe sounded exasperated. "I've even played them the tape. All they said is they'll try to increase the patrols. Then this Sangre calls back and says he knows I phoned them and that we're helpless against his power." She gulped. "It's really spooky how he knows."

"So what does this character want?" Maryann asked. "Did he say?"

"Oh yeah!" Zoe's laugh was hollow. "Among other things, he said he and his group are going to disrupt one of our services this week. They're going to kidnap our babies and rape the women. Then he said they're going to kill us all!"

"Not if we don't let him," Sarah said. "The devil's such a liar."

"That's right. God's in control." Maryann chuckled. "Here I call the church for prayer, and I start preaching to myself."

They heard the young woman sniff. Her breathing sounded better.

"Zoe, you be sure to tell the pastors we're praying for them," Sarah said, "and for them to be strong in the Lord, and in the power of his might. And we'll see y'all tonight." She paused. "You going to be okay now, baby?"

"Yes. God bless you guys. Hey, before I hang up, are Nick and CT supposed to be back tonight?"

"Yeah, they are," Maryann said. "Why?"

"I had a note here, from Pastor Wasson for them . . . shoot, what did I do—here it is." She rattled the paper. "It says, 'Zoe, be sure to call Maryann Castle and Sarah Barnes and tell them that if Nick and CT come to church tonight, I need to see them right after.' That's it. I'm sorry I didn't call you with this earlier, but like I said, it's been crazy here."

"That's all right," Sarah said. "I'm not sure if they'll be back in time, but we'll let them know. Maybe they can call the pastor in the morning. Bye, Zoe. God bless."

"You too. Bye."

Maryann slowly walked back into the kitchen. "Death threats. I can't believe it."

"I do, hon. This talk about the rapture happening this week has got Satan all stirred up. We need to remember what God says and keep prayed up."

"Let's do that. Right now."

Both women sat down at the kitchen table. Holding hands across it, they bowed their heads and went to war.

CHAPTER 29

THE MAN WHO CALLED HIMSELF Sangre de Diablo spit out the chicken's head, then began sucking on the neck stump like a straw. The other man watching him choked back his nausea.

A moment later Sangre let the drained carcass dangle. Seeing the other man's discomfort, he laughed. "Mm-mm-good, Crandall! I think there may be a drop or two left. Sure I can't interest you?" He bobbed the dead chicken softly up and down, his black eyes twinkling in merriment.

"No! Not now." The other man swallowed. "Jesus, Ronnie."

"Ut, ut, ut!" Sangre wagged his finger. "Wrong on both counts. I've said this and said it: If you ever plan to be anything more in the coming kingdom than a flunkie you need to remember never to mention that name. And you also need to remember to call me—"

"Yeah, yeah, I know. Sangre de Diablo," Crandall sighed. "You won't let me forget it. Although after callin' you Ronnie Tompkins all my life—"

"There are a lot of things we need to change and rearrange. Our names included." Sangre leaned forward and laid the chicken on the floor before straightening. "After the ceremony Sunday night you're going to have to come up with one. Why don't you let me help?"

Crandall blew out a breath and shook his head, saying nothing.

Frowning, Sangre slumped back in his chair and folded his arms, dark eyes narrowed, lips pursed. He was trying for tough, and at five-foot-five and 120 pounds it wasn't easy.

"You're not having second thoughts, are you? Turning . . . " He nudged the headless carcass with the toe of his boot. The thing was still moving a little. ". . . chicken?" He grinned, revealing a mouthful of tiny teeth. They were covered with blood.

"No, man!" Crandall stood up and went over to the office door. Opening it a crack, he peered out. The hallway was still deserted. He looked back at Sangre, then down at the bloody chicken. "You gonna clean that up? What if somebody walks in?"

"What if they do?" Sangre stood and stretched so that the tattoos covering his body seemed to dance. "You don't get it yet, do you? Those freaking Christers are history. In less than a week they're going to be gone forever. And then we get our chance." He grinned. "Power, Crandall. The ultimate rush. And girls . . . " Sliding up behind the other man, he began rubbing his shoulders. "I know you like them young. Real young."

Crandall swallowed.

"You'll have them . . . as many as you want." Sangre ran his hand lightly up Crandall's arm. "The Dark Prince rewards his choice servants. All we need to do is show him we're sincere. So be courageous. Now. And Sunday night." Stretching up, he licked Crandall's ear. "Courage and blood," he whispered. "Remember."

Crandall nodded jerkily, sweat running through his hair. It was always the same. Ronnie—Sangre!—had known for years what buttons to push.

Yeah, Crandall remembered, all right.

Ronnie Tompkins and Crandall Weems. Two bent boys everyone shied away from. Boys people crossed to the other side of the street to avoid. They didn't care. Theirs was a brotherhood of sniggers and whispers and wails, a fellowship of fevered, muffled laughter and gray, squirming thoughts.

Crandall remembered the summer all the cats in the neighborhood vanished—into traps the two had laid. The cats' fate was best not considered. And then there was the time when they were both fourteen and they'd lured that trusting little Down's syndrome girl into the abandoned mill for a bit of fun. And then the high school prom their senior year when they'd thrown lit dynamite they'd stolen from a construction site under one of the vehicles parked outside the gym, never guessing that the van held two couples drinking and necking. Those deaths—Ronnie and Crandall's first—were icing on the cake.

And no one had ever even brought so much as an accusation against them. It was like they were invisible—no, better. They were protected.

Courage and blood.

And now it was payoff time. The two had sworn an oath that they'd take lives this coming Sunday night. They'd convince the Prince they were sincere. Their time to rule and reign with him had come at last.

Turning to look at his friend, Crandall smiled. Afraid? Not him. He swung the office door open fully, chest out, daring anyone to find them.

Sangre laughed, a breathy sound, and clapped Crandall on the shoulder. "Good! That's the ticket!" He bent down and threw the dead chicken into a paper sack. Then he looked up and squinted one eye, a smile flickering across his mouth. "You know you're going to have to drink it Sunday night. Are you sure you don't want to practice now?" He wiggled the sack. "Last chance."

Crandall shook his head. "I'm sure. I'll save it for then. It'll be twice as good then, right, Sangre?"

"Right, right." Sangre wiped his hands, standing. "Twice as good." He licked his lips and grinned. "First the chicken, then a baby from the nursery."

Checking the bag one last time for seepage, he twisted it shut and looked up again. "Now you're sure that church thing is handled?"

"It's handled, man. They're not gonna give us problems. Bank on it."

Sangre smiled in anticipation. "That place is going to be a killing ground." He pointed his finger at the other man. "I don't want any last-minute screwups."

"Relax, Ron—uh, Sangre. The only police those people will be seein' will be the ones haulin' their dead friends out." Just then the phone rang, and Crandall swore. "Lemme get that." He picked it up. "Sheriff's office, Deputy Weems."

CHAPTER 30

TO CT, THEIR FLIGHT BACK HOME was every nightmare he'd ever had about air travel, squared. When the ticket agent told him his seat was located in the middle of the plane, she'd been almost geometrically precise. The giant's six-foot, seven-inch frame was shoehorned into a seat that must have been designed by and for an elf.

To make matters worse, on his right side reposed a snoring, drooling old man who kept leaning over on him. On his left, a traveling salesman continually gnawed on the biggest, grossest summer sausage CT had ever seen. Or smelled.

On top of that, the flight attendants had given a new meaning to the term *surly*. Plus the movie, lousy though it was, had conked out halfway through. Plus his reading lamp was burned out, and the airflow knob was stuck closed.

Plus, plus, plus . . . they were five hours into the flight, and he was ready to start tossing bodies.

Three rows back, Nick wasn't faring any better. He had his own fellow sufferers to contend with: a group of loudly jabbering Norwegian geophysicists, all with serious gas problems. He sighed. Just great.

Once again he put his credit card into the airfone slot in the seat in front of him and yanked the phone free. For the fifteenth time in as many minutes he punched in all the required digits and waited.

Still nothing.

No getting around it, the thing was as dead as a hammer; every one of them was, all over the plane.

Nick ground his teeth, his thoughts dark. *I wish I was still a cussing man. A good heat-seeking, paint-peeling cuss would sure help right about now.*

Then he shook his head. No, no it wouldn't. He closed his eyes and softly began praying again.

.. .. ..

By the time they'd landed, both men were exhausted and ill tempered. Standing by the luggage carrousel, Nick glanced up at the airport clock. "Three minutes after twelve. Can that be right?"

"I guess so," CT answered. "So that makes this what—Friday mornin'?"

"Call it Thursday midnight. Keeps my internal clock straight." Nick rubbed his hands in frustration. "Come on, come on. How long does it take to get the luggage unloaded anyway?"

"I dunno, but I tell ya, I'm about done. My internal clock is screamin' for evac." CT yawned hugely. "I guess we missed church."

Nick stared over with bleary eyes. "I'd say that's a good bet. I'm glad I called home when we landed. I hated to wake up Maryann and Tracy and Blake, but I was coming unglued on that plane. I had to find out what's up."

"Funny that Sarah and our kids were there too, huh?"

"Not so funny. I was going to wait until you weren't so cranky to tell you this."

The big man scowled. "Tell me what?"

"Maryann said there's been some weird stuff going on at home. Breathers on the phone. Death threats from satanists at church. Who knows what else? That's why she asked Sarah and the kids to stay with them. Safety in numbers, I guess."

The look on CT's face was murderous. "Satanists? Threatenin' *my* family?"

"And mine too, hot rock. So if our luggage *ever gets here* we can head on home and make sure they're safe."

Several other travelers must have picked up the frustration radiating from the two men. They all gave them some extra room.

"I wish all we'd brought was just our carry-on stuff," Nick muttered. "We'd already be in the car on the way home. But no, I have to be Mr. Practical and pack some clothes in case we had to stay over."

"Notice who didn't pack any," CT told him. "I had a feelin' we wouldn't need 'em."

"Yeah, yeah—finally!"

The first pieces of luggage were now lifting up onto the carousel. Luckily Nick's garment bag was third in view. He grabbed it with a grunt, and they began walking briskly through the glass doors toward the parking lot and home.

CHAPTER 31

THE TRAFFIC AT THAT HOUR WAS LIGHT, and they made it from the airport to Nick's house within forty minutes. Nick sighed as they pulled into the driveway. To him the drive seemed to have taken ten hours. Cincinnati had to be the only major city in the U.S. with its airport clear over in another state.

Scowling, he drywashed his face with his hands. He truly was in a lousy mood. Absolutely beat, the two men slowly climbed out of the car.

"Be quiet when we go in. They're all probably asleep."

CT stopped with a scowl. "Are you for real, man? How old do you think I am, twelve? Cut me some slack."

"I just know how loud you can be," Nick snapped. "We've been friends for nearly forty years. You start stomping around the place with those size sixteen rowboats of yours, and—"

"Rowboats!" CT yelled. "You think it's easy havin' feet this big? I gotta special order all my shoes, even house slippers, and you—"

The front door swung open, and Maryann blinked at the light from the street. She wrapped her housecoat tightly around her.

"Good grief, guys, can you make any more noise? I don't think they can hear you up in Dayton yet!" Across the street, lights went on in a couple of houses. "Get in here, both of you, before somebody calls the police!"

Grumbling, both men trudged into the house. Once inside they saw that Sarah was also up, as were the Barnes twins and Tracy and Blake.

Nick looked sheepish. "Uh, we didn't wake you guys, did we?"

"Nope," Sarah answered. "We were just watching TV and waiting for y'all to get home." Over on the couch, the twins cuddled together, muffling their giggles with their hands.

CT frowned. "What?"

"Daddy has rowboats on his feet!" Toby squealed in laughter, his English flawless.

Snarling comically, the big man ran at them, hands upraised like King Kong. "Yeah, well here comes the rowboat express to getchaaa!"

Grabbing both kids, he rubbed their heads together, their combined laughter making the window glass buzz. Sarah jumped on top of the pile, and the laughing doubled.

Nick kissed Maryann and gave his niece and nephew a hug. "Auntie Em, Auntie Em!" he squeaked. "There really *is* no place like home!"

Maryann smiled as she kissed him again. "Nut. C'mon guys, sit down and tell us all about it."

"You first," CT said. He untangled himself from the pile and gazed at his wife. "You sure you're all right?"

"We're fine. Really. God's faithful, just like he said. Oh, by the way, Pastor Wasson wants you and Nick to call him. Zoe didn't say what it was about."

"Okay, we'll do that," agreed Nick. "First thing in the—well, I guess it's morning already."

"If you break into that "Good Mornin' " song from *Singin' in the Rain,* the way you used to back at Quon Tre," CT said, his tone dark, "life as you've known it is gonna be over, Nick."

"Yikes!" Nick threw up his hands with a mocking laugh, and the others joined in. Sarah was right; the oppression was easing.

"Okay, we'll tell you, but we have to give you the quick version; we're about done in. We found Trevor Ames and also met a new brother in the Lord, an English cop. We prayed for Trevor and God healed him and he accepted Jesus." Nick dug the heels of his hands into his eyes, yawning. "And the rest has got to wait until after we get some sleep."

"Oh, hon," Maryann clucked sympathetically. "I know you're both exhausted. Let's all go to bed. By the way, we've got Sarah and CT in the guest room, with blankets for their kids on the floor."

"The floor?" Nick frowned. "We can do better than that."

"But we wanna sleep on the floor, Unca Nick!" shouted Toby.

"Aunt Mary said was hokay!" Tina chimed in. "It's an adventure!"

Nick still wasn't sure. "Well, if you guys don't mind—"

"Bro, I don't care if they climb up in a tree." Now it was CT who yawned. "I have got to get some shuteye. The sandman is beatin' me to death."

This sent the twins into more gales of laughter. With a final wave, the big man and his family shuffled off in the direction of the guest room.

"Blake and I are going to sleep in here in the den," Tracy said, adding with a devilish grin, "We tossed for the couch, and I won."

"Which leaves me on the floor," the boy grumped. "Just for which, I'm gonna give you a snore concert like you've never heard."

"All right, you two, enough," Maryann said. "Look at your poor uncle. Dead to the world."

It was true. Nick was slumped in his chair, head back, gone.

"Nick. Nicky!" Maryann gave him a gentle shake. He opened bleary eyes. "Come on to bed now."

Groggily Nick stood. Leaning on each other, hips bumping, he and Maryann headed down the hall. Nick had enough steam left to crawl into bed, and then, fully clothed, was gone again.

Maryann smiled and kissed him softly on the cheek, then covered him with the blanket. Nuzzling close, soon she was asleep herself.

CHAPTER 32

TRY AS HE MIGHT, Nick had never been able to sleep past 6 a.m. in his life. Leaving Maryann still asleep, he padded into the bathroom to shower and shave.

As he lathered his face he heard water running down the hall and guessed that CT was also up. The sense of urgency was back this morning. Mentally Nick calculated one hundred and seven hours left. Maybe.

When he went into the kitchen, CT already had coffee and eggs going. "Mornin'. Feelin' more human?"

"You know it. You could have shot off a howitzer in the bedroom, and I would never have heard it." Nick poured some coffee. "Listen, if I was out of line last night—"

"Not a problem." CT took a huge bite of egg. "We were both dead on our feet. Besides, I know ya love me."

Nick blew him a kiss.

Just then Sarah walked in. "Hmm. World travel has made you boys strange."

All three chuckled. Maryann shuffled in, yawning and rubbing her eyes.

"I thought I heard everybody up." She reached for the coffeepot. "So what do you guys have on for today?"

"First we need to call Manny at nine," Nick answered as he sopped up egg with his toast. He leveled a gaze at CT. "If you thought yesterday was a treat, you're going to love the running we need to do today. Manny's setting up the meeting with Mad Jack and his wife for sometime this afternoon."

"St. Louis, isn't it?" Sarah asked, getting some cereal out of the cupboard. "You guys are flying out, right?"

Nick grimaced. "As much as we hate climbing back on an airplane, we really don't have a choice." Longingly he looked at the rest of his breakfast, knowing he wouldn't get to finish it. "Less than a hundred and seven hours left. Then we need to think about getting to Newark to see Frankie."

"I know." CT pushed his chair back. "We're burnin' daylight. You about done?"

"No." Nick took a final slurp of coffee. "But it's all we have time for. Let's move."

He grabbed their jackets, pitched CT his, then turned and kissed Maryann. "We're headed on down to the office to call Manny from there. If we don't get back home before we start for the airport, we'll give you and Sarah a call."

"Okay." She gave him a hug. "Just let us know. Godspeed to you both."

CT zipped his jacket. "We need to swing by our house first. If we end up goin' to Newark after St. Louis, I may just need that change of clothes."

"Good thing my garment bag's still stowed in the trunk." Nick pulled out his car keys, glancing again at Maryann. "You sure you're going to be all right?"

"We'll be fine," she assured him with a smile. "The kids are staying close to home today."

"And I've got the twins here too," Sarah added. "I asked Maryann if us hanging here was going to be a problem—"

"And I said of course not. We do plan to let the machine get all the calls today, though."

"Good thinking," Nick said.

Giving their wives a couple of final kisses, the two men hurried outside and climbed in the car. With a wave and a shift of gears, they were gone. Silently the women watched the car recede into the distance.

Sarah finally spoke up. "You heard it, girlfriend."

"One hundred and seven hours," Maryann whispered, as much to herself as to Sarah. "How can they possibly find them all?"

CHAPTER 33

MOUSE DROPPINGS, Sangre mused. *That's what I'm smelling in here. Mouse droppings.* He drew a deep breath, savoring the odor. *A person could get used to anything. And after a while, learn to love it.*

He looked over at the other people gathered together with him in the old abandoned mill. Smiling, he spread his arms wide. "Man, I love this place!"

One of the women, that new girl—what was her name again? Akeela or something—spoke up. "I think it smells funny." She wrinkled her nose. "And it's dirty. What makes this dump so special to you, Sangre?"

Hot light burning in his eyes, he dropped his arms and slowly walked over to her, until their noses were almost touching.

"Dump?" he breathed, still smiling. "You need to be more charitable, sweetie. This was where Crandall and I first became aware." He looked over at the deputy. "That little retarded girl helped us, didn't she, Crandall?"

The deputy was still touching up the pentagram on the floor. He hoped he had enough red paint.

"Hm? Yeah, that's right, Sangre. It was . . . right over there." He pointed with the brush. "We crucified her to the floor after we were finished with her."

Sangre nodded, pleased that Crandall was finding it easier to remember to use his power name.

"This sacred place," Sangre said loudly as he pirouetted around, "has been anointed with blood. The blood of a virgin." He had no idea, none at all, of how silly and full of himself he was.

"Yeah, but the kid didn't die," one of the men, Nightshade, said. "You yourself said you guys didn't kill her; you just used her till she was almost dead. Does that make a difference?"

"We were young," Sangre replied. "We still were unaware of the surpassing power death holds. If we had known that then, yes, we would have gone ahead and killed her. We did fix her so she couldn't talk at any rate."

He smiled, savoring the memory. They'd fixed her, all right. When he and Crandall had finished with the little retarded girl, they'd deposited her on her parents' front porch, her tongue cut out and neatly stuffed in her purse.

"What we took that night was almost as good." Sangre's smile widened. "Innocence. We took it all, every drop."

One of the men said, "So the killing we're gonna do Sunday night at the church—"

"Will complete our apprenticeship. Exactly so. If we can do this thing properly, and the Dark Prince approves . . . well, our rewards are going to be incredible."

"What if we don't kill them all?" Akeela asked. "There's only thirteen of us, and I heard those Christers are running nearly seven thousand there now. And how are we going to do it? I—"

"Way too many questions, little bird," Sangre broke in, his smile fading. "You know how much I hate that. Are you starting to doubt me?"

She shook her head. "Well, no, but—"

"Let me explain it to you, to all of you," Sangre said, his voice rising. "We don't need to kill them all. We just need to begin killing, and so assure the Dark Prince of our sincerity." They all nodded. "He's coming into his power very soon, quite possibly the day those Christers are dispatched, and we'll ascend with him. As for how we'll do it . . . show them, Crandall."

The deputy set down his paintbrush and lumbered over to a large wooden case. Lifting the lid, he reached in and lifted out a MAC-10 machine pistol. "Here's what we're gonna use. A fence got us nine of these. Believe me, they'll do the trick. Also I managed to get us three .38 revolvers and a big old nasty Desert Eagle .50." He smiled. "That's for me."

"I'll provide everyone with Molotov cocktails in small bottles that we'll be throwing as we leave," Sangre added, and then he laughed, "We'll give them a taste of that hell they keep going on about."

The others joined him in his laughter. All but Akeela. She looked pensive. That didn't escape Sangre's notice.

"Nightshade." Sangre's smile had grown very soft, his eyes never leaving the girl's face. "I thought you said Akeela was all right. You promised me. And you're the one who brought her to us, remember that. I ask you. Does she look all right to you?"

Nightshade shifted uncomfortably, trying to smile. "Aw, she's okay, Sangre. She's just . . . nervous, I guess."

Eyes narrowed, Sangre turned to the girl. His smile faded. "Is that your problem, Akeela? Are you nervous?" His voice took on a singsong quality. "Are you nervous in the service, little bird? Does your liver quiver?"

"Well . . . yeah." She tried putting together a smile, but it didn't work. "Maybe a little, I guess. I just—"

"What?" Sangre grabbed the girl, holding her close. Slowly he began rubbing his hand up and down her spine. "Ooh, come on baby, tell me. Tell Sangre all about it. You just what?"

"Uh . . . " Akeela tried backing up, but the wall stopped her.

"Do you see these people, girl?" he whispered. "They're committed to the cause of our Dark Prince. But I'm beginning to question how strong your commitment is. You know. You being new and all."

Having heard that tone before, many times, Nightshade tried jumping in. "Hey!"

Too late. Sangre cut him off as if he hadn't heard. He went on, louder, "Now my problem, Akeela, and yours too, is your nervousness is making me nervous. And I hate that feeling. I always have. So what do you say, little bird? Let's fix that, all right? Right here and right now, let's you and me fix it for good."

Snatching the girl's head in both hands, he then kissed her hard on the mouth. Her eyes grew huge in surprise.

That was an unexpected pleasure. *They're so pretty*, he thought. *A nice, clear blue, the color of cornflowers in summer.* Odd he'd never noticed that until now.

Before she could pull back, he tightened his grip, just so. Then, still kissing her, he gave her head a sharp twist. The cracking of her neckbones sounded like applause.

Those blue, blue eyes went blank as he let her fall.

"Jesus, Ronnie!" Crandall gasped, dropping to her side.

Sangre wagged his finger at him. "Ah-ah. Remember?"

"Well. That's just marvelous." An older man, Jace, a professor of English literature at the university, shook his head at Akeela's twitching body as he dabbed at his mouth with a perfumed handkerchief. "You've killed our thirteenth, Sangre. How are we going to fill the Circle now?"

"We don't need to," Sangre said. "The Circle remains complete. I've assumed her lifeforce into me. She's still here, but now her attitude problem has been corrected. Her will brought into line. Understand?"

Jace nodded. Say what you will, the fellow knew his business.

Sangre looked over at Nightshade. "And as for you . . . " The young man stepped back, fear gleaming in his eyes. "I'll disregard this." Sangre's smile was magnanimous. "You were just trying to be a good helper, true? Just trying to make the Circle complete. Isn't that right?"

"Right! That's right!" The relief in Nightshade's voice was pitiful.

"Yes indeedy. Oh, Crandall." Sangre turned and looked down at the deputy, who was still feeling for a pulse. "Quit fooling around and get something to put her in. We'll drop her in the quarry later on tonight. The usual spot."

"Okay, Ro—uh, Sangre. I think I got a tarp around here someplace."

"Before you do that, though, we need to pray."

The twelve gathered in a circle and held hands. Sangre tenderly gazed at them, the depth of feeling in his heart nearly bringing tears to his eyes. These were his people, his clan, his brothers and sisters, his *family*.

He did love them so.

Pointing his chin up toward the ceiling, he grinned in unfeigned joy. The dirty morning light filtering down through the high, smudged windows made his tiny teeth glow like foxfire.

CHAPTER 34

IT WAS NEARLY 8:30 A.M. by the time Nick and CT arrived downtown at corporate headquarters. The whisper-quiet elevator deposited them on the thirtieth floor. As they exited, they noticed that the receptionist was at her post behind the mahogany desk, but no other employees could be seen.

Nick frowned. There were usually twenty or more people scurrying around at this hour. Now what? He walked over to the desk.

"Rita, this may be a stupid question, but just where the heck is everybody?"

She laughed, even though he hadn't meant his question to be humorous. It didn't matter; the tiny Hispanic woman laughed at everything that came out of Nick's mouth.

Rita Ybarra's story was unique. Less than a year earlier she'd been a homeless, hopeless junkie, doomed. But then through a ministry outreach of the GCC, she'd been led not only to the Lord, but to a clean lifestyle as well.

When the church asked Nick to help her find work, he did them one better and agreed to try her as a receptionist. To everyone's surprise but her own, Rita discovered she had a talent for communicating with the public. Even better, most people found her efficient, bubbly personality charming.

Her only flaw, and admittedly it was a small one, was that her sense of humor was a bit . . . off. Rita found Nick Castle to be simply the most screamingly funny individual she'd ever met. Call it a personality quirk. That or incipient insanity.

"Almost everyone, they take some days off, Mr. Castle," she giggled. "Vacations, sick days, whatever, you know? I guess to talk to their families about God."

That made sense, Nick had to admit.

"Now, my mama is a Christian many years already. And I think, hey, she okay with Jesus, and she all the family I have anyway, so I might as well come on to work, to answer the phones." She smiled, revealing a mouthful of incredibly bad teeth. "Okay?"

"Okay. Listen, Mr. Barnes will be with me in my office, so hold all our calls." Nick stopped, his hand on his office doorknob. "By the way, did you make any coffee yet?"

"No, Mr. Castle!" Rita shrieked as she collapsed across her desk in helpless laughter.

Shaking their heads, the two men went on in.

"I know I've said this before," CT said, pulling up a padded office chair. "But that's an odd woman out there. She must figure workin' here is like bein' in one long Marx Brothers movie."

"Yeah, but she's sweet, and the customers love her. Plus I believe she may be onto something."

"Yeah, what?"

"I'm thinking I ought to shut the plant and offices down until next Wednesday, making sure everyone gets their regular pay this week, of course. We're not the only ones who could use that time to make final contacts."

CT looked at his friend in genuine admiration. "That's a great idea. I'll put a memo on the company net. So who gets to tell Rita she needs to go home?"

Nick laughed and picked up the phone, switching the speaker on. "Let's call Pastor Wasson first, then Manny."

"Hey guys!" Wasson sounded awfully chipper for a man recieving death threats. "How was England? Did y'all find Mr. Ames all right?"

"Yeah, we did. God not only healed and saved him, he also reunited him with his sister."

"Praise the Lord! That's terrific!"

"Yep. Listen, pastor, I don't mean to be abrupt, but we're kind of short on time here. Maryann said you needed to speak with us."

"That's right. It has to do with this fella Dooley. Any success in finding him?"

"Not yet. After we get done talking with you, we're going to call our contact at the Pentagon to see if he's been able to come up with anything."

"Okay, guys, here's my thought. Back when I was in the service, our company clerk had a nickname: the Keeper of the Secrets. If there was ever a man who had his hand on the pulse of the unit, it was him." Wasson paused, and then said, "Who was yours?"

Nick and CT stared at each other as revelation dawned. "Greer," they answered in unison.

"Sergeant Greer." CT scowled. "Why not? He would have known Dooley's full name, his hometown, the works. Stupid, *stupid.*"

"C'mon fellas, ease up," Wasson soothed. "One of you would have thought of it sooner or later."

"Yeah, but we didn't," Nick said. "We'll run that idea past Manny Alverez as soon as we hang up. We owe you one, pastor."

"I'll make sure I collect too." The pastor laughed. "Say, are you and CT gonna be back in time for tonight's service?"

"I don't know yet. Probably not."

Wasson sounded excited. "Well, do your best. Things are popping here like you wouldn't believe. I could tell you stories. Perfect strangers have been wandering in off the street, asking about Jesus, getting right with God. Most of them have never even heard a gospel message, but they're saying something compelled them to come in. Check the news when you get a chance. It's happening everywhere. We're close, now. Close."

"We know, pastor," CT said. "Around a hundred and five hours, tops; we've been doin' a countdown. Be prayin' for us, that we can get this thing done and be back here quick."

"You've got it. Let's do that now."

The two men smiled. They'd both known what it was like to be in churches where the man behind the pulpit really never had been called to be a pastor. Whatever agenda those men had been pursuing, serving their flocks was about last on their list of priorities.

With Frank Wasson it was different. He had a true pastor's heart. It was evident in everything he did and said. No wonder Satan had targeted him and men and women liked him.

The thing was, it really didn't seem to faze them at all. They'd stay the course, regardless. Nick and CT had both witnessed their share of courage, but this was bravery of a whole different order.

The two men bowed their heads in reverence and gratitude as Pastor Wasson prayed a short, intense prayer for God to grant them traveling mercies and to do a fast work.

After thanking him again, Nick rang off. "Frank's a good man."

"Yeah. He came through for us on Greer, that's for sure." CT shook his head. "Greer. Nick, you and me must be industrial strength dumb."

"Speak for yourself." Nick picked up the phone again. "Let's call Manny."

He dialed the number and waited. And waited some more. The phone seemed to ring for an inordinately long time. He was about to make a remark about it when it was finally snatched up.

"Pentagon. Personnel, Sergeant Alverez." Manny sounded out of breath.

"Manny? Nick Castle. You all right?"

"Nick. Gimme a second."

They heard him cover the phone with his hand and mumble something to someone. "Okay, I'm back. Sorry, but it's a zoo here today. Phones are ringing like crazy, and almost nobody here to answer 'em. Lotta absences."

"How come?" CT asked.

"You tell me," Manny snapped. "Most of 'em are Christians, like you guys. I heard everybody's using their accumulated sick leave and personal days to talk to their friends and families about . . . you know."

"How about you?" Nick asked. "Did you have that sit-down with your folks yet?"

"Yeah." Manny sounded uncomfortable. "I'm still thinking. I guess you guys called about seeing Jack."

Nick decided not to press him. He'd heard the gospel. He'd either take the step or he wouldn't. "That's right. Is it all set up?"

"Between one-thirty and two. I'll fax you the directions telling you how to get from the St. Louis airport to their house." He sighed, "But that's where the good news ends, because as for your buddy Dooley, I'm sorry. I've drawn a complete blank."

"We may have some help for you there," Nick said. "How about our company clerk? Let's see if we can reach him. If anybody would have known Dooley's full name, he would."

"Good grief, your clerk!" Manny groaned. "Of course. Why didn't I think of that? What's the name?"

"Greer," CT said. "Sergeant Robert Greer. G-R-E-E-R. And he was always talkin' about his hometown. Bozeman, Montana. Was gonna get a ranch there someday, he said."

"Robert Greer, sergeant. Hometown, Bozeman, Mon-tan-a." They could hear Manny's pencil scratching. The tradition never changed; sergeants always seemed to prefer pencils to pens. "Got it. This shouldn't take too long. I'll call you back in a few minutes." He hung up.

Nick turned to CT with a smile. "Okay, Security, while Manny's doing that, I've made my decision. Tell Rita to go home."

"Me?"

CHAPTER 35

FRANK WASSON TOOK AN APPRECIATIVE SIP from his battered old Thermos and smiled: Diane had come through again. Over twenty-seven years of marriage, and his wife still hadn't lost the touch of making good coffee. He wasn't sure how she did it, but the stuff she made for him to take to the office every morning was the finest he'd ever tasted. That coffee was his only vice—that and riding Harleys.

And no offense to the kitchen ladies, but the brew from the church was always watery and contained strange aftertastes. This week it was sardines. Wasson took another sip and suppressed a shudder. Definitely no contest here. His reverie was broken by the ringing of the phone on his desk.

Here we go, he thought, resigning himself to the beginning of another exhausting day. Appointments from now until four-thirty, home for a quick shower, dinner, Bible study and prayer, and then back for another service that could possibly go until midnight.

He picked up. "Yes, Zoe?"

The secretary sounded agitated. "Pastor, line two. It's a man. And he says he's going to shoot himself if he doesn't speak with you right away!"

"What? Okay, I'll take it. Give me a second." Wasson muted the connection and bowed his head for a quick prayer for discernment and wisdom. After a moment he opened his eyes and punched line two. "This is Pastor Wasson. How can I help you, sir?"

"You can help me . . . by dying!"

The pastor almost broke the connection, but felt he had to say something to this tormented person. "Too late," he said. "I'm already dead."

There was a silence on the other end, and then, "What?"

"I said I'm already dead. But I'm also alive. The Bible mentions it a lot. Would you like to talk about that? I've been told I'm a pretty good listener."

An even longer silence dragged out, and then whoever it was hung up with a crash. The pastor rotated his head in a slow circle. Nine a.m., and already his neck felt like it had a hundred rubber bands around it.

Again he prayed softly for a moment, asking for strength. Then, picking up his beat-up old Thermos, he took another sip of Diane's superb coffee and asked Zoe to send in his first appointment.

.. .. ..

DEPUTY CRANDALL WEEMS SLUMPED in the swivel chair at his dispatcher's desk, trembling like a malaria victim. That hadn't gone as he'd thought it would. What the pastor had said to him just now—didn't anything rattle these people? The ear Crandall had held the phone to burned as if it had been drenched in lye.

The deputy swallowed, desperately trying to assure himself that everything was still on track. Sangre knew what he was doing. He had to. Just this morning he'd told the Circle that the power was almost theirs and that they all should ignore the news reports of a worldwide move of *him*. Those reports were nothing more than lies, Sangre had told the group. Just lies and fakes. There was simply no way that so-called savior could be doing so much damage to the Dark Prince's kingdom worldwide at the same time.

There was another word Sangre had used, but Crandall couldn't remember it. What was it? A *hoak*. Yeah, that was it. Crandall was pretty sure that was the word Sangre had said . . . or was it *hoax?*

He smiled a little. Hoak, hoax, whatever, it was just some fake stories. Everything was gonna be okay. The Dark Prince had it all figured out, all under control.

Didn't he?

CHAPTER 36

"HELLO. LAZY G."

Nick smiled. Manny had been as good as his word. He'd called back not four minutes later with Greer's home and work addresses and phone numbers. On a hunch Nick had tried the work number—the Lazy G Ranch—and found out, not surprisingly, that the G stood for Greer. Their old clerk had gotten that ranch after all. Owing to the time differential—it was just past seven in the morning out there—Nick had caught Greer as he was finishing breakfast.

"Sergeant Greer? Nick Castle. I—"

"Sergeant Greer?" the man interrupted. "Nobody's called me that in years. Everybody just calls me Bob—wait a minute. Did you say your name's Castle? Not the Nick Castle from Nam?"

"The very one. I'm glad you remember me."

"Sure I remember you! I heard you'd gone into business for yourself. We get our horse liniment from Castle Industries."

"Well, not straight from us. We're just the distributor. Listen, Bob, I know you're busy, and this is going to sound kind of strange, but I've got something I need to ask you."

"Ask away—hold on a sec." Greer turned away from the phone, but Nick could still hear him clearly. "Charlie, you'd better hot walk that mare some more before you put her back in the corral. And make sure you curry her tail this time too, not just her mane . . . Yeah, okay, then grab some chow . . . Edwina's got flapjacks, eggs, and grits on the stove for you guys . . . Sure, you can have seconds!" Greer's voice got louder again. "Okay, I'm back. Sorry about that, but I took the cordless phone straight from the kitchen into the paddock when it rang. The Lazy G Ranch is, well, it's kind of a starting-over place for boys who have gotten into trouble with the law."

Nick remembered now that Greer was a motormouth, but decided that if he wanted this man's help it would be best to let him get his own words said first.

"I worked out a deal with old Judge Boudine a while back," Greer went on, "to see if I could maybe help some kids avoid the mistakes my brother made. For most of 'em it's either a stay at the Gray Bar Hotel or a stint here." He chuckled, "With the way I work 'em, jail starts looking better and better."

They both laughed, and Nick felt constrained to ask, "So your brother got in some trouble with the law?"

Greer's laugh faded. "Yeah, he did. Both our parents were killed in a plane crash right after I got back to the World, and Tom—that's my brother—really took it hard. He's younger than me by a good number of years. My mom always called Tommy her surprise baby. Anyway, when they died, Tom went kind of wild. I guess I'm partly to blame. I was trying to get this place going, and, well, I just missed the signs. Ten years ago he and a buddy robbed a liquor store in Bozeman. Somehow it went wrong, and Tom killed the owner."

Greer paused, then went on, "Tom's in prison for life, with no possibility of parole. But it gets better. About five years ago he got . . . well, I don't know if you've ever heard the term, but Tom got saved. He asked me to take this ranch and make it someplace guys like him could maybe start over."

Nick had the feeling that, motormouth or no, Bob Greer would be a good man to have as a friend. "Bob, that's the very reason I called. I know exactly what the term means. It happened to me back in that MASH."

"Me too!" Nick could hear Greer's smile even over the phone. "I accepted the Lord about three years ago, when Tom asked me to give the Lazy G a new purpose. Matter of fact," he went on with some emotion, "it was Tommy who led me to Jesus. How about that?"

"I'm glad," Nick said, meaning it. "Really glad."

There was another pause, then Greer said, "Not that I'm a betting man anymore, but I bet what you wanted to ask me about has to do with the message we all got Tuesday night, right?"

"That's exactly right, and I'll make it quick because we need to catch a plane to St. Louis. You remember CT Barnes?"

"Sure." Greer said. "Ol' Sluefoot lost a good right arm when Barnes got saved. He told the whole unit about it."

"We still work together and have something we need to do."

"Like what?"

"We need to find some of the guys who were in the 7th of the 115th and make sure they have a chance to hear the gospel before we leave."

"Sounds like a plan."

"We already located Trevor Ames, the reporter who went us with us that day, back at his home in England. He got right with God, but we're not done.

We're seeing Mad Jack this afternoon in St. Louis and then Frankie Malone in Newark, hopefully tonight."

"Yeah, I heard about Mad Jack through the grapevine. Pretty sad. And Frankie. Man, talk about being mad at the world. You guys have your work cut out for you, that's for sure."

"Which brings me to the reason I'm keeping you from your horses. We're supposed to see Dooley too, but we're having no success at all finding him." Nick leaned forward, gripping the phone tighter. "Can you help, Bob? Do you remember anything about Dooley's full name or his hometown? Anything at all? We're running out of options here."

"Yeah, I do. One of the things that helped me when I was company clerk was that I have a pretty good memory. Say, is Barnes there with you too?"

"Yeah, I'm here," CT said. "Nick has this on the speaker. Good to hear your voice again."

"Same here. And I hope you guys are sitting down, 'cause this is flat gonna blow you both away. Ready?" His voice grew excited. "Dooley isn't his name!"

"Yeah, I know he has a first name." Nick thought Greer had misunderstood the question. "We thought you might know what it is. All of us always just called him by his last name, Dooley."

"But that's just it, guys!" Greer sounded really agitated now. "Dooley *wasn't* his last name!"

"What?" Nick stood. "Well, good grief! What is it, then?"

"Are you ready?" Greer paused dramatically. "His full name is Ambrose Dooley Ryan!"

"Ryan? But—" CT shook his head. "His nametag said Dooley."

"I know. Here's what happened. When Dooley—Ryan, that is—was inducted, somehow the Ryan part got messed up on his paperwork, and the name Dooley—his middle name—was put down as his last name. Typical Army foul up."

Nick was familiar with those. Anybody who'd ever put on a uniform was.

"He told me he didn't care," Greer went on. "He said he and his dad had some kind of major falling out before he went in, and he told the quartermaster to just leave it be. Well, they didn't, of course; you know the Army."

"We know," CT agreed darkly.

Greer continued, "By the time Dooley finished basic they finally got it straightened out and had given him the right dogtags with the right name.

But he still had all those nametags already made up for his Class A's and fatigues that said Dooley. And he really hated his first name, Ambrose. So from the time he got to Nam until he was wounded, he just went by Dooley."

Nick looked at CT and shrugged. Without Greer's help they wouldn't have gotten this in a million years.

"He had to tell Mad Jack and me, of course, so his pay and benefits wouldn't get fouled up, but nobody else. So if you want to check with records or the VA, just tell 'em to look it up under Ambrose Dooley Ryan."

There was a long pause while the two men digested this. "No wonder we were stumped," Nick remarked at last, shaking his head in amazement. "That computer brain of yours wouldn't happen to recall his hometown, would it?"

"He used to talk about it, some, yeah. But not so much as you'd think; I guess because of that big fight he'd had with his dad. Anyway, I remember he said he was from Danville, Kentucky. Whether or not he's there now, of course, that I wouldn't know."

"Did you get all that?" Nick asked CT, who was hurredly scratching it down in his appointment book.

"Got it." CT finished writing with a flourish. "Bob, you, sir, are all right!"

All three laughed. "This means a lot to us," Nick said. "And to Dooley. We have to go."

"Here, there, or in the air, Nick. God's blessings on you both."

Nick hung up and immediately called Manny. When he'd told him the news about Dooley's real name, the sergeant laughed.

"And here I was thinking I was losing my touch. I just couldn't figure it. Your guy seemed to vanish without a trace, but I knew that was plain nuts. This'll be easy now. I'll just check with the VA and see where Ryan's checks are being mailed." Nick could hear him scribbling something. "I'll bet you dollars to doughnuts the guy's back in, what was it, Danville, Kentucky? Do you want me to fax it or give you a call?"

"How long do you figure this is gonna take?" CT asked.

"Oh, I dunno . . . give me fifteen minutes."

"CT and I have a couple of things to do," Nick said. "We'll call you back." He paused. "And Manny, speaking of vanishing without a trace—"

"Yeah, yeah," the sergeant replied, a note of exasperation in his voice. "I'm still thinking."

CHAPTER 37

CRANDALL WEEMS FELT LIKE he was about to go in his pants. He'd never been so scared in his life.

Sangre.

He was like a man possessed. Why was he so mad? Hadn't Crandall done like he said? Hadn't he tried to make that preacher doubt his protection? It wasn't his fault it hadn't worked.

His arguments still didn't make it any easier to watch Sangre tearing around the mill, frothing like that. The deputy remembered what Sangre had done to Akeela's neck. They may be friends, but no way was he gonna let the guy get within gripping distance.

Sangre had run out of curse words ten minutes ago. Now he was down to just screaming and running around. Crandall had no idea how long this was going to go on. He'd simply never seen him in such a state.

After a few more minutes, the satanist finally stopped and dropped to his knees, looking up at Crandall with red-rimmed eyes. "Pray with me," he croaked, holding out a shaky hand.

"Uh, I gotta get back."

"Pray with me *now!*" Sangre didn't even look human. With his bloodshot eyes, wild hair, and foaming mouth, he looked to Crandall like something he would have shot had he found him in the woods. What was the word the old-timers used? *Feral.*

Crandall swallowed, thinking about the way Akeela's neck had cracked. He slowly sank to his knees beside Sangre.

"Dark One," Sangre moaned. "We yield ourselves to your purpose. Let blood be our byword and pain our companion. We call upon you, that we may confuse the Usurper's children. Let us, your servants, be filled now, and we pledge to you our souls. Forever."

They waited while Sangre rocked slowly from side to side, his hand gripping Crandall's like clock gears. Suddenly he hissed and smiled. "Yes. Thank you." He stood, pulling the deputy with him.

"Crandall." Sangre's voice was normal now, but still a little raspy. "He wants blood. Stick out your palm."

Without hesitation, Crandall did. He knew what was coming. He felt an excitement trembling deep inside.

Reaching into his right boot, Sangre pulled out a long, thin fillet knife. Crandall remembered it. He'd had it as a boy, and they always used it to seal their oaths.

Sangre drew the blade across his own palm, cutting deep, before doing the same to Crandall's. The deputy sucked in, air whistling through his teeth. The steel was cold and clean, and felt so good.

Sangre clasped his bleeding hand with Crandall's, wrapping a leather thong around both.

"Every time." His eyes danced with light. "Every time we take another step together, we do it in blood. Our blood. The Usurper thinks he's won. He has not. He thinks he's discouraged us." Sangre leaned close, hissing the words. "He has not. Crandall, we'll do this thing, and we'll see our Lord's favor surrounding us and guiding us. We're invincible, and we're his. Are you with me?"

"Yeah, Sangre, I am." Crandall said. "Are you sure you're not mad at me anymore?"

"I'm sure. We're brothers aren't we? Brothers in blood? The victory is ours, Crandall, and the defeat—" Sangre smiled, pointing his index finger upward, "—is his."

Still smiling, he knelt again, looking up at Crandall with an open mouth. All that could be seen of Sangre's eyes were the whites.

With a moan he caught a drop of blood dripping off their bound wrists onto his outstretched tongue.

CHAPTER 38

NICK AND CT NOT SO PATIENTLY WAITED their turn in line at the car rental counter at the Lambert-St. Louis International Airport. While not as fraught with tension as Heathrow, the place was still hectic and tightly wound.

The line snaked slowly, maddeningly so. For the tenth time in half as many minutes, CT checked his watch.

"If this line moves any slower you and me are gonna get raptured right here," he grumbled. "Where is it Manny said Mad Jack—wups, make it just plain Jack—and his wife live? Fenton?"

"Yeah, Fenton. Southwest of the city, right off I-44. It shouldn't be too hard to find, provided we ever get our car."

"What did Betty get us this time?"

"Not another Bentley, if that's what you're hoping. I just told her something big, a Lincoln Town Car or something around that size."

CT smiled. "A Town Car'll work." He nodded sagely. "You don't want to get too spoiled ridin' in Bentleys anyway."

Their turn finally came, and they strode up to the counter. The young woman behind it was polite enough, but seemed distracted.

"Hello. Do you have a reservation?"

"Yes, we do. The name is Castle. I believe you have a Lincoln reserved for us."

"Lincoln, for Castle . . . " The agent punched data into her computer for a moment, and then looked up. "Nope, sorry."

"What?" CT shoved in front of Nick. "Check that thing again, will ya?"

She looked down. "Checking . . . no, I'm sorry, I'm not showing anything reserved for you."

"Wonderful." CT blew out a disgusted breath. "Mr. Castle, deal with this. I'm gonna go have a seat." Stalking over to some plastic chairs pushed up against the glass wall, he sat down with a thud. The glass rattled.

The young woman turned to Nick. "Maybe you'd like to wait as well? Something might turn up. You never know."

He scratched his nose. "How about some of the other vendors? Maybe they might?"

"I'm afraid that won't do any good, sir," the rental agent interrupted, not unkindly. "You see how busy the entire airport is. All the agencies are swamped. There's an outside chance we may get an early return, but no guarantees. You can look at our magazines if you want while you're waiting."

Nick bit off a sharp reply; this certainly wasn't the agent's fault. He knew, of course, what was causing all this: Christians, himself and CT included, were running around like maniacs trying to meet up with long-lost friends and families to give them one last witness. Knowing the causes and dealing with their effects were two different things, however.

He ran a hand through his hair. Time for a taxi. He hoped they got a clean one. With a heavy tread he clomped over to CT.

"Well?" The big man uncrossed his arms. "Are we all set?"

"Nope. They don't have a car reserved for us. I don't know what happened, but something got fouled up, that's for sure."

CT frowned. "Was it Betty's fault?"

"Probably not. I'm not about to lay this at her doorstep, any rate." Nick sighed. "I can't imagine her messing us up like this. Talk about tossing a monkey wrench into the plan."

"So. Cab time, huh?"

"Yep. I guess we might as well head on outside and see what we can find." He smiled, resigned now. "Roll up your pantleg. Show some skin. Maybe we'll get one to stop quicker."

"If I do that I can guarantee you we'll be walkin' to Fenton. Come on."

They were heading for the door when they were stopped by a woman's voice.

"Sir! Mr. Castle!" It was the rental agent, beckoning them. Reversing direction, they walked over to the counter.

"Yes?" Nick said.

"I'm glad you guys hadn't left yet. We just had one become available. You must be living right." The agent lowered her voice. "You see that couple going out the door, arguing? Evidently some new bride wants to go back home to mother. If you'd like, I can give you their car. It's a Taurus. I know it's smaller than you wanted, but will it do?"

"It'll have to," Nick said. "We'll squeeze my friend in somehow. Thanks very much."

.. .. ..

TEN MINUTES LATER they were out of the airport mess and on I-270, looping south of the city.

"All right, where's Manny's fax?" Nick peered in dismay through the windshield at the snarled traffic. "We need it to find Fenton."

"Back home on your desk." The big man gritched around. "Man, this car is a tight fit."

"*What?*" Nick looked thunderstruck. "Forget about the fit! You left the *directions?*" He gipped the wheel in frustration. "That's just great!"

CT glared. "Give me a break. The way we've been runnin' around you oughtta be glad I remembered my underwear."

"You're right. Sorry. This is hard on both of us." Nick rubbed his face. "Okay, let's try this again. Check the glove compartment. See if they stuck a map in there."

CT flipped it open with a smile. "Bingo. Here's one." He studied it for a moment, tracing their route with his finger. "Map duty again," he muttered. "At least this one's in English."

"So was the other one, bugwit. It was in English because we were in England. You see how this works?"

"Sarcasm ill becomes you, Nicholas. It makes one appear small."

"All I want to appear is our exit to I-44."

"Comin' up in about ten minutes. Then the map shows us hangin' a roger on it. First exit is Fenton."

.. .. ..

WITHIN TWENTY MINUTES the men were in the town, and two minutes later they found themselves slowly cruising down Whipple, a nice but narrow street in a solidly middle-class neighborhood.

On his lap CT had his appointment book open to where he'd written down the address. "We're lookin' for 3918—wup, stop, we're right on top of it. This is it." He began drumming his fingers in a rhythmic staccato.

Nick checked his watch. "1:45. Not bad timing."

They looked up at the house. It was an older Cape Cod, well maintained, and the blue trim on the shutters and eaves contrasted nicely with the house's cream color. The lawn appeared freshly mown, fronted by pink sweet pea vines interspersed with vibrant yellow snapdragons.

The place was a far cry from Trevor Ames's dwelling, that was for sure. Nick shut the car off.

"Well, let's go on up." He was halfway out of the car, but CT didn't move. "What's the matter with you? Aren't you coming?"

"Yeah, gimme a second here." The big man took a couple of deep breaths and whispered something.

"What's the problem?"

CT rubbed his face. "Bein' here." He sucked more air, clearly jittery. "I'll bet you never knew this, but Mad Jack and I were . . . well, like friends, kinda."

"What? Friends?"

CT gulped. "He always treated me like a man, Nick, like I had potential. It was almost like he didn't see the tough street kid from Gary, but was seein' somethin' past it, like . . . " He shook his head. "He saw somethin' in me only one other person ever saw. My momma, God rest her soul. It's just gonna be tough seein' him like this, that's all."

"If you were that close, how come you didn't keep in touch with him after the war?"

"I dunno. I guess after his court-martial I didn't exactly know what to say. I should have looked him up, though, when I heard the news. You're right, that's on me." He stared back out the windshield. "This is hard."

"You want to stay in the car?"

"No." CT sighed and gave a resigned smile. "God's in control of this deal, right? Let's go."

CHAPTER 39

PATRICE RUGG LOOKED LIKE A WOMAN who'd seen the backside of hell. Manny had said she was younger than Rugg by fifteen years, but it was tough to tell it; her ordeal with him had aged her terribly. Slight and stooped and grey haired, Mrs. Rugg was polite enough to Nick and CT when they knocked on her door, letting them in with a smile, but behind the smile was a pain the years hadn't eased. She showed them to some nice Early American chairs in the simple living room, asking if their flight had been all right. They all made small talk for a few minutes, neither man knowing how to start.

"Our house, it is not very clean," she apologized with another sad smile. "Manny did not give me much warning for this."

"It looks fine, ma'm." CT wondered if Nick felt as twitchy as he did.

"May I get you some coffee? It is fresh."

Nick answered, "We'd love some, Mrs. Rugg, thank you." In truth, between what they'd had at breakfast and on the plane, he and CT were about coffed out. But the woman was trying so hard to make them feel welcome that they each would have had a hard time saying no.

"Yeah," CT chimed in. "Coffee would be great!"

"I'll be right back. Nick and . . . CT was it?" Mrs. Rugg smiled again, heartbreakingly. It was easy to see the Hispanic ancestry in her dark skin and eyes and the way she pronounced her words. She'd once been beautiful.

"That's right, ma'm. CT is fine."

Watching her head off toward the kitchen, they noticed that she walked with a pronounced limp. They heard her getting cups and saucers out. There was no sign of Rugg yet.

"I wonder how she got that bum leg," CT whispered.

Before Nick could reply, Mrs. Rugg was back, bearing a tray with a pot and cups that clearly were of Vietnamese design. Alongside the coffee on the tray she'd placed cream, sugar, and *sopapillas,* a kind of Mexican dough-nut. It was obvious that she was doing her best to make good of a strained situation. She poured the coffee unsteadily, her left leg sticking out at an awkward angle.

"My Jack, he sent me this coffee set from Vietnam, right . . . before. It is pretty, no?"

"Very pretty," answered Nick.

"I'm sorry if I am slow," she said with an apologetic shrug. "My leg, sometimes it don't do what I want."

"It's no problem, Mrs. Rugg. Really." CT was doing his best not to wince. He looked around, trying to change the subject. "This is a nice place you've got here."

"I have tried to make it special for Jack. And for me." She glanced around her. "This place, it is so much better than the places we lived in when we first were married. We got married very young, you know? Jack, he was so handsome in those days."

Her eyes took on a faraway look as though she was seeing something beyond the house. "So funny. The houses the Army gave, they were not so nice, but we made them so." She paused, blinking the memories away. "When Jack came back I took the monies we had saved and bought this place. Not so big, it is true, but for us . . . " She choked off a cry. "I had hoped . . . " Suddenly she bent over and buried her face in her hands.

"Mrs. Rugg, we—" Nick began, but she stood up, cutting him off.

"Excuse, please." She limped off toward the kitchen, obviously distraught.

Before she got five steps, though, she stopped and turned, fixing them with a hot glare. Her wrinkled cheeks were wet with tears as she pointed at them. "Tell me something! Tell me this now! You can help Jack, *si?*"

"No ma'am, we can't," Nick said. "Only Jesus can."

Her return gaze had forty years of pain in it. *"Si,* but will he? Tell me this! *Will* he?"

Nick nodded. "Yes ma'am. He surely will."

Mrs. Rugg stared at them for another moment, then she hobbled into the kitchen. They heard her rummage around, loudly opening drawers. The two men glanced at each other.

At last she limped back in, clutching a small Bible, and pulled up a small chair. When she spoke her voice trembled, and her dark eyes flashed.

"Do you see this thing I am holding? This is the Bible Jack's mother gave to us when we were first married. I have looked in it. I have asked God many times, why does he not heal my Jack? Why does he torment him so? Do you have an answer for me?" Still staring at them, she waited.

After a moment Nick replied softly, "Ma'm, all I know for sure is that we live in a fallen world. But I also know God's a good God. Soon he's going to take his children home to be with him forever. And I believe he wants to restore Jack."

Mrs. Rugg didn't answer for a few long moments. When at last she spoke, it was in a bitter tone. "I know why my Jack stays sick. It is no mystery. I have cursed God! *Si!* Cursed him!" She quickly crossed herself and hung her head. "God forgive me, it is true."

"Mrs. Rugg," CT said, "God'll forgive you, no problem. But you gotta ask him to. Can we do that now?"

The old woman gave a short, humorless laugh. "Look around you! Does this look like a church? Where are the candles? And the incense? And you and your friend, you are priests?"

Nick smiled, leaning toward her. "Ma'am, I don't want to offend you, and I'm certainly not going to go into a long discussion over church doctrine. But that Bible you have in your hands says God's mercies are everlasting, and he forgives all those who ask him to in faith, believing he will."

"Even me?" she whispered, looking very small. "I, who have mocked him and cursed him? He will forgive me?"

"Even you, Mrs. Rugg. You know the time's short, don't you?"

Her nod was almost imperceptible. "*Si,* I hear the news on the TV. I know this thing."

Nick held out his hands. "May we pray with you, ma'am?"

The old woman considered their words and the condition of her heart. And the hope these two men offered. Then slowly she laid the Bible in her lap and put both her small, leathery hands in Nick's.

The three bowed their heads, and the angels gathered near.

Chapter 40

Mrs. Rugg glowed like a woman transformed. Nick smiled as he recalled the scripture that said hope deferred made the heart sick. For the first time in forty years, Mrs. Rugg had hope.

"*Gracias*, Nick! *Gracias* to you both!" The old woman beamed like a newborn. Which, in a way, was true. "And *gracias a Jesu!* And now, *con permiso*, I will bring Jack to you for prayer as well." She stood and limped off through another door.

Nick and CT waited. And waited some more. CT tugged at his collar, even though he was wearing a yellow open-neck sportshirt. Rapidly he tapped his feet, wiping his hands on his thighs, over and over.

Nick frowned. "You sure you're up for this?"

CT jerked his neck in affirmation. "Yep, I'm cool. Cooler than cool. Cucumbers got nothin' on me." His fingers fluttered. "See, my brain is sayin', 'What if it doesn't work?' But my spirit is sayin', 'Shut up, fool. Stand back and see the salvation of the Lord!' " He laughed, plainly embarrassed. "Sometimes I have real interestin' conversations with myself."

"I know what you mean. Maryann's caught me doing that plenty of times."

Suddenly there was a rustle. It was Mrs. Rugg limping back in, pulling her husband gently into the room by his hand.

The two men hoped their reactions didn't show, but Rugg's appearance was shocking. The man appeared almost to be drugged. His eyes were half shut, or maybe half open, and a thin line of drool hung threadlike from his open mouth. Rugg's formerly red crewcut had gone gray and thinning, and his fissured face looked like a relief map of Switzerland. He was almost fifty pounds lighter than when he'd served in the Army, and his bones now seemed too large for his skin.

Between her limp and his shuffle it took them some time to get into the room. Finally Mrs. Rugg guided her husband in front of Nick and CT. They stood.

"Jack?" She gazed at him intently. "Jack! Look at me now."

Rugg turned his head slowly her way, but his eyes appeared to be looking past her toward the living room window.

"This is Nick and CT. Do you remember them? Nick and CT?"

Rugg stared sightlessly around the room, as if he hadn't heard. When his gaze met hers, he blinked once. "Huh?"

"Nick and CT. They have come a long way just to visit you. That's nice, *si,* for them to visit you?"

Nick stole a glance at his friend. CT was shaking, his fists clenching and unclenching.

Rugg blinked again, slowly, like a lizard in the desert sun. "Uhhh . . . " Without warning, huge tears appeared in his eyes and started running down the lines in his face and off his chin, plopping solidly on his shirtfront.

And as those tears fell, Rugg came alive.

He began shuddering and screaming like a man who'd grabbed a live wire. *"DOOLEY!"* His shriek was deafening in the small room. *"DOOLEY'S BURNIN' ALIVE! MAKE IT STOP! STOP IT! OH GOD, SOMEBODY PUT HIM OUT! PUT HIM OUT! DEAR GOD. DEAR GOD DEAR GOgggggg . . . "*

Like someone had stolen his joints, Rugg collapsed. Curling up in a fetal ball, still screaming, with his hands now covering his head, he started pushing himself across the carpet with his feet. All the while his incredible wailing never stopped.

Rugg's wife put a wrinkled hand over her heart, her face stricken with grief. "Do you see him? Jack has not had a fit like this for weeks! Please end this torment—oh God!" She buried her face in both hands. "Heal him or kill him, dear God!"

The heartrending sights and sounds went on for several more seconds, then CT shot to his feet with a snarl. "Aw, enough a' this! *Enough!"* Roughly he pushed Mrs. Rugg and Nick aside before dropping on his knees beside Rugg's writhing form. "It's gonna be all right, colonel," he whispered. Then "Nick!"

CT's voice carried an edge of steel, and his dark eyes burned with a dangerous fire. At that moment he looked exactly like what he'd once been: an angry, street-brawling tough who'd terrorized an entire neighborhood. "Get down here NOW!"

Nick was instantly on his knees on the other side of Rugg. Drawn by a common purpose, the two men placed their hands on the old man at the same time and looked across him at each other.

Nick nodded once. "Do it."

If the neighbors had thought Rugg's voice was loud, CT's made him sound like a laryngitis patient as he prayed. And then a minute later, it was done. He'd said all he needed to.

The two again locked eyes over Rugg's body, CT's chest heaving as he drew deep, ragged breaths. They waited.

It was God's call now.

Over against the wall, Mrs. Rugg had her eyes screwed shut, praying the Our Father and crossing herself over and over, just as fast as her hand could move.

And then . . .

As if on cue, they all looked down. Rugg had stopped his mindless crawling. He grew still. The moment seemed to stretch, while three pairs of eyes fixed on him.

Slowly, very slowly, Rugg levered himself up on his hands and knees, shaking his head from side to side like a goat that had rammed one too many fences. Raising his torso until he sat upright, he dropped his arms to his sides and studied all three of them in turn, a frown deeply furrowing his already seamed face.

Mrs. Rugg held her breath, hand over her mouth, eyes enormous.

"Who?" Rugg said then, his voice a rasp. "Who are you?"

CT leaned close, his eyes searching the older man's. "It's me, Corporal Barnes, sir. And Corporal Castle. Don't you know us?"

Rugg frowned again, shaking his head. "Help me up."

They got him under the arms and liftied him into the nearest chair. Mrs. Rugg knelt by his side. She gazed up at her husband, tears zigzagging down her ravaged face.

CT peppered Nick with questions. "Now what? What happens next? How do—?"

"Hold on. I think I know." He gave Rugg a stern look. "Name, rank, and serial number, soldier!"

Rugg seemed to stiffen involuntarily in his chair. "John Taylor Rugg, Colonel, United States Army, 2655489!" He glared daggers at Nick. "And you'd better soften your tone with me, corporal, or you'll find yourself polishing every medal I've got. And brother, I've got a ton of 'em!"

The man's eyes grew wide in astonishment at his own words.

"Gloria a Dios!" Mrs. Rugg screamed, wrapping her arms around her husband's legs. She began kissing his hands, again and again.

Hollering their delight, Nick and CT grabbed each other, slapping each other's backs.

"Somebody wanna tell me what the Sam Hill is goin' on here," Rugg demanded, "and why everybody, me included, is so stinkin' old?"

Nick stopped his celebration long enough to wipe his streaming eyes, laughing. "Yeah, I can. I'm glad you're sitting down, colonel."

.. .. ..

Twenty minutes later, Rugg was still shaking his head. "Un-dirty-word-believable. Forty years of my life, gone, right down the toilet." He smiled, "Not that I'm regretting you boys coming to see me of course, but still . . . " Gripping his wife's hand like a newlywed, the colonel gently ran his thumb over her fingers. "To think I've been home all this time, with my wife by my side."

Lovingly he gazed down at her as though he saw her as she once was, and always would. He looked back up at the two men.

"You say Jesus Christ is the one who healed me." He cocked his head to the side and smiled again. "That sounds about right. Because believe it or not, I've seen this kind of stuff before. My dad was a Pentecostal preacher."

"What?" Nick couldn't have been more astounded if CT had suddenly jumped up and began quacking like a duck. "Sir, no offense, but—"

"But I was one of the crudest individuals you'd ever met, right?" Rugg waved the question away. "I understand your confusion. It's the classic prodigal son story, sad to say."

"Prodigal son?" CT asked.

Rugg nodded. "I wanted more out of life than the dusty tent revivals and hand-me-down clothes my dad's life offered. He was a real embarrassment to me, so I left home. In this case, though, I went into the Army instead of a pigpen."

He went on with a smile, " 'Course, the way you boys kept your hootches, there wasn't much difference." His smile faded. "My old man begged me not to go. He said the Lord had put a call on my life to preach. Maybe he did. Who knows? All I know for sure is I broke my dad's heart. When the promotions and the medals started coming, he seemed happy enough, but still, I knew . . . " Rugg looked down at his wife. "He died during my third tour in Nam. His heart. The doctors said it was diseased. I know better."

Stroking the old woman's wrinkled face, Rugg smiled wistfully. "Patrice was the one who called me. She said she didn't want some chaplain I didn't know breaking the news. Even then she knew I was running from God and hadn't darkened the door of a church in years." He turned to the others. "My healing isn't complete yet, is it." It wasn't a question.

Nick met his gaze head on. "No sir, it isn't."

Rugg pursed his lips, nodding. Again he looked down at his wife. "Patrice?"

She kissed his gnarled fingertips. "*Sí*, Jack, I have prayed with them. I am ready."

CT stood up and walked on unsteady legs to where Rugg sat and laid a callused hand on the older man's shoulder, his eyes filling. "Colonel, with the exceptions of Jesus Christ and Nick here, you're the finest man I've ever known. You were there when I got the news my daddy had been killed by that train. You came into the hootch and talked to me that day, talked to me like I wish my daddy would have done when I was growin' up."

CT wiped away a tear that threatened to overflow down his cheek and squeezed Rugg's shoulder. "I didn't find out till later that was the same day you found out your own daddy died. Colonel, you were there for me. Now we're here for you." He squeezed even tighter. "Runnin's over, sir. It's time to pray."

Rugg nodded. Truth was truth. With a deep sigh, he closed his eyes.

The four bowed their heads. Another soul, this time in the form of John Taylor Rugg, had laid down its sword and found its way home.

.. .. ..

NICK AND CT CLIMBED back into the Taurus. CT had a rough time of it, and it didn't help matters that Mrs. Rugg kept going back and forth between them, kissing them repeatedly on their cheeks, while the colonel just stood there beaming.

One of the last things Nick had told them was the news that Jesus was now due to rapture his people in less than ninety-nine hours. "Just made it under the wire!" the colonel joked.

CT finally wedged himself into the car. Nick waved goodbye to their old CO and his wife and watched as they slowly made their way back up onto their porch. He was just shutting the car door, when something prompted him to look over at the couple again.

His eyebrows shot up. "Hey, wait a minute!" he called out.

Rugg turned. "What?"

Nick leaped out, reached back in, and jabbed CT. "Come with me!"

"Huh? I just now got situated."

"Come on." Nick was already moving, yelling as he ran, "Colonel, wait! We aren't finished yet!" He trotted up onto the porch with CT close behind him.

"What do you mean?" Rugg asked as they got there. "I don't—"

Nick pointed. "Your wife's leg!"

"My leg?" The old woman unconsciously pulled it around behind herself. "It has been this way for many years. I fell down while I was trying to—" She looked at Rugg. "To move my husband." She held out placating hands. "It was my own fault. I was clumsy. It don't hurt that much no more."

Nick gently took her hand. "It's all right. Nobody's laying blame here. I just thought, since God healed Jack, why not ask him to heal your leg as well?"

She considered that for a moment, then smiled radiantly. "After what he has done for Jack, I will not question if he can do this thing! Let's pray!"

Nick and CT grinned and knelt. Placing their hands on the twisted limb, Nick looked up at Rugg. "Come on, colonel, you too. You have the right."

Rugg surreptitiously glanced from side to side. All around them curious neighbors had opened their doors and windows and were coming out on their porches to see what was going on.

He shrugged and threw back his head in a joyful laugh. "Hey folks, it's me, the nut! That's right, don't be shy, come on over here! You ain't seen nothin' yet! Watch this!" He joined Nick and CT in kneeling before his wife. "Okay, boys," he smiled. "Let's get it done."

All three men laid their right hands on Mrs. Rugg, with Nick's on her ankle, CT's on her knee, and Rugg's on her thigh. The colonel looked up at his wife, kneading her leg gently. "Gonna be all right, hon."

CT grinned. "Pray like your daddy taught you, colonel."

Rugg nodded and closed his eyes. "Father!" His voice boomed like a cannon across the yards. *Oh, Father!*

Quite a crowd was gathering around the porch now. In response, Rugg's voice grew more thunderous, just as his father's had been half a century earlier. There was a split-second of silence. And then . . . a muffled popping noise. The murmuring of the crowd grew louder.

Mrs. Rugg's small mouth went round in an O, and her dark eyes opened wide.

"Look!" she screamed. "*Look!* It don't hurt no more!" She pulled her dress above her knee. Her left leg was now as straight as the right. "*Gloria a Dios!* Look, everyone!" And she danced out into the yard like she was sixteen again.

Rugg clapped a rough hand over his eyes. "Oh my God!" he wept. "Oh, thank you!"

CT gently pulled Rugg's hand away. "Hey, preacher." The big man's smile was soft as he motioned to the crowd growing on the lawn. "There's your flock, brother. Go fulfill your call."

Chapter 41

(AP) Bulgaria. Instantaneous Healings Increase—Reports of instantaneous healings, especially among children, continue to mount, though not without opposition. Organized churches have launched a vigorous campaign to stop Bulgarians from declaring that Jesus had healed them of such maladies as cancer, diabetes, heart disease, and strokes.

There are also unconfirmed reports of missing body parts suddenly regenerating. In Lubrovnik, a small farming community in the country's hinterlands, a story has surfaced of a young boy having had his limbs instantly regrown.

According to family sources, the boy, aged five, had been run over by a threshing machine on his parents' farm. Consequently all four limbs had to be amputated. This morning he allegedly leaped from his hospital bed, healed and apparently whole, after his uncle, a devout Christian, laid his hands on him and prayed.

Both the State and the recognized church have strenuously denied further reports of healings being attributed to the prayers of the country's evangelical Christian population.

.. .. ..

(AP) Beijing, China. House Churches Report Angelic Guards—Government-coordinated raids yesterday against Christian house churches have resulted in zero arrests of dissidents, state officials report.

"It is insane." So says one of China's top military leaders, who refused to be identified. "I have documents on my desk from regional deputy commanders, all declaring their raids were thwarted by 'angelic beings' surrounding places where dissidents were gathered."

Further unconfirmed reports speak of these "beings" possessing unusual height and strength. Some go on to say that government soldiers were driven back by what appeared to be "flaming swords" allegedly wielded by these creatures.

Meanwhile the evangelical Christians gathered inside the buildings continued their services unmolested. It is also widely reported that many house churches are seeing their ranks swell by upwards of five thousand converts a day.

"These allegations are, of course, all rubbish and lies," says Chinese Minister of the Interior Deng Xiao Po. "We are, even as I speak, devising new stratagems to penetrate the pyschic energy fields these dissidents have erected. They defy us at their peril."

.. .. ..

(Reuters) Port Henry, Alaska. Inuits "Healed" of Fish Poisoning— "It's a miracle. Pastor Miller prayed for us and our whole village was healed."

These are the words of Daniel Nongoluk, chief of the Inuit population of this remote fishing village. Every year the Inuits conduct a village-wide feast of the first catch of the season. What they could not have forseen was this year's fish harvest had been contaminated with an as-yet-unidentified metallic poison.

"It was terrible," Mr. Nongoluk went on. "Within a half-hour everyone of our tribe, all two hundred and eighty of us, was violently sick. Most of us were running fevers, and many had gone blind."

Compounding the problem the tribe faced is the fact that the nearest hospital to their village is over four hours away by bush plane.

"We were doomed," Mr. Nongoluk continued. "Then Pastor Miller showed up to pray for us. He heads a mission here. In the past our people had resisted him and his family for their non-Inuit ways. In fact, many times we had tried to drive them away from us. Thankfully, we failed. Everyone Pastor Miller and his family prayed over was immediately healed. They are now telling us more of this God they serve."

CHAPTER 42

"NO, NO, *NO!*"

Sangre tore the newspaper into tiny pieces, and then threw them as hard as he could. They merely flew a few inches and rained down like snow. Screaming, he fell to his knees in the center of the pentagram painted on the floor of the old mill.

"This can't be! I refuse to accept these reports! What more can we do for you? What more could you possibly want?" He hung his head and wept. "What more do you want?"

This certainly wasn't going as he'd planned.

All he'd ever wanted was to fit in, to be important. He remembered the taunts. Ronnie Tompkins. That was his name, but Little Ronnie was what he'd always been called.

The name fit. He was the useless kid, the runty kid, the kid everybody in town laughed at, the kid nobody wanted. Not handsome, not smart, not big, not a jock, not *anything*.

His only friend in the world was stupid old Crandall Weems. Except for Crandall's size, they were exactly alike. Ronnie wanted someone to boss, and stupid old Crandall didn't mind.

Their symbiosis was perfect, save for a missing piece, an ongoing lack, a *gnawing*.

What both boys craved, like a drowning victim screaming for air, was the one thing neither would ever possess. Power. It eluded them the way beads of mercury dodged grasping hands.

Until the day they were both eight, and fooling around under that highway overpass.

.. .. ..

"RONNIE! RONNIE, WAIT UP!"

Crandall hefted his bulk up the steep concrete incline. High over their heads they could hear the whine of cars passing, along with the occasional thunderous rumble of a semi. Ronnie was already seated on the ledge, something weighty in his hands.

Puffing and sweating, Crandall finally made it up there. Wheezing, he plopped himself down next to his friend.

"Whatcha got?" He bent closer. "C'mon, I wanna see."

Ronnie curled his lip and scooted over a foot. "You stink, Crandall. B.O. Don't get sweat on my book."

"A book? Lemme see." Crandall leaned over Ronnie's shoulder, frowning. His sour body odor was pretty bad. "It don't got any pictures. What kind of a book is that, anyway?"

With a sigh Ronnie closed the book, marking his place with his thumb. He held the book up, cover out.

Crandall shook his head. "I can't read it. You know I can't. The words are too big. You're the only one that can read those big words, Ronnie."

It was true. Ronnie, while not smart in math and geography and history and such things, had a good grasp of English, even then.

"*The Satanic Bible* by Anton LaVey," he answered, in that precise way of speaking he had. "I just found it lying up here." He opened it and began to read again.

"What's it about?"

"I don't know yet. The devil, I think."

Crandall pulled back. "The devil?"

"Yes. Shut up a minute." Ronnie ran a grubby finger under a line of text while his lips moved silently. He nodded. "It's the devil all right."

Crandall pulled even farther back this time. "I don't like it. Put it back, Ronnie. What's it doing here, anyway?"

The other boy hunched his skinny shoulders and gave him a gap-toothed grin. "I don't know what it's doing here. Maybe there's a kind of Satan Appleseed who leaves books like this where kids like me can find them. All I know is I'm going to keep it." He shut the book and slipped it into his KISS backpack. "I'll read it later, after Hank and Eileen are gone."

Hank and Eileen Gitteridge were Ronnie's foster parents. Neither of them was all that fond of children, but the extra bucks the state paid didn't hurt. Plus the fact they'd taken in this skinny loser didn't hurt Hank's standing with his straight-arrow boss at the paper company either.

.. .. ..

RONNIE DID READ THE BOOK when he got home. Many times. He worked out the harder words with incessant logic, and the sex stuff in there was way cool. Whenever Hank and Eileen had asked him what he was doing up in his room for all those hours, he merely sneered and told them to buzz off.

They shrugged. As long as he didn't burn the house down, they couldn't have cared less. The years passed, and Ronnie's curiosity only seemed to grow.

He'd come to the conclusion a while back that this LaVey guy had some good ideas, all right, but never had the will to carry them far enough. Ronnie and Crandall began conducting some half-baked made-up animal sacrifices with cats, but that still didn't fill that empiness deep inside.

As he grew older, Ronnie started seeking out carnival fortunetellers and psychics, trying to blend what they knew, or said they knew, and what he'd learned into an amalgamation of something else.

The blood oaths he and Crandall continually took only showed, to Ronnie's mind, just how serious they were. For their ceremonies they used a fisherman's fillet knife he'd stolen out of Hank's tacklebox, but only after he'd burned the blade over a candle.

It was plenty sharp.

By the time it finally began to dawn on Hank and Eileen just how warped Ronnie really was, it was too late. The boy was nearly eighteen and far beyond their grasp. The day he left the Gitteridge home for the last time, Ronnie decapitated their parakeet in gratitude to the Dark One for having seen him safely to this point in his life.

From then on, Ronnie's obsession with death and darkness grew exponentially greater. The one and only time he'd met some genuine satanists was at an occult convention in New York, but they'd seemed hopelessly wimpy and esoteric. Ronnie was sure the Dark One was pleased with the way he'd scorned them. His satanism was the real deal.

And the name he'd given himself: Sangre. Why, he was sure it had come into his mind from the Dark One himself! It sounded a little bit like Santeria, that religious/voodoo thing down in the Caribbean, only better. Ronnie—Sangre—knew those guys liked blood, but not as much as he did.

Courage and blood, that was his motto.

His best idea yet had been the Circle. It had come to him three years ago: Find others like himself who'd rejected traditional satanism for something with some power. Something that would get the job done and propel them all into the positions of power and prestige they so clearly deserved. They weren't that hard to find, but Sangre always made sure he prayed to the Dark One before they were admitted. No sense asking for trouble.

Which made what had happened to Belladonna so maddening.

Belladonna. Even now her name made Sangre ache with remembrance.

She'd come into the Circle on the recommendation of Charon, one of the women he had personally recruited. The first time he saw her, he was smitten. *Smitten,* a fine word, one that described it perfectly.

Belladonna was twenty years old, the daughter of satanists. She'd been expressly conceived to be given to the devil as a sacrificial baby, but her parents were killed in a fire before that could be accomplished. Thus she had no birth certificate, no Social Security card, nothing. She, like Sangre, was an orphan. No, more: a nonentity.

Maybe that was one reason why he felt a kinship with her. She'd been raised by two old sisters, and it was they who had given the girl her name. The sisters felt that since Satan had spared her life from the fire, he must have had a special purpose in mind for her.

Belladonna and Sangre had become friends at first, then best friends, and finally lovers. He had such plans for her, and for himself. They were going to rule with the Dark One forever. Perhaps even start a dynasty under him. Until . . .

.. .. ..

"RONNIE, LET THEM TALK TO YOU. Please? Just this once? You—"

He spun around and grabbed her. "It's Sangre, *Sangre!* Can't you remember that? Have those Christers got you so confused you can't even remember my *name?*"

"But that's not your name!" Belladonna took a breath and tried again. "Ronnie, let them help you, like they helped me. Yesterday when they came around to the house—"

"*My* house!" he angrily broke in. "You let them in *my* house, after we'd agreed never to talk to anyone like them!"

"But all they wanted was to ask if we needed prayer. I was feeling so awful with the morning sickness. Those herbs you gave me hadn't helped at all." Belladonna's eyes began to tear up, and she wiped her nose with her sleeve. "The ladies said they were from God's Community Church, and they were praying for people in the neighborhood. They asked if we needed prayer, and when I told them I was going to have a baby, I just thought—"

"You just thought you'd invite Christers into my house! After I'd expressly forbidden that! I've told you what they do!"

"And they did what, pray for me?" Her laugh was bitter. "Well, it worked and the pain left! What's he ever done for us like that?"

That was a mistake.

Sangre smacked her hard in the mouth. "Don't blaspheme, Belladonna! Not that on top of everything else!"

She whimpered, putting a hand to her bleeding lip. "Ronnie, please, let them pray for you too. It's not too late, I swear."

.. .. ..

BUT IT WAS TOO LATE, and by a goodly margin. Sangre had beaten her savagely then, worse than he ever had, and then raped her. When he was done he'd hung his spent body over hers and told her he hoped the lesson was well learned.

But no. Those stupid Christers had come back again, the very next day, while he was at work at the bookstore.

Belladonna was ripe for the harvest. Her fears of childbirth had peaked, and, quite frankly, she'd grown tired of being of the object of Ronnie's ongoing frustration.

The women from the church patiently explained that a new life was hers for the asking and told her that GCC had a fine unwed mothers' home. Did she want out from her old life, they asked, to discover what her real purpose was?

With huge, racking sobs, she broke down. She told them she wanted that more than anything. She'd felt her life was one long mistake from her conception forward and could only end badly.

They prayed, and when she was done, Belladonna was a new creation.

Her only mistake had been going to see Ronnie at the old mill, after he'd gotten off work. It seemed he was spending more and more time there, and she wanted to share her newfound joy with him.

Quietly she approached him as he was praying in the center of the pentagram. "Hello, Ronnie."

Sangre's head jerked up. He narrowed his eyes at her. "What have you done?" He jumped to his feet, hate flooding his face. "What. Have. You. *Done?*"

Stalking the three paces over, he roughly grabbed her by the shoulders. "Tell me!" he screamed, shaking her. "You can't keep any secrets from me, Belladonna! You know that! You're a Christer now, aren't you! You're a Christer! Admit it!"

Belladonna was thunderstruck. She had no idea how Ronnie had known, but somehow he'd picked up on the change. At any rate, there was no use denying it.

Her smile made the darkness and stench in the old mill that much more noticable. "Yeah, Ronnie, I asked Jesus into my life. I think you should too." Smiling wider, she reached for him, holding something in her hand. "I want you to read this Bible the lady gave me. You can't imagine—"

Horrified, Sangre slapped it away. "Don't touch me!" he spat. "Filth! So he's 'forgiven' you, has he? Oh, I know the stories! I understand my enemies—you know that!"

His voice took on a mocking, singsong quality. "All the terrible things you've ever done, he's taken away, so on and so on. And now you're all shiny, bright, and new, and you can't wait to tell simply everyone, right? Isn't that right, Belladonna! And make *me* look like an absolute fool in front of the others!"

He began to stomp around, his eyes wild. "What are they going to think of me now? I'll tell you what! They'll say I'm weak! They'll say I couldn't even keep my own mate from joining the ranks of the enemy!"

Sangre's hands whipped around like fan blades. "Have you considered that, Belladonna? What about the plans we had to serve the Dark Prince together? They're all poof, gone!" He lowered his face to hers, spittle flying. "Am I right? *Am I?*"

She simply nodded.

His hands now were claws, eyes murderous, face scorched with rage. "I ought to kill you." He nodded. "I think I will."

The woman stood before him, utterly at peace. She couldn't believe how calm she was. Normally when Ronnie went into one of his periodic rages, she was so afraid for her life she could sometimes taste the fear on her tongue, metallic and harsh. But now . . . now all she felt was pity.

"Do what you need to do," she whispered. "My life belongs to God."

Sangre lost it then. "*Get out!*" Violently he shoved her toward the door of the old mill, repeatedly booting her in the rear as she went. "If you love those Christers so much, get out! Let them take care of you and that unborn monster in your belly! I don't want it or you or anything to do with that church of whatever or any of it!"

Belladonna fell hard, and then clambered to her feet and started running into the night. Sangre bent down to pick up the Bible he'd knocked out of her hands, the one *they'd* given her, the one *she'd* tried to give *him*. He was going to throw it after her, but now found he couldn't even bring himself to touch the dirty thing.

So he kicked it.

It tumbled away, spine breaking and pages flying.

"This isn't over yet!" he shrieked after Belladonna's retreating form. "After that thing in your guts breathes air, you'll see! It's not over! *You hear me, girl? Not over!*"

.. .. ..

SANGRE CURLED UP in the center of the pentagram, staring and weeping and mumbling and whispering hoarsely. "It's not over yet. They're dead, all of them. Her, the baby, and that whole lying church. Sunday night they die. It's not over yet, not by a long shot. Steal from me, will you . . . "

CHAPTER 43

NICK AND CT'S FLIGHT left St. Louis right on time at 5:25 p.m. They were scheduled to arrive in Newark at 7:15. At CT's pleading, Nick had once again sprung for first-class tickets.

"After crammin' me in that Taurus it's the least you can do," the big man had pointed out. "That whole trip I felt like seven pounds of oats stuffed in a five-pound bag."

Nick had asked for, and gotten, bulkhead seats for them both. He opened his notebook, again examining his notes on Dooley—Ryan, that is.

He shook his head. It was no use. Dooley he'd been called, and Dooley he'd remain.

They'd phoned Manny before leaving Nick's office, and the sergeant had confirmed that yes, Dooley had returned to his Kentucky hometown after a year's stay at the Walter Reed burn unit. His parents, Clyde and Ida Ryan, had come and fetched him home to finish whatever recuperation was left.

Manny's last records showed Dooley living with them on a farm outside the town on Perryville Road. Nick reflected on that; it was odd that he was still living with his parents forty years later. Again, beyond that basic information, their friend's condition was a blank.

Nick was puzzling on this when noises began to filter past his conciousness, sounds of a happy muttering. He put down his notebook, listening for a moment.

"Hey, CT. Hear that?"

The big man pulled off his headphones. "Huh?"

"I said, do you hear that?"

CT cocked his head. At first it just sounded like the usual airplane chatter mixed with the rush of the engines, but after a moment he could pick out individual conversations.

All over the plane, people were talking about God, asking questions, giving answers, praying. Lives were forever changed.

The two grinned at each other. Right then a fellow passenger across the aisle noticed them, mistaking their smiles for condescension.

"I'm with you guys," the man sneered. "Those religious fanatics are stupid."

"Think so, huh?" Nick said.

"Yep." The man was small and wiry, impeccably dressed. "It's just a sales presentation, that's all. I should know. I'm in sales, bathroom fixtures." He handed them each a card. "Name's Irv Guelpe. The 'e' on the end is silent. You've probably heard of me. I'm pretty famous. In the Midwest I'm considered the biggest thing you'll find in toilets."

"Really." Nick rubbed his hand over his mouth to hide his grin. "That's impressive."

"You said it. Lotta people think, hey, I push the handle and that's it, good-bye waste." Guelpe shook his head. "Nope, that's when things get the most interesting."

"Son of a gun."

"Yessir! It's ecology!" The man cocked a thumb back over his shoulder. "And you know something else? Those nuts are pushing the same line of junk my toilets are built to take care of."

"So you think all this Jesus talk is a bunch of hooey?" Nick asked.

"Yessir. I do. Tell ya why, too. I've studied psychology. For years and years." Guelpe puffed out his narrow chest. "All this stuff is just a reaction."

"A reaction to what, Mr. Guelpe?"

The salesman spread his hands. "To the world! To the way things are falling apart! People need answers, so they've latched on to this fairy tale." He narrowed his eyes knowingly. "I understand all about how sales strategies work. The key is making sure your prospect is, well, I hate to use the word *trapped,* but you know what I mean. Get 'em in a place where they have to listen."

He leaned forward. "All these people on the plane, going on and on about this Jesus stuff, are using techniques I've used myself. And face it, their prospects are trapped. Where are they gonna go to get away from hearing about it—take a step outside for some air?" He laughed, "They'd get air, all right. About thirty thousand feet of it." Guelpe leaned back, grinning wickedly. "They're trapped, sure as shooting!"

"That's true, Mr. Guelpe," Nick said. "You are."

"Huh?" The grin faded from the man's face, to be replaced by a sick look. "Oh no—"

"Oh, yeah." CT leaned past Nick to wave toodle-oo. He wore a huge grin of his own, like a possum eating a sweet potato, as he turned to Nick. "Mr. Castle, would you like to do the honors of tellin' this gentleman about Jesus, or would you rather leave it to me?"

"Golly, Mr. Barnes," Nick grinned in reply. "I'm all tuckered out. Why don't you do it?"

"With pleasure." CT climbed over Nick and stood beside Guelpe.

The big man had to duck his head beneath the luggage compartment as he pulled a Four Spiritual Laws booklet out of his hip pocket. The salesman looked like a deer caught in the headlights.

"Say, Mr. Guelpe," CT said. "Got some great news. Did you know God loves you and has a wonderful plan for your life?"

CHAPTER 44

BY THE TIME THE PLANE LANDED, Guelpe had turned from a sneering disbeliever into an honest seeker. He promised he'd think on what he'd been told.

"Don't think too long," CT admonished. "This offer'll expire without notice."

Standing at the luggage carrousel, they watched the salesman walk away, shaking his head. But he was still reading the ugly little yellow booklet he'd been given.

"I should've gone into sales," CT said. "I bet I would have been good at it."

"That's kind of what we're doing now," Nick said. "Only ours is the best product ever. If Jesus doesn't satisfy, you get your old life back."

"Not mine, baby. I'm a customer forever."

Their garment bags finally came up, and they headed on over to the crowded car rental counters. "Let's hope Betty isn't two for two," Nick muttered as they walked up to the rental agent.

The young man behind the counter looked up. "Yes sir?"

"Do you have a car reserved for Castle?" Nick's tone was hopeful.

"Let's see, Castle . . . Yes sir, we have a Lincoln being held for you, called in by a Betty Zane from Impetus Travel." The agent held out a hand. "I'll need your license and a major credit card."

CT looked relieved.

After filling out the forms required and paying with a Castle corporate card, the two men went out to the lot and located their car. The gathering dusk made the air seem even cooler, more like early November than mid September.

CT climbed into the passenger side without even being asked. He was beginning to get his role as navigator down pat. Popping open the glove compartment, he found a city map of Newark.

"The address is 129 Boyle Street," Nick reminded him.

"Wait a minute, I'm lookin' . . . Found it. Looks like it's dead center of town." The big man stretched. "So which do we want to do first—find Frankie or get a hotel?"

"Let's find Frankie. It'd be good to get this wrapped up tonight so we won't have to sleep here. Maybe we can catch a redeye home."

"Sounds okay to me. Turn right out of this parkin' lot."

For the next twenty minutes CT read off the directions as they made their way deeper into increasingly seedy areas of the town. After a few false turns, finally they were on Boyle. Slowly they crawled down the nearly deserted street. Boyle was composed mainly of crumbling old brownstones, boarded-up storefronts, and scraggly, weed-infested lots. For being only a little after eight on a September evening, it was eerily vacant. Few lights glowed in the apartments above.

CT stared. "This street's best years are definitely behind it. Kinda reminds me of where Mr. Ames lived."

"Yeah," Nick agreed. "As Yogi Berra put it, it's *déjà vu* all over again. Okay, even numbers are on my side, odd are on yours. Do you see 129 yet?"

"Gettin' close. 123 . . . 25 . . . 27 . . . 129. Wait." CT pointed. "Take a look at that."

One hundred twenty-nine Boyle wasn't a house or an apartment at all. It was a crummy-looking, darkened old garage.

Pulling up in front of the place, they parked and got out of the car. Both men looked up and down the street.

"You think Manny got it wrong?" CT asked with a frown.

"Maybe. Let's see if we can get a better look."

When the two reached the garage, they could just barely make out a name scrawled inexpertly in peeling black paint above the entrance.

Nick walked on up to the crusty old door. The sign read, *Malone's Repair*.

He and CT looked at each other, then Nick rattled the knob, peering through the gloom and dusty glass into the office beyond. With no interior lights on, it was hopeless. Letting go, he looked down to find his hand covered in brown flakes of rust.

CT shook his head. "Classy place Frankie has here."

They walked around the building, doing their best to avoid the rusting car parts and broken glass that littered the alley between the garage and the old dry cleaner's next door. Huge spots of what appeared to be ancient dried oil on the ground made the shadows seem even darker.

As they made their way to the back they saw that the building was deeper than it had appeared from the street. At last they found the apartment stuck like a scummy afterthought onto the garage's rear. Standing ankle deep in ragged weeds and filthy litter, the men peered again through smudged glass into the darkened room beyond. All they could make out in this rotten light was that obviously no one was home. The wind picked up as they crunched their way back around to the front.

CT looked glum. "Now what?"

"I guess we come back tomorrow." Nick rotated his neck. "I'm done. Let's find a place to crash. Preferably clean and without bedbugs."

Approaching the car, they both suddenly stopped. "Hey, listen." CT cocked his head and smiled. "I hear singin'. Gospel singin'!"

"Me too." Nick pointed down the street. "I think it's coming from there."

Further down the block, on the opposite side of the street, light and sound spilled from a storefront. Somebody was having church.

"Whattya think?" CT asked. "Want to go on and find a room, or would you like to check that out?"

"Personally I could do with a spiritual recharge. Let's go."

Crossing the street and drawing closer, they saw the name of the church painted in white letters across the front glass: *First Freewill Sanctified Church of the Blessed and Holy Remnant, Reverend F. Dwight Jasper, Founder and Pastor.*

Smiling, they walked in. They found themselves transported from a world of darkness, gloom, and despair into another place altogether, a place of light and sound and joy. And heat.

The place was stifling. The tiny church had been built to handle no more than forty or so, but tonight it was packed with nearly fifty shouting, singing, happy, glorious black faces. To Nick it felt as if the room temperature was double the crowd volume.

CT's mug lit up in pure delight, and he began clapping. Nick, on the other hand, felt a bit strange. His was the only white face in a sea of black ones. He didn't feel uncomfortable, exactly, more like out of place. Maybe he should—

He started as a tiny, ancient black lady tapped him on the arm. "Mister, does you know the Lord Jesus?"

He smiled down at her. "You bet I do, ma'am."

She grinned, showing a huge expanse of shiny, store-bought teeth. "Well, you one of us, then!" The lady began bobbing her head in time with the music, humming tunelessly. "You know dis hymn, *Power in the Blood*?"

"Yes, ma'am."

The old woman smacked Nick good-naturedly on the back. "Then go stand by your frien' and sing it like you know how to!"

Nick did as he was told. Sweat poured down both of them in rivulets.

"This place is exactly what both of us needed tonight," Nick grinned.

"You said it, bro!" CT clapped his hands in time with the singing, each clap resounding from his huge mitts like a rifle shot. "It ain't home, but it'll do!"

After a few more hymns, it was testimony time. One after the other people went forward to tell of incredible struggles with alcoholism, crushing poverty, or drugs. They also testified of the saving and delivering power of God.

Each tale was punctuated with cries of "Yes!" "Tell it like it is, now!" and "Glory to God!" The energy was electrifying.

Nearly twenty-five minutes later an older man finally bounded up onto the tiny platform. He was striking looking, in his late sixties, ebony black and snowy haired. The man's nearly six-foot frame was well draped in a dark shiny suit, and his mouth was graced with a gold incisor that winked when he smiled.

After introducing himself as Reverend Jasper and making a few preliminary remarks, he asked if there were any first-timers in the crowd with them tonight. Nick and CT raised their hands.

"Hello!" The pastor smiled. "May I have your names, please?"

"Hello back at you, sir," CT answered. "My name's CT Barnes, and this is my friend Nick Castle. We're from Cincinnati."

"Thanks for coming tonight. And are you and Mr. Castle here on business?"

"Aw, call us CT and Nick, Reverend," CT replied. "Yeah, we are, kinda. We're here to look up an old friend of ours from the Army to make sure he hears about Jesus before he comes for us." He looked around the room. "Maybe somebody here can help us. The guy's name is Frankie Malone. He owns that garage just down the street."

A muttering broke out, and finally the piano player shook her head in derision. "My, my! You friends with that nasty man?"

"Yeah, we are," CT allowed. "He really needs the Lord."

"You got that right." It was a voice from over against the wall, a glowering young man. "That dude hates anybody that ain't white."

There were further mutters of agreement, and the pastor held up his hands for quiet. "CT, these people are right. Mr. Malone is the last white man living on this whole block. He says he would have moved long ago, but the fact that he's crippled keeps him from it. And he won't take help from any man, Lord knows. Especially not from any of us." Heads nodded.

"So he still lives behind his garage, then?" Nick asked.

"Yes, he does, but sometimes he goes away for a time." The reverend scowled. "To drink. I've seen Mr. Malone wheeling himself down the street in his chair many a night. He goes away, then you may not see him for two or three days. He always comes back reeking of whiskey. I don't think the man has had any business at that garage of his for, Lord, I don't know when."

Nick looked at CT. "Living on his disabilty, I guess."

The big man shook his head. "Not much of a livin'. Vet disability stinks. It's a cryin' shame how little our bros get."

"You might try him tomorrow morning," Reverend Jasper suggested. "Perhaps he'll be back by then." He looked out at his flock. "Will you all help us keep an eye out for these gentlemen, to help them find their friend, Mr. Malone?"

There were assents from the crowd, and Jasper smiled. "Thank you! Now, I'd like to tell you all about my friend Jesus."

"Amen!"

"Say it, pastor!"

"Preach it well, now!"

CHAPTER 45

AFTER REVEREND JASPER HAD FINISHED his message, there were a few more songs and then an altar call. Six young men went up with their mothers to pray, and the whole church joined in.

When that was done the pastor jumped back up onto the platform again, his smile dazzling. "Praise Jesus! More souls were added to the kingdom tonight!"

"Yes!"

"That's right, that's right!"

Jasper held up his hands. "That's about it for our service, but before we're dismissed there's one more order of business we need to address. Sister Lutrille, would you come up here please?"

"Yes, pastor."

An ordinary-looking, mocha-hued woman in her forties with her hair done up in cornrows made her way up onto the platform and stood beside the pastor.

Smiling, he placed a fatherly hand on her shoulder. "Well, we all know Sister Lutrille, and what a miracle she is. How the Lord Jesus delivered her from a life of drugs and sin on this very platform not six months ago . . ."

"Yes!"

"Mm-hmmm."

"Glory to you, Lord!"

His smile faded. "It's been told to me that Sister Lutrille has a need. She'd like to go see her brother in Detroit to tell him of Jesus, but she has no money for the bus." The pastor turned to her. "It costs how much and leaves when, sister?"

The woman looked down at the floor, obviously embarrassed as she mumbled in a low voice, "I don't deserve no help, pastor, after the life I done lived."

The crowd gasped. "No!" "Say what?" "No, no, now don't you listen to that old devil!"

Reverend Jasper held up a hand for quiet, and then he smiled at her. "They're right, sister. That old person you once were died all those months ago, never to be seen again. You are our sister now. Won't you let us help you?"

After a second, she nodded. "I ain't seen Anthony since we was little kids, but the Lord ain't leaved me alone 'bout him." She swallowed and gazed back down at the floor. "The buses leave here tonight in a hour, nonstop to Detroit. It cost fifty-nine dollars, and I ain't got it."

Placing both hands on the woman's shoulders, the pastor looked out at the congregation, his voice quiet. "How many of you will help?" Without another word came sounds of purses being opened and pockets dug into.

Nick leaned over to CT. "How much money do you have on you?"

"Eight bucks and some change," the big man whispered back. "I don't carry much cash, you oughtta know that."

"Neither do I, unfortunately." Nick checked the contents of his pockets. "Twelve dollars and thirty-nine cents. Pretty shabby."

CT tightened his lips in resolve. "Let's give it all, bro. God knows that lady needs it more than us."

The old brass plate came their way, and they did just that. After everyone in the church had had a chance to give, the plate was placed on the platform at the woman's feet.

Reverend Jasper bent down, put in the money he had in his hand, then straightened and turned to an elderly man. "Count that out, Deacon Marsh, and let's see what we've got."

Marsh upended the plate and began to count, putting the bills into piles by denomination. After a few moments he grinned up at the pastor. Marsh didn't have a tooth in his head.

"Praise the Lord, Reverend Jasper! Eighty-one dollars and forty-three cent!"

The place went bats.

"Glory to you, Lord!"

"Thank you, Jesus!"

"Yes, yes!"

The grinning deacon poured all the money into a paper sack and handed it to the pastor. He turned to give it to Sister Lutrille, but she shook her head, stepping back away from it. "I don't need but fifty-nine dollars, pastor." She held up placating hands. "I didn't ask for more than that."

"Get yourself some Co'Colas and sandwiches, sister, to eat on the way," Jasper smiled. "God is a good God, and he is more than enough!"

Weeping then, but also smiling for the first time, the woman took the bag and made her way through the cheering crowd to the front door. When she got there, she turned to them. "Y'all be prayin' for me, and God bless! And I thank ya, for Anthony's sake!" With that, she was gone.

When the tumult had died down, the pastor smiled. "Well, well, mercy, I would say we have had a time for ourselves in Jesus to*night!*"

"Yes!"

"Mmm-hmmmmm!"

"Glory, glory!"

He looked out at the two new arrivals. "Nick, would you please close us in prayer tonight, my brother?"

"Sir, I'd be honored."

"Well, come on up here, then!"

Nick made his way to the platform, receiving pats on the back from those he passed. Standing in front of the congregation, he closed his eyes.

"Father, thank you for this evening, and for all my brothers and sisters here tonight. They've sure made a couple of lonely travelers feel right at home. But that's to be expected. In you there's no male or female, rich or poor, black or white. In you there's love, joy, peace, and acceptance. Now I ask for traveling mercies for each of us. Come quickly, Lord. And we know you are. In your name we pray, amen."

Chapter 46

IT WAS WELL AFTER MIDNIGHT when Nick and CT said goodbye to their new friends and trudged back to their car. The temperature by now had dropped even further. Like a whirling dervish, the gusting wind swirled dried leaves and debris around their feet as they walked.

"Man!" Nick shuddered, pulling his thin jacket closer around himself. "After the heat in that church, it feels like it's freezing out here."

"You know it." CT climbed into the car, his teeth chattering. "Kinda stupid we didn't bring warmer clothes, huh?"

"Yeah, well think about it." Nick started the Lincoln and turned the climate control to max heat. "This whole operation was kind of thrown together. We only got the message about the rapture Tuesday night."

"Man, you're right." CT shook his head, amazed. "Been some week, hasn't it?"

"Yep, and we're not done yet. Let's head on back out to the airport and get a couple of rooms at the Skyway Inn. I'd like to be back out here tomorrow morning around seven."

"Seven?" CT sounded appalled. "It's after midnight now!"

Nick put the car in gear and headed toward the freeway. "Don't hand me that. You can't sleep in past six any more than I can."

"Don't bet on it. I could sure use about twelve solid hours of beauty sleep."

Nick grinned. "Too late, Godzilla."

.. .. ..

WHEN THEY GOT TO THE MOTEL at the airport, they found, to their not very great surprise, that the place was nearly full.

"We just have one room left, guys," the teenaged night clerk said, "and it's only got a queen-size bed." He leered, "I guess if you guys want it you'll have ta cuddle up, huh?"

CT squeezed in front of Nick and towered over the boy, his voice rumbling with menace. "Don't crack wise with us, sonny. We could always take your room."

The kid gulped and smiled weakly. "Just having some fun, gents. That's all. Late night, y'know?"

"And it's gettin' later." CT snapped his fingers. "Form."

Wordlessly the clerk handed him the registration card.

"Pen."

The boy slid that to him as well. CT filled out the card, then turned to Nick. Smiling sweetly, he batted his eyelashes.

"Pay for the room, honeybun, while I get our luggage."

Grinning, Nick complied. The kid didn't a word while he processed their registration.

As they walked down the long hallway to their room, CT suddenly stopped. With a huge sigh he turned and trudged back to the desk.

The kid gulped hard once more, eyes huge, expecting the worst. "Y-yes?"

CT smiled at the boy. "Sorry, kid. I was outta line." He handed him a tract. "Read that."

He grinned sheepishly at Nick as he came back down the hall. "The Lord wasn't gonna let me get away with that."

"I kind of thought he wouldn't." Nick slid the keycard into the slot in their door, and they went into the room.

.. .. ..

THE NEXT MORNING both men were awake by 5:30. CT gave Nick a bleary look.

"Well, sport, did ya win?"

"Hah?" Nick smacked his lips and slowly ran his fingers through his hair. "Win what? What are you talking about?"

"Your bike race, bro." CT stood and stretched, his joints creaking in protest. "You rode the bike all night long, and your knees kept poundin' my back. I hope I don't have kidney damage."

"If I did—and I'm admitting nothing, by the way—it's only because I was trying to get as far away from your snoring as humanly possible. Lord, I thought you sawed the logs in Nam, and here I find it's only gotten worse. Poor Sarah." He got to his feet. "Dibs on the bathroom."

.. .. ..

LATER, AT THE COFFEE SHOP NEXT DOOR, while waiting for their waitress to put their breakfast order in, Nick glanced outside. The weather had turned colder overnight, and the day was drearily gray and blustery.

"Excuse me, sir," he said to the man at the next table. "Have you heard what it's supposed to get to today?"

The man folded his newspaper with a grimace. "Yep. Only gonna get up to maybe forty-five. It's forty out there right now, according to the radio." He slurped the last of his coffee. "I'm catching a flight back to Dallas, where it's ni-i-ice and warm." He held the paper out. "I'm done with this. You guys want it?"

Smiling, Nick took it. "Thanks." He turned back to the front page, glanced at the headline, then held it up so CT could see. "Take a look at this. The president is supposed to give a speech tonight."

"Huh. Lemme see." CT took the paper and continued reading. "Says here he's not releasin' any details yet, but says the speech will be a, quote, watershed event for this administration, unquote." He looked up. "That could mean anything."

Nick grimaced. "Maybe Pastor Wasson'll patch it in for the service, and we'll all be pleasantly surprised."

CT folded the paper and set it on the chair next to him. "You don't care much for President Harcourt, do you?"

Nick took a sip of coffee before answering. "That's a good question. I just have to wonder if the stories about his conversion are real, that's all. You and I have both seen too many instances when a supposed man of God did wrong in public and thought it was no big deal. Their walk didn't match their talk." He shrugged. "Who knows? Maybe I'll hear something that'll nail it down for me."

When their food finally came, they didn't dawdle over eating a huge breakfast of steak, hashbrowns, and eggs. While Nick paid the check, CT said, "Before we head over to see if Frankie's at home, how's about we give our women a call?"

"Good idea. I was just about to suggest the same thing. There are a couple of pay phones over by the door."

They drew up short when they reached the phones. The things were ancient, with old rotary dials.

CT appeared flummoxed. "Man. No way we can use our cards on these babies. And we gave all our money away last night."

"I'll just dial 0 and let the operator take my card number verbally."

"My man! Hope the gals are up."

"There are six people living in that house," Nick pointed out, "including two hyperactive twins. They'll be up, all right."

CT's expression was pained. "Toby and Tina aren't hyperactive. They're just . . . lively."

When the call went through, Nick heard the answering machine kick in. It went through its spiel, and then beeped.

"Hello?" he said. "Anybody there? It's us."

Sarah picked up. "Nick?"

"Hey, Sarah. Yeah, it's me. Here, talk to CT. He's standing right here." Nick handed the phone over.

"Sweet thang!" Sarah yelled. "How's it goin'?"

CT grinned. "Good, you?"

"Great! Maryann told me Nick called her from the airport. He said y'all had some good news about Mad Jack and his wife."

"Yeah, that was really somethin'! God did it again!"

"So, big fella . . . " Sarah pretended to scold, "how come you didn't call me from the airport? Wait, don't tell me, let me guess. You were seeing a man about a horse, right?"

"What are you complainin' about, girl? I'm callin' you now!"

"That you are, you rowdy monster!" They both laughed, then in a more serious tone she went on, "You guys are coming back tonight, right?"

"Dunno yet. So far we haven't caught up with Frankie. After that we gotta fly from here to Lexington and snag a car to Danville. Odds are we won't be back till tomorrow afternoon late. We'll call you later today when things are more settled."

"Oh." Sarah tried unsuccessfully to hide the disappointment in her voice. "Well, here's Maryann. I love you, CT."

"I love you too." He handed the phone to Nick, then went outside to wait by the Lincoln.

CHAPTER 47

NICK AND CT SAT IN THEIR CAR, engine running, trying to get a better view of Frankie's garage than they'd gotten last night. His business didn't look any more prosperous in the cold, gray light of morning. Truth be told, it looked a hundred times worse. The place still had the appearance of a building long since deserted. As Reverend Jasper had pointed out, Frankie hadn't had any trade in quite a while.

"What are we gonna do if he's not home this time?" CT asked.

Nick shrugged. "Much as I'd hate to, we'd have to leave here and head on down to Danville. I don't know what else we could do." He opened his door. "Come on, let's check it out one last time."

They clomped around to the back of the building, negotiating the rutted ground more easily this time, at last stopping at that same cruddy entrance.

Frankie's apartment door, if that's what in fact it was, was in far worse shape than the shop door in front. The thing was warped and streaked, with rust stains running from the doorknob to the ground. Nick balled up his fist and knocked. They waited.

Nothing.

He knocked again, harder this time.

Still nothing.

"Well." Nick was stumped. "Guess that's that."

Stepping in front of him, CT said, "Lemme try." Then with the side of his fist he began pounding on the door as hard and as fast as he could, screaming at the top of his voice. "*FRANKIE MALO-O-O-O-N-N-E!*" Dogs began to bark and howl.

Nick was aghast. "Good grief! You want Newark's finest coming to haul us away?"

"In this neighborhood? Not likely."

CT was filling his lungs for another yell when they heard the door rattle. A muttered cursing came from behind it, and then it rattled again.

"Kick it!" came a muffled voice from inside.

CT obliged, nailing the door with one of his "rowboats" so hard it nearly tore the thing off its hinges. The door swung violently inward, hitting the wall behind it. It began to ricochet closed, and Nick stopped it with his hand. They stood there then, trying to peer into the gloom beyond. Just inside they could see a dim figure seated in a wheelchairr.

"Who are ya?" the chair's occupant slurred. "Whattya want?"

"Frankie?" They stepped inside and gazed around in amazement. Brother. This room was a worse wreck than Trevor Ames's.

Empty pizza boxes and crushed beer cans littered the floor, and the tiny sink at the back overflowed with dishes heavily crusted with unimaginable muck. The whole place reeked of cigarettes, rotgut whiskey, and general filth. It appeared that this one small room was it, with possibly a bathroom beyond that far door. What it looked like didn't bear thinking about.

CT walked over and flipped a switch on the wall. A lone, bare bulb in the ceiling popped into life, throwing the room into a stark relief of light and shadow.

Before them sat Frankie Malone.

At least, they assumed it was him. The slight build was the same, and the fact that he was in a wheelchair seemed to confirm their guess. But the intervening forty years had been less than kind, to put it charitably.

Frankie was balding, the wispy hair around the fringe of his skull hanging gray and limp, and his lined face made him appear years older than he really was. To Nick, the man's legs looked so thin it seemed he could have inserted them into paper towel tubes and still had room to spare.

Dirty and unshaven, Frankie blearily blinked up at them. "I said, who are ya? You with Newark Power and Light?" He belched, blowing out sour breath. "Cut me off, I don't give a—" He finished his sentence with mumbled curses.

Nick squatted down, searching the man's eyes. "Frankie, it's me, Nick Castle. And CT Barnes." He stood up and went back over to the door, so the light hit them better.

Frankie squinted up, shaking his head. Then recognition dawned, and he sneered. "Well, I'll be. So it is. Whattya know? A blast from the past. This calls for a drink."

Wheeling the wheelchair backward, he thudded into an ancient cabinet behind him. Opening the cabinet door with shaky hands, he pulled out a bottle of some nameless liquor. He unscrewed the cap, then upended the thing into his mouth, taking three good swallows that ended in a gasp.

"I'd give ya some," he said, his grin mean, "but I don't feel like it." He raised his head to get a better look. "My bros!" He belched again. "Nearly forty years on. So how come you're here ta visit little ol' me? Wanna see the crippled freak? Talk over old times?" He took another long swallow and wiped his mouth. "Screw ya—"

CT stalked over, scowling. "Gimme that," he barked, yanking the bottle out of Frankie's hand.

"Wooo, big tough guy!" Frankie yelped. "Still the same! Wanna take a poke at me while you're at it, *Mister* C. T. Barnes?" Frankie spread his hands to either side. "As the man said, ya have me at a disadvantage, sir!" Rubbing his face he laughed, a raspy, smoky sound. "What am I sayin? I must still be drunk. You guys ain't really here—"

CT reached down and slapped him, a ringing head shot. "How's that, man? Real enough?"

Nick almost stepped over but stopped when he saw Frankie shaking his head, blinking. He was all right; more surprised than anything else.

"That hurt," he whined.

"I meant it to." CT softened his tone. "Listen, I didn't wanna hit you that hard, but Nicky and I have somethin' we need to say. It's important, and we don't have a lot of time for you to get sobered up. So are you with the program here, Frankie? Firin' on all cylinders? Up to snuff? We need to know."

Frankie nodded. "I think so." He put a hand to his face. "I think ya broke my jaw."

"If I had you wouldn't be talkin' about it. Nick?" CT stepped aside.

Nick squatted down again. "You look like percolated swill, Frankie. CT and I are here to fix that."

"What's that supposed ta mean? What are you guys doin' here, anyway, after all these years?" He seemed to be tracking with them now.

"It's a long story," Nick said. "First off, were you sober this past Tuesday night?"

"More or less. Why?"

"Do you remember hearing a story on the news, either Tuesday night or sometime Wednesday, about a message? A really strange message?" Both men looked closely at him.

Frankie rubbed his chin, his whiskers rasping against his hand. "Seems like I do . . . much as I can remember anything these days . . . " He narrowed his eyes in suspicion. "Why?"

"I'll tell ya," CT replied, and then he changed tack. "Do you remember when I got saved?"

"Yeah." Frankie almost looked like he was about to spit on the floor, but reconsidered it. "I thought you were crazy, Barnes. Still do." His eyes widened. "Hold on, wait a minute. Don't tell me *that's* what all this is about? Ya came here ta get me *saved,* glory, glory?" Frankie did spit then. "Save your breath, holy joe."

"That's what we're here for," Nick said. "The same thing happened to me in that MASH."

Frankie flashed Nick a look of pure hate. "Well, I wouldn't know anything about that, seein' as how I was on the *Kitty Hawk* at the time, havin' my guts stuffed back inside me." He laughed bitterly, waving his hands in the air. "So Nick Castle got 'saved,' praise de Lawd! Ain't that a kick? Me, they took the best parts and threw 'em overboard for the fishies."

His laugh vanished as his eyes filled with sudden, unwanted tears. "Don't be tellin' me how wonderful your lives have gone since ya met sweet Jesus. Save it for the rubes. The day we walked from the briefin' hut over ta my slick was the last day I walked anywhere, period."

His tears flowed freely now. "Oh yeah, my life has turned out great! Look around! I live like a king here! Great place ta bring a date, right?" Violently he wiped his face. "Not that I've ever tried it! I haven't had a woman since 1972!" He slapped his groin. "Dead! Nothin' works down there! Yeah, baby, the docs really fixed ol' Frankie up!" He held up a hand, manic now. "Wait, I haven't showed ya the best part yet!"

Yanking up his blue workshirt, he unsnapped his pants. On his abdomen hung a colostomy bag, swollen and fetid. "Don't get too close 'cause this thing stinks!" Frankie dropped his shirt, burying his face in his hands as he mumbled the rest. "Go on—get out! Take your smiles and your sweet Jesus and get outta my life, willya?"

"We'll leave if you want," Nick said, "but before we do, I'm curious about something. You always seemed to be such a hard case, not letting anybody get close. Back at Quon Tre you said you'd transferred there from another unit where you'd been a tunnel rat. Scuttlebutt had it you'd done or seen something your last time in that you couldn't get past. Do you mind telling us what it was?"

Frankie wiped his nose on his sleeve. "What's it to ya?"

"I'm just trying to understand you. Look, man, your problems are more than just physical, that's obvious. You were already carrying a huge chip on your shoulder the day you first showed up at the unit. Whatever was chewing on you then is eating you alive now. CT and I would just like to know what it is."

Frankie blew out a ragged breath, and then seemed to cave. "Sure. Why not?" He nodded, more to himself than them. "Nothin' matters anymore. My troubles are about over anyway."

The two weren't sure what he was talking about, but kept silent.

Frankie looked past them to the dirty window beyond. "I was always a tough street kid. I grew up close to here, matter of fact. That was back before the coloreds took over."

Realizing what he'd just said, he shot a look at CT. The big man's face was a mask.

Doggedly Frankie went on. "When my draft notice came, the guy at the induction center cracked up. He said there must have been a mistake, that I was too little for the Army." His laugh was bitter. "They took me anyway. I guess they were desperate. So I took the oath and joined up. I don't have to tell ya that basic was a real treat for a guy my size. I had ta hump it twice as hard as anybody else, just ta show 'em I could. I made it, though. I showed 'em all. When I graduated, my MOS was infantry rifleman."

Frankie's next laugh was even more bitter. "But that didn't last 'cause when I got over ta Nam the cap'n took one look at me and made me a tunnel rat. I didn't care as long as I got ta kill gooks. Like I said, I was tough, I was strong, and I thought bein' underground wouldn't bother me." He swallowed. "But it did. First time inside I was scared ta death. It was like I couldn't breathe or somethin'. The smells and the wet and the feel of all that dirt pressin' on top of ya . . . I just wanted ta run right back out and not stop. But I didn't. I didn't."

He drew a shuddering breath, wiping his mouth with his hand. "Somebody once told me a guy can get used ta almost anything. I guess that's right 'cause after a lot more times inside it started not ta seem so bad. Kinda familiar, like. After a while I began ta like it. In the end, I loved it. It became my whole world."

The little man's face glowed with a sick light as he rushed on. "See, I found out that in the tunnels I could be as big as I wanted. In there it was always night. And when ya got right down to it, the job was simple. All I had ta do was keep quiet and keep killin' and keep goin'. Pretty soon I'd gotten me a rep as a real hard man."

His grin was harsh. "I loved it. For the first time in my life, guys looked up ta *me*. 'Send me in, Coach, I'll win this thing for ya!' But then came that last time . . . I don't even know why I'm tellin' you guys all this."

He reached down beside him, where CT had set the whiskey bottle on the floor. Picking it up, he took another big drink and wiped his mouth with the back of his hand.

"I'd been in for an hour, and I'll admit it, I was spooked. Somethin' about the whole job just didn't feel right. I'd heard another unit had lost three rats just the week before, so along with my .45 and some extra clips, I'd started totin' a white phosphorous grenade." He leered horribly at them. "A little hot potato in case things got hairy."

His grin faded, and his voice grew low and ragged. "I'm crawlin' along, listenin' ta water drippin' somewhere, not even mindin' the bugs that went across my face. Bugs could be good company. Good eatin' too, in a pinch. The tunnel's cool, but I'm sweatin' bullets. I come around this bend . . . and then I hear whispers."

For a long moment he was silent, then he muttered, "Troops. A slew of 'em. Had ta be. This time it wasn't gonna be just me against some slope." He looked up at them, haunted. "Remember, it's black as night down there. Ya did everythin' by sound and feel. So like I said, I'm hearin' whispers . . . and all of a sudden I feel the air change across my face. That always meant I was headin' into a bigger chamber. I stop . . . and the whispers stop."

He swallowed. "They knew I was there, all right, and I knew my number was up. Too many ta fight, and too far ta crawl. And then I remembered my grenade. And ya know what? I decided forget it, if they wanted Frankie dead it was gonna cost 'em, big time. I jerked the thing off my belt, yanked the pin, let go of the spoon, and chucked it. Then I flattened myself against a wall, and a second later it cooked off. And then—" His voice caught. "And then I hear all this ungodly, hellacious screamin', and there's white-hot fire everywhere and I . . . I take one quick look into the room ta make sure I got 'em all—*Oh, God!*"

He slapped his hands over his face.

"It was a *nursery!* God help me, a VC *nursery!* Oh Jesus God, the sounds, the sounds—" He stopped, unable to go on, rocking back and forth, his hands still clapped over his face.

Neither Nick nor CT could speak. Both of them struggled to absorb the horror.

With a shudder Frankie dropped his hands. "I don't even remember gettin' outta there. The next thing I know the cap'n is slappin' my face. 'Snap out of it, Malone!' he says. 'Shake it off!' Yeah!"

Frankie rubbed the back of his neck. "The next day I found him and said, 'Up yours, Cap, do whatever ya want with me, but no way I'm goin' back in. No way.' That tore it. He threatened major stockade time. I told him ta shove it, I didn't care. Finally he asks me, real calm-like, what I want. I told him a transfer ta AirCav. As far away from those freakin' tunnels as I could get. And whattya know, they did."

He gazed at them. "There's your story. Pretty, ain't it?"

CT started, "Listen, man, we—"

Frankie held up a weary hand. "Aw, stow it, Barnes. Ya started ta say we all did things over there we ain't proud of. But I'd lay odds I'm the only man in this room that ever burned up a nursery full a' babies!" He began to sob. "In my dreams I still hear 'em. God almighty, I hear 'em. I got what I deserved, all right."

"There's an answer to this, Frankie," Nick said, his tone soothing. "There is. See, God's given us this mission—"

"A mission?" Frankie broke in. "Ya want a mission? I'll give ya one!"

Wheeling over to a rickety desk covered in various papers, he violently rooted around. After a moment he found an envelope and threw it at them with a sneer. It flew end over end, landing between their feet.

"That ain't a love letter, guys. That's what I owe Salvatore Frinessi. Sal's our friendly neighborhood loan shark. A bill from a loan shark. Ya gotta love it. A thousand bucks is what I owe Sal, due and payable on demand. And he's comin' over tonight with two of his 'associates' ta make good on the tab. Guess I don't have ta tell you boys I don't have it—not even close."

Yanking open the desk drawer, Frankie pulled out something else. A chrome-plated Ruger P90. His laugh was tinged with madness.

"But if Sal's lookin' to collect, I'll give him a collection he'll remember. It's simple, guys! I shoot them, they shoot back at me, and then everything's over for everybody, get it? All my problems are done!" With a snarl he slammed the gun back in its drawer and wheeled around again, pointing at them. "Your *mission*, should you decide ta accept it, is ta either shoot those boys for me or pay 'em their thousand bucks. And I'm bettin' you holy joes ain't shot nobody in years. My guess is it'll be money, then."

He crossed his arms over his skinny chest, breathing rapidly. "So will ya do it? Will ya help? Come on, you guys have ta be doin' better than me!" He smacked the arms of his wheelchair with both hands. "This life I've got stinks, but I ain't got another, and I'd like ta keep it just a little while longer. But that all depends on Mr. Frinessi, don't it? And you."

He leaned forward. "So whattya say? How's about helpin' out a bro that's down on his luck? I need cash, and I bet you guys got plenty. How's about givin' me some?" Frankie held out his hands, palms up, eyebrows raised in hope.

Nick and CT stared at each other, a strange smile breaking out on their faces. Both men felt a supernatural rush of power flowing like molten heat in their limbs.

Nick shook his head. "Oh, man, CT, do you suppose—?"

"This is too weird to be anything but God, bro!" the big man grinned.

In three steps they stood before Frankie.

"Look at me!" Nick commanded. He blinked up at them, baffled.

"Silver and gold, we ain't got!" CT yelled.

"But what we have is yours!" Reaching out, Nick grabbed the smaller man by the right hand and jerked him out of his wheelchair. "In the name of Jesus Christ of Nazareth, walk!"

A crackling noise filled the air. Instantly Frankie's legs filled out with muscle, sinews, and skin, completely normal.

He screamed in disbelief. Simultaneously, with a tremendous rip, his now too-small pants split clear up to the crotch, the rags dropping away.

Suddenly there was another sound, wet and squishing. Frankie's colostomy bag had popped free and fallen to the floor, somehow miraculously keeping its foul waste intact as it rolled. The wound where the bag had hung was now smooth, clear skin. The jagged bullet hole scars that had puckered his abdomen, another reminder of that disastrous afternoon those many years before, were gone as well.

"Oh my God!" Frankie yelled, eyes bulging as he ran incredulous hands over his stomach and legs. "What's goin' on here?" He stared down at himself, then at his hands, and then back up, his mouth agape.

Grinning their encouragement, Nick and CT stepped back a few paces to give him room. His entire body shaking, Frankie pushed himself up to his feet.

"Yeah, you can do it!" Nick shouted.

Flexing his fingers, sweat beading his brow, Frankie swallowed a lump the size of a tangerine. Tentatively, he took a shaky step.

Two . . .

Three . . .

And then he was tearing around the tiny room, clad only in his shirt and shoes and underwear, laughing and weeping and knocking things over with a crash. "Look at me!" he screamed as he jumped around, giggling and crying.

"Look at this, my God, *look at what I can do!*" He leaped up and down, up and down, bellowing his joy.

Nick and CT grinned at him like idiots.

After a few more minutes, Frankie finally stopped. He was gasping, sweating, weeping, and spent. "How did this happen?" he croaked. He grabbed their shirtfronts, his eyes searching theirs. "I don't understand. What did you guys do?"

"Not us, Frankie!" Nick yelled, slamming the little man in the chest with the palm of his hand. "It was sweet Jesus!"

Frankie dropped to his knees in surrender then, his long war with himself finally at an end. He wrapped his arms around the two men's legs and began to cry. "Show me what I need ta do, guys. Please show me . . . "

They did.

CHAPTER 48

NICK AND CT SAT IN THEIR CAR, waiting for Frankie to come back out after finishing his shower. They'd decided that they needed to put their friend on the next plane out of Newark, going anywhere. After they broached the subject, a grateful Frankie had told them that yeah, he appreciated their offer. He said he'd always wanted to see Seattle, so if it was all the same to them he'd like to go there.

It made sense, Nick thought. A guy couldn't get too much farther from an outraged Salvatore Frinessi than Seattle.

Frankie had asked them to sit tight, said he'd be right out in a minute. CT checked his watch. A minute, right. Just like back in Nam, the guy was taking his own sweet time getting dressed. CT was about to make a crack about it when the door finally opened.

He and Nick stared in amazement.

Frankie, decked out in his faded forty-year-old Class A dress uniform, strutted over to them, his grin a mile wide. "Can you guys believe this thing still fits?" Laughing, he opened the car door and climbed in the back seat. "I forgot I still had it!"

"Yeah, I was wonderin' if you had any clothes that would fit your brand-new body," CT said.

Frankie held out his arms. "Except for this, I didn't." He frowned at them. "Do I look stupid?"

"You're fine," Nick assured him. "Do you feel as great on the inside as you look on the outside?"

"I feel like a million bucks! You guys've got no idea—" Frankie's grin faded as he began to choke up again. "Almost forty years I spent in that chair, and in one second—boom!" He looked away, staring out the window. "I just wish I had some friends or relatives I could tell."

"Well, you got us. We're family," CT smiled. "Matter of fact, you got family you haven't even met yet."

Frankie climbed back out of the car. "Hey, speakin' a' which, I got some unfinished business before we head out. Will you guys come with me while I do somethin'?"

Without waiting for an answer, he began walking down the street. Nick and CT hurried after him.

"What?" Nick asked as they caught up with him.

"Just somethin' I have ta do—there it is!"

Frankie angled sharply across the street toward that same storefront church Nick and CT had attended the night before. He strode on in with Nick and CT right behind.

At the front of the church, Reverend Jasper was sweeping up. Hearing the men enter, he turned.

"Hello, may I—Lord God A'mighty!" Jasper dropped his broom.

"Reverend Jasper!" Frankie hollered. He ran up and grabbed the astonished man in a bear hug. "God bless ya!"

Jasper's eyes grew huge. He stood speechless.

Grinning, Frankie let go and stepped back. "See what God did for me?"

The pastor finally found his voice. "But . . . but how on earth?"

"It was Jesus! He saved my soul! What you talked about! And healed me to boot! Ain't that a kick?"

The pastor sat down heavily on the edge of the platform, his hands on his knees. "It's . . . wonderful! But . . . that is . . . what I mean is . . . I've preached that God doesn't do healings anymore. Physical ones. At least, up until this week I did." He shook his head. "Like most everyone else, I've heard the news of worldwide miracles, but I've never witnessed one." He shot another look at Frankie and then jumped to his feet with a yell, shooting his hands in the air. "Until now! Bless you, Lord!"

"Amen!" Nick and CT said simultaneously.

Jasper dropped his arms. "Gentlemen! I didn't see you standing there!" He pointed at the smaller man. "Did you have anything to do with this?"

CT rubbed his nose in embarrassment. "Yeah . . . kinda . . . well, not really, no. We just prayed for him. Jesus took it from there."

"Amazing." For the first time Jasper noticed Frankie's uniform. "Are you leaving us, Mr. Malone?"

"Yeah, I am. I'm goin' ta Seattle. Ya might say it's for health reasons. I'm in Dutch for some money with Sal Frinessi, and Nick and CT are helpin' me beat feet."

"Did they tell you about Jesus returning for us?"

"They sure did," Frankie said. He turned to Nick. "How much more time did ya say we have?"

"Eighty-four hours now, maybe less," he answered. "Of course, it could also happen in the next second. No one really knows but God."

Frankie turned to the pastor. "That's the reason why I wanted ta stop by before I left, Reverend. I wanted ta apologize ta you and your people. Just tell 'em I said so, huh?"

"Apologize? Whatever for?"

"Come on, Reverend. I've always hated ni—uh, colored . . . that is . . . you know," Frankie finished lamely. "And somethin's tellin' me I treated you and your people pretty bad over the years. Before I go I needed ta tell ya I'm sorry. So—" He held out his hand. "Friends?"

Reverend Jasper stepped past Frankie's outstretched hand and enfolded the smaller man in an embrace. "Of course, Brother Malone, of course."

Frankie returned the hug, and then both men broke free with a laugh. "These guys have been tellin' me about eternity, Reverend, and how it's forever," Frankie said, "so I guess I'll have a real long time ta unlearn a bunch a' junk I've been carryin' my whole life. They also said I'm gonna have my own mansion up there. How about that? No more livin' in the back of a stinkin' garage. So tell ya what, when we all get settled in, I'm gonna have you and all your folks over ta my place for a big cookout, okay? My treat!"

Frankie gave a boyish grin, looking a lot like the kid who'd played stick-ball on these very streets, all those years ago. He snapped his fingers. "Hey, I got it! We'll make it a real party! Barbeque and watermelon, maybe some ribs, whatever ya want! How's that sound? Pretty good, huh?"

CT winced, wondering how the kindly pastor would take such a remark.

He needn't have worried. Reverend Jasper must have realized from Frankie's open look he hadn't meant anything hurtful because he replied with a smile, "We'll do that very thing, Brother Malone. People always said my grandmother made the best pulled-pork barbeque you ever tasted."

"Good deal!" Frankie grew serious. "And since I'm pretty sure I don't have any family up there, maybe you wouldn't mind showin' me the ropes, Reverend. Helpin' me learn, you and your people. Whattya say?"

Sudden moistness appeared in Jasper's eyes. "It would be an honor, Brother Malone. Both of us will be learning. Wait a moment—"

Going back up on the platform, Jasper squatted down, reached in behind the lectern, and brought out a plain, new, paperback Bible. He brought it to Frankie.

"We always like to make sure that new believers have one of these. Please accept this in love."

Frankie's eyes grew large. "Ta keep?"

"Of course."

"Wow." Frankie fingered the lettering as if it were bound in top-grain leather. "I've never had one of my own. Thanks! I'll read it on the plane!"

Reverend Jasper shook hands with them all one last time. "Goodbye, Brother Malone. And to you gentlemen as well."

Frankie grinned, "See ya up there in a little bit, Reverend. We'll have us a big time!"

He and Nick and CT walked outside into the chilly September morning, climbed in the car, and drove away.

Leaning his broom against the doorframe of his little church, Reverend Jasper looked up at the sky and shook his head. "Lord, you're always full of surprises, aren't you?" he said, smiling. "We all still have a lot to learn."

CHAPTER 49

"HELLO, AND WELCOME BACK. You're listening to NPR, National Public Radio, and the program is *Digital Reality*. I'm your host, Jack Kellogg. For those of you just joining us, the past hour we've been speaking on the subject of the so-called 'message from God' that has sparked interest worldwide.

"I'd like to take this opportunity to thank our last guest, Ms. Ruth Ella Pierce, of the Society of Gaia, who had many salient comments to offer. Unfortunately for our listeners, Ruthie, as she likes to be called, had to leave suddenly during our break, as she said she needed to confer with her spirit guide, Meshazaroth, concerning new developments. Our thanks and best wishes go with her.

"Now I'd like to welcome Dr. Alan Minch. Dr. Minch, as many of you may know by now, was formerly humanities chair at the Yale School of Divinity and currently serves as senior pastor of the Union Free Church in Manhattan. Doctor, thank you for joining us."

"My pleasure, Jack."

"To bring our listeners who have just joined us up to speed, we've been discussing this latest round of religious faddism that appears to be sweeping the globe. Before our station break we were debating where such fanaticism could possibly lead. Doctor Minch, comments?"

"Thank you, Jack. First let me say that all this lunacy has reflected quite badly on historical orthodox Christianity. That the Bible is good literature but undoubtedly written by mere men has never been in question. Sadly, there are those of the evangelical and pentecostal persuasions who take issue with this, but thankfully they are, and continue to be, the exception rather than the rule.

"Also thankfully, biblical debunking has for some become more than an avocation, rather surely and steadily transmogrifing into life's work. I myself have written a book entitled *God's Fools,* which has enjoyed not a little success in major markets and can be found in local bookstores. It explores an area rich with hitherto untapped veins of hermaneutical and apologetical wisdom. Unlearned and ignorant simpletons, to the ongoing detriment of freethinking men and women everywhere, have appropriated these areas in the past.

"I would hope that my efforts, in some small way, have been instrumental in rescuing our faith from those who would pervert its truth, consigning it permanently to the ash heap of hayseed mentality. But I digress. To answer your question more fully, Jack . . . Jack?"

"Huh? Uh, yes, Doctor. A very good point, and very well articulated. In sum, your way of answering this end-of-the-world hysteria would be . . . ?"

"Education. Without a doubt, education is the bedrock of any rational civilization. Unfortunately, the more—how does one say it?—*radical* methods of inculcating wisdom into the young have been fought, hammer and tongs, by those of the so-called religious right—and I would go so far as to call them religiously wrong-headed—who would hamstring the very feet of the future."

"Radical methods consisting of what, in particular, Dr. Minch?"

"Inter-vivos indoctrination for one. Education beginning in the womb, pre-birth, accomplished with stimulation probes inserted into the fetus's skulls as soon as verifiable brain-wave activity has been ascertained. Now admittedly, this is an area rife with controversy—"

"Yes, I quite agree. Didn't Josef Mengele attempt such things at Auschwitz, Bergen-Belsen, and Buchenwald?"

"He did, but before any of your listeners take umbrage with me, let me elaborate that we are nearly sixty years past that time, with concurrently greater technology. Plus, it must not be overlooked that whereas Dr. Mengele was doing his experimentation in trying to advance the, quote, Master Race, unquote, we must realize that we are the master race now, on the very fringes of godhead, if I may be so bold. And because that's true, anything we would undertake in the lives of our young would be done, as Scripture admonishes, 'decently and in order.' In order for what? Why, nothing less than the facilitation of the soon-coming achievment of God's status ourselves . . . "

CHAPTER 50

IT WAS 12:30 P.M. and Nick and CT were at yet another airport, this one Bluegrass Airport in Lexington, Kentucky, standing at yet another baggage carrousel, waiting yet again for their luggage to appear.

CT wiped his face and sighed. "Man, I gotta tell ya, this flyin' around business has lost its charm."

"I heard that," agreed Nick. "It sure would be sweet to get this wrapped up by this afternoon so we can get on home. Another night of me listening to you snoring, and you're going to experience the phenomenon of the sudden laying on of hands."

Rolling his massive shoulders, CT arched an eyebrow. "Threats, Nick? I think not, m'friend." His grin took the edge off his words. "While you hustled over here to get our bags, I called your house and talked to Maryann and Sarah and the kids."

"How're they doing? Everything copacetic?"

"Yep. Since they turned on the answerin' machine, that's pretty much eliminated the nasty phone calls. I told 'em about Frankie, and they flipped. They said they're expectin' good news about Dooley too." CT scratched his chin. "Which reminds me. There's somethin' been botherin' me about that Frankie business."

Nick was still staring at the conveyor belt. "What?"

CT considered his answer for a moment. "Well, us puttin' him on that plane to escape that Salvatore guy. Was that the right thing to do?"

Nick looked over at him. "What are you asking? Do I think the thousand bucks Frankie owed was a legitimate debt, and we helped him skate?" He shook his head. "I don't know. What I can tell you for sure is that Frinessi's a criminal, and sounds like a pretty rough character to boot. So what that we helped Frankie escape a beating, and maybe worse? Who cares? Frinessi might, but I don't plan to lose any sleep over it."

"Forget him if he can't take a joke, right?"

"Right."

Nick cast another glance toward the conveyor, but their bags were still nowhere in sight. "If our luggage comes up anytime in the next ten hours we can get on the road to Danville."

"Poor old Nick. You and luggage carrousels don't mix well, do ya?"

"No." Nick placed one hand over his eyes, assuming a dramatic pose as he intoned in a stentorian voice, "but The Great Nickini predicts our bags will be coming up . . . now."

He jerked his hand away. Nothing.

He did it again. "Now."

Nothing.

"Now."

Up popped their bags from the conveyor belt onto the carrousel.

"Hah!" Nick smirked, grabbing them and handing CT's bag over. "I knew they'd come up then. Nickini never fails."

CT shook his head. "You've been standin' here for fifteen minutes waitin'. Odds alone say they were due to come up next."

Nick narrowed his eyes. "Infidel. I—"

Right then the intercom called his name, and they trotted over to the car rental counter to pick up their ride. Although people were lined up five deep in front of each agent, it was not as busy as they'd been experiencing.

"Somethin' else I'm not gonna miss," CT said. "We are just drivin' this one back to Cincy when we're done and leavin' it at the airport, right? You weren't gonna make me fly *again* were ya?"

Nick shot him a sly grin. "Why not? You and airplanes don't mix well?"

Ten minutes later they were on the Bluegrass Parkway, heading toward the exit to Danville. "I don't think we're going to need a map this time," Nick said. "Dooley's folks live right outside of town on Perryville Road, not too far from the Civil War battlefield. Hey, remember the last time the four of us with all our kids rented a van and came down here for a picnic and to tour the site?"

"Yeah. It was almost two years ago exactly. October. The weather was gorgeous, kinda like today, and the leaves had turned. Maryann made a huge thing of that German potato salad, and Sarah fried enough chicken to feed us all for a week. After we got done eatin' like pigs, we had us that big ol' touch football game, where Sarah and I shellacked your guys' butts. What a perfect day."

"Except for us losing that game, it was pretty good, all right."

CT shifted in his seat, suddenly growing serious. "Y'know, it's kinda sad. I mean, that we're not gonna be around to see the leaves turnin' this year . . . "

"Yeah, so?" When CT didn't reply, Nick glanced over at him. "What about it?"

CT shook his head, staring out the windshield. "Forget it. I shouldn't have opened my yap."

"Come on, you were going to say something. What?"

"Well . . . it's just that I like the fall, and I'm gonna miss it, that's all."

"So what are you saying—that you want to forgo the rapture for this year's leaf turning?" Nick almost laughed in disbelief, but checked it at the last second.

CT pursed his lips. "Nah, man, 'course not. In a coupla years the planet's gonna be so blown up and burned over fall won't be worth mentionin' anyway. It's just that . . . Do you think we'll have 'em in heaven? Seasons, I mean? Like fall with drinkin' cider and lookin' at punkins? And wintertime when the night air is so cold and crisp and quiet you can hear each snowflake as it lands? And then spring with plantin' corn and beans and okra, and then summertime with softball games and horsehoes and fishin' at dawn on the lake when the water's like glass?" He cleared his throat and finished lamely, "You know, stuff like that."

Nick didn't reply for a moment. "You've really given this some thought, haven't you?"

"Yeah, I have. So whattya think?"

Nick paused before answering. "All I can tell you for certain is that the equation's simple: Heaven equals paradise. The Word's clear on that. So if, mind you, *if* there aren't any seasons there, I don't think we'll even miss them because God loves his kids. He knows what it'll take to make it heaven for us. Besides, you're forgetting something."

"What?"

"After the tribulation is over, the Bible says Jesus is going to remake the entire earth back into the way it was at the start, and then we get to rule the whole thing with him for a thousand years."

CT frowned, still not getting it.

"What I'm trying to say," Nick explained, "is that after the millennial reign is done, we're still eternal beings. Think about it, CT. The universe is a huge place. I mean huge. Trillions of light years wide, maybe more. Who knows, maybe there are entire planets where it's fall forever and you can drink cider and look at pumpkins all you want. Then when that gets old, you and Sarah can find another planet and fish for a million years, pulling out lunkers by the ton."

"Nah, not for a million years. Knowin' Sarah, she'd get tired of it after a hundred thousand." Nick chuckled, and the big man went on with a laugh, "Plus you know how squeamish that girl is. With that much fishin' I know I'd get awful tired of always havin' to bait her hook."

Both men laughed now as they tooled on down the highway.

CHAPTER 51

ROUTE 127 WAS A STRAIGHT SHOT from the Harrodsburg exit to Danville. Almost exactly forty-five minutes after they'd left the Lexington airport, Nick and CT pulled up in front of a neat little 1950s-style cedar-shake shop whose bright neon sign bore the legend: Danville Donuts—None Finer! They had to agree; both families had stopped there on their way to the Perryville battlefield and had found the shop's coffee to be singularly good.

Nick shut the Caddy off and got out. "I'll grab us a couple of cups of the management's best."

"Make mine heavy-heavy, the way I like it," CT called after him.

A few minutes later Nick climbed back in the car and handed CT his cup. "Heavy-heavy, as ordered."

The big man took a sip, smacking his lips appreciatively, and nodded his thanks. "Yumbo! Mighty tasty. This place sure hasn't lost the touch."

Nick grimaced and gave his friend the fish eye. He'd always taken his coffee hot, black, and unadorned, while CT preferred his nearly half cream and sugar.

"How you can take a perfectly fine cup of coffee and ruin it is beyond me."

CT drained his cup in a huge swallow, wiped his mouth, and stuffed his napkin inside the empty. "Well, I'll tell ya. I drank so much bitter, muddy, nasty brew in Nam that I promised myself when I got back to the World I'd always have mine the way I like it, and my momma always told me to keep my promises."

"A dutiful son. I like it." Nick gulped his coffee down as well, and they both tossed their empties into the back. He looked over at his friend. "You ready to go? All prayed up?"

"Yep." CT pointed forward. "Let's roll, Kato."

.. .. ..

WITHIN FIVE MINUTES they'd left the town and were deep into farm country. Perryville Road had built up some during the last two years, but it still managed to maintain its bucolic charm. The area they passed through was mostly rolling fields, ripe with feed corn and soybeans ready for harvest and dotted with small, well-tended family farms.

Nick powered down the windows. Rich, sweet air washed into the car. "Ah, nectar!"

CT sniffed. "Smells like manure ta me. Well, ta each his own." The appointment book open on his lap, he looked down at the Ryans' address. "Manny said Dooley and his folks live at box 166-A. There's box 125-B. We got a ways."

"Don't be too sure of that. These rural numbers have a way of jumping at random. Keep a sharp eye on your side."

The majority of the mailboxes they passed were either rusty or battered beyond belief, and the numbers on their sides were, for the most part, nonexistent.

CT frowned. "How does anybody find their way around here?"

"It's the country. Everybody knows everybody else, including the mailman, so I guess they don't see a real need for numbers. Plus, it keeps city slickers like us at a disadvantage."

"Yeah—hey, look."

They'd just crested a small hill. At the bottom of a gravel drive a newer-looking mailbox in the form of a tractor stood proudly erect next to the road. The number read Box 166-A RYAN. Nick pulled the car into the base of the drive, and both men looked up at the farmhouse at the top of the hill.

The place was pretty, but in an odd, bright way, as if a child's farm playset had been blown up lifesize. The house loomed large, boasting white paint that shone even more brilliantly against the clear blue of the sky and a newer-looking black shingle roof.

Blue and red windowboxes, full of flowers, adorned nearly every window, and a trellis festooned with dark ivy graced the house's near side. Beyond the dwelling Nick and CT could see the barns and outbuildings, and they too looked well built. They were painted black, but contained no "Red Man" or "Mail Pouch" tobacco ads on their roofs or sides, as was so common down South. All in all, it was quietly impressive. Somebody had gone to a lot of work to keep this farm up.

CT was about to make a remark when he saw a curtain move on one of the downstairs windows. "I think we've been spotted, Ace."

Nick shrugged. "Might as well go boldly."

He stepped on the gas, and they made the long climb up the drive. Finally reaching the house, they pulled around and got out, then strode up onto the well-kept porch. The bell mounted next to the door was one of the old-fashioned twist kind. Nick reached out and wrenched it around.

Almost instantly the portal flew open. Before them stood a pinch-faced older woman, tall and frowning, her hair done up in a tight bun at the base of her neck. The woman's dress was blue gingham, old but clean, and she looked as if she hadn't smiled since Nixon was president.

She eyed them suspiciously. "Yeah?"

Nick put together one of his better smiles. "Mrs. Ryan?"

The woman didn't budge. "Who's askin'?"

"My name is Nick Castle, ma'm. This is my friend CT Barnes. We're friends of Doo—uh, Ambrose. Is he here?"

He arched his eyebrows in what he hoped was an open, honest look. It didn't work.

The woman's frown deepened. "If you really was friends of Ambrose," she said, her speech as flat as roadkill, "you'd know he don't see nobody. Now get."

She began to close the door, but CT stopped it with his hand. "Ma'am, we—" he began.

She cut him off, her eyes stony as she growled at them in a low voice through gritted teeth. "Now if I was a smart boy like you, I'd get my hand off this door. My husband's got hisself a shotgun, and he ain't shy about usin' it."

Boy? CT balled up his fist in reflex. Before he could spit out a reply, they heard a man's voice from inside the house, growing nearer.

"Ida? I thought I heard—oh." The man who came up behind the woman stopped speaking when he saw Nick and CT standing there.

Balding and sun-reddened, Clyde Ryan, if that's who he was, was nearly a head shorter than his wife, but saddled with the same pinched face. He was clad in bib overalls, also worn and spotless, and his shiny head sported round, Mr. Peepers-style glasses.

Nick fought down a sudden urge to laugh. Except for the size reversals, the Ryans were a carbon copy of the couple on Grant Wood's painting *American Gothic*. All the man lacked was a pitchfork, and his compact size made it obvious where Dooley had gotten his own short stature.

"Who're you?"

"They said they was friends of Ambrose, Clyde," the woman said, her eyes never leaving Nick and CT's faces. "I told 'em to get, but they ain't."

Nick held up a hand. "Sir, if we could just talk with you—"

"Oh, now Ida." The old man's smile took years off him. "If they was friends of Ambrose, I'd at least like to meet 'em. Be sociable now." He stepped aside, effectively pushing his wife away from the door. "Won't y'all come on in?"

"Thank you, sir." Nick stepped inside, CT following closely. "We won't take up much of your time."

The woman was still shooting darts at them, and Clyde noticed it. "Ida . . . Ida!"

She tore her eyes away to glare at her husband.

"Why don't you get these men somethin' to drink?" he said.

She looked back at the men, snarling in a gutteral voice, "Y'all want some lemonade?"

"Boy, I bet that hurt." CT grinned.

"Y'all want some lemonade or not?" she snapped.

"That would be fine, ma'am," Nick replied, giving CT a warning glance.

The old woman turned and stomped off, presumably to the kitchen.

Clyde smiled apologetically. "Don't mind my wife, fellers. It's just Ida is a mite . . . well, protective of Ambrose, is all."

"I hope we haven't come at a bad time, Mr. Ryan," Nick said.

"Naw, she gets like this around strangers. At least since Ambrose come back from the war she has."

He looked as if he was going to say more but clamped his lips shut as Ida stomped back into the room, bearing two blue aluminum cups, which she thrust at them. "Here."

Each man took his with a smile, but inwardly Nick grimaced. Aluminum cups. He remembered them from back in the fifties, when they were all the rage. People may have liked the colors they came in, but even as a kid Nick had hated the way they felt on his teeth.

Gingerly taking a sip, he tried to keep the cold metal from touching enamel. It didn't work. He hoped his wince didn't show. Fingernails on a blackboard were pure bliss compared to this. Strangely enough, the lemonade was quite good.

Clyde leaned forward in his chair, eyes alight. "Y'all like that lemonade?"

"Really tasty, sir," CT said, meaning it.

"Heh! Tell you why." Clyde lowered his voice to a conspiritorial whisper. "It's got honey in it, from our own hives. Yep, I been keepin' bees for—"

"Aw, shut up about them bees!" Ida snapped. "Just let em drink up so's they can get!"

"We'd still like to see your son," Nick reminded them.

"Heyyy . . . hold on . . . " Ida leaned forward, squinting her eyes at him. "Wait just a minute here. What did you say your name was again?"

"Nick Castle, ma'am."

She straightened up and put a hand to her throat. "Oh, my Lord . . . It's *you!*"

"Ma'am?"

Her eyes were huge. "You're the one that saved Ambrose's life over in Vee-het Nam!"

"He sure is!" CT stated with pride. "Won the Bronze Star for it, too!"

Ida dropped her hand back in her lap. Her voice hollow, she said, "You should've let him burn."

Clyde Ryan shot to his feet. "Ida! Good God, woman!"

She swiveled her head toward him. "You know it's true. It'd been better if he'd died there. You know it."

It was a moment before Clyde found his voice, then he sputtered, "I'm not listen' to this!" Storming out the front door, he slammed it shut behind him with a crash.

"Old fool," Ida muttered. "He knows I'm right . . . he knows." She raised her voice. "And as for you two, get!"

Nick set his cup down. "Ma'am, if you really want us to go, we will. But please, you owe us this much. Tell us about your son. CT and I lost track of Ambrose after he was hurt—"

"Burned up, you mean," the old woman said sharply.

"Yes. Can you at least tell us how he's doing?"

"Aw, he's doin', all right!" she cackled. "Yeah, he's doin'!"

She fixed them in an odd gaze, and her voice grew strangely calm. "All right. I'm gonna tell this but once, so you both better listen up right smart. You won't get another chance. Then the two of you are gonna leave here and never come back. Ambrose is me and Clyde's only child, and I won't have him hurt no more. Not no more."

She held up a warning finger. "Mind! Now then. I guess y'all know Ambrose never was the sharpest knife in the drawer, but he was sweet. Loved animals."

Nick and CT remembered that well. Dooley was always finding stray dogs and cats around the camp. He'd protect them, feed them scraps from the mess tent until their skinny ribs fleshed out, then he'd either send them on their way or give them to children from the surrounding villages. He got plenty upset one day when Cookie snottily reminded him that many of those same dogs and cats had probably ended up in the family stewpot.

"And lovin' animals is what caused the problem." Ida cleared her throat and settled back deeper in her chair. "I remember the whole thing like it was yesterday. It happened the night before Ambrose was to go into the Army. Boy'd been talkin' for weeks before he left about what he was gonna do when he got out. He was all cranked up, said he was gonna be a veterinarian, like old Doc Fontaine, and doctor farm animals."

She barked a short laugh. "Now ain't that a crazy thought? Poor boy didn't hardly graduate high school, but yet he wanted to go to vet college. Well, Clyde and me had been tryin' to talk him out of it, of course, but he said he'd been talkin' to Doc, and Doc had filled Ambrose's head with all kinds of nonsense about how he was gonna help him get set up when our boy got out."

She shook her head at the apparent stupidity of it. "Tomfoolery. And like I said, it all come to a head that last night. Him and Clyde was yellin' at each other, goin' round and round. Finally Clyde says we already got enough horse doctors, and he needed him a son to help him keep this here place up. Besides, he says to him, you're too dumb to ever go to college."

Ida tightened her lips at the memory.

"Lord, Ambrose gets this awful look in his eyes, and then he swings his fist and hits Clyde square in the face. Knocks his glasses clean off his head. And him a foot shorter than Clyde." The old woman stared in remembrance. "Ambrose is cryin' like a baby, screamin' that we just don't understand, and we're screamin' back. Lord, it was bad. Worst I ever seen. Then he storms out. He ended up walkin' the eight miles on into town to catch the bus for the Army.

"Well, after a few days Clyde and me cooled off, and we started feelin' terrible, of course. We tried writin' him at boot camp. But Ambrose wouldn't write back." Ida's voice caught. "Even when he got on over to Vee-het Nam he wouldn't write. It was like he was dead. Purt' near a year passes, and then we get that awful letter . . . "

The tears started coming now. "From somebody named Greer, some sergeant. He said Ambrose's colonel woulda wrote it, but he'd got hisself in some sorta trouble over there. I never did figure it out . . . but anyway the sergeant told us about how Ambrose'd been burnt, and he was bein' sent back here to the States to Walter Reed Hospital in Bethesda, Maryland, and by the time we got the letter he prob'ly be there already."

She wiped her eyes. "Clyde and me hopped in the car and drove all night to see him. When we got there, some fat old Army doctor stopped us in the hall and said Ambrose had been drugged real heavy and the doc wanted to talk to us in his office, private-like, before we went in. We knew somethin' was bad wrong then. Clyde and me sat down in some chairs acrost from that doctor's desk, and I just fixed him a look and said 'Doc, I got me one question, and you best answer me honest. Is Ambrose gonna be all right?' Then that doc looked at me and Clyde all sad-like and says, 'Well, Mrs. Ryan, that's tough to say. Ambrose's life is gonna be *different* from now on.' And then we knew."

Ida stopped. Nick and CT thought that might be all she was going to say, but she gulped and drew a ragged breath. Nick wondered how long it had been since she'd told anyone this story. If ever.

"Then that doc takes me and Clyde on down the hall and into Ambrose's room, and . . . oh my God! There our sweet boy lay, on his back on some kinda waterbed. He's burnt black as sin and has tubes goin' in and out and machines a-pumpin'. His arms and legs is all drawed up like he's fixin' to box, and there's some sorta plastic shield-like thing over his bed, and they tell us that's to keep him from evaporatin' because the only skin our boy has left on him is on his stomach and the backs of his legs!"

Ida did stop then, burying her face in both hands. Nick and CT said nothing, stunned. She pulled her hands free.

"I musta swooned clean away, 'cause I come to back in that fat doctor's office, and he's got a cold cloth on my head and is pattin' my hand. After a while Clyde and me up and left. We spent the night at some cheap motel. But we didn't sleep. Not hardly. The next day we come back. This time Ambrose is awake. His eyes—" Ida gulped. "His eyes is all swole shut, but he knows our voices. He tries turnin' his head, and then he . . . he starts moanin'."

Her voice broke at last. "Moanin' about how he's sorry, and how much it hurts, oh God, it hurts, and beggin' me *please*, mama, *please* make it not hurt."

Tears ran in rivulets down Ida's face. The pain radiating from her had a weight of its own. Somehow she got herself back under control.

"That was just the start. For the next year me and Clyde drove out to see Ambrose as much as we could. Neighbors helped us get that year's crop harvested and the spring seed in. He went through I don't know how many operations and skin grafts, then when the year was up they said that was it, they'd done as much as they could do, and for us to take him on home." Ida swallowed again. "So we did."

She fumbled for a tissue. CT handed her his handkerchief, which she wordlessly took.

"They give us some cream and told us to rub it into him as often as we could and as much as he could stand, and to stretch him to keep him limber. He'd scream bloody murder each time we did it, but he wouldn't quit." She shook her head. "So much like his daddy. Stubborn as a red mule. I guess our doin' him that way musta worked 'cause a year after he was home he was walkin' the property. Six months after that he started helpin' Clyde some with the farm."

Ida folded her hands in her lap. "And that's how it's been. Ambrose is back livin' in his old room upstairs, and each day it's the same. He gets up at dawn, does his chores all day, then at night he listens to the radio or watches some TV. Then he goes to bed and starts it all over again the next day. It ain't much of a life, I reckon, but it's his, and like I said, I won't have y'all upsettin' him. That's all they is to it."

"But that's not all, Mrs. Ryan," Nick said gently. "CT and I have a greater reason for being here today than just seeing Ambrose and talking over old times."

She squinted at him. "And what would that be?"

"You say he listens to the radio and TV. I'm sure you've been hearing about what happened last Tuesday night"

"You mean about that message from God?" Ida broke in with a snort. "Tommyrot."

Nick went on as if he hadn't heard her. "Also there've been reports on the news about God doing miracles these past few days—"

"Hold on!" Ida interrupted again. "Don't tell me that's what all this is about! You sayin' God is gonna *heal* Ambrose?"

"Yes ma'am," Nick replied. "That's exactly right."

She jumped to her feet. "No! I won't have it! Not a bit of it! Y'all waltz in here and—No!" She pointed at them. "Do you know it took me and Clyde purt' near a day and a half to get Ambrose calmed down after he saw that report on the TV the other night 'bout them healin's? A day and a half! And now you boys think I'm gonna let y'all get him that upset again?" She pointed toward the door. "Get out!"

The two men stood, but Nick felt he had to make one last effort. "Mrs. Ryan, Ambrose is over fifty years old. Don't you think he's old enough to—"

"*Get!*" she shrieked.

They got.

CHAPTER 52

SANGRE STEPPED LIGHTLY into the center of the pentagram. The early afternoon sun's warmth streaming in through the high windows in the old mill felt good on his naked skin, and he idly wondered if there now were enough tattoos covering him so he possessed a permanent blue and red tan. He hoped so. He didn't care for the idea of any burning rays being able to reach through his inky covering and scorching his white Aryan flesh. But it didn't really matter. He hardly ever went out in the daylight anyway.

He looked over at Crandall and nodded.

The deputy, equally naked (though untattooed except for the globe and anchor on his left shoulder), walked silently up to the Satanist and handed him their ceremonial fillet knife.

Sangre took it in his right hand and held out his left. Into it Crandall placed a squirming, mewling kitten. He then stepped away, leaving his friend alone in the center of the pentagram with their sacrifice.

Glancing down at the tiny cat, Sangre shook his head a millimeter; he really needed to work with Crandall on his trapping skills. For something as big as the Circle was planning Sunday night, he should have procured a bigger sacrificial animal. Oh well, at least it was alive.

Sangre held the knife and kitten away from his body and nodded again. Crandall padded around the five points of the pentagram, placing a stubby black candle at each and setting them alight. When he'd finished, he again stepped back.

Sangre closed his eyes in prayer. "Dark One. We approach the hour of your ascension. Let the small blood we shed now merely be an earnest of the great blood we will shed that night. Yours is the power, and yours is the glory. Forever."

Bringing the kitten close to his body, Sangre gently placed the tip of his razor-sharp blade against its throat. He could feel the furious pounding of the kitten's tiny heart thrumming through his palm as it stared up at him with enormous eyes. And then it mewed.

The piercing noise it released sounded, at least to Sangre's ears, like a baby's cry, and he smiled. In his mind he'd already fast-forwarded to Sunday night's coming carnage.

That's when he felt something else coming from the animal, something . . . warm. He looked closer. It was the kitten's urine, pouring through his fingers and running down his wrist. He smiled again. Pure terror.

Perfect.

Sensing its doom, the panicked kitten jerked, twisting in Sangre's palm. As it did, the point of the knife pierced its skin. The blade didn't even draw blood, but for the kitten that was close enough, thank you. With a minature growl and hiss it pulled deep on its heritage, laid its ears back, and sank its tiny teeth into Sangre's thumb.

"Yow!" Sangre's eyes popped open.

The bite didn't hurt so much as it surprised him, but the result was the same. He relaxed his hold on the kitten's fur just enough. The little beast flew out of Sangre's hand, down his chest, and leaped hard off his groin, its sharp back claws drawing blood at last. Sangre's, that is.

He yelled and dropped his knife, clattering, to the floor. Clapping his hands over himself, he danced on one foot, and then the other, screaming and cursing a blue streak. Crandall didn't know whether to be concerned or laugh his head off.

In the confusion the kitten scampered unnoticed through a rotted hole in the wall near the floor, picking up speed as it made its break. A flash of white from its tail, and it was gone.

Crandall chanced another look at his boss. Okay, enough comedy. He decided for his own sake he'd go for concern.

"Yo, Sangre, are you all right?"

Sangre gave out one more bellow of rage before squatting down and picking up the knife. "Yes, no thanks to you! Why didn't you catch it?"

"No way I could'a!" Crandall went to get their clothes off a chair. "The thing was like a rocket with feet!"

Sangre sneered at the deputy in disgust as he pushed him aside to get his clothes. "Crandall, sometimes I don't know about you."

The deputy put his clothes on without answering. It wasn't his fault the kitten escaped, but Sangre was trying to make him feel that it was. It was always the same, ever since they were kids. The guy never took responsibilty for anything. Never did, never would.

He was bending down to tie his shoes when suddenly another thought hit him and he straightened. "Hey, Sangre!"

"What?" Sangre was having trouble fastening his pants over the raw furrows the kitten's claws had left.

"Since we didn't get the sacrifice done, do you think that's gonna make the Dark One mad at us?" Crandall sure hoped not.

Sangre finally got his pants snapped. "Maybe not. I'll have to put in a good word for you with him, I know that." He clapped a hand on Crandall's shoulder. "You know, it's a good thing I'm your friend. Perhaps you can redeem yourself by trapping another animal. We'll try again later this afternoon or this evening.

"And listen, Crandall." Sangre fixed the deputy with a pitying look. "I know it will probably strain your faculties, but this time could you come back with something a bit . . . larger?" He smiled and patted the top of Crandall's head. "I know you can do it. I have faith in you."

When Sangre started for the door, Crandall scowled and bent down to pick up his deputy sheriff's hat. Placing it firmly on his head, he tried to imagine what would happen if he brought back a full-grown wildcat tonight. Watch that thing do a half-gainer off old Sangre's crotch.

Rubbing the laugh off his face, Crandall snuffed out the candle and followed his friend out the door.

CHAPTER 53

THE TWO MEN STARTED down the porch steps. CT headed for the car, but Nick suddenly cut the other way. He was walking around the side of the house before the big man noticed, and by the time CT shifted gears, Nick had gone into the backyard.

"Hey!" CT called out. "Wait up!"

Nick kept moving until CT grabbed him by the shoulder. The big man cast a fearful glance back at the house, then back to Nick.

"Just what do you think you're doin'?" he demanded in a hoarse whisper. "You wanna get shot?"

Nick pulled away. "I'm going to see Dooley. It's what we came here for, isn't it?"

"Nicky, come *on*, man! Ida said her husband has a shotgun!"

"This is a farm. Of course, he has a shotgun. I'd be surprised if he didn't. Let's go."

When Nick moved forward, CT again looked back toward the house, and then hastily followed. At the end of the yard, a metal gate blocked their way. Nick sprung the latch open, pushed the gate wide, and strode through.

"I'm telling you, Ida is bluffing."

After a second's consideration, CT followed. "All right, man. I'm washin' my hands. But ya do know I went through a whole tour in The Land of the Bad Things without gettin' a scratch on me. If I get blown away now by some crazy farm woman, you're gonna have one H of a time explainin' that to Sarah."

Hearing a shout, they turned.

"Hey, you! Stop!" Ida yelled at them from a back window. "I done told you to get! Don't you be talkin' to Ambrose now, I mean it!" She turned away, her voice growing fainter. "Clyde, don't let 'em, please!"

They could just make out Clyde's response. "Now, Ida, it's all right. I got a feelin' this is how things are s'posed to be workin' out for the boy. Could his life be any worse than it is? Think, woman."

The window slid shut, and they resolutely started moving again.

"Told you we weren't gonna get shot," Nick said.

"I heard you." CT looked dubious. "Good thing we're out of range, anyhow."

They crossed the dirt barnyard to reach the back fields and began to make their way through brush and hip-high weeds, finding the grade slowly growing steeper. Thistles, cockleburs, and itchy seeds of various kinds attached themselves to their pants and socks, and to top it off chiggers, big ones by the feel of them, had discovered their legs.

"Yowch!" CT slapped at himself. "Man, I hate bugs!"

"Hey, remember that bug repellent battalion sent to us that one time? That nasty-smelling stuff? HQ said it was supposed to be some kind of miracle formula."

CT smiled now in spite of himself. "It was lousy. The bugs liked it, though. They musta thought it was some kinda bug salad dressin'."

Nick laughed. "And do you remember what Mad Jack said? That it must be more effective in the dark? So that night the four of us smeared it on right before lights out—"

"And five minutes later we were all jumpin' around and scratchin' like crazy!" CT hooted. "Dooley was the funniest one! He was flappin' his arms like a bird and wigglin' his butt—"

"Like some kid doing the latest number on *American Bandstand!* I thought I'd bust a gut!"

CT howled, "And then you started singin' 'La Cucaracha.' The more you sang, the madder Dooley got!"

They crested the hill and looked down. The laughter died in their throats.

A hundred yards away a slight figure bent under the open hood of a tractor, peering inside. It was hard for them to make out any details, but from the man's small size, it had to be Dooley. He was wearing faded overalls, and a battered straw hat covered his head.

They glanced at each other, and then started down the hill.

"You think it's him?" CT whispered.

"Has to be."

As they drew closer, Nick thought it odd that they couldn't make out any details of the man's face yet. They were ten feet away when they stopped.

He had finished with whatever he was looking at. Slamming the hood closed, he took off his hat and waved away some flies with it.

He must have seen them then out of the corner of his eye. He whipped around, then just stood there, staring.

Nick gulped back his shock. He now saw why it had been so hard to make out any facial details.

This man had no face.

His entire hairless head appeared to be nothing more than a mass of puckered red scars. He had no ears to speak of. Where his nose should have been were instead two slits, garnished with a nub of flesh gathered at the top. His lips were gone, his mouth only a slash. Hanging from the ends of his shirt-sleeves protruded two twisted flippers, all that was left of his hands after his fingers had melted together.

The man regarded them with dull, reddened eyes. "You from the gov'-ment?"

His voice was a rasp, the result of inhaling flames, Nick guessed. The man waited, watching them. CT's mouth hung open, but absolutely nothing came out.

Nick finally found his own voice. "Uh, Dooley?" He took a step forward. "It's me. Nick Castle."

There was a second of incredulity, then the man came to life with a gasp.

"Oh my God! *Nick!*" He pulled his hat over his face. "What're you *doin'* here? *Don't look at me!*"

The man—Dooley—turned and ran the few steps over to his tractor, trying to see through his hat as he did. He scrambled up onto the seat but didn't start the motor. He just sat there with his hat still on his face, breathing heavily.

"Hey, Dooley," CT said gently. "It's me, CT. How ya doin'? Nick and me just wanted to—"

"Get away!" Dooley screamed at the top of his lungs, nearly incoherent. "For God's sake, have some pity, guys. Don't look—I don't even have my hood on that Ma made me. I don't want you here—leave me alone. Please, oh God, don't look, please, please!" His narrow shoulders shook with grief and shame.

"Listen, Dooley," Nick said softly. "It's all right if you want to keep your hat over your face, but CT and I have something we need to say."

"Just go away," came the muffled reply.

"Come on, man," CT said. "We've come a long way to tell you this. Climb down from there, will ya?"

Dooley hesitated another moment, then with a groan he did as CT asked. But he still kept his hat where it was.

Nick had been praying for guidance for this moment, for the right words. Of all the men they'd ministered to, he'd dreaded this meeting the most. But he decided that since candor had worked with the others, it would here too. It had to.

"Dooley, I'm sorry I didn't keep in contact with you after I got back home."

" 'Sall right, Nick." The man's voice sounded dead. "I didn't much expect anybody to. Kinda hoped they wouldn't. I reckoned nobody knew my real name. You and Mr. C. T. Barnes is the only outside people I've spoke to since I got back to this here farm."

"Call me CT," the big man said. "Keeps thing simple."

"All right. Don't matter none to me."

Nick asked, "Your mom said you listen to the radio and watch TV a lot, right?"

"Ma says a lotta things," Dooley muttered. "More'n I can listen to."

Nick smiled at that. "So I guess you heard about the message from God that people got this past Tuesday night?"

Dooley didn't answer. When he did, his words were clipped and muffled. "Radio an' TV says a bunch'a stuff, too. You goin' somewheres with this?"

"Yeah." Nick shook his head. "I changed my mind from what I said before. If we're going to talk, get that hat off your face."

"No way."

"I want to look you in the eye and say this."

"You'll see more'n you'll ever want," Dooley warned. "Guaranteed. I'm a-tellin' you."

"We've already seen it. You weren't quick enough on the draw with your hat."

"You ever see *House of Wax?*"

The apparent non sequitur threw Nick for a second before he could mentally switch gears. The pain in his friend's tortured voice was raw, but Nick knew that what was needed here was grace, not sympathy.

Dooley's tone dripped with self-derision. "You know the one I mean, with Vincent Price?"

"Yes." Nick knew it well.

"I saw it as a kid," Dooley said, "me and Bobby Rymer. Skeered the whiz outta me, tell you that. But the part at the end, when Vincent Price's mask gets knocked off was the worst. People screamin' all over the theater, women cryin' . . . wild."

Nick didn't reply, letting Dooley get this out at his own pace.

"Anyways, after the movie is over me and Bobby're havin' some ice cream at Spoonamore's, and Bobby says, 'Man, I would not want to end up with a face like that, scarin' babies and such, and people runnin' away.' And I says, 'Me neither. I'd rather be dead.' Well—" Dooley suddenly flung his hat away. "Just call me Vincent!"

He took several limping steps toward them, wagging his flipper-like hands on either side of his face until his ghastly, red-eyed visage was only inches away. "Skeered yet? I'm gonna kill ya!"

Nick just looked at him. "Are you done?"

"Come on!" Dooley howled, dropping his hands. "Hollywood people'd pay big bucks to have me in their monster movies. What a face! And I work cheap too! No makeup needed!" He spat to the side, vintage Dooley. "Ask Ma all about it, how it is with her. Forty years later, and she still cain't look at me."

"Listen—" CT started to say, but their friend charged on, heedless.

"She made me this here hood, see, and I have to wear it all the time around her. Pa don't seem to mind as much. Soon's we're out of sight of the house, he has me pull it off so's I can work easier and not pass out. I cain't sweat no more, see, and . . . " Dooley sighed. "Nick, what the heck are you and CT doin' here, anyway?"

"Getting you healed and right with God."

There was a pause, and then"What?"

"I'm not sure if you know this," Nick said, "but I got hit on that last mission too."

"No, I didn't know."

"Well, I did. It happened right after I tossed your carcass in the slick. Mister Charles darn near blew my head off. While I was laid up in the MASH, CT told me about Jesus, and I accepted him too."

Dooley silently took this in.

"Anyway, Tuesday night we both heard God say he's coming back for his people sometime in the next seven days. The Lord gave us the idea to find certain guys we knew in the war and give them a chance to get straight before that happens."

"You're the last one," CT broke in. "We've already seen Trevor Ames, Mad Jack, and Frankie. And now you."

Dooley stared at them, still not saying anything. When he finally did speak, his words were low and measured.

"Nick, you saved my life, what they is of it, that's true. And most days I appreciate what you did." He paused. "Most days. So I reckon I owe you at least a fair hearin'. But man, I gotta say, the whole thing sounds squirrely to me."

"What's squirrely about it?"

"Well . . . maybe that part about comin' to know Jesus is real. I ain't sayin' it is or it ain't, mind. And maybe, *maybe* God can heal people." Dooley shook his head again. "Those testimonies I heard on the TV sure got me riled up, tell you that. But . . . "

He held up his hands. "Look at these now. Take a good look. We ain't talkin' about God healin' lumbago or crossed eyes, boys. We're talkin' about me gettin' new skin. All over. And a nose. And ears. And some fingers. And— ahhh."

He put his hands down, his voice hollow with defeat. "They ain't no hope, Nick. I know it, and so do you. So why don't you and CT get on outta here, and lemme fix this here tractor?"

With a sigh he limped over and picked up his old hat. Placing it on his head, he turned and walked away.

CT looked sick. "We can't just let him go, man."

"I don't—wait a minute. Come on." Nick trotted after Dooley, CT right behind.

Their friend once again had the tractor's hood up. His hand was deep inside the thing's guts, evidently trying to turn something.

"Need some help?" Nick called out.

Dooley twisted around. "Thought I told y'all to get." He turned back and again grunted with the effort of trying to free whatever he had hold of.

"I just thought we'd give you a hand before we leave. CT knows all about tractors."

"I do?" CT's eyebrows went up. "Uh, that is, yeah, Nick's right, I do. Me and tractors are good friends." He shot Nick a look as if to say, *What are you doin' to me here, slick?*

"Sure," Nick said expansively. "You remember it from Nam. Just give CT a manual and some tools and he can fix anything."

"We ain't . . . got . . . a manual," Dooley grunted again. "I cain't hardly get a grip with these here useless hands."

"No manual?" Nick faked surprise. "Well, a manual would sure be helpful." His tone grew light. "Yeah, you know what they say. With the manufacturer's handbook and the right parts, anything can be rebuilt good as new."

Dooley stopped what he was doing. "We talkin' about tractors or some-thin' else?"

"You know what we're talking about," Nick answered, all frivolity gone now. "God made you, Dooley. The Bible says he knows our parts, that he knew us even before we were born." He placed his hand on Dooley's shoulder. "Those things you've been seeing on the news are true. It's happening all around the world, in cities and at sea and on farms, just like this one." He put his other hand on top of the first. "This game's about up, man. Last call. God loves you. He wants to heal you and save you from hell. Will you let him?"

Dooley didn't answer.

"Come on, what have you got to lose?" CT pleaded as he lifted one of Dooley's hands. "Only this, man. This. And the pain in your heart."

Dooley was quiet for a moment, his look haunted. Finally he said, "You know what I wish? I wish I could cry. I try, but I cain't. The fire, somethin' . . . my eyeballs got burnt. I ain't had no tears for forty years."

"You'll cry today, Dooley," Nick promised. "Can we pray?"

Dooley swallowed hard. "But . . . that is . . . what I mean to say. . . ." They could barely hear his next words, they were said so softly. "What if it don't work?" He shook his head, staring at the ground. "I don't think I could bear it."

"You let God handle that." Nick gently squeezed the smaller man's shoul-ders again. "You ready?"

Dooley didn't reply. Then he gulped once, his body tense. "Oh, I reckon. Let's get it done."

Nick smiled to himself: Colonel Rugg's very words. He began to close his eyes, but then decided, no, he wanted to see this. CT must have agreed. His gaze was fixed on their friend.

"Father God." Nick's voice was clear and carrying as he looked up into the bright blue mid-September sky. And as he prayed, he found his eyes filling with tears. Somehow, he wasn't sure how, he suddenly knew the pain Dooley had known and lived with for all those years.

"Oh God," he wept, "give Dooley his face back. And his fingers and his hands and anything else . . . Oh God, I don't know even know how to—just have mercy. In Jesus' name, amen."

The words seemed to hang . . . and then there was the oddest sound, like someone rubbing a balloon with his hands. Dooley gasped, looking down.

Very quietly and without a fuss, his skin was falling off.

CT clenched his fists, speechless as he stared. Nick took a step back.

"Do you see that?" he croaked, pointing. "God almighty, take a look at *that*."

Because they now realized it wasn't Dooley's skin sloughing away. It was his scars.

And he whimpered as they fell. He wasn't ready for this, not ready. He was seeing pieces of himself, pieces he'd lived with and endured for forty years, falling dead on the ground, and he didn't know what to do.

"Jesus, help me!" he moaned. The rubbing, stretching sound continued, and suddenly he held out his melted hands. "Pull! For God's sake, *pull!*"

Nick and CT each grabbed a hand and did just that. And with the wet sound of tearing paper, the wrinkled red scar tissue peeled off like work gloves, revealing normal fingers and hands.

"Oh, God!" Dooley held them up before his face in wonderment, wiggling them. Then with a grunt he slammed them on top of his head, new fingers digging in. He gave a mighty yank. With more wet sounds the skin on his head split and peeled, dropping away.

Revealing something underneath.

Nick could now barely process what he was seeing. Before his eyes he was viewing an incredible thing: a scar-free, tow-headed, freckled, fifty-six-year-old, normal Dooley face—ears, eyes, nose, lips, and all—grinning back at him. Through tears of his own.

That was too much for CT, and with a massive thud he fainted away. Nick simply dropped to his knees, face to the ground as he poured out his thanks-giving to God.

And as he did, Dooley began running around the field in circles, around and around and around, whooping with joy.

He was quite a ways off when Nick finally roused himself. He looked over at CT. The big man was still out cold, and Nick got up.

On shaky legs, he stalked over to the tractor. Yep, just as he thought. Lying on the ground in the shade was a canteen. He picked it up and went to stand over his friend. Unscrewing the cap, he upended the contents on CT's head.

Spluttering and coughing, the big man jumped to his feet, balling up both fists. "Hey, what the—!"

"Easy, man. You back among the living?"

"I was almost among the drowned," CT growled, dripping. "So where did Dooley go?"

Nick pointed. "Thataway."

Off in the distance, merely a speck now, their friend was running and doing cartwheels. They could just barely make out his laughter.

"God did it again, man! Wonder how long Dooley's gonna keep that up?"

"Not long, I hope. The job's only half done."

They waited, and in a few more minutes Dooley came walking back across the field, fastening the bib on his overalls as he came. His limp had disappeared, and he was drenched with sweat.

"Wooo-eee!" he yelled. "I bet I smell ripe! Over forty years of sweat all comin' out at once! And I'm sorry I took so long, but I went over beyond the ridge and took my clothes off and shook out all that dead skin. My, but they was a sight of it!" His smile slowly faded. "I bet there's more to this, ain't there?"

CT nodded. "God's taken care of your outside, Dooley, but now you gotta let him do his work on the inside."

Dooley thought on this for a second. "Seems only fair. Guess if one part of the Bible is true, it just makes sense it's all true. Ain't that right?"

"That's exactly right," Nick agreed. "Are you ready?"

"Yep." Without another word their friend dropped to his knees on the tromped-down grass and folded his hands under his chin, his eyes shut tight.

Nick and CT grinned at each other as they sank to their knees on either side of him.

"Just repeat after me," Nick said. "Father . . . "

.. .. ..

CLYDE RYAN PULLED HIS GLASSES OFF and laid his *Stockman's Weekly* in his lap. "Ida. You hear somethin'?"

"What?" She laid her knitting aside.

"I said I'm hearin' somethin'. Singin', like . . . "

Ida picked her needles back up. She was making Ambrose another hood, a blue one. Winter was coming, and his old knit one had worn plumb out. The needles clacked as she worked.

"Old fool. You're always hearin' things these days. Best be callin' Doctor Beetoe for a checkup."

"Woman, I am not makin' this up!" Clyde jumped up and strode over to the window. He pulled the curtain back and peered out. "I tell you there's singin' comin' from the back pasture."

"Ohhh!" With a disgusted shake of her head, Ida put her work down again and joined her husband. "I don't—oh."

They both could hear it now. And see it as well.

Ida Ryan put a hand over her mouth. Clyde's eyes bulged. "Oh . . . my . . . God."

For the old farmer and his wife were seeing themselves a sight, yes they were.

Coming over the crest of the hill loped those two strangers—Nick and CT they'd called themselves—walking three abreast along with . . . *Ambrose?* No. No, it couldn't be.

Because this was a *different* Ambrose coming their way, a *fine* Ambrose, a healed, whole, completely *normal* Ambrose, freckle-faced grin and all.

His parents stared at each other. How in the world?

And to add a final, surrealistic fillip to the incredible scene was the fact that all three men were flapping their arms as they came, wiggling their backsides, laughing like lunatics and singing.

"La Cucaracha."

CHAPTER 54

REVEREND JASPER SIGHED as he surveyed the interior of his church. Only room for eighty chairs, and that was going some. The problem was, last night's service had seen nearly sixty worshipers, with many more expected tonight, so earlier today he'd entreated the manager of a strip bar down the block to donate twenty of his more dilapidated chairs.

At first the man laughed, but then he relented and told Jasper to help himself to whatever he wanted in the storeroom. He'd also told him to be sure to put in a good word for him with "the Man upstairs."

Eagerly agreeing, Jasper had carried those chairs two at a time back to the church and arranged them all as best he could. He stepped back and shook his head. Eighty chairs was a mighty tight fit. He sure hoped the fire marshall didn't surprise them tonight.

He was in the process of moving them around for the twelfth time when a shadow darkened the doorway. He turned.

It was Frankie.

"Yo, Reverend!" he bellowed cheerfully. "Guess who's back?"

Jasper walked over and wrung Frankie's hand in welcome. "Brother Malone! This is a surprise!"

Frankie grinned. "Ain't it? Bet ya thought the next time ya'd see me was in heaven, huh?"

"Yes, indeed." Jasper regarded him with a puzzled expression. "I don't mean to appear rude, but didn't I hear your friends say they were taking you to the airport this morning to put you on a flight to Seattle?"

"Ya sure did, Reverend." Frankie's smile faded. "But I couldn't go through with it. I had a taxi bring me home."

"Why?"

"Well, they dropped me off at the terminal, all right, after they'd already called ahead and bought my ticket. Then they said they had to head on over ta catch their flight to Kentucky. But after they left, I had some time ta kill. And ta think."

"What did you think about?"

Frankie raised his chin in defiance. "I realized I'm not a runner, Reverend. Never have been. This is my home. This street. The old grocery store. Mondello's pool hall. Even that stinkin' garage where I live. Anybody I've ever known has lived here at one time or another. And that includes you. So I decided I'm not gonna go lookin' for trouble, but if Frinessi wants me, he'll know where ta find me." He tightened his fists and gave a dark and dangerous smile. "Maybe I'll surprise the guy. Give him a thrill. Maybe I'll use my brand-new feet ta stomp his lousy, loan-sharkin' guts out."

"Brother Malone!"

"Just a joke, Reverend." Frankie paused. "I think. But you can rest easy. I won't bring any trouble here. I just wanted ta stop by and say hello and ta tell ya I'm back." He turned to go.

"Frankie?" Reverend Jasper's use of his first name caused him to stop and turn around. "Your troubles are ours, brother, whatever they may be. Let's face them as they come, together, shall we?"

Frankie looked hard at him. "Ya mean that? Don't be messin' with me, now."

"I'm not. I do mean it." Jasper's eyes twinkled with merriment, even as his tone became brisk. "So. Service starts in two hours, and I still haven't figured out how to arrange these chairs so people won't be tripping over each other's feet. Do you have any ideas?"

With a nod and a grin Frankie picked up a chair. "Let's try 'em this way."

.. .. ..

"I AM PLEADING WITH YOU PEOPLE." Colonel Rugg's voice was harsh and raspy. "Time as we've known it is over. Jesus Christ may return any second."

He licked his dry lips, suddenly feeling lightheaded. Only allowing for short bathroom breaks and to take sips of water, Rugg had been preaching from his porch for over twenty-four hours straight.

He gazed at the crowd on the lawn, mentally counting them. Nearly seventy. The pattern hadn't varied: Rugg would preach, his booming voice carrying for blocks, until a crowd of several dozen of the curious, the smirking, and the profane gathered on his lawn. He would then lead as many as were stirred by the old words into a profession of faith in Jesus.

After that Patrice would take the new believers around the back of the house to their old, above-ground swimming pool, where she'd baptize them and give each of them a Bible some local churches had provided, after first taking their names for follow-up from those same churches.

Meanwhile, on their front porch, her husband would start preaching again.

But now Rugg suddenly stopped speaking. Narrowing his eyes, he watched in disapproval as a TV news truck carelessly pulled up in front of their house, two of its wheels coming right up on the lawn.

Earlier today it had been a radio newsman, and now TV. He didn't expect any better treatment from this bunch of yahoos than he'd gotten earlier.

A young woman, dressed to the nines and coiffed within an inch of her life, got out of the truck. She strode up to Rugg, smiling at him in a pretty, plastic way, a bored cameraman wearily following in her wake.

"Okay, Freddie, roll tape," she muttered, then her voice grew louder. "Mr. Rugg? I'm Leah Delvecchio, TV3 news. May I have a moment?"

"No." He began preaching again, right where he'd stopped.

That threw her. Leah had been told that all these nuts that had been popping up like crazy wheat for the past few days loved publicity. Camera hounds. So what was with this guy?

"I beg your pardon?"

Rugg stopped his sermon again. "Were you born rude, miss, or did you have to work at it?"

Leah blinked rapidly. "Mr. Rugg, I—"

"First off, the name is *Colonel* Rugg. Colonel. Check your records. You'll find I'm still carried on the Army reserves roster, though I have no idea why. Second, I'm right in the middle of speaking with these people. So until I'm finished, you are just gonna have to sit your pretty self down on the grass and wait until I am by-God done."

Leah reddened, and the cameraman perked up. Nobody talked to his boss that way. Leah Delvecchio was well known as an up and comer in the TV3 organization and, like most twenty-five-year-old news reporters, had her eye on a network slot. She deeply resented having been assigned this fool to interview and hadn't been shy about telling Freddie about it.

She recovered nicely, however, and put together another ersatz smile. "Well, since I *am* on deadline here—"

"Miss, you probably have never spoken truer words."

Leah frowned, going for serious and no nonsense. "Colonel Rugg, I—"

"Are you an investigator, Miss Delvecchio? A searcher? A seeker? A pursuer of truth?"

Chewing his gum furiously, Freddie grinned as he taped. This was great.

Leah's face colored. "Well, yes, I like to think so, colonel, but I'm here to ask you—"

"A great many things, I'm sure," Rugg finished for her. "And maybe we'll talk when I'm done speaking here. But the thing is, since you're an admitted seeker, as are these folks," Rugg motioned to the crowd, who were listening to the exchange in rapt attention, "my advice to you would be to shut your pie hole, make yourself comfortable, and *listen.*"

Leah began to fire off a smart reply, one that would really skewer this old coot, but it died in her throat, unsaid. There was something compelling about this strange old man, compelling beyond the sense of just news. And the reporter inside her intended to find out just what that was.

She found herself simply nodding. "All right. Point taken. I'll listen." She cocked her head. "Tell me a story, Colonel Rugg."

He smiled. "I will. A singlular story. I'll tell you all. Now . . . "

.. .. ..

"ALLY, I HAVEN'T THRASHED YOU since you were twelve, but by all that's holy, you are sorely tempting my good nature." Neville Woodhaven took another pull of his dark Guinness and regarded his brother under lowering brows. It was 10:30 p.m. on this side of the world, and the village pub where they were sitting was packed with curious townsfolk all wanting to see and hear Trevor Ames's testimony. Provided Neville would let him get it said, of course.

Alastair didn't flinch. "Rave all you wish. You know what I'm speaking is true. Simply take a hard look at Trevor, here—"

"I *am* looking!" Neville roared.

The chatter in the old pub dropped several decibels, and most of the patrons seated near the three scooted their chairs a few inches further back. The big constable's temper was legendarily volcanic, and only his younger brother seemed to be able to withstand it. Still and all, even Alastair's luck had to run out sooner or later, and it wouldn't pay to be too close to him when it did.

Neville wagged a disparaging hand in Ames's direction, and the old man heartily wished the floor would open up and swallow him whole. He'd never been one to draw attention to himself, and this evening was turning into a real pip.

"I am looking," Neville said again, "at a fraud." Disgust hissed from his voice like a rusty radiator.

"A fraud?" Alastair raised an eyebrow. "A forty-year practical joke? Trevor Ames feigns madness for four decades just to make a fool of Neville Woodhaven? Are you that far gone in disbelief, then?" He raised his voice. "Are any of you? Come now! What you are seeing is a living, breathing, walking miracle. Honoria sees it, his own sister. This is a work of God! Who here believes it?"

There was a pause, and then, "I do." The voice was a woman's, faint, from the back of the crowd.

"As do I." A man speaking this time.

"Aye. The same."

"Aye."

"Me also."

The voices were growing, and so was the redness of Neville's countenance.

"Tell us, Trevor!"

"How did this come about?"

"Don't keep it to yourself!"

"Tell us, man!"

Ames's eyes darted from side to side in fear. Then he saw Alastair smiling at him, nodding his encouragement.

"It's all right." The young constable winked. "I think God's primed the pump!"

"Well." Ames licked his lips as he silently whispered a prayer for strength. And then, like a curtain rising, the fear lifted and his vision cleared. In a firm voice, he said, "My story begins in 1972."

With a scowl and a shake of his head, Neville pushed his chair back and stalked out.

.. .. ..

"IN JESUS' NAME, AMEN."

"In Jesus' name, amen." Clyde Ryan reached into the back of his overalls and pulled out a tattered, stained handkerchief. He wiped his tearing eyes and with a mighty honk blew his nose and smiled. "And that's all they is to it?"

Nick patted him on the shoulder. "That's it. Welcome to the family, Mr. Ryan."

"Whew." Clyde sat heavily in his chair.

Dooley bent down and kissed his father on the top of his head. "Way ta go, Pa!"

"I should have done this years ago, years ago. Guess it took me seein' you healed up to bring me around, Ambrose."

CT laughed. "After the way we found you fainted away when we walked in, they almost had to bring me around. I thought you were dead."

"CT doesn't pass out more than twice a day, Mr. Ryan," Nick grinned. "Honest."

"Ahh, mercy." Clyde reached up to pat his son's hand, still seemingly in shock over his appearance. "This is like a dream—"

"Old fool, it's a dream, all right."

All four men turned their heads to look at Ida, seated on the sofa across the room. She glared at them as if she were spoiling for a fight, a mad light gleaming in her eyes.

Nick bit off a sharp reply. Things had gotten mighty strange in this house. He and CT and Dooley had come in here not twenty minutes ago, expecting hugs and kisses and tears of joy. What they found instead was Clyde Ryan unconcious from shock and his wife bent over him, fanning him with his *Stockman's Weekly*.

She'd looked up, frowning. Nick was forming words of greeting when she'd pointed at Dooley with a long, bony finger.

"Ambrose Dooley Ryan!" she spat. "They's company here and you're runnin' around without your hood on! How many times have I told you? Now get upstairs and put it on, and I mean right . . . this . . . minute."

They stared at her, blinking in incomprehension.

Dooley smiled placatingly. "Ma, it's me, Ambrose." He walked toward her with his hands out. "Ambrose!"

"I know who you are!" Ida yelled. "You think I don't know my own son? Now get that hood on like I told you! Mind!"

"But, Ma." Dooley was trying to sound reasonable. "I don't need it no more. I'm all healed up. It was God. He done healed me." He wiggled his fingers at her. "See?"

"Tommyrot!" she screeched. "What sort of nonsense are you spewin', Ambrose? I done told you a million times. No comin' in this house without wearin' your hood. You know the rules. I will not have the neighbors talkin'."

"But I don't need it no more!" Dooley began to cry. "Don't you see? I done been healed! I got all my skin back! And my face! Aren't you happy for me?"

"Tommyrot! Tommyrot!" She put her hands over her ears. "I ain't listenin' to you no more, Ambrose, until you get that there hood on! I mean it! Mind!"

"But Ma—"

Nick and CT had each then put a hand on their friend's shoulder, quieting him. "It's the shock, man," CT said. "We all saw it in Nam. Just give her some time, okay?"

"Well . . . okay." Dooley seemed uncertain. He turned to his father, who was still out on the floor. "Let's get Pa up."

They brought Clyde around with cold cloths on his head. When he'd opened his eyes and looked upon his son, they thought he might conk out on them again, but to their surprise Clyde merely placed a hand tenderly on Dooley's cheek.

With tears coursing down his wrinkled face, he whispered, "It's a miracle, a blessed miracle. I been prayin' for this for purt' near forty years."

Nick explained what had happened to Dooley out in the pasture and how God had obviously restored everything that had been taken from his son. Nick then asked Clyde if he'd like to know the joy of sins forgiven too. The old man answered yes. And now . . .

"I said, it's a dream." Ida folded her arms so tightly across her body Nick thought she might cut off her own breathing. "It ain't real." She pointed her chin at him. "I gave you a chance to leave before. Now I want you and your friend out of here."

CT took a step toward her. "Good grief, lady, don't you believe your own—"

"Hold it." Nick stopped him, gripping CT's arm. "Look."

Ida, arms still clenched and staring straight ahead, had now begun rocking, back and forth, muttering.

The two men exchanged looks, and Dooley and Clyde jumped to their feet.

"Ida?" Fear filled the old farmer's voice as he took his wife's hand. But his touch didn't help. She kept up her strange movement.

"Guys?" Dooley sounded frightened. "What's the matter with Ma?"

"It's her mind," Nick said softly. "She's had control of you for almost forty years. For some reason, this has sent her around the bend."

"Well, cain't you help her?" Dooley's eyes were wild. "You did with Mad Jack and Mister Ames. You told me so on the way back here."

"That was different," CT replied. "Those guys had somethin' awful happen to them. But your mom's been sowin' seeds of bitterness and resentment and manipulation for a long time. I think today the crop's come up."

"But. . . " Dooley turned anguished eyes toward his parents. Clyde Ryan was speaking soothing words to his wife and patting her hand. Dooley's voice sank to a ragged whisper. "They ain't no hope?"

"I don't know," Nick said. "The Bible says you reap what you sow."

Ida stopped for a second, looking at them, squinting her eyes. "I won't have this in my house, I say. Stuff and nonsense is all it is." She began to rock mindlessly again.

"You and your dad keep praying for her," Nick said. "I wish I could say something more comforting, but that's it."

Clyde looked up at them, eyes glistening. "Ida weren't always mean and hateful, you know." He glanced over at his son. "Ambrose remembers, don't you, boy?"

Dooley nodded.

Clyde began stroking his wife's hair. "When we was first married, Ida was the sweetest thing. But after Ambrose got . . . burnt . . . she started changin'. Day after day, gettin' meaner and bossier, always afraid the neighbors was gonna see him, like what happened was somethin' shameful. Day after day, growin' from worse to worse." The old man swallowed. "Them seeds you boys was talkin' about, I guess they done put down some deep roots, didn't they?"

"Mr. Ryan—" Nick began, but Clyde cut him off.

"It's all right," he said. "I knew this day was comin'. A person don't pickle themselves every day in hate and resentment and foolish pride without some-day the brine killin' 'em, and—oh, Ida."

He buried his face in her lap and wept for the lost years. Ida now began to mutter curses mixed in with her moaning.

Nick leaned over, whispering in Dooley's ear. "Keep them lifted in prayer. Maybe . . . just keep praying. CT and I and the rest of our church will do the same."

The two men embraced their old comrade one last time and made their way out the door. "See you soon, man," Nick said as he started down the porch steps.

CT hung back and turned. "Do your folks have a home church they attend?"

Dooley shook his head.

"Well, find one. One that preaches the Bible. And you and your daddy put her in the car and get her there. Now!"

CHAPTER 55

NICK GLANCED AT THE CLOCK on the GCC foyer wall as he and CT hurried in. Eight o'clock, straight up. They'd mashed the gas to get here, thankfully finding that they'd only missed some of the opening music. The place was absolutely jammed, including the parking lot. They'd had to park Nick's Lexus nearly a half-mile down the road, on the shoulder.

As they trotted into the sanctuary, they found everyone standing in worship. The noise level was incredible.

"You see our wives?" CT yelled in Nick's ear.

"Not yet!" Nick shouted back. "When we phoned them from the doughnut shop before we started back I asked them to hold us two seats. With this mob that may have been tough to do." He looked and pointed. "There they are. See 'em? Left center, about five rows from the front. Looks like they've got the kids with 'em, too."

Making their way to their families, they were happy to see that their wives had managed to hold two seats open by laying Bibles on them. They scooted in beside the two women and gave Maryann and Sarah, respectively, long, lingering kisses, then hugged and kissed their kids as well. Earlier on the phone they'd told their families the bittersweet news about Dooley and his parents, so there wasn't any need for further explanations. Both men were just heartily glad to be home.

When the last song ended, Pastor Wasson asked the congregation to be seated. He signaled to the media crew up in the top level of the balcony, and a second later the big screen above the choir loft began to lower.

"Folks, it's almost 9 o'clock," he said, "but don't worry; we're not nearly done yet. As most of you know, President Harcourt is going to be addressing the nation tonight. We're patching it in here. Now . . . " He nodded at the media crew again, and the lights dimmed.

"Many of you've heard reports these past few weeks about the president's supposed conversion to Christianity. From the man himself, though, we've heard nothing. Maybe tonight those questions will be answered. Maybe not.

But whether or not he identifies himself as a brother in the Lord, keep him and all our leaders in your prayers as these final hours wind down."

Suddenly the screen flickered. The great seal of the United States appeared. The pastor ducked out of the way and found his seat on the platform.

"Ladies and gentlemen," intoned a disembodied voice from a speaker mounted above the screen, "the President of the United States." The seal disappeared, replaced by a shot of the president seated behind his desk in the Oval Office.

"Good evening, my fellow Americans."

From the tired way President Everett Harcourt said those opening words and from his unusual clothes, everyone viewing tonight knew this wasn't going to be an ordinary address. Rather than sporting his customary navy pinstripe suit, he instead wore an open-neck, blue denim workshirt. He'd also forgone the usual TV makeup. The acne scars deeply cratering his face were plainly visible, and although dark circles colored the skin under his eyes, the eyes themselves were clear and his smile seemed genuine.

"This isn't going to take long," he said. "I know many of you are piping this signal into your churches this evening and, contrary to popular opinion, I've never been one to try to compete with God."

Harcourt's smile faded. "Tonight I'm going against every piece of political advice I've ever been given, including advice from my own wife, who's helped guide me these past three years. The words I'm about to say are the hardest I've ever had to utter, but I'll say them plainly. Many of my predecessors had the unfortunate habit of trying to weasel out of uncomfortable situations by using misleading speech. This I will not do."

He cleared his throat. "Tonight, at the conclusion of this address, I will make my way to the chambers of Congress, where I've called an emergency joint session of both the House and the Senate. They're watching this as well, and none of them has obtained an advance copy of my remarks, as is customary. There, upon my arrival, I will tender my resignation as president of the United States."

Harcourt paused as though giving time for what must surely be baffled and disbelieving reactions to richocet back and forth across America and around the world. Inside the GCC, thousands of voices chattered excitedly. Nick, CT, and their families looked at each other in amazement. Nobody had expected this. Finally the president again began to speak, and a stunned silence descended on the GCC.

"The reason for this decision is as simple as it is gut-wrenching. Three years ago, I was elected president of all of the people of this country. And, until recently, I thought I'd done a pretty good job. I tried to prefer no creed or lifestyle above another, thinking all truth was relative. I believed man was the final arbiter of his destiny on this planet.

"Tonight I say publicly, and with deep regret, that I was wrong. The twin mindsets of relativism and humanism that guided my thinking my entire life have been obliterated. Six weeks ago, through the ongoing prayers of millions of you—and, to be honest, much to the chagrin of my wife and my staff—I turned off that path and onto another when I gave my heart and life to Jesus Christ."

The church exploded again, this time in cheers and tumults of praise.

"Normally," Harcourt continued, "it would present no problem for a president who took this step of faith to continue in office. Indeed, in times past, a president's Christianity was considered an asset to the office rather than a liability. Sadly, those days are gone. What we used to jokingly refer to as political correctness has turned into the *de facto* law of the land, and more, George Orwell's Thought Police have gone from fiction to reality. In the name of open-mindedness and fairness and tolerance, our society—our very world—has slowly and surely turned from common sense and sanity and started its long, destructive march toward the vilest sort of self-gratification. Until recently, I had no problem with that turning. In point of fact, I embraced it. And then . . . my life was changed."

The president's smile was disarming. "Some would say it was a change for the worse. I disagree. These past few weeks have been at once the most joyful and the most difficult of my life."

Harcourt leaned forward slightly, pain etched deeply in the lines of his face. "Before I continue, however, I need to address certain rumors you may have heard. Let me say this plainly: The rumors are true. First, my dear wife Millicent has today filed for separation, citing irreconcilable differences. The agony this has caused us is indescribable." Harcourt's voice caught. "Please keep us in your prayers. Millie is, and always has been, not only my wife but my best friend.

"Second, my chief of staff, Stan Rolfe, has insisted that I check into a sanitarium for observation, citing grave concerns about my mental well-being. Unfortunately for Stan, I'm not going to do it." The president's smile now seemed sad and tight. "Sorry, old buddy.

"Third, the rest of my staff is in nearly open revolt. They are justly concerned that if my presidency falls, so do their jobs. They may be right. Worst of all, in the name of political expedience and to protect my faltering poll numbers, I confess that I hesitated to let my new life be made known publicly. It's amazing. I was willing to let the possibility of losing my job take preference over acknowledging my Lord. Many nights I lay awake, wrestling mightily with when and how I'd finally make known to the world this step of faith I've taken and how to protect myself politically. And had things remained as they were, I might have been able to put off that confession indefinitely."

Harcourt folded his hands on his desk, again leaning slightly forward in his chair. "I no longer have that option. The events of last Tuesday night have changed everything. I'm resigning as your president because, simply put, in less than seventy-two hours I, along with millions of other Christian believers worldwide, will be gone."

More cheers broke out in the church. Pastor Wasson had to hush the congregation so the rest of the president's speech could be heard.

Harcourt continued, "Why resign? many of you may ask. Again, the answer is simple. Should I be mistaken about our homegoing and Wednesday morning arrives with us all still here, then obviously my effectiveness as a leader would be lost, as well it should be. But should the prophecy be correct and we are gone, it would be grossly unfair to leave Vice President Caprill with the daunting task of calming a frightened populace and assuming the duties of the chief executive at the same time."

His voice even, the president added, "Of course, I like Bob Caprill a lot and would vastly prefer that he come with us. But Bob made known to me in private his vehement disagreement with my conversion—which is his right. He suggested that I take this step. After prayerful consideration, I concurred. So then . . . "

Harcourt reached up to adjust the knot in his tie, a nervous mannerism he was well known for, but stopped with his hand halfway to his throat. "Forgot I have my weekend clothes on." He smiled, then sobered.

"Many years ago Theodore Roosevelt described the office of the president as a 'bully pulpit,' a platform for expressing ideas near and dear to a president's heart, ideas as far ranging as the reasons for going to war or the neccessity of putting a man on the moon or why welfare reform was needed. Strong ideas. Important ideas. Ideas worthy of perusal and discussion. So I will use this pulpit and the remaining moments I have as your president to plead with those of you listening to me worldwide to hear and consider this idea. The idea that in this vast cosmos you have worth, worth not only to your fellow man, but worth to the God who created you. The God who breathed life into you. The God who knows your faults and loves you still.

"I would implore each of you to take a long, critical look into your hearts, as I did. To regard the sin found there as a hateful thing, as I did. To realize you've completely and utterly lost your way, as I did. And to seek the free gift of God's forgiveness and your way back to the life you were created to live, through his son, Jesus Christ, as I did."

The president's voice roughened, and he rapidly blinked back tears. "That's it. That's all I have. God bless you all in Jesus' name."

The screen faded and went dark.

CHAPTER 56

AT THE SAME TIME the president was holding the folks at GCC in thrall with his words, a meeting of quite another kind was taking place not two miles from the church.

"This blueprint shows all the exits," Crandall said, pointing out each of them with a stubby yellow pencil. It was a little hard to see by the fluttering candlelight in the old mill, but Sangre had insisted on candles. "There's three main double doors leadin' into the building from the parkin' lots here, here, and here."

Crandall used the point of the pencil to scratch an itch on his head before continuing. "Once we're inside, we cross the foyer here, and then there's seven doors goin' into the main sanctuary." He straightened. "So twelve of us can secure the place, easy."

Sangre frowned. "How do you figure that?"

Crandall immensely enjoyed having Sangre ask him some questions for a change. Being a sheriff's deputy had made it child's play to steal these documents from the county recorder's office. Crandall had keys to almost everything at city hall.

"Take a look," he replied, again bending over the blueprint. "See, the doors into the sanctuary go double, single, single, double, single, single, double. Get it?"

"No," Sangre snapped. "You're about as clear as mud."

"Okay, here's what I mean. Even though most of the doors are doubles, it'll still only take one of us to guard each of them. Seven doors, seven guards. Plus the balcony only has stairs at both ends, so two of us can secure that whole thing."

"So?" said one of the others.

"So the way I see it, we all saunter in like poor old sinners, then when Sangre gives the word, seven of us take the doors. Two of us take the balcony. One of us, I guess you, Sangre, heads for the nursery. That still leaves two of us for whatever. See?"

"Seems easy enough," Nightshade remarked.

"I agree," Jace chimed in. "As long as we all look to Sangre for our cues, I don't see how we can go wrong."

This remark pleased Sangre to no end.

"So twelve of us can really hold off thousands?" Charon mused.

"Yeah," Crandall assured them. "It'll be a snap because this state still hasn't done much with concealed carry. I'd be willing to bet none of those guys'll be armed." He went on with a snicker, "Closest thing to a weapon those holy rollers'll be carryin' is a Bible."

They all laughed, even Sangre.

Crandall smiled, savoring the limelight. "If our raid was happenin' some-place other than here, this deal would be a lot tougher. Half those good old Christian people might be carryin' who-knows-what in shoulder rigs or purses, and we'd have to come up with a whole different plan. But here?" He shook his head. "It'll be a duck shoot."

"Speaking of weapons," Sangre jumped in, eager to draw their attention back to him, where it belonged, "I think it's time we passed them out and familiarized ourselves with them."

The others readily agreed. Sangre motioned for Crandall to get them out of the crate.

The deputy did and laid them on the desk by twos. Sangre chose one of the MAC-10 machine pistols as his own. Crandall, of course, kept the Desert Eagle .50 for himself, as he'd promised, leaving the rest of the group to claim the remaining weapons. Not surprisingly, the women chose the .38 caliber revolvers, leaving the remaining MAC-10s to the men.

Crandall took the next twenty minutes to show them all how their guns worked, dry firing them repeatedly, even though he hated doing that. Dry firing weapons was really hard on them, but there was no way he was trusting these greenies with live ammo until they had gotten more familiar with their pieces.

Finally satisfied, he handed speed-loaders to the women for their revolvers and two 32-round magazines apiece to the men for their MAC-10s, showing both groups how to load their guns. They were all disappointed that they couldn't fire them but understood that the noise would be horrendous and might draw attention, even clear out there at the mill.

When they were done, Sangre gathered everyone around him. "You've done well, my friends. We've done well. I think the Dark One is pleased with us . . . even though we weren't able to secure another sacrificial animal." This was directed at Crandall, who took the rebuke stoically.

"At any rate, the hour is upon us at last." Sangre drew himself up to his full height. "The time has come for us to show that our deeds more than match our words. Tomorrow night our destinies begin."

This led to excited grins and chattering. Sangre held up a hand for quiet.

"I've always believed a simple plan is a foolproof plan. You're each to go in your own cars, parking wherever you can, while I drive our van. I'll leave it under the tall sycamore tree near the south graveyard entrance across the road from the church. This will be our getaway vehicle." He chuckled at the melodramatic phrase. "At 9:30 we will all meet at the church's center exterior door. As we go in, I'll immediately make my way to the nursery to secure a baby for the sacrifice. While I'm doing that you, Crandall, will lead the others into the main sanctuary. But do it quietly."

Crandall nodded, his chest swelling with pride. A leader!

Sangre went on, "Jace, I want you and Nightshade to make your way to the front of the sanctuary, also quietly. Take your places at each of the front corners."

They nodded their assent.

"Crandall, you and the others will secure the foyer doors. Nobody is to make a move until I come in. When I enter with the child, the fun starts. We'll allow ourselves no more than five minutes for everything, starting with the baby's kidnapping and ending when we've exhausted our ammunition. Upon arriving back here, we'll all partake of the child's blood."

Crandall grinned. He was finally ready to drink.

"Here," Sangre said. "I've made something for you all. Take one of these as well." He handed them each a small bottle containing an amber-colored liquid. Every bottle was stuffed closed with a rag that was left hanging out.

"Molotov cocktails," he explained. "I mentioned them to you earlier. The last thing we'll do on our way back out of the sanctuary is to light them and throw them into the crowd. The survivors will already be insane with grief, and the fire will just add to their pain. We'll scatter during the confusion, meet at the van, and drive away." He gazed around at them. "Any questions?"

There were none.

Sangre smiled with pleasure. "Our time has arrived. Tomorrow night the lives of those upright, pious folks at that useless church are forfeit, and we enter a new plane of existence." He looked meaningfully at Charon. "And now, before we disperse to our homes, a prayer of consecration."

Wordlessly, they all began to disrobe.

CHAPTER 57

"MMM, THIS IS NICE." Maryann snuggled closer to Nick, pulling her sweater more tightly around her shoulders. "Don't you think?"

"You bet," he said. "Sure beats the way we used to unwind after a mission, doesn't it, CT?"

"No comparison, bro." The big man leaned over Sarah, picking the pitcher up off the plastic table. "Anybody want more lemonade?"

Nick and Maryann both demurred, and all four went back to their slow swinging. The Barneses' front porch boasted not one, but two wooden swings, and both couples would have been hard-pressed to think of a more pleasant way to end their evening.

It was well after midnight, and they were alone at last. Toby and Tina were in bed, and Tracy and Blake had elected to go with their college and career group to a local pizza place. After tonight's joyous and raucous service, it was enough now to sit on this fine old porch, rocking away, drinking cold lemonade and listening to the crickets and peeper frogs holding court down by the pond.

Maryann broke the silence. "I was online today, going through some of the Christian news services, and was really blessed by some of the things I saw."

"Like what?" Nick asked.

"Well . . ." She leaned forward, set her glass on the floor, then straightened. "Have any of you ever heard of the Tree Church?"

"Tree Church?" That was a new one to Nick. "Is that really its name?"

"Yes. It's in China, somewhere. And it really is a tree, so they say, with a white cross painted on it. People walk for miles every Sunday just to meet under it and have services. Of course, the tree's exact location is kept secret so the believers won't get arrested, but reports say the group meeting there has grown from fifty to over three thousand, with most of those being new converts."

Sarah looked amazed. "And nobody's let on to the authorities where this church is?"

"Not a word." Maryann picked up her glass again, rolling it between her palms. "Isn't that great? All those brand-new Christians, and the police still don't have a clue how to find them." She went on with a grin, "I bet God has angels confusing the government officials to keep them from locating it."

"Well, yeah, he'd have to be." This from CT. "I mean dig it, three thousand people meetin' in the woods for church, and nobody can find 'em? Does the Lord have a great sense of humor or what?"

Nick remarked, "After we get to heaven, it's going to take a long time just to hear all the stories of God's miraculous protection of his people."

"Especially what he's been doin' this past week." CT looked over at his wife. "You never heard any more from those satanists, huh, and their threats against the church?"

Sarah shook her head. "No, haven't heard a thing from them today. Maybe they've given up. Maryann and I were talking about it, and we think the intercessors finally gave them their walking papers."

"Don't be too sure," Nick warned, his tone serious. "I think it'd be a mistake to write these guys off so quickly. If anything, I'd hope the intercessors double their prayers. Before we all get free of this place, I think the devil's got at least a few more stunts he'd like to pull. We'd all be stupid to let our guard down now. Not this close."

The others fell silent as they considered his words.

.. .. ..

THE OLD MILL WAS DARK. The lights were off, the black stubby candles had been extinguished, and the Circle had long since dispersed to their homes. The only illumination penetrating the Stygian gloom was pale, wan moonlight streaming in through the high, dirty windows, landing on the floor and painting it a ghastly white.

In the center of the pentagram, Sangre crouched, naked, humming tunelessly. Using his trusty fillet knife he slowly and with great precision sliced narrow, shallow slits into his left arm, from his shoulder to his wrist, every eighth of an inch.

Periodically he nodded and smiled and licked the blood from the blade.

CHAPTER 58

NICK CRACKED ANOTHER EGG into the skillet. Were two eggs apiece enough? He didn't have a clue. Breakfast had always been Maryann's department, but he'd decided to let her sleep in a bit this morning and try it himself. Their niece and nephew were still sacked out as well, not having rolled in until nearly three.

Truth be told, Nick had toyed with the idea of them all staying home this morning and grabbing some extra family time, but just as quickly tossed that notion. He'd never knowingly played hookey from Sunday church services since he'd become a Christian. He even found a church to attend when he was out of town on business. And since their homegoing was due to occur in less than sixty hours, he felt he would have been an idiot to start now.

About then Maryann shuffled in, rubbing her eyes. She gave Nick a sleepy smile. "Morning, sweets." Coming up behind him, she put her arms around him and nuzzled his back with her chin. "Why don't you let me do that?"

"I've got it, baby. Did I wake you up with my banging? I was doing my best to keep things quiet, but you know how it goes."

"No, I just woke up by myself. Was it you that turned off the alarm?"

"Yeah. I was up at six, as usual, and I thought I'd let everybody get a little extra sleep while I fixed breakfast for us all. Surprised?"

Her grin was wry. "Shocked is more like it. In the thirty years we've been married you've never even made cereal. And from the looks of things . . . "

She peered around the kitchen. The eggs cooling on their plates were brown and crispy, every piece of toast burned black, clotted pancake batter congealed in the bowl, and the coffee viciously bubbling away on the stove had a distinctly scorched odor.

Shaking her head, she looked at her husband. "Nick, how long have you been president of Castle Industries?"

"You know the answer to that. Why?"

She raised one eyebrow and pushed him aside. "Play to your strengths, hon. Go set the table while I toss this mess and start over."

.. .. ..

"WELL, WE GOT HER IN THE CAR, SON." Clyde Ryan wiped the sweat from his brow. "Took some doin', but we done it. Thing is, I'm not so sure that hog-tyin' and gaggin' your Ma was such a good idea. When we cut them ropes, she's liable to try tearin' both our heads off."

Dooley shrugged. "They just wasn't no other way, and you know it. She sure wasn't gonna get in the car by her own self, now was she?"

"Naw, I expect you're right."

Dubiously Clyde considered their work: Ida Ryan was well and truly trussed and gagged. They'd tried placing her as gently as they could in the bed of their old Ford pickup, but she was still mumbling curses at them a blue streak under all that duct tape, and her glare could have taken off barnacles.

"So now what?" he asked his son.

"Well, we take her to church, I guess."

"Yeah, but where?" Clyde looked perplexed. "We ain't been near a church since before you left for the Army."

"Is that place you and Ma took me to as a kid still around?"

"Yeah, why?"

"Because we ain't takin' her there, that's why. That dump was a tomb for folks that didn't know they was dead yet. Lotta high-falutin' dry old crap that didn't mean a spit in the soup, and as for that preacher feller in charge, I could've carved a better man out of a banana." He shook his head in finality. "Nope, we're gonna do like CT said. You and me are gonna get Ma to a church that believes God is still able to help folks like us out."

Clyde rubbed his hands in frustration. "But where are we gonna find a place like that?"

"The rapture's s'posed happen in less'n sixty hours," Dooley replied. "So I guess we find us one with a buncha cars parked outside and a lotta shoutin' inside."

.. .. ..

THE EARLY SERVICE at Reverend Jasper's church had just started when three large white men appeared, filling the doorway as they stared inside.

Deacon Marsh tottered over to greet them. "Mawnin', gentlemen! Welcome to the—"

"Move out of our way," the smallest man said as all three shoved past him. A few steps further in he stopped and gazed around, shaking his head.

"Room full of nearly a hundred black faces," he muttered to his hulking compatriots. "It won't be too hard to find a white one." Then he squared his shoulders and bellowed, *"Excuse me!"*

As one, every person in the room turned around to see who was making all the racket.

"My name is Salvatore Frinessi," the man snarled. "Most of you in here have heard of me. And you've probably heard I'm not big on patience. So I'm going to ask this just once. Have any of you seen Frankie Malone in here today?"

Right about then Frankie, who'd been helping Reverend Jasper fill the communion cups in the back room, sauntered out. His grin was tight as he wiped his hands on a small towel.

"Sal Frinessi, as I live and breathe. I thought I heard somebody dyin' out here, like they was stranglin' on a fish bone. Here I find it's only a poor stupid idiot, talkin' trash in his usual way."

"Malone," Frinessi said, his voice as flat as a hubcap. "So the stories are true. You can walk. I also heard you've become some kind of religious freak. Is that right?"

"Right enough. Ya got a problem with that, Sal?"

"The only problem I have is the one you created. You welshed out on me. You owe me a large. I want it back."

"Well, Sal, it's like I told Stan and Ollie here, yesterday. I ain't got it. Truth is, I drank it up." He shrugged. "Sorry about your luck."

The two men standing on either side of Frinessi had gone as tense as German shepherds. All they needed from their boss was the high sign, and Frankie was toast. Meanwhile the people in the chairs shifted nervously.

"My friend," Frinessi sighed, "you're about to be a lot sorrier." He stared at his henchmen. "Tony, Larry, abuse that fool, and make it hurt." He paused, then added, "A lot."

As the thugs started forward, Frankie held up his hand. "Wait a minute, fellas. If we're gonna dance, let's take it outside. Our business don't involve these people."

"I don't care who it involves," Frinessi said. "All I know is my boys are about to take your teeth out through your eyes." He again looked pointedly at his men. "Well?"

With grim determination they began moving once more toward Frankie.

"Now, see here, please—" Reverend Jasper tried to block their way, but Frinessi's men roughly pushed him aside.

Tony's left hand was already graced with a set of nasty-looking brass knuckles. Larry pulled out a switchblade, springing it open with a deadly sound. They both had sickening smiles on their faces as they came.

Then suddenly those smiles vanished.

They were staring at something past Frankie, something horrifying, something that caused them both to stop and drop their weapons. Yelling incoherently, eyes bulging, feet tangling, and screaming in terror, as one the two turned and tore back through the crowd toward the door.

Frinessi tried to stop them as they ran past. "Hey, what are you—"

And then he saw *them*: two immense men, each at least nine feet tall. The swords they held blazed with an unearthly fire, and they were glaring at Frinessi in a distinctly unfriendly way.

Yelling incoherently, he tried to back up and fell on his rump. Flipping over on his hands and knees, he procceded to set a land speed record crawling toward the church entrance.

Before he could get far, it seemed as if an invisible foot slammed him in the backside, launching him ten feet forward. The contents of his pockets scattered across the floor as he clambered to his feet. With a backward glance and another cry of terror, he rocketed through the door, laughs and cheers following. No one in the congregation had seen anything, but they all knew a miracle had happened to frighten those men like that.

Frankie was still chuckling when an object on the floor caught his eye, something Frinessi had dropped in his haste to exit the church. Bending down, he picked it up with a grin. It was a roll of money, layered with twenties on the outside. Judging from its thickness, if it was twenties all the way through, he had to be holding at least ten thousand dollars.

Frankie held it high. "Hey!" he laughed. "Who else needs ta go ta Detroit?"

·· ·· ··

FREDDIE LEANED OVER, his whisper loud in Leah Delvecchio's ear. "How's he doing it? What's holding him up?"

Leah shook her head in amazement. She had no idea what force sustained the old man. She and Freddie were standing with a crowd of nearly eighty people in this suburban neighborhood front yard on this brisk mid-September morning, listening to Colonel John Taylor Rugg as he moved into his fortieth hour of preaching. The marathon session showed no signs of stopping; in fact, Rugg appeared even stronger than he had the day before.

The previous day Leah and Freddie had fulfilled their end of the bargain they'd made with the colonel, refraining from asking him questions until he'd finished preaching his sermon. In turn, during the five-minute break he'd allowed himself after he was finished, he'd granted Leah the interview she sought.

Strangely enough, at the end of their talk Leah had more questions than ever. It was bizarre. Even though he lacked the long hair and flowing beard of an Old Testament prophet, Rugg seemed, at least to Leah, the personification of one.

When she and Freddie had arrived back at the TV station later that day, Leah had convinced the news director that she wasn't finished with the old man and needed more footage. But in truth, what she craved was more of what Rugg seemed to possess in limitless quantities.

Peace, power, and indominatable purpose.

Now her curiosity was at a fever pitch. That some unearthly force was not only sustaining the man, but also renewing his strength, was never in doubt. The only question remaining was how could she appropriate that force for herself?

As if in response to her unasked request, Rugg looked over at the two reporters. He never broke stride as he preached, but, unbelievably, he winked at them.

Leah felt a strange stirring in her heart. Oh, yeah. Colonel Rugg knew what her question was, all right.

·· ·· ··

ON THE OTHER SIDE OF THE WORLD, it was already Sunday afternoon. Teatime had arrived for Trevor Ames, Honoria, and Alastair Woodhaven, who were using Honoria's set of old Wedgewood china.

Honoria's small Victorian apartment above Throckmorton's Apothecary Shop was warm and cozy, snug against the chill and driving rain hammering outside. She smiled. Now with her brother living with her, the apartment was cozier still. Earlier that morning the three of them had located a small church in a neighboring village and attended services there. Safely back home after a harrowing drive through the storm, they enjoyed their tea in comfort.

Honoria was just passing the plate of buttered scones and marmalade to the others when they heard a knock at the door.

"I wonder who that could be." Ames took another sip of tea. Oolong and orange pekoe blend. Delightful.

Honoria set her cup down and stood. "I suppose while you sit on your bum I'll find out," she chided in mock exasperation.

She pretended to be upset, but in her heart she was so glad to have her brother back after his nearly forty-year exile that he could have played "God Save the Queen" on a kazoo in his underwear and she wouldn't have minded . . . much. She went to open the door.

Neville Woodhaven waited outside.

Honoria blinked. Ames and Alastair had filled her in on the row at the Twin Ravens pub the night before and how Neville had stormed out, so she found it odd that the hulking constable should appear here now.

She quickly composed herself. "Neville! What a pleasant surprise! Won't you come in? Look at you—you're dripping wet!"

Alastair stood up in alarm. "What is it? Is everything all right?"

Neville seemed at a loss for words, a first for him. "No," he finally managed to croak. "Everything's fine. No problems. It's just that—" He looked at them all, one at a time, finally settling his gaze on Ames. Neville's mouth opened and shut several times, but nothing further came out.

Ames set his tea and biscuits down and came over to the door. Tentatively he put a hand on the bigger man's shoulder. "You can talk here. You're among friends."

"Friends." Neville seemed almost to strangle on the word. "Do I have any friends? Real ones? I don't think I do." His hands opened and closed spasmodically, seemingly on their own.

"Yes, you do," Alastair told him. "Even though I'm your brother, Neville, I'm also your friend. All of us are. Now won't you tell us what's the trouble?"

The constable stared a moment longer, then finally nodded. "Last night," he began, his voice halting, "last night at the Twin Ravens, I was listening to the both of you. Oh, I know I was mocking, but I was listening, all the same." He swallowed. "All this talk about what appears to be taking place around the world. You called me a fool, Ally." Surprisingly, Neville's tone wasn't harsh as he said this; to the contary, his voice had sunk to a whisper. "And so I am. I didn't set out to be, but that's what I've become."

"Now, Neville," his brother soothed, "I—"

Neville held up his hand. "Please, Ally, don't humor me. I came here to say something, and I'll do that very thing. I won't be coddled." With an effort he softened his words. "I . . . I just needed to tell you, Trevor . . . to tell you all . . . " Nervously he licked his lips. "I was wrong."

"About me?" Ames asked.

Neville shook his head. "All of it. You. Ally. Me. Jesus. All of it." He looked at them with haunted eyes. "I didn't sleep last night. This morning I took the patrol car and just drove. Drove and thought. As I did, I remembered, Ally." Neville fixed the younger man with a look of pain. "I remembered Father's friend, the missionary. I remembered our talks. Our walks. I remembered his prayers for us boys. I remembered it all." He rubbed his face with his hands. "I can't go on. I need help, Ally. God help me, I do. I need what you all have."

"And so you shall, Neville." Alastair, tears stinging his eyes as he contemplated what the power of effectual, fervent prayer could do, placed both his hands on his brother's massive shoulders. "And so you shall."

CHAPTER 59

PASTOR WASSON HAD SOMETHING IN HIS HAND, and he held it high. He wanted to make sure everyone in the sanctuary could see it. This Sunday night service was the largest he'd ever preached, with the crowd numbering a shade over seven thousand.

"This is called a shofar. As you can see, it's a ram's horn. Shofars come in many types. This particular horn has been straightened some so that it has only three twists running its length. A lot of people, me included, believe something very much like this is what the Lord is going to blow when he comes for us. I'd blow it myself to show you all how it sounds, but I've never been able to get as much as a squeak out of the thing. I know a lady in here who can, though. Julie?"

A woman stood and made her way to the podium. Julie Loudon, along with her husband, Mike, were Messianic, or completed, Jews. They headed up a ministry called Elijah's Bond, which was dedicated to the task of grafting the Jew and the Gentile together in Yeshua, or Jesus.

And nobody could blow the shofar like Julie Loudon.

Pastor Wasson held the horn out to her. Taking it, she whispered a quick prayer. Then drawing a deep breath, she placed the horn's smaller opening to her lips, closed her eyes.

And blew.

From the shofar's larger open end erupted one long, sustained note, a tone of such piercing sweetness and raw power it made the hair on Nick's arms stand up. Nobody in the building moved as they listened, transfixed, to that sound going on and on.

Incredibly, Julie managed to hold it for nearly twenty seconds. When she finally stopped blowing, it seemed as if the ringing still hung in the air, echoing from the podium to the rear of the sanctuary and back again.

A few moments passed before Wasson seemed to rouse himself. He nodded his wordless thanks to Julie. With a smile, she laid the shofar down on one of the podium chairs and quietly made her way back to her husband.

"And that, people," the pastor said, his voice roughened with emotion, "is the sound we're going to hear in less than forty-eight hours. The sound that's going to call us home."

.. .. ..

OUTSIDE, AN OLDER MAN AND HIS WIFE ARGUED with each other as they approached the church doors. "Walking nearly half a mile to church," the man said, his voice gruff. "Carla Sue, I can't believe I let you talk me into this. I'm not as young as I used to be."

"You're the same age as me," his wife snapped. "If I can do it, you can."

He stopped, facing her. "But why are we doing it? Here we are, on our way from Florida to Michigan to have a nice visit with your sister, and then blam, clear outta the blue, you decide to visit this church." He shook his head. "You and your whims."

"It wasn't a whim," Carla Sue said primly. "It was a billboard."

"Yeah, a billboard. I know. I saw it too. 'Visit God's Community Church, the Most Welcoming Church in America.' " He snorted, "You're the one into all this Jesus stuff, not me. So why this particular church? It's not even the denomination you go to."

"I know it isn't. I'm just following the leading of God, that's all."

"And dragging me along for the ride."

The man was about to say more when something caught his eye: a group of people, a dozen or so, strolling nonchalantly but silently into the church.

The one in front, a smallish man, had what appeared to be tattoos covering his arms down to the tips of his fingers. For some reason he couldn't fathom, this made the older man nervous. There was something . . . off . . . about that bunch.

He glanced at his watch, trying one last tactic to get his wife to listen to reason. "Look at the time. It's almost 9:30. We've missed everything. The service is about over, I'll bet."

"You may be right. But I don't care. All I know is I have a leading from God that you're supposed to be here tonight, husband of mine." Carla Sue smiled. "This is your night."

"You've been saying that for nearly a week."

"But tonight it's true," she replied, deflating whatever remark he was about to come up with next. "Let's go in."

The man and his wife passed through the foyer, and then into the main sanctuary, where he stopped with a scowl. "Look at this crowd. Not only did we have to park half a mile away, but now we gotta stand all—"

"Dear," she interrupted, pointing. "Seats."

And so there were. Two seats, together, on the aisle, six rows from the front.

Carla Sue looked up at her husband, a triumphant grin on her face. "God knew we'd be here tonight. He's held those seats just for us."

The man dropped his head. He knew when he was beaten. "All right. So we sit."

They took their places in the pew, and the man tried as best he could to concentrate on what was being said. He figured if he acted interested enough, maybe Carla Sue would leave him alone for a while. She was always bully-ragging him to go to church with her. And he always fought back like a Turkish prisoner of war. *Why can't she just leave me be?* he thought miserably. He worked hard, always had. Let a guy have his Sundays for the lake and fishing.

Then suddenly the pastor said something, something incredible, something that made Carla Sue's husband sit up straight and his mouth drop open in shock.

CHAPTER 60

"FOR THE PAST FORTY-FIVE MINUTES," Pastor Wasson said, "I've been telling you about God's love and what that love means to us. But I've got a concrete example of that love right here to show you. Nick Castle and CT Barnes, I know I didn't prepare you for this, but could you come up here?"

It was the mention of those names that caused Carla Sue's husband to react so.

With sheepish grins, Nick and CT left their families and made their way up onto the podium. When they got there, Wasson put a hand on each of their arms. "Embarrassed yet?" He laughed.

Nick and CT just shook their heads. The pastor was always unpredictable. Once, to make a point in a sermon, he'd ridden a horse down the main aisle. What did he have in mind now?

"Seriously, guys," Wasson went on, "the reason I called you up here was to tell everyone what you've been doing these past few days. Now before you stop me," he held up his hand, "I'm not trying to make out like you two are some kind of super saints because we all know you're not."

The whole church cracked up over that, Maryann and Sarah most of all.

"No," Wasson said, "I'm just using you both as an example, an example of what Christians around the world have been doing to reach their lost friends and loved ones."

The pastor's smile faded as he turned to address the crowd. "Most of you in here have never heard Nick and CT's story. It's an incredible one. But they're too shy to tell you, so let me summarize. Back in 1972, in the closing days of the Vietnam war, they served together in an air cavalry unit. For those of you unfamiliar with that term, what Nick and CT did was ride as gunners in Huey helicopters.

"One day, a day like any other, they went up on a mission. They had no way of knowing how that day would end. Their unit had received a call to rescue the survivors of a Marine outpost that was about to be overrun by Vietcong. That rescue was successful, but at a terrible cost.

"One of their friends was horribly burned when his helicopter was shot down. Another man was shot and paralyzed. An English reporter covering the story lost his mind, and Nick and CT's commanding officer was court-martialed for having let that reporter ride along without official permission. The commander consequently lost his mind as well. And Nick didn't escape unharmed. He was shot in the head right after he'd rescued the burned man. If the bullet had gone another inch to the left, he would have died."

The congregation took this news in stunned silence. Most of them had known the two served together in Vietnam but had never heard the particulars.

"I'll let them finish this story themselves," the pastor said. "Guys?"

Nick took the mike, nervously clearing his throat. "Well, it's pretty simple. Last Tuesday night, after we'd all gotten the message, God kind of dropped into my heart that CT and I should go and find our old Army buddies to minister Christ to them. So we did. I guess that's all."

He turned and tried to give the pastor back his mike, but Wasson just grinned, taking a step back. "Not so fast, hotrod. You know me. I'm not letting you guys off that easy. Tell it all, now."

Nick, who would have rather eaten peanuts with the shells on than speak in public, had had enough. He shoved the mike into CT's hand. "You heard the man. Make yourself useful." The crowd laughed.

"Uh," CT started, "yeah. It's like Nick said. God gave him that burden for our bros, and Nick shared it with me. Now I gotta admit, at first I thought Nicky was nuts, but then God kinda dealt with me about it too. So to cut to the chase, we ran our butts off and found every one of our guys. And guess what?" He grinned hugely. "God saved and healed . . . every . . . one . . . we . . . found."

The church erupted in applause. After a few seconds, Pastor Wasson held up his hand. "I invited Nick and CT up here tonight not to praise them, but to praise the Lord who so instructed them." He narrowed his eyes. "People, here it is. Sometime in the next two days, an astounding event will take place, the likes of which this world has never seen. In less than forty-eight hours, you, me, all of us, will be gone. What does that mean? Very simply it means the earth's hold on us is loosed forever and we head home. But here's the point I'm trying to make. *We're not going alone.*"

Wasson's voice took on an impassioned tone. "What Nick and CT did these past few days was wonderful, but it's also just an example of what Christians around the world have been doing, Christians who've sacrificed their very lives to rescue their friends and loved ones from being overrun by the enemy of our souls. So in proxy I just want to say thanks to you men on behalf of those you fought so valiantly to save, both in the past and the present. Thanks."

The man who'd been arguing with his wife earlier had heard enough. He jumped to his feet. "Sir? May I say something?"

Pastor Wasson frowned as he searched the congregation for the speaker. Locating him, the pastor motioned for the man to continue.

"None of you people in here know my wife and me," the man said. "We're visitors from Florida, heading to Michigan to see my wife's sister. My wife's been a Christian for the past few years, but I was never really all that hot about about it—no disrespect intended, sir."

This was directed at Wasson, who shook it off with a smile.

"Anyway," the man went on, "Tonight Carla Sue saw a billboard out on the highway about this place and said . . . well, she said God told her we needed to be here. Said it was my night. I didn't know what she meant. I thought she was loopy. But then, Reverend, you said these guys' names here, and I almost had a stroke."

Nervously he began kneading the pew back in front of him. "Y'see . . . I know them."

Surprised, Nick and CT looked at each other. They had no idea who this guy was.

"Yeah," the man continued, "I know them, or at least know of them, because I was there that day. I was one of the men these guys rescued." He cleared his throat. "My name is Yancey Wheeler, formerly Gunnery Sergeant Yancey Wheeler, USMC. And I never got the chance to say thanks." Tears coursing down his weathered face, he added, "Until tonight."

CHAPTER 61

SANGRE TURNED FROM THE CHURCH MAP located on the foyer wall. He nodded at Crandall. "You know what to do. I'm heading for the nursery."

The deputy nodded back, then turned, and with a gesture sent two of the Circle members on upstairs. Sangre began strutting purposefully down the long corridor, listening for the sounds of infants. It didn't take long. After a bit of a hike and only two wrong turns, he finally found what he was after. The nursery door.

This will be sweet. Pasting a smile of befuddled innocence on his face, he jammed his hands into his pockets and wandered on in. Just inside the entrance he stopped and looked around, trying to appear confused.

Over in the corner a young teenaged girl struggled with the job of diapering a bellowing six-month-old. She stopped long enough to glance up.

"Hi, do you have a baby in here? Or are you looking for someone?"

"Both, actually," Sangre smiled, faking his relief. "I think a friend of mine has a little one in your nursery. She's a young lady, a bit older than you, around twenty-three. About so tall, long black hair. Her name is Belladonna. Somebody told me they saw her come in here. I hope that's true." And he smiled again, pure charm.

"Oh sure, Belladonna. Yeah, I know her." The teenager, both hands occupied with her task, blew a piece of stray hair away from her face. "She's in the back, nursing Matthew-Mark. Want me to go get her when I'm done?"

Matthew-Mark? Sangre mused. *What a stupid name. What a stupid, stupid name.*

"No thanks. Back there, is it? I'll get her myself. You keep on with your noble calling." He moved toward the door.

The girl's eyes opened wide. "But sir! That's the nursing room! It's just for women! You can't go back there!"

The smile left Sangre's face as if it had never been there at all. "Child, you simply have no idea of what I can do."

.. .. ..

CRANDALL GLANCED ABOUT HIM NERVOUSLY. He hoped everyone remembered what they were supposed to do. If there were any screwups, he knew full well where the blame would fall.

The deputy mentally ticked off the assignments: two of the women, Charon and Asphyx, had taken their places in the balcony. Nightshade and Jace were down front, blending in pretty well with that whole weeping, praying bunch at the altar. The rest of the Circle had manned their positions at the doors, and Crandall was at the center entrance at the top of the main aisle. Now all they had to do was to wait for Sangre to come in with that kid.

When he gave the sign, all hell would break loose.

.. .. ..

THE ALTAR COUNSELORS WERE LEADING hundreds down front to the Lord, Yancey Wheeler among them. He'd come to the conclusion that God must want him pretty badly to have put the idea into Carla Sue's heart to come here tonight.

Yancey was a gnarly old combat vet, but he wasn't stupid. Meeting his rescuers here from a battle forty years past was simply beyond coincidence. His wife was right. This was his night.

After he finished praying, he started to head back to his seat, but Pastor Wasson motioned for one of the ushers to get his attention. They did. The pastor then asked Yancey and Carla Sue to join him and Nick and CT on the platform.

When they got up there, Wasson said, "We really appreciate y'all being here tonight, Gunny. I thought maybe you'd like to thank these men personally after all these years."

"You bet I would, Reverend." Yancey wrung Nick's and CT's hands in turn. "You bet I would."

.. .. ..

ONE OF THE ALTAR COUNSELORS approached Jace. "Sir, would you like to have a personal relationship with Jesus Christ?"

Jace took an involuntary step back. Something about this simpering fool repelled him, and it wasn't just his smile. "Uh, no," he stammered. "That is— what I mean to say is—I mean, not right now." Where the deuce was Sangre?

"The Word says today is the day of salvation," the man said. "Don't harden your heart."

"Too late for that," Jace muttered. He looked across the sanctuary to the other side.

It appeared Nightshade was also trying to fend off one of these grasping Christers. He wasn't having any better luck.

Jace resisted the urge to look at his watch. He was sure they were running late. He was equally sure he didn't want to have anything more to do with this walking dead man who kept yammering so incessantly at him. Where was Sangre?

"But sir." The counselor appeared confused. "I don't understand. If you don't want a personal relationship with the Lord, what did you come down here for, then? That's what most of the people—"

Jace had had it. "Oh, bugger off!"

The other man was about to reply when they both heard something, confusion at the back of the sanctuary. Then Sangre strolled in, bigger than life, his face plastered with a self-satisfied grin. Seeing what he held, Jace heaved a sigh of relief. It was about bloody time.

Sangre clutched a shrieking Matthew-Mark in his left hand.

His MAC-10 was cradled in his right.

.. .. ..

BACK IN THE NURSERY, pandemonium reigned as dozens of terrifed infants and toddlers screamed out their fear. Sangre had locked the young girl he'd just met in a nearby storage closet, along with three of her helpers who'd been back in the nursery's small kitchen. He wasn't shy about killing them; he just didn't want to kill them here. But Belladonna, on the other hand . . .

No, she was another story entirely. He'd found her in the nursing room, just as the helper had said. The young girl had foolishly tried to stop him as he reached that door. A savage backward elbow to her face stopped her chattering and dropped her in her tracks.

And then Sangre entered and found Belladonna suckling her *thing*.

He fairly beamed with joy at the sight. Anyone seeing that smile would have rather taken poison than see it again.

The girl's eyes grew huge as she screamed. Pulling the infant off her breast, she tried shielding him with her body. The baby, sensing her terror, joined his cries with hers. It didn't do any good. In two strides Sangre was on her.

Laughing maniacally, he ripped the child from her arms, and then savagely backhanded her across the face, all the frustration he'd felt these past months contained in that single blow. Stunned, she fell out of the rocking chair and crashed to the floor.

Sangre leaned down close, his breath foul and eyes insane. "I told you, Belladonna," he giggled. "I told you you would see." He shook the terrifed, wailing child in her face. "This creature was ours . . . and now it's *mine*."

CHAPTER 62

THE MOMENT SANGRE HAD COME IN with the baby and the gun, the people in the congregation began to scream. In response he grinned, aimed his MAC-10 at the ceiling, and pulled the trigger.

The two-second burst he fired was more than effective. For a moment, except for the baby's shrieks, shocked silence reigned.

"No one moves, no one blinks, no one talks, no one even *thinks* about activating a cell phone." He placed the still-smoking gun barrel against the baby's head. "Or the child dies."

There were muffled, anguished sobs from men and women alike, but they obeyed.

"Very good," he crooned. "Very, very good. You all just may live through this. And what a story you'll have to tell."

Insolently he began to wander down the aisle toward the platform, all the while keeping the gun barrel tightly screwed into Matthew-Mark's forehead. The baby's sobs were heartrending.

"Sir." Pastor Wasson could barely speak the words. "Please. What do you want?"

"Oh, my." Sangre said airily as he came. "That's the question of the year, isn't it? What do I want? What *do* I want? Golly gee whiz, I suppose I want understanding for my poor sinner self. That's what you sell, isn't it? Understanding, acceptance, a clean slate, hallelujah?"

He stopped at the base of the podium. Wasson didn't respond.

But Nick did. "Listen to me, whoever you are. Why don't you put that thing down? This is nothing that can't be worked out. Let's talk. Maybe we can help you." He hoped his tone sounded reasonable.

" 'Maybe we can help you.' " Sangre mocked. "Like you 'helped' Belladonna deny her destiny? With me?"

"Oh, my God," Nick croaked, sudden recognition dawning. "Is that Matthew-Mark? Is that Belladonna's baby you're holding?"

"Let's see . . . " Sangre put the infant up to his face, ignoring its cries as he pretended to examine it. All the while the gun never wavered. "Doesn't look much like me, does it? Ugly, red creature." He gazed back at Nick, fluttering his eyelashes. "And me, so handsome and debonair. But it's my baby, all right. Such as it is. It was mine and Belladonna's, more's the pity, but," he broke into what he was sure was a funny TV evangelist's voice, "Ah have shown, yay-yuh, Ah have shown that young lay-dah the er-rah of her waze! So pa-raze him! Pa-raze him all ye peoples of this doomed old world!" He giggled at his own wit.

"If you've done anything to hurt that young woman—" Pastor Wasson began, but Sangre cut him off.

"Oh, please," he said, his voice gone flat. "Notice who's holding the gun."

Now it was Nick's turn to smile. "I bet we can fix that."

Sangre gave a light laugh. "Oh yes, I forgot. You're some kind of big-cheese-army-hero-type, aren't you, Mister Nick? So I heard tonight. You and your large, dark, slack-jawed friend there."

CT gritted his teeth, clenching his fists so tight he felt his nails drawing blood. He didn't trust himself to respond to the taunt. All he needed was two seconds. Two. If that punk would just swing that gun away from Matthew-Mark's head . . .

"You're forgetting something, scumbag," somebody else said in a loud voice. "Me."

Sangre frowned. "And you are?"

"Gunnery Sergeant Yancey Wheeler, USMC."

Sangre responded with unexpected glee. "A Marine? Goody!" He chanced a glance backward. "Crandall! Crandall, old chum, come here and come running. I've got a treat for you. One you'll like."

The deputy came trotting down the aisle in his usual lumbering, flatfooted way, his Desert Eagle .50 held loosely in his hand. "Yeah, what?"

"Take a look." Sangre motioned at Yancey. "Sergeant Wheeler, meet a teammate. I give you another sergeant, Sergeant Crandall Weems, one of your fellow—leathernecks, I believe the term is." His grin grew wider. "Crandall was a Marine, too."

"You were in the Corps?" Yancey regarded Crandall with disgusted and disbelieving eyes. "When? What did you do? What was your MOS?"

"It was awhile back," the deputy evaded. "I was in supply."

Yancey crowed a derisive laugh. "Socks 'n' jocks! What's the matter, tough guy, you couldn't get a job at the PX? Well, lemme tell you something."

His voice grew menacing. "After I served three tours in-country, the Corps made me a DI on Parris Island. Pukes like you I ate every day for breakfast. Sometimes two, with a little syrup on top. I didn't even break a sweat." He went on with a sneer, "You don't impress me, Weems, not a bit. Truth is, you hanging with this momma's boy here makes me sick. You're a sorry excuse as a civilian. I got the feeling you were a sorrier excuse as a Marine."

Crandall's eyes grew wide at the unexpected rebuke.

Sangre regarded the deputy with a mocking smile. "Well, now! Such words. Surely you're not going to take that from him, are you, Crandall? You were a Marine too. Make him pay."

"Make him pay?" Crandall didn't get it.

Sangre blew out an exasperated breath. "Yes, you idiot! Must I do all your thinking? Shoot him!" From the front row, Yancey's wife screamed.

"Shoot him?" Crandall looked appalled. "But—"

"I said shoot that man, Crandall! Right now! Shoot him between the eyes or in the heart or right in the belly. I don't care; just *shoot him!*"

Yancey stood tall, eyes hard. "Do it, boy. If you can."

"Well?" Sangre's tone turned mocking. "The Marines did teach you how to shoot, didn't they?"

"Well . . . yeah. But—"

"Crandall." Sangre had grown deadly calm. "I've given you a direct order. I expect that order to be obeyed. I'm warning you, do not fail me. Shoot this man. Now."

The deputy started to plead, rushing his words. "I'll do anythin' you say, Sangre, you know I will. I always have, ever since we were kids, but I can't kill a fellow Marine, I just can't."

Sangre shook his head in disgust. This wouldn't do.

"Stupid old Crandall," he sighed. And swinging the MAC-10 away from the baby, he shot the deputy squarely in the chest.

He fired less than a one-second burst, but in the echoing church it sounded like he'd emptied the magazine.

Crandall never knew what hit him. His body, jerking and spurting blood, arms windmilling, blasted back several feet before slamming to the floor and slipping down it with hard momentum, only stopping when he slid to a halt against a pew, his eyes dead and staring up at nothing at all.

Terrified screams broke out, redoubled. Some of the people jumped to their feet, eyes darting wildly, searching for escape.

"*Shut up!*" Sangre ground the gun's barrel against the screaming baby's skull. "*Shut up or he dies! Right! Now!*"

Nick groaned as he saw the man's finger tightening down on the trigger, his knuckle quivering and growing white with force.

The situation was at flashpoint. Several people, heedless of Sangre's warnings, had begun to jostle each other, seconds away from taking their chances and bolting from the pews.

"Oh well," Sangre sighed, compressing the trigger even further. "I suppose I'll just have to procure another baby."

Nick had had enough. More than enough. He'd had a bellyful of this demonic jerk, this human hemorrhoid, this—

Enough!

"Hey!" he yelled, leaping off the podium. In two steps he stood before the incredulous man.

The would-be satanist, gasping at the utter cowboy temerity of this fool, dug the gun barrel deeper into the baby. "Stop! I'll kill him!"

"You?" Nick snorted. "You don't pack the gear."

Several women in the congregation screamed their dismay. Nick tried to ignore it, hoping his goading would make the satanist fumble and give him a chance to take him out.

"You think I won't? Watch me!"

"Sure, you can kill him. But then he'll be beyond your grasp, and then what?" Nick shrugged. "Enough talk, little man. Do it already."

The crowd screamed again.

"Idiot!" Sangre howled. "You're so smart. Don't you know a ruse when you see one?" In a flash he swung the gun away from the baby, training it now on Nick. He grew deadly calm. "Of course, I'll kill the child, if that's your wish, sir. But . . . you first."

Nick went cold. The maw of the gun he stared down looked as big as Mammoth Cave.

So this is how it ends. Nuts. Sure would have been nice to have been alive for the rapture.

Tormented cries erupted from the crowd, Maryann's and Tracy's and Blake's the loudest of all.

CT stood frozen in despair. He knew what Nick was planning. To anyone with combat training it was obvious: He meant to sacrifice his life to give CT a chance to sieze control of the situation. He could tell it by the odd thumb-cocking motion Nick made down at his side in Sangre's direction, and in a lightning flash of intuition CT knew what he was expected to do. As soon as Sangre fired, he was to jump off the podium and pummel that tattooed freak straight through the floor.

Nick was now inches away from Sangre, desperately trying to push him over the edge. He hoped it worked. He hoped CT was quick. He hoped death didn't hurt.

"Sanka?" Nick sneered. Sweat pooled in the small of his back. "Is that what they call you? What kind of a stupid name is that? I don't think you're man enough, Sanka."

"Don't push it! You have no idea of the forces I control!"

"Who cares, you little, dried-up twit? If you had a hair on your chest, you'd pull that trigger. But you don't, so you won't. As they used to say in the Old West, pal, you're all hat and no cattle."

"Nick, please!" Maryann sobbed. "Leave him alone!"

He ignored her, his heart pounding like a hammer. "So anyway, Sanka." Nick glanced down at the weapon an inch from his navel, and then he grinned recklessly. "Are you—"

"No!" A new cry came from the back of the sanctuary.

Belladonna.

As if on cue, Jace and Nightshade and the rest of the Circle all slipped their guns from under their clothes, unseen. As soon as Sangre fired, so would they.

"No!" Belladonna gasped as she stumbled toward the men, her hands outstretched. "Please, Ronnie, give me back my baby! Don't kill him, please!"

The young woman was obviously hurt, as was evident from the blood running down her face. Nick knew he couldn't let her get much closer or his plan would be useless.

Endgame. Time to go.

And with that final thought roaring through his brain, he grabbed the scorching-hot gun barrel with both hands, disregarding the heat, and jammed it deep into his own gut.

"Do it!" he screamed, his eyes locked onto those of the madman.

Sangre grinned. "Suits me."

And pulled the trigger.

.. .. ..

THE NEXT TWO THINGS happened at exactly the same instant. Sangre and the Circle fired their guns . . .

. . . and a shofar blew.

CHAPTER 63

IN HIS PLUSH MANHATTAN APARTMENT, Doctor Alan Minch leaned back with a sigh and kindly regarded the blood-red glass of port gently cradled in his palm. Life was good and only getting better.

Like a king of ancient days cloistered in his money room, he added up his good fortune. Every Sunday his church was full to the rafters with credulous, old-monied blue-hairs hailing from the Hamptons and its evirons who took every word he said or wrote as holy writ, whatever that was. His recent radio and TV appearances had resulted in his latest book, *God's Fools*, going into its third printing, his airtight larder was loaded with the best food and drink in the land, and his latest conquest, a young, gorgeous delivery man, was proving to be his most energetic and imaginative lover yet.

Minch sighed again . . .

. . . and a shofar blew.

.. .. ..

MANNY ALVEREZ FOLDED the sports section of the Sunday *Washington Post* back into order and shook his head. Almost 9:30 p.m., and only now was he was getting around to reading the thing. His father had pulled the paper apart earlier this afternoon when he read it, like he always did, leaving it for Manny to redo later. Usually when Manny had his parents over for Sunday lunch, they only stayed an hour or so, leaving him with the whole afternoon to watch the games and reconstruct and read his beloved *Post*. But today they were still here, for lunch and supper both.

He supposed he shouldn't begrudge them his time or his food or his newspaper. He knew they weren't getting any younger, and he owed them. They'd taken him in as a kid when nobody else would. But their constant harping on religion had gotten mighty old over the years, and tonight they'd been in rare form. The tears, the pleading, the arm waving—it finally had worn them, and him, out.

And now here his mom and dad were, both softly snoring in the wing-back chairs in his living room, leaving Manny alone with his paper at last.

He growled softly. It was no good. Now that he'd finally gotten them to shut up, he found he couldn't concentrate. Their words kept swarming around his head like bees.

With a sigh he laid the paper on his lap, regarding them both with a pitying look. Manny knew they loved him, sure, and he loved them. But all this rapture stuff—sheesh. They'd almost talked his ear off tonight. He really shouldn't have been so brusque with them, though. They meant well enough.

And how about all that work he'd done for Nick Castle these past few days, and his rapture talk? That had taken it out of him too.

He yawned as he regarded his parents. Silly old crocks. Next Sunday they'd all go out for lunch. That'd be a treat for all of them. Interlacing his fingers above his head, Manny stretched, his knuckles cracking. Definitely time for bed.

He yawned again . . .

. . . and a shofar blew.

.. .. ..

"IN JESUS' NAME, AMEN." Ida Ryan wiped her eyes as the tall elderly pastor gently pulled her to her feet.

Smiling, he turned to Clyde and Dooley. "She made it, boys. By the skin of her teeth and the grace of God, she done it."

Dooley and his father hugged and kissed her, murmuring their thanks to God into the shoulders of her dress. As the three broke free with smiles and chatter, Dooley wiped the sweat from his face again. The little church was stifling hot and crowded as all get-out, but he didn't mind; he'd waited forty years to sweat like this. And to see his Ma get saved and delivered from her craziness like she just did—shoot, he'd have sweated days to see it. Dooley reached out to shake the tall preacher's hand . . .

. . . and a shofar blew.

.. .. ..

SMILING, Frankie set the small plastic cup on the floor between his feet. He'd taken communion this morning, and now in this service he'd just taken it again. He didn't care: Reverend Jasper had told them that Jesus commanded his followers to do it as often as they could in memory of him, and Frankie wanted to take communion a million times.

Because he remembered, all right.

What he really couldn't wait for was what Reverend Jasper had preached on this evening, the marriage supper of the Lamb, up in heaven. Frankie grinned. A seven-year supper with Jesus made his cookout plans with the reverend and his people sound kinda stupid, but he figured God would understand.

Then he remembered he was still holding the plate with the little cups on it. He started to pass it to the man on his right . . .

. . . and a shofar blew.

.. .. ..

LEAH AND FREDDIE HELPED another person into the Ruggs' backyard pool, this time a tall skinny black kid singing at the top of his lungs. Leah smiled. The kid had a pretty good voice. He'd do well in heaven's choir. Freddie too. He was always singing in the TV truck.

Leah wondered about her own voice. It wasn't much, never had been. Would she have a nice singing voice in heaven? It was something she'd ask the colonel, when she got a chance. If she got the chance. If he'd ever stop preaching.

She didn't mind. It was Colonel Rugg's simple, impassioned telling of the gospel that had finally won her and Freddie over this morning. This morning! Leah still couldn't get over it. This morning her search had ended in light.

Patrice Rugg lifted the shouting, singing kid's head from the water, and a cheer rose from those who had gone before.

Leah laughed . . .

. . . and a shofar blew.

.. .. ..

IN HIS ROOM AT HONORIA'S, Trevor Ames lay soundly asleep, his sister in her own bed down the hall. Mercifully, neither could hear the combined buzzsaw snoring of Alastair and Neville, who reposed comfortably on the living room floor.

All four had taken turns testifying at the Twin Ravens tonight. Being a pub, it was somewhat of a miracle that the landlord had allowed it, but the man had appeared as awed by Neville's talk as the rest. It was agreed: If God was big enough and strong enough and loving enough to win over such a formidable brute as Neville Woodhaven, it would be best to listen to his call.

And listen they did. By the score.

When Trevor, Honoria, Alastair, and Neville had finally given a combined altar call, more than fifty patrons had crowded the bar rail to get right with God. It had been exhilarating, but also tiring. One of the biggest surprises of the evening had been seeing Mr. Dales, the pub landlord, crying like a baby as Neville, formerly his best customer, led him to the Lord.

Trevor chuckled in his sleep at the memory . . .

. . . and a shofar blew.

CHAPTER 64

AND MANNY'S PARENTS VANISHED. Right before his eyes, gone. Just. Like. That. It wasn't until some long minutes later that he realized the screaming he was hearing was his own.

A shofar blew . . .

.. .. ..

AND ALAN MINCH HEARD and felt nothing. Just the slightest whisper of a quick chill, perhaps, but that was nothing on a night as good and fine as this. The delivery man was due later tonight and said he was bringing scented body creams. Lifting the port to his lips, Minch drank deep.

A shofar blew . . .

.. .. ..

AND DOOLEY AND MA AND PA and the tall preacher and most of the folks at the Danville Christian Center . . .

Blinked out.

A shofar blew . . .

.. .. ..

AND THE COMMUNION PLATE Frankie had been holding clattered to the floor, spilling the grape juice and making a real mess. There was no longer a hand holding it. Frankie and Reverend Jasper and Deacon Marsh instantly disappeared, along with most of the people with them.

A shofar blew . . .

.. .. ..

AND THE WATER IN THE RUGGS' POOL slopped in aimless motion, disturbed when the bodies in there only seconds earlier vanished.

Colonel Rugg, Patrice, Leah, Freddie, the skinny black kid, scores more. In that neighborhood, the disappearance rate was nearly 100 percent.

A shofar blew . . .

.. .. ..

AND IN HONORIA PEET'S HOUSE the snoring in the living room abruptly ceased as Honoria and her brother and Alastair and Neville Woodhaven departed in an instant. As did most of the people in South Essex.

Trevor Ames finished his chuckle in the sky.

.. .. ..

AND AT THE CHURCH . . .

Sangre dumbly looked down. The baby he'd been holding . . . gone. *What the—*? And his right hand, hanging limp and shattered by . . . bullets? But how? And what about his gun? Why was his gun on the floor? He remembered firing it at that Castle idiot, right before. So where had he gone?

And what was that noise he was hearing? Dripping? What could possibly be dripping? He felt sudden weakness along his bones, and he looked at the floor again. He frowned. It was red. Red?

Blood. The puddle of blood between his feet was the size of a chafing dish and growing larger.

But where was it coming from? All that blood, from just his arm? He looked down again, trying to see where the leak was. As he did, the pain started. In earnest.

Three more bullet holes. One in his collarbone, one in his shoulder, and one . . . parked right in his chest.

But who—? Then he realized who. Of course. When everyone had vanished, the crossfire had caught him. And not only him.

Sangre blinked in amazement around the sanctuary.

The rest of the Circle lay in crumpled heaps, dead. Jace, Nightshade, Charon, Asphyx, the others, not to mention, of course, stupid old Crandall . . . all dead as yesterday's dreams.

Sangre smiled. What a joke. Hoo boy. This was rich. He started to giggle, and the giggle turned into a gurgling retch as bright red arterial blood gushed richly from his mouth. His vision darkened around the edges. Hey now, this wouldn't do. He wouldn't . . . allow it. Courage and . . .

Blood?

Sangre's eyes rolled back in his head. Oblivious now to the pain, he dropped to his knees, his arms outstretched to either side in a parody of supplication, seeking . . . something . . .

Air hissing like a snake from the hole in his chest, he flopped face-first into his own gore, his blood flow slowing, his body growing numb as the gathering, hungry darkness closed in.

What happened to my plans? What happened to my plans . . . ? Why doesn't the . . . Dark One help me . . . ? I'm a . . . good . . . servant. . . . I . . . don't . . . understand . . .

And then, beneath his dying gasps, Sangre heard something else, an altogether different sound, a sound he knew now would taunt him throughout eternity, a mocking noise he thought he'd left forever back in his dark, sad, twisted childhood.

The diabolical cacaphony of someone . . . *laughing* at him.

CHAPTER 65

NICK CASTLE, EYES CLENCHED SHUT, checked his body with his hands. What was going on? He'd heard that nut open fire. Why wasn't he dead? He should be. He should be like a fine, aged Swiss cheese.

He wasn't even hurt. What happened?

Slowly he opened his eyes. And found himself gazing into the face of . . .

His jaw dropped.

It was him. Jesus. Immanuel. The Son of God. And he was smiling. At Nick. Smiling at him, accepting him completely and loving him utterly, with eyes that went on forever . . .

The air all around began swelling with awesome music, growing incredibly sweet. Nick filled his lungs deep to join in. But now he couldn't speak. There simply were no words.

Then, like an explosive wave, like the light from ten thousand suns, the final knowledge hit him, blasting him to his core over and over and over again. He'd made it. *He'd made it.* He'd—

But not only him. No, not only him. Because Maryann and their kids and CT and Sarah and their kids . . .

And Pastor Wasson and Colonel Rugg and Bob Greer and Dooley Ryan and Rita Ybarra and Trevor Ames and Frankie Malone and Irv Guelpe and Reverend Jasper and Deacon Marsh and multiplied hundreds of millions of saved, blood-bought children of the King of kings and Lord of lords, every blessed one of them suddenly found themselves *flying.*

They were rolling and twisting and *flying,* and tumbling and soaring and *flying,* and laughing and chasing and *flying,* going farther and farther and deeper and deeper into a cloud of pure, sweet glory, on their way to a destiny beyond imagining, into a realm of endless, incredible life, rocketing along at God's own speed. *Flying . . .*

And below them the earth tilted and swung and fell away. They were above the guns, above the death, lifting higher.

Heading home.